SHURA

SHURA

BATIA COHEN

ISBN 979-8-9947412-0-7 (Paperback)
ISBN 979-8-9947412-2-1 (Hardcover)
ISBN 979-8-9947412-1-4 (Digital)

Library of Congress Control Number: 2026902633

This book is a work of narrative nonfiction. All historical events and dates have been researched and are presented as accurately as possible. Some scenes and dialogue have been reconstructed to convey the lived experience of the events described.

Shura is a translated and revised edition of *Una Amapola Entre Cactus*, originally published in Mexico in 2012.

Front cover image and book design by Samantha Cohen.
Printed in the United States of America.

Batiacohen.com

Acknowledgements

To Szura—thank you for trusting me with your story; without you, this book could never exist. Your courage, your memories, and your voice are at the heart of every page.

To Rafa, my pillar, and to Natalie, Vanessa, and Samantha—the quiet strength that lifts me, the steady force that carries me forward.

To my father, whose memory I carry every day, and to my mother, who shaped my love of history.

Masza, I can never thank you enough for your generosity in sharing the details of your story that made these pages possible. And to Victor, who walked by my side in the Belarusian forest as we pieced together Szura's memories.

To my brothers, my sister, and my extended family—your presence, love, and support have been a constant light along this journey.

Felipe Solís, your mentorship shaped the person I am today; your dedication to education inspired my path as an art historian and inspired me to teach. Paul Azaroff, your passion for Jewish culture has been contagious, and your encouragement has lifted me when I needed it most.

To friends who cheered me on along the way—thank you. Samara Walman and Alexis Summer, your thoughtful feedback at just the right moment helped guide this book to its final form.

I am also deeply grateful to the Holocaust Documentation Center for welcoming me and opening its doors. Through them, I met Frida, a survivor whose memories of the Bielsky brothers brought history vividly to life, and I was also reconnected with Mike and Bella Stolowitsky, who generously shared their own testimonies, reminding me of the enduring power of bearing witness.

And a special thank you to my daughter, Samantha—you have been my companion, my editor, my translator, and my inspiration. Every time you read these pages, corrected them, and helped me translate them from Spanish into English, you infused them with care, love, and attention. This book carries your spirit as much as mine.

Author's Note

While this book is written as a novel, it's grounded in the real events of Szura Pupko's life. Over the years, Szura shared with me many episodes of her journey, and through this book, I have tried to honor her life and capture her spirit. Most of what you'll read comes directly from those memories, along with the recollections of other Holocaust survivors I was fortunate enough to speak with. Of course, I have added dialogue and details to bring the narrative to life, but the core of the plot and the dates are real—these events did happen.

Some names have been changed for privacy and others because they were lost to time. To shape these stories into a cohesive whole, I spent years researching the locations mentioned here, as well as how they were affected during World War I and II. Because the borders of this region shifted so often, you may see different names for the same place. Russian, Hebrew, and Yiddish terms appear as transliterations, as they were part of the way Szura shared her memories with me.

My hope is that this book allows Szura's incredible story to be heard for generations to come. Her legacy lives on not only in these pages but through her family. Szura lived in Mexico, surrounded by her eight great-grandchildren, through the age of ninety-six. Her life was marked not only by survival but also by love, family, and an enduring spirit.

Contents

SHURA

Prologue

A bow holds together the few thin strands of hair that fall against the back of her neck, the shiny ribbon reminiscent of her coquetry and her taste for luxury. She might be old, but her appearance still evokes the essence of the dazzling woman she once was. That afternoon in September 1999, when I began to untie the mysteries of her life, she was looking through the window of her apartment in Mexico City—watching the rain at dusk, not thinking about her losses or her achievements. Little by little, she began remembering: her sufferings, her anxieties, the uncertainty of a troubled, evil world, and her lost love.

The clock was ticking; the rhythm of her words carried her beyond the walls of her apartment, and my presence was no longer relevant to her. My questions or exclamations didn't matter; she was not listening to me anymore. The uninterrupted flow of her voice filled the space. Her experiences gathered inside her body, beating strongly as they tried to burst out—transgressing the barriers of her mind. Suddenly, she would raise her head and notice me. I was trying to write down her words, but she would gesture a sign forbidding me to do so. I wanted to capture her stories in my mind, eager to remember every detail, every episode she was recounting. I placed myself in her shoes and imagined what she felt, trying to recreate the images she was describing to express them on these pages...

I see the world with injured eyes. My soul endures through the sleepless nights. Fragments from my childhood come to life. Faceless memories suddenly arrive. Lost friends and family members appear as ghosts. The hidden shadow of the truth is there: it is the truth, my truth! It is my past. There is a fence I cannot hurdle—the nostalgia that will not let me die. I have lived in that past, a past that gets into my wounds and prevents them from healing.

Introduction: 1914

Masza Nechama Rapoport was the eldest daughter of Shabtai and Leah Rapoport, who was a descendant of the Talmudic scholar Nachman Meishe Soloveitchick from Brisk. Masza and Shmuel Bernstein met and connected instantly. Not very long after, they decided to get married in Anykščiai, Lithuania.

Under the *chuppah,* the wedding canopy, the young couple looked radiant, listening attentively to the blessings of the rabbi. The ceremony ended traditionally with Shmuel smashing a wine glass with his foot, breaking it into pieces to remember the destruction of the Second Temple in Jerusalem. The crowd pronounced a loud, *"Mazel tov,"* and the celebration started.

Men began to spin to the beat of the *klezmer* and *freilajs* melodies. Shmuel did not wish to dance. All those traditions were old-fashioned and pointless. He was more interested in nature and science.

For Shmuel, Yiddish represented the *shtetl*, the small Jewish village. The language was a reflection of the past, a display of the backward ways by which most Jews still lived. He knew he was more sophisticated than that. He had a higher education degree and had worked at a major pharmacy in Vilna. Shmuel was a man who was up to date on the advances of the twentieth century. The music that the Jewish group played pierced his ears; the pace of the clarinet and the vocal wail of the singer were not for him. He found the whole thing cacophonous and the dancing leaps of the crowd ridiculous.

Masza's younger brother took the hand of his newly pronounced brother-in-law and placed him inside the circle of dancing men. That gesture of affection was more powerful than Shmuel's rational mind. He gave into the rhythm of the music and jovial atmosphere, leaving behind his logical principles. Shmuel searched for his bride with every turn, trying to lock eyes with her as she blissfully danced with the women. They were a couple in love and were about to begin a new journey together.

***

Thanks to the dowry provided by Shabtai, Shmuel and Masza built their house with an adjacent pharmacy in Nemenčinė.

Shmuel was received with open arms the moment he arrived in Nemenčinė—the town didn't have a doctor, and his study of pharmacology in Russia was highly regarded. He immediately earned everyone's respect. Masza adapted easily to the circumstances. Nemenčinė was a small village, smaller than her native Anykščiai. Beautiful and well-educated, she quickly became a local celebrity. The village women joyfully visited the young couple daily to pay their respects. And Masza certainly enjoyed their attention.

In early August of that same year, Germany attacked Russia. The Jews of the *shtetl* were fearful of what would become of them. As history had taught them, the Jewish community would pay the price whenever there was conflict in the region.

The Russian army was composed of Cossacks and young men who had been drafted. As the soldiers paraded through the streets of Nemenčinė on their way to the front, children came out of their houses to greet them. They marched through the villages, spreading their seed and leaving traces of unfinished love affairs.

The Great War grew into a powerful monster that raged through Europe. Nemenčinė was affected by the lack of food and supplies. Masza learned that she was pregnant during those days. The good news was accompanied by a bad omen; life and death were wrestling. Starvation and uncertainty were followed by yet another matter: Masza had developed a small lump in her breast. It was cancer. Without any medical resources, the disease progressed. It invaded Masza's body, destroying every cell in its path in the same way the Kaiser's army was annihilating Lithuania.

The war reawakened Europe's antisemitism. Lithuanians and Poles blamed the Jews for their misfortunes and ruthlessly and repeatedly attacked them.

***

November 7, 1914 (18 Cheshvan 5675 in the Jewish calendar). Masza drank an herbal tea to induce labor, but the baby refused to greet the world. After a long struggle, Szifra Bernstein Rapoport— or Szura, as she would later be known—was born in Vilna. Shmuel, the new father, gave donations to the poor. Feeling blessed, he was generous with the *tzdoke*, thanking God for the health of his newborn daughter.

A few months after the delivery, Masza's skin—usually a velvety lustrous white—became ashen. She was rapidly dying. They tried everything to save her, even going so far as to giving her a new name to fool the Angel of Death. Nothing worked. Masza lost the battle to an aggressive breast cancer on the twenty-first of *Tishrei* of the year 5676 at the age of twenty-seven. She left behind a trail of pain, a widowed husband, and a newborn.

Friends and acquaintances accompanied the mourners at their home before the burial. They didn't leave Masza alone, not even for a minute; there was always somebody praying Psalms beside the corpse. In the living room, some whispered the latest gossip, overlooking the still-warm body above which death hovered. The murmur lulled the little child as she slept in the arms of her grandmother Leah.

Masza's body, covered with a light sheet, was transported to the cemetery in a one-horse-drawn carriage. Everybody walked in an orderly fashion up to the gates of the old cemetery of Vilna. The trees, lined up in rows, observed the flow of time, absorbing every regret, every affliction, and every sorrow that passed through. Surrounded by tombstones with epitaphs in Yiddish and Hebrew, the cortege waited for the last rites to be completed before Masza's burial. People of the *Chevre Kadisha*, the Jewish burial society, washed the body, wrapped it in white linen, and placed it in a wooden coffin with sand brought from *Eretz* Israel.

The close family members ripped their clothes in mourning, a tradition that allowed them to release their frustration and grief. The ritual served as a poignant sign of suffering over Masza's premature fate. The widower Shmuel Bernstein, Masza's parents Shabtai and Leah Rapoport, and Masza's siblings surrounded the burial until the completion of the funeral prayer.

Before exiting the cemetery, Shmuel washed his hands three times, letting the water drain his tears. He looked down and noticed his shoes soiled with dirt—the same dirt which had just covered his lifeless wife. Downcast, he headed back to the apartment he had temporarily rented in Vilna.

Shivah, the period of mourning, was observed in the strictest manner. Leah covered all the mirrors in Shmuel's house and prayed so Masza's soul wouldn't be trapped in the reflection: "God, save us from seeing the Angel of Death hanging around here." She pushed the chairs into a corner and sat down on the floor. Shabtai, Maisei, Shayna, Sonja, and Meyer joined her. Shmuel was the last one to sit.

The neighbors brought food to the house: herring, plum wine, hard-boiled eggs, and peas—all symbols of mourning. The silence was broken only by the baby's cries. An echo of enormous grief was felt around the room. The little girl was inconsolable. Her cries were interpreted as a sign of despair, as if she knew the fate that awaited her. Shayna, Masza's sister, took her niece into her arms, calming her down as she fed her a bottle of milk. Only thus did the baby fall asleep. Szifra would grow up with fortitude forged by adversity, which gave her the skills to fight. That was her *bashert*, her destiny.

Shmuel choked back tears, trying to prevent them from flowing down his cheeks. He felt isolated from the world. He regretted not knowing how to keep his baby safe. He feared he wouldn't be able to fill the maternal void. As a pharmacist, he worked long days; maybe he was not cut out to be a good father. Little by little, he convinced himself that the child would be better off in the care of her grandparents.

With an absent mind, Shmuel hugged his daughter goodbye and handed the child to Leah, his mother-in-law. Wrapped in wool blankets, Szifra, by then only a few months old, could not realize that this simple act would mark her life. The Great War would modify the borders; suddenly, familiar places would become hopelessly impenetrable, forbidding communication between the newly imposed boundaries, separating father and daughter.

Leah, Shabtai, and the baby departed for Anykščiai in a

horse-drawn cart. Shmuel left for Nemenčinė feeling lonely and empty.

Szifra thus became the "daughter" of Shabtai and Leah Rapoport; she would call them Mom and Dad. Szifra would grow up without knowing anything about her deceased mother or the existence of her biological father. Until she turned thirteen years old, she lived a happy fallacy beside her grandparents and uncles.

This is her story from Lithuania to Mexico:

A poppy among cacti.

And if no more Jews remain in my city—

Their souls live on in its alleys.

And he who thinks a house is empty

And walks in

And puts up an idol, a table, makes a bed,

Puts on an abandoned shirt,

A dress,

A shawl—

At night, he will hear the crying of children,

And the shirt will become a grater, shredding his skin.

Until he runs madly out of the house

Abraham Sutzkever

"Farewell"

Written in Zazherye forest

October 13, 1943

Chapter One: 1914-1923

My *mother* Leah had shiny and beautiful hair, but she always wore it hidden under a scarf. She would move constantly, from one side to the other, back and forth, cleaning here and there, always humming to herself. Shabtai, my *father*, wore on his face the perfect portrait of sadness. His kindness was noticeable through his sweet little watery gray eyes, ready to cry but eternally repressing the urge just before giving into it. As a good Lithuanian, he took everything with a grave and serious

tone; but with me he was always tender and good. His beard, as white as flour, matched his friendly features, and his soft and melodious voice made my soul happy.

 Mama was devoted to the *midrashim*, the rabbinic commentaries, so she sewed a red ribbon around my tiny bed to protect me against Lilith. The amulet worked! The 1915 cholera epidemic that swept the streets of Anykščiai passed without greeting us. In 1917, typhoid hovered over the town for over nine months and killed hundreds of children. But the illness never touched me. Typhoid, influenza, chills, and high fever took many children during the Great War; red signals on doors pathetically adorned houses and announced quarantines. Wagons would constantly pass to take the coffins off the streets. It was said that in Vilna, one Jew died for every ten inhabitants. During those years, the flu failed to weaken me, and diarrhea never shared my crib—all thanks to my *mother's* talismans.

The Germans had taken over Anykščiai. Petroshka, the young Lithuanian girl who helped my *mother* at home, took me by the hand to the Yavnoson's guesthouse, where my *parents* were. From their house, we could better observe the military deployment progressing down the main avenue.

There was always a nice buzz in my *parents'* friend's house. They often received travelers who'd spend the night and leave the following morning for the next town. Merchants, messengers, rabbis, and young students left only fleeting traces of their stay: crumbs on the dishes, dirty sheets, and a distant murmur that faded when they were gone.

As soon as we came in, I rushed to the Yavnoson girls to show them my doll. Brachana, Fin, and Aida gathered around me to play. We then sat down, drank tea, ate babka, and played while our parents dined and talked about the current political situation, which we were far from understanding.

What did I know of Vladimir Lenin, who had led the Bolshevik army and taken hold of the city of Petrograd? Or of the pressure that the British government imposed on Zionism, the national movement that wished to establish a Jewish state in Palestine?

We looked out the window at the German soldiers patrolling the streets. We were amused, admiring their uniforms and the black, red, and yellow horizontal stripes on their flags.

"When will the war end?" asked my worried *mother* while she said her goodbyes, embracing me as we walked back home.

***

The Germans left Anykščiai when the western front collapsed. The army withdrew on February 16, 1918. Lithuania's independence was declared on that very same day.

The town's respite only lasted five months. On July 16, 1918, Tsar Nicholas II was assassinated, and the Bolsheviks invaded Lithuania. Tyranny and deprivation knocked at the door.

The Bolsheviks made the people feel the iron sickle and persecuted anyone who had an aristocratic or bourgeois past. This new "egalitarian" society treated all capitalists as a danger to society; the punishment was banishment to Siberia. Many were deported, others were shot in public places, some fled and found shelter hiding in remote farms, but most preferred anonymity and poverty.

"Comrades, long live the proletariat, we'll finish the bourgeois." Those were the words that resounded through the muddy alleys of Anykščiai. Smugglers and swindlers owned the city.

The stores, like my *father's*, were emptied by the invaders only to be forced back again into terrible shortages. Beggars took over the streets, living on the sidewalks and asking for bread.

We often gathered at the Yavnoson's guesthouse. Fear and confusion invaded their living room. As kids, we understood nothing; the dimensions of this crucial historical moment were beyond our simple comprehension of the world. It was difficult for us to feel the contagious fear spreading amongst the adults.

In January 1919, we received news that Vilna had been taken by the Polish legionaries. Five days later, the Bolsheviks drove out the Poles and nationalized the factories. By April 19, the Polish legionaries returned and expelled the Russians. The lack of control was exhausting.

General Józef Piłsudski, the Polish head of state, had no control over his troops. Many took the opportunity to turn their anger against the Jews. News came from Vilna: the ancient Jewish cemetery Beth Olam, located on the opposite side of the Vilija River, had been desecrated. A mob attacked and ransacked the Jewish neighborhood, taking whatever they wished. The chaos was so great that men, women, and children were snatched and taken to the

Lipuvka suburb, where they were forced to dig their graves before they were assassinated.

I was still very young; I did not want to listen to adult conversations; their worries made me feel uneasy, and I tried to block out their voices. Somehow, even so, their conversation seeped through my ears, disturbing my thoughts.

"Some were buried alive," they said.

"Others were thrown into the river Vilija with their hands tied."

"A Jew was tied to a horse and dragged through the streets of the city of Lida."

"Three men stabbed a Jewish family in Białystok."

***

Elections were held in Lithuania on the first day of February 1921. Everything was so confusing. Poland had annexed several territories, including Vilna, and Lithuania had been divided into two, but Anykščiai was still located in an independent region.

Bordered by a forest of black alders, aspens, and cottonwoods, whose shadows framed the river Šventoji, Anykščiai had the air of a provincial town. We all knew each other, and we all lived in our own reality, isolated from the outside world. It was a small Jewish village, with Yiddish as the common language.

We would wake up at dawn during the winter and have an early breakfast of black or rye bread smeared with *schmaltz*, the chicken fat saved as a little treat. Shayna and Sonja, my *sisters,* were my role models. Sonja counted the days until she could leave Anykščiai to attend the *gymnasium,* the higher education institution in Riga. Shayna would make sure that I ate a healthy meal before she left for work at the bank in the main square. Meyer, my older *brother,* had married Leye Wolchick and worked with my *father* in his grocery store. I'd entertain myself by helping my *mother* or visiting my *father* in his store. Then I would wait for Petroshka or Shayna to play with me or go for a walk.

I enjoyed every minute of watching my *mother* prepare herring with cream or organize the pickles and jams in different glass jars. She'd put them on a high shelf in the kitchen so they were out of my reach. I felt special whenever she entrusted me with any task, especially if it had to do with finding something in the cupboard located at the back of the room where she kept all the *chachkes*—different objects that were seldom used—or even when she would ask me to arrange the coats along the rack at the entrance of the house. I could spend hours cleaning my *galoshi,* my rubber boots, which were usually dirty with mud, or running around the simple wooden dining table in the center of the house.

Anykščiai was an enchanted city, especially because it was powered by electricity, making the dark mornings magical. At home, a single bulb flickered timidly, illuminating the main room. I would fix my eyes on the light and pretend it was the spring sun. When my eyes would tire, I would look down and then at the walls. Different colors appeared around the pictures that decorated the room.

"It is my ancestor, Rabbi Soloveitchick. He was a Talmudic scholar and a renowned religious intellectual," my *mother* would state proudly when she caught me looking at his portrait. I can still see the sublime eyes framed by the bushy eyebrows.

"*Zichrono lebrajah*, blessed be his memory," she would whisper.

***

The public entrance to my *father's* store was down the street of Birutes. It was a small place with miscellaneous items sold in bulk. Shelves were stuffed with items like soaps, perfumes, wax, wool, matches, needles, thread, sacks of caraway, poppy, kasha, and millet. The floor was covered in bags of potatoes, rock salt, and honey, along with barrels of wheat and barley.

During the early days of winter, the wholesale store was even more crowded as farmers delivered large bags of produce to sell before the first frost. My *mother* would also make sauerkraut and pickled beets to sell. In the summertime, blackberries, plums, raspberries, cherries, blueberries, and peaches accentuated the colorful store. The highly priced fresh and dried mushrooms were stored in glass jars on the shelves. We had apples and pears all year round, and occasionally, my *father* procured oranges and grapefruit. Those fruits were a real treasure: exotic, imported from Spain, and sold at exorbitant prices. Bananas were also a treat and usually sold to a sick person or a rich pregnant woman. During the month of

September, a sole pineapple was sporadically offered. Only the very rich could afford it and would buy it to say a special prayer during Rosh Hashanah, the Jewish New Year.

Some afternoons, when I ventured to visit my *father*, I would enter quietly so as not to bother him, trying my best not to make noise when stepping on the seeds that had accidentally fallen onto the wooden floor. I would lean close to the cash register next to my *father's* feet, hoping he'd take a break and let me play with the register. I would stroke his white beard that contrasted with his dark suit and take refuge in his sweet eyes.

"*Papa*, can I have some candy?" I would implore.

"Bubbala, my little doll, not now, I'm busy."

"Please, *Papa*."

"Szifra, I told you to wait, I cannot attend to you now." My *father* would speak softly but impose his authority. "Go look for your *mama*, or Petroshka, or Shayna. She probably has come home from work by now."

I would disappear quickly through the connecting house door and go to the room I shared with Shayna to wait for her. She would give me comfort. She spoiled me, and I adored her.

My *father* had difficulty being strict with me. His gentle character would surface instinctively, and before the end of the day, he would take a break just to bring me a whole piece of chocolate. Those few moments were sublime. They were minutes to cherish until a customer would ring the bell again—and then the magical moment would evaporate.

The nights were quiet in our house. Every night, around the same time, my *mother* would sit down at the table in the main room of the house and dedicate a few moments to balance the accounts. In her little black book, she would calculate the finances of the store: the expenses, the income, and the credit that was granted to certain customers. In a separate list, she inscribed everything that was needed for our living. She saved every penny and never spent any money on luxuries or banalities.

In our room, Shayna would invite me to sit beside her on the couch while she lit the kerosene lamp. The dim light drew shadows on her face, announcing small premature wrinkles on her visage. She would read aloud from her book *Ze'enah U Re'enah*. I listened carefully to the mysteries and legends. I liked hearing her soft, melodious voice narrating the miraculous events of our ancestors. Shayna shared her knowledge, and I tried to stay awake. I fought against the sleepiness that came over me, but my eyelids weighed too much. Finally, I would give into slumber. Shayna would turn off the small lamp and put me tenderly into bed. I would feel her lips barely brushing my forehead. She would whisper affectionately: "*A gute nacht, mein kind*, good night, my child." Without hearing the end of the story, I would fall asleep.

***

My family was convinced that the future for the Jews was in *Eretz* Israel. I was required to learn Hebrew in order to settle in the land of my ancestors. In 1922, I was enrolled at the Tarbut school, located three blocks from the house. Each morning, I would walk through the small streets of Anykščiai armed with a pencil and a small notebook. I'd pass by the *cheder*, the study hall of *melamed* Kaplan who taught the foundations of the Hebrew Torah, and then I would wave at the butcher on the corner. Walking through the alleys, one by one, friends would join the group, and we would walk together to school.

I started learning Hebrew and some Lithuanian. *Morah* Chayele Konitzki, my teacher, recited the verses from Nahman Bialik and taught us about Eliezer Ben-Yehuda, who devoted his life to composing the first Hebrew dictionary.

One day, *Morah* Chayele asked for silence, and her gentle but excited voice filled the room as she started to recite the poem "Vilna" by Shneour, published only a few months earlier. The rhythmic words transported us to the Lithuanian capital across the Black Border created after the Great War. Vilna was not far from Anykščiai, but it was impossible to visit as it was occupied by Poland. We imagined the prosperous city, the center of Jewish spirituality, in which the Gaon—the wisest of the Jews of Vilna—had introduced his disciples into philosophical Talmudic dissertations.

Classes would end at noon. Accompanied by several friends, I would walk straight to my house. One day, while talking, we did not realize that several boys had been following us. They did not look Jewish and disdainfully shouted at us in Lithuanian. I tried to understand what they were saying, but we mostly spoke Yiddish. I only managed to hear "dirty Jews." There were many of them, older and stronger. We were frightened as they approached us, and we ran as fast as we could. Without asking permission to enter the house of an acquaintance of my *parents*, we took refuge there until the boys ran off and it was safe to return to our homes.

I was panting when I arrived home and waited anxiously for Shayna to return from work. Night came. Already in my bed, I took out my book *Sipurei HaMikrah.* The book had been given to me by the school and explained the stories of the Bible. I couldn't concentrate; I was distracted. I kept thinking about what had happened on the street and what it meant.

When Shayna arrived, she noticed my nervousness. She stroked my hair and asked gently, "What is it, Szifra?"

I told her what had happened.

She replied assertively, "We as Jews have had to learn to live with the hatred of our neighbors. We must be grateful for what we have now. We don't suffer from hunger or poverty, and we can enjoy our health. If this happens again, do not answer them, just ignore them, try to walk fast, and get close to areas where there are more people. Promise me you will never walk in deserted streets again."

I looked at her incredulously. "Shouldn't I defend myself? They insult us like we don't have any dignity ...."

"Promise me you'll do as I tell you." Shayna steadied her gaze, looking straight into my eyes until I nodded.

The next morning, the young assailants were waiting at the corner. This time, they were armed with stones. They threw them at us like bullets. We tried to take cover, but we were inevitably beaten. A stone hit my leg, and my knee bled a little.

Frightened, we told our *morah* what had happened. She promised to accompany us back to our homes after class. Down the road from the onslaught, the same boys waited for us once again, this time with sticks. When they saw an adult accompanying us, they gave up and disappeared in a flash.

From that day on, I was afraid to go out alone. I was so innocent, I believed in spirits and gnomes and thought that if I pronounced an incantation against evil, it would be enough to protect me. It occurred to me that I could wish them to lose all their teeth, leaving them with only one ever-aching tooth. I pictured myself spitting on their faces and cursing them to grow like onions, with their heads underground. In my imagination, my ideas were simple and easy. But I never did anything. Whenever I bumped into those boys, I would fall silent and run across the street for safety.

They never attacked us again; however, we knew that people didn't like us. Hatred grew each day. We chose to ignore it just to survive.

***

Wednesday was market day. I accompanied my *father* to the main square with a big basket to carry the vegetables we would buy. We passed just in front of the church on our way there. My father pointed at the door and warned, "Szifra, *mein kind*, my dear, the Jews should not look in there."

"Why?" I asked, turning with curiosity toward the open door of the church of Saint Mathew. I knew the answer wouldn't be a simple explanation but rather a Talmudic lesson. I was eager to peek inside the immense space filled with impenetrable darkness.

What will I find that makes it so forbidden to us? I thought without externalizing my curiosity. My *father* realized that I had slowed my pace and was snooping, trying to guess what was hidden inside the church walls.

Pulling my arm, he exclaimed in a trembling voice, "The church is not for us; our eyes should not see what's inside, and our ears should not hear what the Christians preach." He continued pulling my arm and hurried toward the main square where the market was.

The plaza was filled with horse-drawn carriages, some rickety from their heavy weight. Ragged peasants and savvy traders came from far away to offer their products. Sellers roamed the improvised alleys with wicker baskets loaded with produce—each one of them shouting, offering their merchandise.

"Half a *lita* for a *beigl!*" shouted a woman with a flowered cloth covering her head. She took the basket with both hands and showed me what she had inside. It was full of bread; the smell got my attention. I looked back at my *father* for approval, and he nodded. I chose a *beigl*. As my father paid, the woman took out her *knippl,* which was nothing more than a dirty handkerchief where she kept her earnings, and placed into it the money she had just received.

It was a harsh winter day, but even so, the market was full of life. A group of men were gathered around an open drum in which a fire burned. Most women sellers were sitting and had placed a brazier inside their petticoats to keep warm. Everybody was there: the *pákntreger* selling used books, the supplier of kerosene, the merchant who offered marinated herring at an affordable price, the seller of secondhand clothing, and even an avid "feather plucker."

I was spellbound by the spectacle of peasants, who spoke only Lithuanian, haranguing and negotiating with Jews who answered in Yiddish. I enjoyed the excitement and the intricacies of negotiations and bargaining between Jews and Christians, who would usually close a deal with a universal handshake.

We bought milk and salt and walked toward the section where they were selling fish. A pungent and peculiar smell emanated from the place, impregnating my nose. The stench of dead fish increased until it became almost unbearable. Enduring the discomfort, I watched my *father* as he used the basics of the Lithuanian tongue to get the best price for a live carp.

The tannery was located on the opposite side of the square. On that corner, at the end of the plaza, there were other small shops selling clothes, fabrics, hats, and some other trinkets. These shops would open every day of the week, but they would take advantage of market day to make their best sales. Merchants and peasants would come at the end of the day to spend their earnings. I wanted to explore these places and see the array of things they offered, but we had our heavy baskets full of purchases, including a live fish.

We hurried home. Upon arrival, I helped my *father* fill a big bucket of water to preserve the carp until the next day so we could have it fresh.

***

It was Friday. Classes ended early, as was customary in the Jewish schools. An astringent smell hit me as I opened the front door of my house. My *mother* and Petroshka had thoroughly cleaned the house, as they always did before *Shabbat*. The young Lithuanian girl had scrubbed the floors with bleach until they were shiny, leaving an antiseptic odor hanging around the room. But as I entered the house, more pleasant aromas surfaced. The smell of the food cooking on the stove soothed me, and I remembered that I only had a pickle for lunch ... and now I was starving.

I came close to the stove and opened the pot of *cholent*, a meat stew with lentils, potatoes, and barley. The *tzimes*—sweet carrots—were ready, expelling their fragrance. On the table, my *mother* kneaded small *knishes* stuffed with mashed potatoes; they would be ready for dinner. In the center of the table, the challah dough rose slowly under the cloth. My *mother* flattened the bread dough with just one strike then took a small piece and threw it into the fire saying the blessing, "Blessed are you, Lord our God, King of the Universe, who has sanctified us with His commandments and commanded us to eat challah." Then she braided the rest of the dough together.

Szifra is growing rapidly. I am old, my back is hunched, my eyes don't see clearly anymore, and my hands tremble in an arrhythmic beat. My beautiful granddaughter: Who will take care of you if I die? Who will explain to you the facts of life? Will your aunt Shayna be able to take care of you? It's not fair to doom Shayna for a life of solitude, taking care of others, without ever experiencing love. It's not fair .... Please, God, give me the strength to shape Szifra's character and allow me to see her turn into a woman. I beg you, God, don't take my health away, I need to go on.

"Szifra, pass me the poppy seeds, I need to put them on the challah."

I took the jar full of black seeds from the shelf. She glazed the braided dough with egg wash and let me sprinkle the seeds over it. She put the two loaves on a brass tray and placed them in the oven. The fine aroma of the *Shabbat* bread soon began to cover the walls of the house.

I wanted to see my friend Abrasha Evenson before *Shabbat*, so I quickly put on my wool tights, slipped on my *galoshi*, and asked my *mother* for permission to leave. I ran to meet him, and we went to play in the snow before nightfall.

As we scampered through the cobbled streets, we saw Perchik, the Russian beggar who always came to visit the house before *Shabbat*. I hurried back home before he knocked on the door.

The small box that hung on the door frame, the *mezuzah*, greeted me every time. In an automatic gesture, I brushed it with my fingertips and brought them to my lips.

I greeted my *mother* while inhaling the aroma of the food on the stove. Coins were already set on the table, ready for the *shnorer* to ask for charity. The beggar would look in through the window in a matter of seconds. Before he even knocked on the door, I took the money and put it in his open hand. He smiled at me and went on his way without saying a word.

Mama was busy, like every Friday. She wanted to flatter the family with a beautiful *Shabbat* meal. She was hurrying to finish everything before sundown and the appearance of the first star in the sky. The last rays of sunshine were starting to vanish; not much time remained before the day of rest. The sanctity of the moment started to envelop the atmosphere of our home.

The voice of the *shames*, the assistant rabbi, announcing the arrival of *Shabbat* was heard through the streets. Sounding his bell, he urged men and women to go to the *mikveh*, the ritual bath. *Papa* picked up the clean clothes that *Mama* had laid for him on the chair, took his hat, his prayer shawl, and his book, and off he went to the *mikveh*.

Today I managed to close the store in time to go to the *mikveh* before heading to *shul*, the synagogue. The bath has revitalized me; I feel that youthful energy and momentum again. "*Baruch Atah Adonai*, blessed are you, Lord." I get my head through my garment; I feel the rough wool of the *tzitzit* over my shoulders. I am old and tired, my eyes no longer work like they used to, and still, I must educate a child, *mein* Szifra. The strings of the *tzitzit* fall on my hip. I put on the white clean shirt that Leah has prepared for me and put on top the black caftan to finish my outfit. Today is *Shabbat,* and I, Shabtai, am a happy man!

I wanted to go with my *father* to the *shul* to pray beside him; I hurried and put on the dress with red embroidered flowers that my *mother* had bought for me especially for *Shabbat.* I left the house with my coat and my *galoshi* and found *Papa* on the road near the *eyruv*, the enclosure that the rabbis had placed around the village. As we walked, he greeted friends and acquaintances with a nod. The number of men in black caftans grew the closer we got to the Street of the Synagogues, and the more it looked like a uniformed parade. The mass split almost as quickly as it had united—with each person heading to the house of prayer of their choice. Some would enter the small synagogue of carpenters while others went to the Sephardic synagogue. My *father* and I went into one of the *misnagdim*, where my *father* was the honorary manager, the *gabai.*

The *shul* had a sober look on the outside. Small steps indicated the entrance and guided congregants into a large open space. In the center of the room was the *bimah*, a platform made of wood with carved railings, which had been donated last year by the shoemakers' guild. *Papa* was happy to get into this synagogue, built in part with funding sent from America by my *half-brothers* Leibn and Yosef.

I headed to the top section, the *ezras noshim,* where a few women were seated. I sat in my usual spot. On the wall, facing *mizrach*, east toward Jerusalem, I could see the ark in which the Torah was kept. It was an elegant cedarwood cabinet with a complicated etched design that seemed endless. The door of the ark was covered with a velvet fabric, ornamented with the coat of arms of David, the *Magen David*, and framed with Judea lions embellished in gold and silver.

My *father* sat in his customary place, surrounded by friends and acquaintances. I sat watching him from above as he hurried to cover his head with the *tallit* before the beginning of the prayer. The humming started as a lullaby; the rhythmic swaying of the bodies accompanied the songs and prayers. While some prayers grew louder and seemed sad lamentations with rhythmic moans, others had the tone of afflicted groans, and the rest were quiet supplications. Passion and spirituality filled the room. The congregants prayed with great fervor as they completed the eighteen prayers. After that, the prayer culminated in pure silence only to be interrupted a few minutes later with melodious songs, leading eventually to the last prayer, *Adon Olam*.

As we walked back home together, we saw *Shabbat* candles glittering languidly through our neighbors' windows. As it was every Friday night, the table was covered with a white cloth and adorned with challah and wine. My *mother* looked beautiful in her black silk dress and pearl necklace. My *father* came in after me and left his black hat at the entrance, replacing it with a *kippa* over his head.

"*Gut Shabbos*, have a good Sabbath," he said.

We sat around the table, my *dad* at the head, my *mama* next to him. Singing in unison *Malachei Elyon* in honor of the *Shabbat* angels, we felt the richness of the moment. My *papa* blessed the glass of wine, which was filled to the very top. With skill and expertise, he sipped without spilling even one scarlet droplet on the tablecloth. Then my *mother* tasted the wine from the same cup, as was customary. The cup was passed on to me. The sweet wine barely touched my lips.

Mama placed the jar with holders on the sink so we could do the ritual of washing our hands. After rinsing our hands and saying the appropriate prayer, we returned to the table without uttering a word and waited for the blessing of the bread. As always, my *mother* removed the napkin covering the challah, and my *father* grabbed the two loaves to bless them. Then he cut the bread into small pieces and distributed them. Everyone murmured the prayer, breaking the silence, before we each ate a morsel of bread. *Mama* hurriedly brought the cooked carp, giving the fish's head to my *father* as an honor.

"Leah, please, you eat the head!" *Papa* said.

Mama smiled, satisfied with my *father's* respect for her and just as pleased when she saw my *father* savoring the juicy meat. It was strange to see those little signs of affection between them, which were hardly visible to the untrained eye. These subtle gestures were part of their communication. Rarely would their hands touch; just a gentle smile, a sweet twinkle in their eyes, or a nod sufficed … their small actions were just as sugar and raisins sweetening the dough of the *lokshen kugel.*

The conversation veered between the problems of the people of Anykščiai, the livelihood of the Jews in *Eretz* Israel, and the *lokshen* and fish that my *mother* had prepared.

I was hypnotized by the almost-extinct flame of the *Shabbat* candles. I had the urge to blow them out, but I refrained, as I remembered that *Mama* had warned me that doing so was a sin and could cause great grief for the family. Instead, I just stood there, without moving, watching the wax melt. *Mama* cleared the table, and I watched her add the leftover meat to the *cholent* on the stove.

***

When I woke up the next day, my *father* had already left for *shul.* I hurried to get ready to catch up with him.

I looked for Shayna upon returning home after the prayers. I had many questions swirling inside me, and I thought maybe she had the answers.

"*Mama* told me that we have an additional soul that adheres to us on *Shabbat* and that this glorified being helps us solve our problems. Shayna, you have no idea, every week I try to find this *neshomeh yeseireh*, that very soul that helps us to think of God, that second soul that *Mama* talks about so passionately. I try very hard to concentrate on God, but my mind always tricks me, and I end up thinking about my friends at school and the games we play together. What can I do, Shayna?"

"Oh, my dearest Szifra." Shayna sighed. "*Mein kind*, do not worry about the *neshomeh*, she is with you, but she's still just as playful as you are. You will grow soon enough, and your *neshomeh* will help you clear your thoughts, you'll see."

Shayna fell asleep soon after our talk, she worked so hard at a local bank a few blocks from our house. Silence crept on the walls; the stillness of a *Shabbat* afternoon was rising like the sweet vapor of a perfume. The rhythmic movement of the branches of the tree outside my window began to lull me to sleep.

Suddenly, I heard someone calling my name. It was my friend Abrasha Evenson! Without anyone noticing, I quickly went outside to join him. We held hands and ran through the muddy street, laughing all the way. We did not realize we had strayed away from our homes and found ourselves in the middle of the Christian quarter. We were a little afraid though thrilled to be on unfamiliar turf.

A group of scruffy older boys stopped at the corner just in front of us. We felt threatened as they shouted obscenities at us. We crossed quickly to the opposite side of the road, trying to avoid them, but to no avail. They started to chase after us as we ran faster. There were quite a few of them. My heart was pounding incessantly. Nobody was nearby to help us; we were not in our familiar Jewish neighborhood anymore. None of our acquaintances would leave home at that hour; people were either taking a *Shabbos* nap or concentrating on the religious rituals of the holy day. We were on our own and terrified. Fleeing, we reached an alley. The boys surrounded us, measuring our fear, and defying us. Their faces came close to ours. They were wolves with sharpened teeth gleaming with irony and malice. Luckily, something unexpected dissuaded them. I didn't know what happened—they just turned their backs, leaving us there, confused and shaking.

I arrived back at my house without being seen, took the prayer book my *mother* had left in the room the night before, and started to read, pretending that nothing had happened. Time came for *Havdalah*, the last *Shabbat* prayer. We gathered around the table waiting for *Papa* to recite the blessing. He was saying goodbye to the holy day and welcoming the first working day. He filled the glass with wine and, as he did every *Shabbat*, handed me a small box with aromatic spices for me to smell. I brought the braided candle from the side table, and my *father* took a sip of wine after saying the blessing, wet his fingers with wine, and touched his eyes and ears. With his wet fingers, he pressed the wick of the candle and extinguished the light. The ritual finished with the usual phrase: "*Gute voch*, have a good and healthy week."

"Amen," we answered in unison.

We ate rye bread, a symbol differentiating the daily routine from the holy day, hoping to return to our daily chores and looking forward to the week ahead.

The next day, I went with Petroshka to the main square where the well was located. We took two empty tin buckets to fill with water. As with every Sunday, we would hear the bells announcing the beginning of mass.

Petroshka took me by the hand along the road that followed the curve of the river and led to the church. We arrived at the large wooden door. Petroshka asked me to wait on the sidewalk as she went into the church. A man was playing the mandolin at the entrance, and some onlookers came by to give him a few coins.

From the threshold, I could hear the harmonious, sublime songs of the Christian ceremony. I wanted to go in but remembered my *father* explaining that it was forbidden for us Jews to enter a Christian place of worship. I took a step with the intention of entering but was surprised by Mr. Yavnoson, the hostel owner and friend of my *parents*.

"What are you doing here, Szifra?" he snapped with bewilderment.

"I am waiting for Petroshka."

His gaze condemned my sin. "I'll tell your parents not to rely on that girl so much. I'll wait here with you until she comes back. You should never dare to enter that place, you are Jewish!"

When Petroshka came out and saw Mr. Yavnoson standing beside me, she understood she was in trouble. I feared my *mother's* reprimand. I did not know for sure what I'd done wrong, but the nervousness of my companion was palpable.

On the way to the square, Petroshka did not say a word. When we reached the well, she moored the rope carefully, slowly lowering the vessels down until we heard the click of the container as it came in contact with the water. I could hear the grinding pulleys as they worked to bring up the load of filled containers.

As we walked slowly home carrying the heavy buckets, drops of water danced their way out of the containers. I focused my attention on this detail to avoid the thought of the scene that was about to happen upon our arrival. I rushed to my room. I heard my *mother* strongly rebuking Petroshka, warning her to never again take that route with me. She received her pay and left the house without saying goodbye to me.

After this incident, and totally ignoring our previous cordial relationship, Petroshka became sullen toward me. This attitude was not ephemeral or stormy; it became the norm. She became solely devoted to cleaning the house. I got used to spending every evening alone in my bedroom, waiting for Shayna to come back from work.

Mornings became darker as the winter approached. Our exhaling breaths became cold before leaving our mouths. Bristles of snow painted the streets, and roofs became a white reflection.

My friend Abrasha discovered an abandoned wobbly sleigh, which we used and cared for throughout the winter. We would launch it on the knoll on Synagogue Street, picking up speed and pushing the sled past the building that housed the Tarbut school. I especially enjoyed seeing how the white powder spattered against our faces and how it melted the second it hit our bodies. We laughed happily on those days; our only thought was to repeat the same activity every afternoon.

Finally, winter started to abandon us. Some days, the faint sun defeated the chilly weather. The snow began to melt, and everything turned into mud. Without complaints or sadness, we stored the sled to be used the following year. From then on, we focused our energy on hopping between puddles on our way to school and trying to step on them on our way back home.

Spring made a great entrance, splashing the land with heavy rains that were cheered by the peasants. Life became lighter, and my *parents'* humor brightened again. We were all smiles.

I usually walked back from school with my friends. But one afternoon, *Mother* asked me to go to the market to buy some groceries before heading home. Clouds accompanied me all the way to the main square. Suddenly, heavy rain fell over the town. I hurried to find a roof to cover me. As I ran, I noticed the open doors of the church. Mass was in full swing, and I heard the voice of the priest giving his sermon to the congregation. As he addressed the parishioners, he made a statement blaming the Jews for Christ's death. Surprised and a little bit scared, I hid in the shadow of a column as I tried to listen better. The accusatory words were ringing in my ears; I could even hear the loud rhythm of my beating heart as my soaked clothes dripped on the ground.

Almost petrified, I sneaked away without anybody noticing me. I didn't care about the downpour; it was preferable to the antisemitic speech that had opened my eyes: the Jews were not welcome here despite our history in this land, and no matter how many centuries ago our ancestors had settled in Lithuania, they hated us. We were outcasts.

***

The forests surrounding the city seemed rather sleepy and magnetic; sometimes I ventured out with my friends to the great legendary rock that hid a terrible tale. We all knew it had served as an altar to the pagan cult of Perkonus, but others said that it was the devil who had thrown the rock from heaven.

We didn't care about those stories; it was a thrill to go there and, after a difficult climb, admire the scenery below.

In a soft whisper, I began to share my thoughts: "There's an old cabinet in my house that has never been opened. I wonder what is hidden inside." I said this almost to myself, almost like a confession.

Abrasha relentlessly responded, "Ask your mother to open it. It's that simple."

I looked at him without thinking about his words. I wasn't sure I wanted to uncover all those old mysteries. Somehow, I sensed that what was stored there was part of my past, protected with great zeal. My *parents* would speak between them in a kind of code; they used sentences that were left broken, and they would look at me from the corners of their eyes to see my reaction. I pretended not to notice, but I knew they were talking about me. I didn't worry too much; I knew they loved me, although I perceived that everyday life was becoming inexplicably tense. Incongruous looks, truncated sentences, a sudden interrupted chatter, and hushed talks led me to believe that something was floating in the air. The cabinet remained there, consistent, concealing the sentences that were left unsaid. I sensed that the puzzle of my life was hidden within it.

"Szifra, it's time to go, the sun is setting, and we don't want the *dibuk* to appear in front of us, right?" said Abrasha, taking me out of my reverie.

We hurried down the hill; this time we didn't stop to find clovers or cut lupines along the way. I went in through the backyard door, being extremely careful not to step on my *mother's* berries left to dry in the sun. I reached my bed thinking of the time when I would ask about that locked armoire.

Chapter Two: 1923-1927

My *parents* built a two-story house on #4 Church Street, Bažnyčius Gatvie. In 1923, we left the small house we were leasing to start a new chapter.

We took almost every item we had, including the old furniture that was part of my *mother's* dowry and the mysterious cabinet, which we placed on the second floor. We diligently filled boxes with pots, pans, knives, and sheets, taking them from our old house to the new one. I was busy helping when Mrs. Katz, our previous landlady, appeared in front of me. She was complaining, but none of us were listening to her grumbles. At a moment's notice, I was left alone in the room with her and was desperately trying to avoid her rant.

"I cannot believe you are leaving this beautiful house. How am I going to find somebody to rent it? The situation today is difficult, nobody will want to pay. It is not fair."

I tried to ignore her and kept putting things in the box. She became increasingly angry. Envious and mad, she continued with her lamentations. She wanted to provoke, and suddenly, she fired a wounding dart:

"You know, Szifra ... you know that you're not really Leah's daughter? Your mother's name was Masza, and she died a few months after you were born. Leah is your grandmother, not your mother! I'm telling you this, just so you know."

I looked at her blankly without understanding her words. Was she suggesting that I was not Leah's daughter?

"That's not possible!" I cried, trembling. "That's a lie!" I stammered, barely in a whisper. "Leah is my mother," I managed to say almost in a catatonic state.

"I don't lie. Go on, go and ask Leah. She will confirm what I say!"

I left immediately. With tears pouring down my face, my life was presented through blurred vision. I don't know how I got to the new house where my *mother*—or was it my grandmother Leah—was cleaning the shelves.

I stood at the threshold and with my fists clenched, between sobs, I cried, "*Mama*, you're my mother, right? How can anyone say that my mother died a few months after I was born? Mrs. Katz said that you're my grandmother. Is it true? All my life has been a lie ...?"

My *mother* remained motionless, weightless, floating in the middle of the room. Without a word, she held me for a long time as I moaned and swallowed my misfortune. Little by little, reality filled the room. Leah sobbed; the salty liquid dripped down her face, washing her cheeks. My relief and uncertainty were mixed in a cauldron of emotions.

After reinforcing a fallacy for so long, my grandmother was finally showing great sadness. At that moment, every misery in her life became present. She lamented the death of her daughter that had happened years ago. Anxiety, instead of sweat, was coming out of her pores. The undefined future of her motherless granddaughter, me, came to life. Our tears joined without comfort; no dike existed that could contain so much drain.

I cried alone in my bedroom, feeling as though the floor had been pulled out from beneath me. I heard my grandmother coming up the stairs, then she stealthily entered my room. She took out a crumpled handkerchief from her apron pocket and carefully unfolded it. A pair of coral earrings appeared within the linen fabric. I had never seen those! With a melodious voice, extending her hand toward me, she pronounced her statement:

"These belonged to your mother, her name was Masza Nechama."

She placed the earrings on the bedside table and left the room. Soon enough, she came back with a sharp object in one hand and a plate of cookies in the other. She made an incision in my lobes, and I moaned a little but had no time to react further before she placed my mother's earrings in my ears. I touched the gems with my fingertips, reconnecting the umbilical cord to my mother's womb.

I ate the cookies left on the night table. They were full of sugar and cinnamon, but they tasted salty. I reached maturity in that very instant. Grief would settle forever in my chest.

"I have to confess something," said my grandmother.

Is there more? I thought.

"Your real father is not Shabtai. Your father's name is Shmuel, and he lives across the Black Border. That is why he's never come to see you, but he regularly writes and always asks about you. When your mom Masza got sick, there wasn't enough time to take her to a specialist. The cancerous tumors in her breasts were too big and had already invaded her whole body."

The light coming through the window accentuated her old age. Her dominant personality was broken under the shadow's spell. The wrinkles framing her eyes betrayed her. Every word she emitted diminished the glow of her gaze. She realized I had to digest the new information about my life and the changes that were coming. I had to process it all in just one blow. She kissed me and went out of the room, leaving me alone with my confused thoughts and a cluster of entangled feelings. I looked out the window. The browning leaves were waiting for their certain death as the autumn winds blew our way.

It was already late, but I longed to go to *shul* to pray. I wanted the spirits of the dead to be with me in the synagogue; I wanted to meet my deceased mother. I had so many questions for her.

My grandmother barely managed to ask where I was going.

"Do not worry, I will return soon."

With no fear, amid one of the darkest nights, I arrived as a sleepwalker at the Street of the Synagogues. I entered the small lobby of the New Synagogue and walked through the first floor, where the presence of women was usually prohibited. There was no one on the premises, so I approached the *bimah* directly. I climbed the three steps to stand on top of the small platform and prayed aloud.

"Mother, listen to me! I do not know how to tell you that I need you. I do not know who I am anymore. They say Shabtai is not my father. I don't know my real father, the one who lives behind the so-called Black Border .... I want to be the daughter of Leah and Shabtai, I love them, but now everything has turned upside down, and I do not know what to do. Please help me!"

I heard a creak behind me. My heart jumped. I quickly turned. A voice came out of the shadows:

"What are you doing here, at this hour, *mein kind?*"

It was Rabbi Gordimer. I replied humbly explaining that I needed God's comfort and advice from my dead mother. The rabbi came closer and patted my head, trying to console me.

"Girl ... you are surrounded by love. Your grandparents have educated you with the deepest affection. Embrace that feeling, it will strengthen you in the future. Go home, take care of them, they are elderly, and they need you."

I looked into his eyes. So, he knew. Everyone in town knew except me!

My soul felt empty. I walked back home, trying to replenish

my heart and convince myself that everything was going to be fine. I kept repeating to myself reminders of the kindness of my grandparents. They loved me and looked after me. When I turned around the corner, where the Street of the Synagogues and Church Street intersected, I reassured myself by repeating the rabbi's words, which gently penetrated my pores.

I tried to deduce the parts of the axiom: *So, Shayna ... is my aunt, not my older sister. She plays with me in her spare time, brushes my hair and puts ribbons in my braids. She loves me ... they all love me, I know! I will try to do what the rabbi has recommended: to just love them back.*

When I got home, my grandmother was busy preparing a *krupnik*, a soup with barley and buckwheat, for dinner. I gave her a kiss on the forehead, she smiled, and I offered to help her chop the onion.

"Who is my father?" I asked.

"Your father lives in a small town called Nemenčinė. It is impossible for him to come or for you to go, the borders are closed. Lithuania has been cut to pieces, and his village has been annexed to Poland; it is unthinkable to cross over. Your father cares about you, and he sends money continuously for your support. He is a well-respected man in his *shtetl*; he is a pharmacist, and people appreciate him."

I hope I can meet him one day. Those were the words that first came to me and would be engraved with a burin in my heart. But I couldn't imagine then that to achieve this, I would have to lose my home and my family.

Full of hope, but also frustration and despair, I waited for the right moment to write to him. Shabtai was not my father. My biological father lived in a distant village. I was trying to face this reality. My skin would convulse in reaction; my entrails were filled with mistrust. My confusion intensified in crescendo, and my anxiety built up inside me. I remembered the drawing of the Solomonic Judgment that we had just picked up from the corridor of our old house. There was King Solomon, magnanimous, in front of two women who each claimed to be the mother of the same infant. Two disconsolate women, waiting for the king's decision, who fought over the possession of a son .... He was lucky; he had two mothers who wanted him. I didn't even have one. Who would fight for me?

My brain was like a honeycomb, an orderly array of hexagonal cells, each one of them containing infinite questions that I did not dare to ask. But the armoire, that old closet that was off-limits—maybe there I could find some answers.

During one of my days of musing and twirling around the house, I found a small box. I opened it with great care and found a key. Could it unlock the dresser? I looked around to make sure no one was watching me. The doors of the old armoire, complaining, squeaking, opened in front of me. I was paralyzed, and my head was spinning.

The objects that were hidden inside that ancient piece of furniture looked forgotten, untouched for years. There was a wedding dress with small applications and delicate embroidery ....

It was the trousseau of her wedding! From HER wedding! That wardrobe was a gem. I thought that her garments still preserved part of my mother's soul; I realized that she had been beside me all this time. My mother, Masza Nechama, had worn these clothes! The smell of moths and dust was transformed into the scent of a sublime fragrance.

As my mother had been dying with an agonizing cry, I had been smiling to the world for the first time. Surely, when I'd learned to sit, she had been languishing in bed, and when I'd learned to crawl, her eyes closed forever ....

I did not remember anything about her, not her face nor her hands nor her caresses, but those earrings meant everything to me.

All her things! Her silk and crepe dresses, a fur coat, the trousseau she could not enjoy. White tablecloths with embroidery and lace, even a hat with feathers and her bridal veil. I took the clothes that had been kept there for so many years and wrapped myself in them, one by one. Covered in delicate fabrics, I felt comforted by the satin and velvet that had belonged to my mother.

I was absorbed in looking at the treasures I had discovered. The forbidden past that had been kept from me was preserved, frozen in front of my eyes. I found the books my mother had read and flipped through them, imagining that she was reading them aloud to me.

I couldn't stop. In a tin box, I found some letters that Shmuel, my real father, had written over the years to my grandparents. They showed an address in Nemenčinė. I read carefully, for I wanted to savor his expressions, to know what he ate, what interested him, what he did in his spare time. I wanted to merge with the words of my father and establish an eternal symbiosis with his affection. But his messages were short and concise. He asked my grandparents about their health and mine, and he sent them greetings and said goodbye politely, not mentioning anything about his personal life.

I scanned the letters one by one, and one by one, they disappointed me. He was not an eloquent writer, not even expressive, so I felt incomplete, lonely, and greatly uncertain. From then on, I would search for a feeling of wholeness.

Shayna found me surrounded by the clutter of trinkets that I thought brought me closer to my mother. Sensing my distress and confusion, she hugged me tightly.

"Szifra, enough of this," she said gently, trying to comfort me.

This house is full of uncertainty and disarray! The girl does not know who to turn to. She never knew her mother. She learned the truth abruptly. My parents should have told her earlier. Masza Nechama, my older sister, was a beautiful young girl; she was intelligent and vibrant until she got sick. All that remains of her are these drilling memories; they are like needles that only serve to weave mystifying crossroads for her daughter Szifra. The recollections kept inside this closet are like pins that pierce the body, like those used some time ago to secure Szifra's diapers. How it hurts to see Szifra grow up quickly, disconsolate .... My parents adore her, but they are getting old and tired of raising children. I am resigned to dedicate my life to watch over them. I have chosen not to marry to take care of this girl whom I love with all my soul; she gives me the courage to live. However, there are times when the burden is too much.

"Here, Szifra, enough …. All this you see here are the memories of the past. It must be put aside for now but not forgotten."

***

The floating snowflakes announced the arrival of winter. Dawn was still a distant glow, but the white that covered the ground was enough to brighten the day early in the morning. The stove, which also served as a chimney, heated the cold room. The samovar boiled water, always ready for a hot tea. Still in almost complete darkness, I went out of the house with my grandmother to make the last purchases before Chanukah.

When we came back home, I noticed that Shayna had just ironed and laid some clothes on the bed for me to wear. I put on the nice dress and, seeing my reflection in the mirror, noticed something amiss.

"I lost an earring!" I exclaimed, frightened.

I searched the four corners of the bedroom and scanned the floor, trying to magnify my eyes; it was nowhere to be found. Could I have lost it on the way to the market? Or maybe it had fallen while I was in the Yavnosons' house?

I hurried out into the street and retraced the path I'd taken during the day. I returned breathless and crying.

I tried to explain to my grandmother what had happened, but no words came out of my mouth. My brain was working at an accelerated pace, and my anxiety was building. I had lost a part of my mother's soul.

My chest expanded sharply between sobs. My grandmother was waiting for me to calm down. Finally, between mutilated words, I managed to say, "I … lost … the … earring …."

Shayna and my grandmother joined the search. Under the bed, between the chairs, inside the drawers, on the kitchen counter, even inside the oven … we searched everywhere; the earring did not appear.

I couldn't suppress my anguish. I couldn't hold in the pain any longer. I cried. I expelled through my tears all the feelings that had lain dormant since I'd learned about my real mother. I suffered my loss through my eyes and my nostrils—not for the earring, but rather for the mother I'd never had. I cried to my loneliness. I wiped the drawers with tears and scrubbed the closet with sad fantasies. I swore to myself that I would never take off the earring I had left, and to this day, I carry it with me.

My pain finally receded but never vanquished. When the guests arrived, I was calmer. My grandmother lit the first Chanukah candle. From our window, I saw the candles magically illuminating our neighbors' homes. My friends, the Yavnoson girls, invited me to play with the *dreidl*. While playing, I daydreamed that my mother had come to tell me to forget the lost earring. I turned to see Brachana and Aida, who were waiting for me to spin the toy and try my luck.

I was exhausted and ready for bed when my grandmother, in her nightgown, handed me a sealed envelope. It was a letter from Nemenčinė; it was my father's, and it was addressed to me. The small, round lettering, written in Yiddish, made me forget for a moment the sadness I felt. I focused my attention on the Hebrew letters, which I had just learned. They seemed engraved on the white paper.

Dear daughter:
I am glad that you are well. I am sending you a few dollars; your grandparents can exchange them for litas.

Your father,
Shmuel Bernstein

My grandmother was still standing next to me, watching over my shoulder. I gave her the bills, and she understood. My father had not been very eloquent or effusive with his words. Money meant nothing to me. I would have preferred a warmer message, but for the moment, I would have to content myself with those informative and precise letters.

My father would continue to send letters with money for my livelihood. My life in Anykščiai did not change much; what changed was only the titles with which I would refer to my loved ones. I had trouble getting used to calling Shabtai my grandfather and Leah my grandmother, but their love and the care they gave me remained the same.

***

The heat warmed our bodies in that summer of 1924. I ran to the edge of the river. The poppies adorned the fields; those beautiful *mak* brightened the landscape with their red petals. The Šventoji River awaited me with its murky backwaters. "Where the Šventoji River runs / Where the Niemen River runs / There is our country, the beautiful Lithuania ..." said the poem. I reached the place where my friends were gathering. We approached a small, eroded beach. The grounded stones allowed us to get closer to the shore without getting wet. The girls and boys separated; we took off our clothes and, in our underpants, ventured into the water. We managed to get some logs that were drifting downstream to use as floats. The older boys taught me how to go against the current and not drown, so I kicked and stroked until I began to swim happily.

The sun was burning intensely; the dark waters of the river helped us refresh. I was having a blast! With the water running through my thighs, I felt a pleasant tingling rising from the soles of my feet to my chest. I swam; I drifted without thinking, closing my eyes and letting the water take me away ... before alerting with a sudden jolt when I heard loud shouts nearby. My eyes opened and confronted the mid-day, dazzling rays of the sun.

"Hey, Jews! Yes, you! Get out of the river, you are polluting it with your filth!" shouted a boy from the shore.

None of us turned to see him. Hypnotized, I did not react until someone pulled my arm.

"Let's go, Szifra!" It was Abrasha Evenson. "More hoodlums are coming looking for trouble! We shouldn't fight, someone could get hurt. Let's get out of here!"

I looked at him incredulously; I didn't understand what he was saying.

"We must avoid fighting, it's not worth getting beaten up. Those kids are ignorant, they don't even know how to read and write. They don't have the Torah to guide them, but we do," insisted Abrasha. He would change his mind on violence later on when he started working for the NKVD, the precursor of the KGB, but at that moment on the river in Anykščiai, he preferred to give in.

We got out of the water, dried ourselves as fast as we could, and rushed back home. I couldn't run; my legs trembled in a dancing zigzag. Abrasha took my arm again and pulled me until he delivered me to my front door. Had it not been for my friend, I would have been left alone, and who knows what would have happened to me.

I was filled with rage and frustration. We should have defended ourselves. But I understood that Abrasha was right: it was better to run away than fight a lost cause. We had to find another way.

***

The damp earth was drying out once more, the first scents of autumn arrived, the days became shorter, and the flowers disappeared from the wooden fence in front of the house.

There was a mild frost after Rosh Hashanah, and the fast of Yom Kippur was approaching. Fortunately, Petroshka and I had pulled up the cabbages a week before. We had been careful to wash the leaves, stopping to examine if they had any worms.

My grandmother took the cleaned cabbages and grated them, preparing them with salt and caraway seeds to be pickled. While I stirred them with my hands, as I usually did, the cold wind carried away my childhood. Although my body was still standing there watching my grandparents work, my mind was possessed, without warning, by gloomy dreams of solitude. Awake, I dreamed of gigantic shadows that suddenly appeared around me.

In a second, everything darkened. I perceived a shadow. The face was unknown to me, but I sensed that it was my biological father who, with long, dark hands, had come to fetch me.

My grandfather began to hit the barrel with a stick so that all the juices could run through the holes he had made previously; little by little, he added apples, carrots, and beets.

I watched my grandparents without really seeing them, immersed in my thoughts. I swallowed the cries exploding inside me. I wanted to hide. I imagined my father taking me far away and hoped he wouldn't find me. I wanted to disappear. I felt my feet becoming roots, my thighs the trunk of a tree, my arms sprouting branches, and my body covered by the wood of the Anykščiai forest.

Lost in a hazy dream, I saw my grandparents through a fog. I rubbed my eyes, conscious of the fact that I had not moved from the garden behind the house where they had placed the fermentation barrels. The smell of the gases from the fermenting cabbage penetrated my nostrils. My grandmother looked at me questioningly.

"Is something the matter, Szifra? You look a little pale."

"No, Grandma, I'm fine."

I turned around and went into the house. I imagined my future; I saw it as the frosts that precede the harsh winter, when the snow stomps over the few green leaves that remain on the shrubs. My grandparents were finding it harder and harder to take care of me. My father wrote more frequently asking about my day-to-day activities with greater interest, and I sensed that things would change from one day to the next.

Weeks passed, divided into intervals marked by the prayers: *Shaharith, Minchah, Maariv* .... The echo of the songs resonated off the walls of the synagogues, giving a fine voice to the silence and the sighs that were left between the prayers.

My grandfather was busy in his grocery store, my grandmother toiled with the accounts, Shayna worked in the bank, and Petroshka was in charge of the housework while I went to the Tarbut school. Sundays were different, for those were the days when my uncle Meyer brought grains and flour to fill the store, and I went with my friends to the *Shomer Hatzair* meeting.

Shabbat rolled around again, and we went to visit the Yavnosons at their inn. On one occasion, Brachana—the liveliest of the three sisters—invited me to play in the back of the inn while her sisters, Fin and Aida, fought over some colored pencils.

The topic in the dining room was something related to the possibility of collecting money to build a library for the *Shomer Hatzair*.

Struck by the rising noise, we approached the dining room slowly to hear what was happening. From the door that led to the kitchen, my friend and I listened to the explosion of ideologies and beliefs. We picked up pieces of the conversation and looked incredulously at each other.

The heated discussion became louder. We knew nothing about the mechanisms that pointed to a war; we were unaware of the imminent military conflict that was growing. Every day, all around us, antisemitism was becoming more aggressive and more dangerous. Who could imagine that those enthusiastic discussions would be silenced and that Jewish ideals would be buried under a pile of ashes in the concentration camps?

As young girls, we felt far removed from the concerns of the adults, and we preferred to continue enjoying an afternoon together, dreaming about our next excursion with the *Shomer Hatzair*.

***

"There's a letter for you from Nemenčinė," my grandfather said, handing me the envelope. My father wrote often, but this time his missive announced that he had gotten remarried, and he and his new wife would have a baby soon.

I hope one day I can bring you home with me.

Your father

Blood rushed through my veins, the temperature in my temples rose, and my head throbbed with pain and anger, ready to explode.

This time the letter contained more dollar bills than usual. I rushed to my grandfather and showed him the money. We both knew what it was; my father had sent extra money for my transportation to Nemenčinė. It was only a matter of time before he found a way to take me through the Black Border to his village.

As I handed the bills to my grandfather, I exclaimed nervously, "Grandfather, tell me I'm not going anywhere! Promise me that you will not send me to Nemenčinė. I'll be good, and I will try not to be a bother! I want to stay here in Anykščiai forever!"

"*Bubbala*, my little doll," he said, embracing me, "everything's going to be alright, do not worry."

But he did not promise that I could stay.

I rushed to my room, closed my eyes, and tried to forget. The shadowy nightmares returned, larger than ever, crossing the walls, easily pulling out my birch tree roots, and crossing mighty rivers until they arrived at unknown lands I could not identify ....

Soon the inevitable would happen. I would have to leave my home and the security that my grandparents, aunts, and uncles in Anykščiai provided. I was afraid, suffering, and unable to escape the dark and black destiny that persecuted me. I knew I had become a burden. My grandparents began to discuss the possibility of sending me to live with my father. I still had time to sort out my feelings before the imminent separation, but I felt more anxious as the day of leaving Anykščiai approached.

***

When I finished elementary school in 1926, my nightmare came true. There were no opportunities for advanced education in Anykščiai. My grandparents agreed to take me to Marijampolė, where one of my father's brothers lived. There was a school, Am Ami, where I could continue my studies and eventually finish the *gymnasium*. It was all arranged: my father would pay for my education, and I would stay there.

My uncle Meyer took me to Marijampolė. The trip wasn't long, but it was silent; my uncle answered my questions in sharp monosyllables. Uncle Yankel Bernstein's wife greeted us when we arrived at their house. Two small children were playing in the living room.

Will this be my new home? I asked myself. I could get used to living there. My uncles stepped aside to speak to each other. Uncle Yankel raised his voice, unconcerned who would hear him:

"Meyer, Szifra is still a little girl ... I neither want nor can take care of her. It's not about the expenses; I know that Shmuel would send the money for her support. The responsibility of having a young girl in the house weighs on me. I have small children, I don't have a big house, and moreover, I am dependent upon my father-in-law and—"

Irritated, Meyer interrupted him. "Say no more," he said briskly. "Let's go, Szifra."

He grabbed his hat and abruptly said goodbye. The plan hadn't worked. I breathed a sigh of relief, though sadly, I realized that I would still be a burden on my grandparents, aunts, and uncles. We traveled by train, via Kovno, back to Anykščiai.

A week later, I got word from my father. He demanded that I make the trip to Nemenčinė as soon as possible. He was furious with his brother Yankel. My father wrote that he would assume his responsibility as a father. He was aware of the risks involved, yet he was determined to orchestrate my secret crossing of the Black Border so that we could be reunited.

My grandfather spoke to me tenderly: "Szifra, here in Anykščiai, there are no schools for you to go on studying. We are old now. We want to give you a better future. Your father has married a good woman, and he wants to have you close. He wants to get to know you and has the means to support you and give you a good life and education. He has offered to send more money, if necessary, so that you can cross the border."

I was paralyzed. I touched the prayer book *Sipurei HaMikrah* that was on my nightstand and picked it up. As if not in control of my movements, I caressed its worn leather cover and passed my fingertips over the engraved title. I opened the book. The first page revealed its provenance: it had been printed in Vilna, at the renowned Romms family publishing company. It made me wonder about the famous city on the other side of the Black Border. I thought about that legendary city with its two rivers: the Vilija on one side and the Nemenčia on the other. Maybe living in Nemenčinė with my father wouldn't be so bad. I could go to Vilna, the capital of Lithuania, as it was nearby.

Vilna was called the Jerusalem of Lithuania. It was the home of the Gaon, the erudite Talmudic and Kabbalistic scholar, who had curbed the influence of Hasidism in Lithuania. It was in Vilna where the Vilner Trupe, the theatre company, had been founded. It was a city that Napoleon had visited and admired.

The following months went by in a blur. The day of my departure was approaching, and every night, as I tried to sleep, I fought against insurmountable walls and countless feelings trapped in my chest. The unknown road ahead kept me awake in the darkness.

I had nightmares. I acted like an automaton. I feared that the *dybbuk* had attached itself to my body and that my soul had abandoned me. I imagined myself surrounded by *ruhin*, spirits without bodies, that danced around me. I thought that Lilith and her daughters were coming to get me. Almost every night imps and devilish beings appeared in front of me. My father would materialize like a volatile shadow accompanied by intangible forms. I felt a great sorrow; I lived submersed in anxiety.

We waited until the summer of 1927 for the propitious moment. I was thirteen years old by then. The political situation

changed as Vilna welcomed the new Polish president Ignacy
Mościcki. It became more favorable to cross the border
clandestinely. My father arranged for a smuggler to take me from
the railway station in Anykščiai to the door of his home in
Nemenčinė.

My friends all came to bid me farewell and wish me good
luck. My grandmother helped me pack. Given the danger of the
crossing, I could only carry a few of my belongings, so I chose my
most precious possessions to put into the suitcase: my book of the
Sipurei HaMikrah (the prayer book); *Likutei Mizmorim*, which my
grandfather had given to me; my *tilboshet* (my uniform from the
Shomer Hatzair); and the dress my grandmother had bought me for
Rosh Hashanah.

I touched my ear, making sure I still had my mother's
earring. My tears polished my face, which was flushed from crying.
I closed the *luvianka*, the brown suitcase, and Shayna carried it to
the front door.

***

The departure was sad. My uncle Meyer and the Yavnosons came to
say goodbye. My grandmother was busy cooking who knows what,
and my grandfather was occupied in a corner, pretending to read.
He looked pale and thin. He raised his stricken face to say goodbye,
kissed me on the forehead, and hugged me tightly. My cheeks
clashed with his chest; I heard his rapid heartbeat and felt his tears

bathing my hair.

I said goodbye to my grandmother, too. Her face was stained with soot from the stove. More tired than usual, she hugged me affectionately and gave me one last kiss. She knew that she would never see me again.

Shayna called me from the doorway. She was carrying my suitcase, waiting for me so she could accompany me on a wagon to the train station. We had to hurry. Before leaving, I caressed the *mezuzah* with my fingertips. I wanted to be blessed. Slowly, I brought my fingers to my lips and kissed them, feeling a terrible emptiness.

From the entrance, I looked back for the last time at what had been my home, at my grandmother who had pretended to be my mother in order to protect me, at my grandfather who had stuffed me with candies and sat me on his knee, spoiling me. My sobs were unable to soothe my tangled emotions as I faced the uncertainty of meeting my biological father.

I didn't make a fuss. I forced myself to look at my grandmother as she cooked. I felt my heart shrink in despair when, for the last time, I smelled the aroma of the house impregnated with familiar spices.

The horse-drawn vehicle dropped us off at the entrance of the terminal. Shayna once again carried my *luvianka,* and we walked toward the train tracks.

My aunt tried to cheer me up by talking jovially about trivial matters, but I was reluctant to follow along. I tried to swallow my sadness but instead locked myself in it.

The platform was almost deserted. We had to be careful to avoid suspicion. Smuggling a little girl across the Black Border could be fatal, unforgiven by the authorities. My aunt walked steadily, with a determined step. She had identified a man in a gray jacket, hat in hand, who rapidly approached us. She quickly said goodbye to me without shedding a tear. She hid her face so I wouldn't see her sadness. I knew that I had to restrain myself, so I tried to remain impassive, controlling the emotions that threatened to burst out of my pores. The train was blowing white steam, announcing its imminent departure. The man took my hand as we boarded with haste.

Under the cover of a moonless night, I would be led by a stranger through perilous territory. I would leave my loving home. Once I crossed the river, I would be separated from my loved ones forever.

My little niece is now traveling down an unknown road; I hope she arrives safely. Please, God, take care of her, do not let Szifra suffer, let her have a happy life. My mother and father are waiting for me to return and have dinner at home. I feel so much pain that I don't know if I will be able to have a regular conversation with them. We have lost our beloved child. We do not know if we will ever see her again. It was not up to my parents to give her up; she had to go back to her father. It is her *bashert*, her destiny. My future is already set up: I will stay at the small Jewish bank in this town and never marry. My *bashert* is to take care of my parents and live a self-effacing existence in Anykščiai whilst the fate of my siblings is quite different: Sonja has left with the Bolsheviks; she has this impossible ideal to make a better, just world. Meyer, on the other hand, has a stable life and a lovely family. Szifra brightened my days with her childhood innocence. Now the hours remain empty; I am empty. I see the train pulling away. And me ... I am bound to loneliness.

Chapter Three: 1927-1929

We boarded the Kleimbaum train. Once we were in the stateroom and without him saying a word to me, I understood the man's swift head movement indicated I had to hide for the night. I slid under the bunkbed and, without any complaint, endured the rest of the train trip in that little space.

We sneaked off the train at one of the stops and headed for the inhospitable forest. It was dark, and I was very scared. *Are there wolves hiding behind the thick, wild shrubs?* I wondered. Without making a sound, I walked beside my guide. He noticed I was exhausted and was kind enough to carry me on his back to pass the most difficult stretches. Nobody, not even the clouds above us, saw us as we reached the riverbank.

The ground was swampy. My feet would come out of the mud only to sink back into the next puddle. The man took me to a place where there was a lush tree. Its wide roots drank water directly from the stream. I recognized the tree; it was the same one from my nightmares, the one that had appeared to me as a premonition, distressing my sleep.

I could hear the waves splashing near the shore. A large log was conveniently placed between the two riverbanks. The smuggler took my hand, and we walked along the wet and slippery tree bark. I was afraid of falling to the bottom of those raging waters. The dark and mysterious river could swallow me up with one false move. One wrong step! The smuggler momentarily lost his footing. As his body contorted to avoid tripping, he unexpectedly let go of my hand, causing me to fall into the water while he managed to stay standing. Waving my arms and legs to avoid drowning, I heard his voice coming out of the blackness.

"Grab my hand!" he shouted, alarmed, concerned that the river's current was dragging me away.

If he doesn't take me to my father's house, he won't receive the rest of his payment, I thought, as I tried to swim toward him. I swam strongly upstream, fighting for my life. He grabbed my arm, pulling me up to the tree trunk again. We did not exchange another word for the rest of the night.

We walked until we reached the Polish border and came upon a pair of officials who appeared to be expecting our arrival. They offered me a blanket to dry myself. They told me that my father had been in touch with them and that they would call him to let him know of my arrival. One of the guards offered me something to eat. They put me onto a cart pulled by two horses, and, still accompanied by the smuggler, we began the journey toward Nemenčinė. Night dissolved into the horizon, melting with the morning fog that wrapped the landscape.

Nemenčinė was twenty *versts* from the border. Although dawn was breaking, sleep came over me. I imagined my father and my stepmother and thought about what was about to come: a new home and a little sister barely two years old.

When I woke up, I could make out a blurry vision of a bridge over the Niemen River and, after that, the entrance to the city. I managed to distinguish the house with the *apteka* sign, my father's pharmacy. It was located on the main street of Nemenčinė, the same street that leads to Švenčionys, the next town, which is famous for its sawmills.

A man and a woman holding the hand of a little girl stood outside the house. It was almost seven o'clock in the morning. I was very sleepy as I got out of the cart and gathered that the tall, good-looking man was my father. His wife Esfir greeted me politely, and the child, my half-sister Tanya, with her blond hair and blue eyes, smiled innocently. She immediately delighted my heart.

The smuggler turned to my father. "Mr. Bernstein, I have complied with our agreement. Here is your daughter."

I looked at my father. I had a strong impulse to go over and hug him, but I remained where I was, petrified. Shmuel Bernstein thanked the man in the gray jacket for his services and paid him five hundred dollars.

My father approached me and held my head in his hands to examine it. He separated my hair from one side to the other, inspecting it as if trying to discover something. He found a birthmark on my cranium, a mark of authenticity sealed on my scalp.

"*Ya, ya, sis mein kind;* yes, yes, you're my daughter." I was able to detect a spark of joy in his eyes.

I never asked why my father hadn't come to the border to meet me. A silent wind went deep into my soul; it tasted like solitude and longing.

"Tanya," says my father, nervous and tense, "your older sister is coming soon, her name is Szifra. She's going to stay with us."

My blue eyes open without comprehension. I'm only two, but I see my father is full of different emotions. I babble some syllables to express my happiness.

"The cart is approaching," my mother exclaims.

"Let's go and meet them," my father answers.

I run through the front door between the two lions that adorn the entrance. I stop when I see that it is not a woman who gets out of the wagon but a corpulent man with broad shoulders. My mother takes my hand. A young lady peeks out from behind the cart. She must be Szifra, my sister. She approaches us. She is beautiful, but how very sad she looks! I smile at her as my father says, "Welcome, *mein kind.*" And, taking her by the head, he inspects her scrupulously, probably checking for lice.

The door of the house was open, and I noticed that there was no *mezuzah* on the doorframe. We went in through the living and dining area, which had a simple table with six wooden chairs around it and a couch on the side.

My father proceeded ahead of me to show me the room that would become my bedroom. It was quite spacious and had a *tachta*, a sofa where I would be able to sit and read. The little kerosene lamp burned weakly, causing our faint shadows to tremble on the wall. Daylight streamed in through the window, and the wind blew as if to extinguish the flame.

Alone in the bedroom, I looked at my reflection in the small mirror on the bedside table. As I sat down in a corner, I felt a profound sadness growing inside me. I took the book of Psalms my grandfather had given me and pressed it close to my chest. I thought about my dead mother, my family in Anykščiai, my friends at the Tarbut school, and Abrasha Evenson, my playmate.

I heard my name called and emerged from my reverie. I combed my hair, straightened my dress, and went into the living room—encountering practically all the Jews in the village who were there to meet the pharmacist's daughter.

Standing in the doorway, my hands crossed, I nodded, greeting everybody. My body was there, but my soul wanted to flee, to dissolve into oblivion; I wanted to run and shout, but my legs did not respond to my wishes. I hoped my despair would explode in front of all those curious people. My lips became swollen and full of hypocrisy, and my tongue froze with fear. I remained there, fossilized until my father dismissed the last nosy guest.

I tried to gain courage and challenged my father: "I don't want to stay here. Tell the man who brought me to come back and pick me up. I want to go back to Anykščiai."

Without bothering to utter a word, my father, with a distant air, strode through the door that connected the pharmacy to the house. He returned with a bottle, got the boiling water from the samovar, and ordered me, "Drink this infusion of valerian, it will do you good."

My father diagnosed me with "impulsiveness." Over time, I learned that this was not a real disease but rather a condition that would be part of my unpredictable and sensitive personality.

The herbal tea was effective, calming my uncertainty and volatility. I barely heard my father's advice as if he were far away: "Szifra, my wife is kind. You will not lack anything here." But he was lying; I would always lack a mother's love.

Dinner was ready. We sat down at the table, and I was served cream of carrot soup. I was very hungry and ate it quickly. Esfir then served me *cacletn*, chicken patties. I couldn't believe it; we Jews never mix milk and meat! That soup was made with cream. That was *treyf!* According to the Laws of *kashrut,* that was forbidden.

Everything my grandmother had taught me crumbled in the blink of an eye. I hadn't eaten well for the last few days, and I didn't have the strength to turn down the chicken. I could not bear fasting until the next morning, and I was trying to make a good impression; I feared they would think I was rude, and I didn't want to be a nuisance. I wanted to be invisible, to slip under the wooden floor and sneak out the door onto the road back to Lithuania. I wanted to be in Anykščiai.

SHURA

It was the first time I would transgress the rules, but my appetite overcame my ponderings as I prayed in silence. I gobbled up the pieces of the chicken patty, each bite adding to a long list of sins. God would never forgive me for this. It was torture. A hopeless sigh escaped my mouth; it was a last blow of air that separated me even more from my grandparents and my past.

Is it possible that my father is an epicoires, *a nonbeliever?* I was afraid of the wrath of God. *This is not my family, my family is in Anykščiai,* I thought.

I withdrew early to my bedroom; shortly after, and quite suddenly, Tanya came bursting in. With her bright blond locks and fleeting smile, she sweetened that sad room; she hugged me with her naïve curiosity and stroked my hair. I hugged her, squeezing her against my chest, feeling her warmth, breathing in her sweet smell. She seemed to be the only one who was not judging me. I inhaled deeply, trying to sink into her fragrance. Like a chamomile flower, her aroma was a peaceful balsam. A tear came out at last, triumphant, rolling down my face until it exploded on the parquet floor.

Tanya showed me her rag doll, babbling some unintelligible words. Her luminous, beautiful face provided me with a shelter that soothed my anxiety. From that day on, I filled many dreary afternoons with her unconditional company and candor, for which I was eternally grateful.

***

Friday was approaching, and Esfir was not busy preparing the challah or polishing the floors as my grandmother did before *Shabbat*. It seemed strange to me. Didn't they feel Jewish? Wouldn't my father go to *shul* to pray?

He came through the door that connected the house with the pharmacy, kissed me on the forehead, and said, "*Gut Shabbos, mein kind*; May you have a good *Shabbat*, my child."

We had dinner together, and I went to bed awaiting the arrival of my second soul, my *neshomeh yeseireh,* who, according to my grandmother's teaching, visited me every Saturday.

The sun was rising. My dreams started to dissipate, and I realized that my *neshomeh yeseireh* had faded away. I sighed gloomily and thought of my grandmother who observed the Sabbath as a sacred day, rejoicing when my grandfather returned from the synagogue. She was careful not to concern herself with money on *Shabbat* and followed all the traditions of Jewish ritual. My father, on the contrary, was removed from religion. His life transpired amidst prescriptions and medications, seemingly without any time devoted to thanking God. He did not pray to God like my grandfather Shabtai did. He didn't even attend synagogue on Fridays.

Every *Shabbat*, my grandmother would take out her book *Tz'enah Ur'enah* to explain a Torah verse to me. Esfir didn't seem to care about any Jewish precepts; instead, she strolled along the river with Tanya.

I spent the rest of the afternoon reading the book *Sipurei HaMikrah*. How I missed my home in Anykščiai, my grandfather's embraces, my conversations with Shayna, and helping my grandmother prepare the challah! In Nemenčinė, in Esfir's house, everything was strange to me. My father was busy all day long mixing chemicals and remedies, and I, not knowing anyone, stayed in my bedroom all alone.

I began to explore my father's pharmacy several days later. The white and transparent jars with lotions and herbs, remedies for all sorts of illness, had bizarre names—*Angelica archangelica, infusion of Cnitus Benedictus, Matricaria recutita, Viburnum opulus*—all of them equally unpronounceable.

I began to silently observe my father from the doorway. Patients came in looking for cures for stomach pains, toothaches, and insomnia. I had a thousand questions for him.

"Doctor," they called him. "Do you think that raspberry syrup is enough to cure a sore throat? Can seltzer water settle my son's stomach?"

The people who visited the pharmacy had all kinds of complaints, not only about their maladies but about life. They worried about their economic situations, grumbled about their work, and very often whimpered over a relative in bed rest. My father listened to them calmly and prescribed, advised, or suggested home remedies. Not only was he the village's pharmacist and "doctor" but also a confidant and a friend.

Loneliness became my natural state and seclusion my only

companion. Books gave me comfort, and I spent hours reading. My father bought me the stories of Méndele Mocher Sforim. He didn't understand that I needed company and people to talk to rather than more ways to isolate myself.

As time went by, I realized that my stay in Nemenčinė was becoming as complicated as it had been in Anykščiai. There was no school for me, and, although my father was supportive of furthering my education, he couldn't find a solution for my future. I understood Yiddish, Hebrew, and some Lithuanian, but I needed to learn Polish, the current language of Nemenčinė. In the meantime, my father hired a private teacher.

The private Polish tutor brought me a dictionary. The first word I searched was "adoption." I don't know what prompted me to do so, but the definition and description didn't fit what my grandparents had done for me when they'd assumed my custody. "Adoption: legal act by which a familial relationship is created." No, it wasn't adoption. I then looked up other words: "abandonment," "lie," "isolation" … I closed the book, not wanting to think any more about it.

I couldn't find the answers to my existence in the Polish dictionary. While my father was visiting a patient, I went into the pharmacy, took out a fat medical compendium, and looked up the word "cancer." My mother had died of breast cancer; that was what my father had said. The cold explanation froze my body. How distant everything seemed: a mother unable to breastfeed me, her nipples exhausted from fighting the reproduction of malignant cells.

A mother unable to hug me when I took my first steps. I felt the presence of someone behind me. It was my father. I felt a sudden fright, as I was snooping in his precious books.

"If you want to learn medicine or pharmacology, I can teach you some things," he said in Yiddish with a decisive tone.

I began to spend more time in the drugstore. My admiration for him grew. My father was an important man in the village, loved by all. He took care of anyone who needed it, regardless of their religion. He had studied botany, anatomy, and herbology, and he functioned as a doctor in a place where there were only midwives and healers. He was known as Dr. Shmuel Bernstein. He accepted any type of payment: loaves of bread, raspberry jelly, pickled cucumbers, and even chickens. But he also helped people who could not pay. He would keep every penny, putting them meticulously in a specific medicine jar. At the end of the day, exhausted, he would close the pharmacy and prepare for the next day.

He was like a magician: with a potion, he could make the pains decrease, the migraines diminish, and the insomnia disappear. Watching my father work, absorbed in his thoughts, I sometimes felt like hugging him, but I always held back to avoid arousing my stepmother's or my little sister Tanya's jealousy. Every day I looked forward to a hint from my father inviting me to come into the back part of the pharmacy so that I could watch how he prepared medications and unguents. He compressed powders in a pill maker, ground herbs in a mortar, and heated potions to create balms and cures that were stored in porcelain jars.

"*Stramonium*," I managed to read on one container.

"Szifra, don't touch that jar," my father cried. "It must be used very carefully." He explained further: "If you ingest even a small amount, it can kill you. *Stramonium* is known as a toxic plant that can induce hallucinations. During the Middle Ages, witches used it in brews for various spells, including so-called love potions. Today it is used as an analgesic; you can drink it in a tea, and it relaxes the respiratory muscles, preventing asthma. But if used in excess, it can be poisonous and dangerous." He then placed it on the tallest shelf, along with other potent medications, such as *belladonna*, *mandrake*, and *henbane*.

"Szifra, if you have any questions, ask me anything you like," he said in his deep, clear voice. "But please, don't snoop around without my permission. Some of these herbs and crystals are imported from faraway places and are very expensive. For example, the *Imula Helenium* is brought from England, and when dissolved in alcohol, it can reduce phlegm. I wouldn't want it to be wasted or lost. Ask me if you want to learn."

I understood that the pharmacy was his refuge, his space, and I should not be there without his authorization.

***

Esfir had prepared a succulent meal to begin the Yom Kippur fast. It was the only Jewish holiday that my father observed.

I managed to put on the dress my grandmother had bought

for me. In such a short time, I had gained a few pounds; the dress was a little tight, and I was uncomfortable in it.

We ate fast and hurried to the synagogue. It suddenly hit me that today would be my first time attending services in Nemenčinė, I would sing *Kol Nidrei* in a new place. The little *shul* was located just around the corner, behind the pharmacy. Neighbors hurried past us, wishing that we be inscribed in the Book of Life on this Judgment Day. My father proudly introduced me to them and responded with "*A Gut Yor*, Happy New Year!"

The cabinet where the Torah was kept was covered with a *parohet* that my father had donated; it was a dark velvet curtain embroidered with gold thread. Even though he didn't follow the rules of *kashrut* or study the Torah, he was invited to stand at the podium to read from the sacred book. I was surprised to see how much honor was bestowed upon him.

While the prayers were similar to the ones recited in Anykščiai, I felt strange among so many unfamiliar people and without any friends. I became absorbed in thinking about my past: the city of my childhood, with its forest and its river, the faces of my grandparents, Shabtai's eyes, Leah's smile ... I struggled to remember them. They quickly disappeared through the rhythm of the prayer.

When we arrived home, my father scolded me: "Szifra, Esfir complains that you answer her brusquely. You must change. I don't want you to be rude to her, she deserves respect, she is my wife, and moreover, she only wants the best for you. You must make an effort;

I would like you to call her 'mama.'"

My father paused, awaiting my reply. I wanted to protest, but I kept quiet, fearful of altering the cosmic order between father and daughter. My words died before coming out of my mouth. I asked to be excused. I tried to see myself in my little bedroom mirror, but I only saw a hollow image. I tried to say the word ... "mama." I said it aloud, but it was not Esfir whom I saw, it was my grandmother Leah.

When I was called to dinner I tried again, but my tongue was caught between my palate and my teeth. From that day on, when I referred to Esfir while speaking with my father, I added the article "the": *die muter*, the mother. I gave her a title; she was a mother all right but imposed by force. My father never mentioned the subject again.

***

The constant tedium wrapped me in a taciturn veil. Melancholy and solitude blended with the memories I had of my grandparents. Enduring every minute of the sad boredom plunged me into a deep depression. Occasionally, I would talk to my father, but these conversations only revolved around herbs and medications. He was knowledgeable about the body but unfamiliar with the sorrows of the soul. Believing that I was ill, he searched for medical formulas and rational remedies to cure my loneliness. He rummaged through papers and books searching for potions and infusions that would alleviate my anxiety. Only a magic spell could help me convert into the happy and gay daughter he wished for.

The days got dark earlier as winter approached. All the shutters of the houses in the neighborhood were drawn, the winds were swirling, and the chimneys worked continuously. Mud and snow mingled; the surface of the snow was tinted with shades of brown. I was eager for the landscape to be embellished with winter's white blanket. I had no friends my age, and I spent the days alone; at home, everyone was canning food and plucking goose feathers to make quilts, anticipating the freezing climate to come. Obscurity would take over, dimming the light of the afternoons that passed slowly between boredom and longing.

By now, I had learned to understand Polish but still preferred to speak in Yiddish. I spent my time in the pharmacy, asking my father questions and learning from him. Our conversations were technical, with little affection, and never sentimental. During one afternoon filled with a toxic lethargy, my father was grinding remedies in a mortar when I exclaimed, "Papa, I decided that I want to study pharmacology. I would like to know as much as you do so I can help and take care of the sick."

The news fell like snow in spring. I saw the confused expression on his face.

"Don't you want to get married? A husband doesn't want someone who knows too much, a wife shouldn't surpass her husband in knowledge. I want you to have a family. I want to have grandchildren. Be careful what you do and what you say."

We didn't mention the subject again, but I continued to visit the pharmacy, asking questions and learning ceaselessly. In the *apteka*, surrounded by small jars with medicinal powders, bottles of chemicals, yellow pills, and unguents, I believed I could achieve the highest level of knowledge. I could differentiate the morphine ampoules inside a glass jug, the mercury ointment in the blue container, and the acetylsalicylic acid. I was learning the benefits of one and the effects of another. In the pharmacy, I was away from the everyday world. My father was a sorcerer, and I was his apprentice.

The autumn snow dyed the earth white while the sun fought to warm the soil. Weak and dying, the summer bid us farewell, still managing to occasionally melt the white flakes. A crowd gathered on the main street of the village across from the pharmacy. They wanted to witness the miracle of the newly installed electric lights. Everybody looked up at the Polish workers hanging from the poles above as they connected the last wires before nightfall. By then the temperature had dropped, and it was freezing, but no one wanted to miss that moment. When the workers gave the signal, all the streetlamps lit up brilliantly at the same time. We sighed in unison. The admiration was a contagious feeling. Bewitched by the light, I joined the street celebration with Esfir and little Tanya. Little by little, the street began to empty. That day, in 1927, was unforgettable.

I had more freedom as the weather improved, and I was able to go on walks around the village. I found myself more able to tolerate the dense atmosphere that usually obscured the house. *Dir muter* no longer seemed as evil as I had judged her initially. The slush dried up prodigiously with the warmth of the sun. The snow melted—making the roads muddy again.

I wrote to my grandparents and Shayna almost every week. I told them about the Niemen River and its slow and mysterious flow; I described how I enjoyed watching tree trunks floating down the river as they made their way to the Baltic; I wrote about the little beach where young boys gathered to swim and talk and about the number of vacationers who came to spend the summer near Lake Gela. My long letters illustrated the lush landscapes from my solitary walks.

The feeling of freedom, however, did not last. When I ventured out on a walk, I inevitably would return with severe coughs that were the result of bronchial allergies, which my father tried to cure, to no avail, with herbal teas.

***

Children and young adults swam on the small beach formed by the river. One boy, hugging a tree trunk, invited me to grab onto the log and float down the river with him.

"My name is Asher; I live in Vilna. I come here with my family every summer."

"Hi, I'm Szifra, daughter of Shmuel Bernstein, the town's pharmacist," I introduced myself, happy to meet someone my age.

Enjoying the conversation and laughing raucously, we gradually floated downstream, leaving the village. We had to swim back, and Asher was surprised at my ability to dodge the river currents.

When we returned, we sat in the shade of the tree chatting animatedly, and then he walked me home. I was thrilled! It had been a long time since I had felt so happy! For several days, Asher came to pick me up to swim in the river or Lake Gela, about two kilometers from the village, where we met with a group of other young people.

He spoke enthusiastically about his life in Vilna, his native city. He described how big and cultured it was and how excited he was to go back to study there at the end of the summer. I bombarded him with questions that he answered without hesitation. Half flirting and half joking, he made fun of my effervescent fits of laughter.

One day, as we returned from the river, I overheard a conversation in Polish between my stepmother and my father.

"Szifra is becoming a young woman, she's flirtatious and has a passionate nature. It's not appropriate for her to run around with those boys from Vilna. They are beginning to talk about her in the village. I don't want them to judge us as liberals without scruples or moral values," Esfir argued explosively. "That boy Asher is interested in her. She has too much time on her hands, and I'm afraid that leisure will be an invitation to licentiousness. The wisest thing is to send her to Vilna to study and to continue her education in the *gymnasium*."

My stomach turned over. The next day, my father and Esfir invited two young girls to the house to have tea so I could meet them.

"These are Mindel and Franya," my father said to me.

Mindel was my age; her eyes were an intense green, contrasting with her reddish hair and her pale skin. Franya was younger and had a darker complexion. I learned that they had lost their mother a few years back and were both going to Vilna to study.

"Hello," I greeted them awkwardly.

"Dear Szifra," my father said casually, "wouldn't you like to go and study in Vilna with Mindel and Franya?"

My future was thus decided. I would go to Vilna in the fall.

***

The summer ended, and the moment arrived when my father took me to Vilna. I left the idleness behind, and with it, my dreams of Asher's friendship. My father hired a horse and carriage at the train station. We crossed over the Vilija River via the Green Bridge until we arrived at Wileńska Avenue. At the top of the hill, we were able to see the ruins of King Gediminas's Castle, once majestic, and today only the memory of a legend. The *Shlosberg*, castle hill in Yiddish, was at the end of Adam Mickiewicz Avenue. We stopped at the square across the street from the magnanimous neoclassical cathedral and started walking on Ulica Wielka until we came upon the great City Hall.

Turning right on Stikly Street, we entered the Jewish Quarter. The Polish language disappeared, and only Yiddish was heard. The horses' hooves clanked, and the haranguing of the peddlers became a deafening hubbub. The winding little streets became narrow and twisted, limited by tight passageways in which one could hardly breathe. The houses facing each other shaded the cobblestone streets. Small public squares appeared unexpectedly here and there; those *hoifs* were the only respite in that crowded space.

The entrance to the old Jewish ghetto was through a medieval arch covered with ancient moss. We immediately came upon the *Groyse Shul* on Ulica Zydowska, the Street of the Jews. The monumental Grand Synagogue had a capacity of more than five thousand congregants. Across the *shulhoif,* the synagogue's patio, I could see a conglomeration of buildings devoted to religious institutions: dozens of *yeshivot,* schools dedicated to learning the ancient precepts of the Torah; a small building that had been the study of Vilna Gaon; a few charitable societies; the *mikvek* where people had the ritual bath; the Rabbinical Court; and the Society for Assistance to the Poor. The ghetto also contained more than a hundred little synagogues, each affiliated with a different labor guild.

Three clocks adorned the wall outside the synagogue. One of the clocks, proudly displaying the date 1640, marked the precise moment when the first star would appear—signaling the exact time to light the *Shabbat* candles. On the other side of the wall were the daily announcements of deaths, births, and important Jewish festivities. And in the lower part stood two small boxes where donations were collected for the maintenance of the synagogue. Its balconies on the upper floor were adorned with a Renaissance colonnade while the Greek columns contrasted with the heaviness of the building.

I was enraptured with the city of the great Vilna Gaon where he had taught the precepts of the Talmud. Many students with long beards, dressed in black, ankle-length cassocks and large hats, were coming and going; they were so absorbed in their biblical axioms that they didn't raise their heads while walking. Nothing of what was happening in their surroundings was relevant to them; the fervor and the melancholy of their prayers crossed the borders of time. While the Lithuanian *maskilim*—intellectuals like my father—distanced themselves from the Gaon, those young men faithfully followed the ancient teachings of the Torah, eager to discover its secrets.

My father hurried along, ignoring the young men carrying copies of the *Chumash*, the Pentateuch, beneath their arms. He didn't care about the religious environment.

We crossed the street at the corner of Ulica Zydowska and came to a commercial area. Coats and old clothing hung from wooden doors. There were trinkets everywhere: combs, soaps, perfumes, secondhand clothing, shoelaces, linen handkerchiefs, wooden planks, and pots of different materials—aluminum, copper, brass, or iron. Overwhelmed and excited, I didn't know where to look first. An old woman offered me a loaf of bread, and a young man sitting outside the small door of his shop tried to convince me to look at the secondhand clothes that were being delivered. A heavyset woman, standing in the doorway of her store, insistently showed me the buckets and other cleaning utensils she was selling while my father hurried through the streets.

We went to Ulica Niemiecka, where Rev Perelman's *cheder* was located. The street led us to the concrete wall of the Dominican building; and farther on, we could see the church dedicated to St. Catherine. We arrived at the *milchiks* restaurant that my father frequented. Following kosher laws, the diner served only foods that could be accompanied with dairy. We sat down at a table, and he ordered fish. Without hesitation, he took a big bite from the plate. I was ecstatic. I had never been anywhere with so much bustle and activity. I stopped to watch my father as he savored his food. I wanted to ask him a thousand questions and get closer to him. I wanted to know how much he had loved my mother, whether I looked like her, or if he remembered her when he looked at me.

I tried to initiate a casual conversation: "How can so many Jews live together in such a small space?"

My father looked up and replied, "Did you see the *shulhoif?* In that courtyard, there are more than eight *batei tfilah*, houses of prayers, including the *Groyse Shul* and the Strashun library, where one of the greatest collections of Jewish books is housed, as well as other buildings like the Gaon synagogue. That quarter is where the Orthodox Jews come together to be as close as possible to the holiness and wisdom of the late Vilna Gaon. This city is full of surprises, you will see."

There was no time to talk about feelings or any other intimate subjects. My father stood from the table and hurried us out hastily. We stopped on the corner of Jatkowa Street. "Majorka brand tobacco, please," he said to the store owner. Then he turned around and commented, "It is the best quality." It was a dull detail, but that brought me closer to Shmuel Bernstein, not the pharmacist but my father. We took a *drosky*, a carriage, to a building on Ulica Rudnicka, the place where I would live during the upcoming school year. With my *luvianka*, my light suitcase, in one hand and the new coat my father had bought me for the winter in the other, I waited for the landlady to open the door.

Mrs. Rivkah Koplevich, with a body round like a sphere but crowned with a kind face, led me to my room across a narrow corridor. I managed to see the small kitchen and, above the stove, a picture of the Vilna Gaon. My father and Mrs. Koplevich agreed on a price for my lodging that included my room, meals, laundry for my bed linens, and the purchase of schoolbooks. He handed her a few *zlotys* in advance before we headed out.

We then went to the *Gymnasium Pedagogow*, a high school founded in 1924 by the Teachers Association. It was located on #4 Ulica Portowa, almost at the corner of the intersection between the Jagiellońska and Zawalna streets, near the Eksztejn Tarbut School. I was enrolled, bought my school uniform, and was informed that classes would begin the following morning.

Before returning to my new home, we visited the Fair of the North, where different booths promoted a wide range of businesses and products. The mayor's office sponsored the fair with an appropriate slogan: "Between savings and work, the nation will be enriched." But the stall that attracted my attention the most was the one from the Jewish community of Vilna. Funded by the ORT organization, it offered people the opportunity to study different occupations.

It was dusk when we returned to Mrs. Koplevich's apartment. My father entered the bedroom without speaking, quickly and coldly kissed my forehead, said that he would come to visit me soon, and hurried off. I was left alone in my room, surrounded by abysmal nothingness that made me want to vomit. Although the walls and floors of the bedroom had been scrubbed with bleach and smelled clean, I was disgusted. I ran to the bathroom and washed my face several times, rubbing it harshly with my hands and trying to free myself from my father's unexpected rejection. After a while, I distracted myself by thinking about Asher, about his smile, about the likelihood of finding him in this enormous city. Somehow, I managed to control my anxiety, at least for the moment.

I see her and remember Masza, my first love .... They are so alike. I don't know how to talk to Szifra, how to earn her affection, or how to communicate with her. I would like to embrace her, to recover the lost time, and yet, I ask myself whether it's appropriate to hug her because she is now a young lady, and while I am her father, I am still a stranger to her. I want to give her all the best so she can have a good education and then choose a good husband. Marriage is complicated, and Esfir is not an easy woman. She didn't want Szifra in Nemenčinė any longer; she thought that my daughter was an intruder in our lives and continuously argued with me about her. I prefer that Szifra continues her studies in Vilna, and perhaps, in the future, she will be able to study pharmacy as she wants to do. Perhaps one day we can become closer.

***

I placed and replaced the red cap of my school uniform on my head for the fifth time. It was my first day of school. I looked in the small mirror, adjusted the beret, tilting it a little more, and tried to smile. I said goodbye to Mrs. Koplevich, and I walked to school.

I encountered a marvelous scene: the city of Vilna was dressed in all sorts of colors. The black caftans of the Orthodox Jews contrasted with all the different hues of the school uniforms. There was an effervescence boiling in different directions: some took the Swedish Arbon bus, others walked hastily, while some strode slowly toward the *yeshivot* in order to concentrate on their Talmud studies.

I turned down Jatkowa Street, made a left turn on Strashun, and then walked along Zawalna until I reached Portowa, where my school was located. I ran inside and strode up to the second floor. Panting, I crossed the long corridor with a row of numbered classrooms. I managed to sit down at my desk promptly at eight o'clock in the morning as the metal bell rang. I saw the familiar face of Mindel, one of the girls who had been introduced to me in

Nemenčinė. Her friendly smile welcomed me.

The teacher asked us to write an essay on any subject we chose. I considered writing about the sad farewell I'd had with my grandparents in Anykščiai. Our separation had been abrupt and had left me heartbroken. Shabtai and Leah appeared continuously in my mind, growing older behind the border. My anxiety and painful loneliness flowed easily onto the paper.

I turned in my work with unclear handwriting and ink overflowing the page. I was afraid the teacher would reprimand me, but to my surprise, I was congratulated. The teacher showed my manuscript to the director and then circulated my text throughout the school. My life was now transparent. I had never imagined that my feeling of emptiness would be made so public. On that day, unexpectedly, my pain became known to the entire school, and everybody became aware of my inner thoughts.

"I would like to introduce Szifra Bernstein Rapoport," the teacher said to the class.

"Are you a relative of Shloyme Zaynvl Rapoport, better known as An-ski, the writer of the play 'Der Dibek' that was staged a few years ago?" one of my classmates asked.

Surprised by the question, I wrinkled my forehead and shook my head. Of course, I had heard of the famous play by An-ski, but I'd never realized the author shared my last name. The distraction calmed my nerves, and the teacher asked me to begin reading my paper. Facing my classmates, I reviewed each line. My past life seemed remote. In perfect Hebrew, I concluded with the sentence,

"*Harei sela yajlú ligboa!* Stone mountains can also grow!"

From classroom to classroom, I read my thoughts as if they were someone else's story, little by little, unconsciously separating myself from the pain. Without warning or any help from Freud, my grandparents were left marginalized in a corner of my memory.

The weeks passed between classes in mathematics, physics, Jewish history, Hebrew, Yiddish, and German. At two o'clock in the afternoon, I would leave school, often taking with me several books including the Yiddish grammar of Zalman Rajzen, a play by Schiller or Goethe, or the poetry of Adam Mickiewicz. Twice a week, I rushed to my private Polish lessons with Professor Kochanovich, as I was still far from mastering the language.

One afternoon after school, as I was walking along with some friends on the streets of Vilna, we stopped to buy sunflower seeds. We then approached the garden of the Saint Bernardine convent to listen to a rehearsal of the philharmonic. As we strolled back along the charming little Sawyca Street toward Wielka, I unexpectedly ran into Asher!

"Asher!" I shouted in excitement. "Asher, it's you!" I ran to hug him.

"I thought your father would enroll you in the Eksztejn Tarbut *Gymnasium* and that we would be together at school," he exclaimed. "I didn't know where to look for you. The only thing that occurred to me was to wait until the summer to meet you again in Nemenčinė. Now we can see each other every day after school."

Hand in hand, we walked along Ulica Wielka, where flowery

ornaments clashed with the gray pavement. In the cathedral square, the bells that marked the hour could be heard, calling the faithful to prayer. As we passed the ruins of the Zamkowa Castle, I noticed someone playing the violin on the sidewalk. The melody added magic to our already beautiful day. We continued walking toward the Green Bridge that crossed over the Vilija River.

It was Friday, market day, and Lukiškės Square was bustling. Absorbed in our conversation, we continued walking until we arrived at the entrance of the Rasos Cemetery. A red brick wall encircled the little Gothic chapel. As we entered the graveyard, I felt awkward. It was somewhat disturbing to wander among the tombstones, and I asked Asher to walk me home before it got dark. Twilight surrounded us as we came by my lodgings. I hurriedly said goodbye to Asher and ran upstairs.

I kept on seeing Asher regularly. He would wait for me at the school gate every day so we could stroll around the city together. We avoided returning home late so Mrs. Koplevich wouldn't scold me.

One of those days, we met up with some friends at the ruins of King Gediminas Castle. Although I had seen the castle from afar on numerous occasions, I had never ventured to walk inside. The place inspired more fear than curiosity. But Asher and the others encouraged me to go in.

"I'm afraid," I confessed. "Don't you think this castle might be haunted? Lilith might be wandering around here. She can harm us!" I exclaimed in a high-pitched voice.

Asher burst out laughing and took my hand, guiding me

farther up the dilapidated steps. "Don't be so provincial. I've been coming here to play since I was little. It is here where the dreams and the legend of a king come together."

He excitedly told me the legend of King Gediminas who unified Lithuania in the fourteenth century. He told me that the king had organized a hunt in the nearby woods of Trakai, where he lived. Gediminas had spotted and shot a fawn but missed. Instead, his arrow had pierced a calf on top of a little hillside near the Vilija River. The king walked toward the wounded animal and decided to spend the night there. A wolf appeared in his dream; it was wearing an iron shield and was howling sonorously. The king woke up frightened and asked one of his priests to interpret the dream. Lezdeika, the priest, told him that he should erect a fortress on that same spot. King Gediminas thus ordered the construction of his castle and founded the city.

We climbed the hill through the collapsed walls and finally reached the summit. From there, I admired the immensity of the city of Vilna. The Vilija and the Vilnia rivers flanked the center. Asher's eyes focused on me; he brought his face close to mine, and I felt his lips on mine.

"Children! What are you doing there?" yelled the guard. "Get out of there this instant!"

It seemed like the castle crumbled beneath our feet; the energy that had drawn us there a second before had vanished. Frightened, we ran hand in hand, out of breath, until we reached the chocolate factory located on Adam Mickiewicz Avenue. Our mutual attraction dissolved.

I said goodbye to Asher. Amid confusion and excitement, I ran to the apartment to get there before sundown.

Mrs. Koplevich was there, waiting for me at the gate.

"Do you think I don't know what you do every afternoon?" Her index finger almost touched my face as she spoke. "People talk, they see you hanging out with that young man, Asher. Your father won't like you spending so much time alone with him. You should mind your reputation."

With tears in my eyes, I went to my room and closed the door to avoid hearing any more of her moralistic haranguing.

My father arrived the following week. He forbade me from dating Asher. I complied with his strict rules and did not go out alone with him again. I was afraid I couldn't control my emotions, yet at the same time, I was afraid of my father's wrath. From time to time, I would go out with groups of friends up to the ruins of King Gediminas Castle. From up there, it was possible to see the cathedral tower, tall and straight, bearing witness to centuries of Lithuanian history. Sometimes Asher went along, but we never again went walking by ourselves around the streets of the city. The magic of our love disappeared. Only an affectionate friendship remained.

The school year was filled with friends and teachers, visits from my father, perfecting my Polish, and practicing my Hebrew. 1927 turned into 1928. I met a group of young people through the Zionist youth organization of *Shomer Hatzair*. They met two or three times a week in an apartment near Makowa Street.

Mindel, my friend from Nemenčinė, attended the meetings regularly and offered to go with me on my first visit. I took out my old *tilboshet*, the uniform I had worn in Anykščiai when I went to the *Shomer* with the Yavnoson girls and with Abrasha, and off we went.

The apartment was crowded. A group was arguing enthusiastically and all at once about humanitarian ideals, *Eretz* Israel, and the defense of Jewish rights. I was eager to understand every passionate and heated opinion around the room. I wanted to be a part of it all, but shyness overcame me, and I didn't want to be separated from Mindel.

Mindel greeted a tall young man holding a drink in his hand:

"*Salutaton*, Moishe," said Mindel, who had become obsessed with the study of Esperanto.

"*Shalom*, Mindel," he replied in Hebrew.

"I'd like to introduce you to Szifra. She comes from Anykščiai and Nemenčinė and studies in the teachers' *gymnasium*," she continued in Polish.

"Hello," I replied hesitantly, trying to hide my ignorance in front of all these well-educated teens.

"This is a secret meeting, is that clear?" Moishe stated.

I cast a questioning glance at Mindel, sitting next to me. I had just read *Quo Vadis* in my Polish literature class, and I felt like the Christians in Nero's time.

From the back of the room, a young man wearing glasses

raised his voice:

"Comrades," he began slowly, "we all know the history of Lithuania, the conflicts with czarist Russia, the Polish partitions, and the revolt organized by Tadeusz Kościuszko." His curly hair, despite having been combed down with grease, shook impetuously. His flushed cheeks showed his energetic passion for the Zionist cause. "We believe that Lithuania is our home, we were born here and went to school here, but our land is *Eretz* Israel. We must go to Palestine to work hard and have a better future!"

Everybody applauded and cheered enthusiastically for the future of Israel. They had different opinions, but they mostly revolved around the writings of Engels and Marx. They argued about the equality of men and women and the importance of knowing agricultural techniques. Although their discrepancies continued, I sensed that they were friends.

A small group organized an excursion to Lake Trakai for the following Friday. I immediately signed up to go.

Early Friday morning, we took a bus to Kovno. As we left the noise of Vilna behind, the group's mood lightened. When we arrived in Trakai, a sandy path led us to the village's main street. The tranquility of the hamlet bestowed serenity onto us.

We meandered along the streets, bought pickles from the *Karaim*, and then rented some rowboats on the lake. The wind picked up, penetrating our bones. Amidst songs and laughter, we hadn't realized that we were about to run aground. The boat stopped abruptly and jerked some of us out into the frozen waters of the lake.

Soaked, we climbed back onto the boat to continue with our fun. I began to cough and have chills. By the time we took the bus back to Vilna that afternoon, my head was on fire.

I was late coming home. The Koplevich family was waiting for me for *Shabbat*. I rushed to my bedroom to change my clothes.

"We were waiting for you to pray and have supper together," Mrs. Koplevich reprimanded me sullenly.

Mrs. Koplevich forced me to drink a cup of hot water that tasted like garlic. In a dreamlike state, I walked over to my bed. The doctor came, examined me superficially, and pronounced decisively: "Szifra must stay in bed. She will benefit from the application of suction cups with methyl. She has phlegm and fever, and the temperature changes have affected her respiratory system. She needs an alcohol rub, and I would advise that Mrs. Gervinsky come to apply the *bankes*."

Every breath of air was a triumph. Through the fever, I remembered my father saying that *bankes* were a thing of the past, that studies of modern medicine indicated they didn't help in the slightest, but I was too weak to complain. I couldn't express an opinion. I prayed for my father to be notified, thinking he could come from Nemenčinė to cure me, but that didn't happen. Sometime later, a woman came into my bedroom with a clinking bag, took out some small glasses, lit a candle, and in an authoritarian tone ordered me to undress from the chest up.

Somewhat embarrassed by my prematurely developed bust, I slowly did what she asked. Suddenly, I felt the edge of a hot glass stick to the skin of my back. Four or five glass cups were stuck to me. After a few minutes—pop! The lady pulled the little cups that held on tight to my body, leaving marks of red circles on my skin—which stayed for several days as a testimony of the treatment.

The woman immediately left the room and announced, "She will be cured in a few days; otherwise, call me, and I will come back."

I prayed to God for my prompt recovery only to be free of this torment. Mrs. Koplevich prepared a *goglmogl*, a nauseating yellow brew made of hot milk and raw eggs, that she forced me to swallow. Between all the coughing and the fever, I finally managed to fall asleep.

My father never came to see me. I got better soon enough, and I returned to my daily routine: waking up, studying the scientific advances of Maria Sklodowska, memorizing Józef Szujski's poems, reading the play of Pan Tadeusz, strolling the streets of Vilna with friends, attending the meetings of the *Shomer Hatzair,* and immersing myself in the socialist ideology.

***

The trees changed their dress and stayed naked during the winter. I received a letter from Nemenčinė signed by my stepmother in November 1929. It informed me that my father had traveled to Carlsbad and Berlin to undergo special treatment for an acute ulcer attack. According to Esfir, he had invested a large part of his savings in the stock market in the United States. When he learned of the crash, the shock of the news affected him so much that he fell ill. *Dir muter* ended the letter in a dry tone, sending me greetings from my father.

I did not hear from him for several weeks until he returned to Nemenčinė. He sent a letter informing me that he was feeling better and was hoping to see me soon.

When I went to visit him, I was surprised at his appearance; the last time I had seen him, his visage had shown a wise and assured man. Now, he looked sad and tired. He was overworked, spending even the holidays in the laboratory of his pharmacy. He feared the economic losses of the Great Depression of 1929, complaining constantly about the cost of my education and the expensive rent he paid for me in Vilna. Still, no matter the circumstances, my father always welcomed me home with a smile.

***

I spent Rosh Hashanah and Yom Kippur in Nemenčinė then returned to Vilna in time for the debut of the film *Mata Hari* with Greta Garbo as the star. Mindel and I were eager to see it and planned to go to the Helios Theater on Wileńska Street.

I bought an orange at a small stand just outside school and savored the slices of the fibrous exotic fruit. On the Street of the Bernardines, where the monument of the musician Stanisław Monisuzko was located, we encountered a long procession of parishioners coming to pray to the Virgin of Ostra Brama. Her visage, carved into a niche in the arch of the eastern gate, welcomed everyone into the old city.

The pilgrimage had filled the road that bordered the river toward the Gate of Dawn. Mindel and I were trapped by the religious parade. It was useless to try to get out of the garden of the Bernardine monastery, where the Gothic Church of Santa Ana's flaming needles scratched the sky. The fervent crowd forced us to follow in their footsteps.

The smell of frankincense and burned wax made me sneeze, and I lost sight of my friend, who had walked ahead of me. I was afraid; I knew that the crowds often turned against Jews during Catholic festivities.

I kept on marching with the tumult. I was pushed onto the street in front of the church of St. Casimir, on Wielka Street, near the Hotel Astorja. If only I could reach the door of the hotel, but the throng continued relentlessly along Ulica Ostra Brama. I tried to get away from the procession onto one of the streets neighboring the Greek Orthodox Church of the Holy Spirit, but it was impossible. I was immersed in the incense, the crying, and the people beating their chests.

Someone cried, "They threw a stone, and they've broken a window in Mrs. Müller's shop on Szopena Street!"

Taking advantage of the bedlam, I slipped away from the crowd. Frightened, I ran to Koplevich's apartment and took refuge inside, hoping that Mindel had managed to escape as well. The celebration ended at dawn, and the festive commotion subsided slowly until it finally died out altogether in the dark alleyways.

The next day, I walked to the *gymnasium* in a dense fog and found Mindel in the classroom. I was relieved to see that she had suffered no harm from the day before. We forgot about our determination to see Greta Garbo and went to the *Shomer* meeting together later that afternoon.

Our comrades were engrossed in a bitter argument. They were debating about the different Jewish organizations in Vilna, suggesting that they unite. Some people felt that a merge would be impossible, given the egos, ideologies, and specific interests of each organization that vastly exceeded the emergency of the moment.

I approached my old friend Asher who was arguing heatedly with a curly-haired boy. His face was familiar to me—I had seen him in the corridors at school and at the *Shomer* meetings.

"Do you think it's possible that someday Orthodox *Mizrahis* could get along with Zionists? Or the people affiliated with *Beitar* could get along with those belonging to *Shomer* or *Poalei Zion*? Do you think that people associated with the *Bund*, who are opposed to Zionism, would be able to agree with Zionist youth organizations like *HeHalutz*?"

"Itzhak," argued Asher, "it's impossible for the *Shomer* to unite with *Beitar*. We have very different ideals; they support capitalism, we're Marxists."

"No, Asher, you don't understand the issue here, our coreligionists in Palestine are suffering," Itzhak Zuckerman replied convincingly. "We must make a greater effort, and besides working the land, we must be united to fight, to defend ourselves. The British have become our enemies, they have blocked the entry of Jews into *Eretz* Israel …. If what you want is to strengthen your muscles to farm the land, then maybe you should enroll in *Maccabi*, where the only thing that they do is morning calisthenics."

"Calm down, Itzhak. It is possible that we may agree on some points, but for the moment, it is unlikely to bring all factions together. Forget it, and let's concentrate on our activities."

A young man, about twenty years old, tall and good-looking, stood up in the center of the room. In a firm voice, he proposed the weekend's activities: "On Saturday we will go on an excursion to the forests near Volozhin where we will learn about first aid."

He was very handsome, and I asked Mindel if she knew who he was.

"He's Eksztejn, Yudko Eksztejn. He is a medical student at the University of Vilna," my friend replied.

My gaze was fixed on him. His voice was captivating. His soft demeanor and his slow speech enchanted me. When I arrived home, I thought about Yudko Eksztejn, and my heart began to beat uncontrollably. Yudko Eksztejn was in my destiny. My love for him had no explanation; it suddenly appeared inside me as an insatiable vice that would not find fulfillment. Uneven breathing and restlessness prevented me from sleeping. Even though I didn't know him well, I was already in love with Eksztejn. Those bewitching sentiments would become part of a labyrinth of complex passions.

Chapter Four: 1929-1933

My father came to Vilna to buy raw materials and insisted on waiting outside the school gate every afternoon to take me to dinner. All I wanted to do was attend the meetings of the *Shomer* and be with the young medical student Yudko Eksztejn. I couldn't get him out of my mind. His visage would appear in my dreams unexpectedly. A pleasant yet distant love persisted within me.

I saw Yudko again one morning after visiting the Šnipiškės cemetery with my father for the first time. The old Jewish cemetery was on the other side of the Vilija River which bordered the city. Fifteen years ago, my mother had been buried in the old *Bet Olam*. Although the cemetery had scarcely been used since the beginning of the century, my father had managed to have his beloved Masza Nechama buried there.

It was the first time I visited my mother's tomb. We walked

among the tombstones down a straight path of poplar trees. Dating from the seventeenth century, the graveyard bore witness to the deaths in the community. The place contained the enigmas of time and possessed a mysterious beauty. Its Gothic sculptures sparked legends of lost spirits that swarmed among the graves, or so people believed. The great Gaon was buried in a mausoleum, safeguarded by an iron-bar fence. Orthodox Jews visited the grave, leaving notes written in Yiddish and Hebrew on his tombstone, asking the Gaon to intercede with the Almighty on their behalf.

Sheltered by a leafy tree, the tomb of Potocki stood proudly—despite the continuous acts of vandalism. Graf Potocki had been burned at the stake in 1749 for converting to Judaism. The sign on the tombstone said: "This tree resists any savagery." Many Jews believed that the sap from that tree had the power to predict the misfortunes of the Jewish community in Vilna.

My eyes scanned the writings chiseled on the stones in both Yiddish and Hebrew—unknown names, deaths from another time, and people who meant nothing to me. Even after death, some boasted about their social status or the work they had done in their lives. The Cohanim, the ancient temple priests, were represented with a symbol of two hands outstretched with a peculiar space between their fingers. The Levis, second in the biblical hierarchy, had engraved the basin in which they'd washed the hands of the Cohanim. A doctor's profession was indicated with a mortar and pestle. A tall column pointed to the gravesite of the victims of the Bund, massacred in 1905, and a sculpture of an eagle adorned the tombstone of the recently assassinated writer, A. Weiter.

My mother's tombstone was engraved in Hebrew with the letters *pei* and *nun*, the initials of the phrase *po nikbar* meaning "Here lies," followed by her name: Masza Nechama Bernstein *bat*—daughter of—Shabtai Rapoport. My father motioned for me to pick up a little stone from the edge of the path and place it on the headstone. *My mother will know that we were here!* I thought. *This little stone will remain with her.*

As we walked toward the exit, the cry of the mourner's prayer, the *Kaddish*, could be heard in the distance. My father took out a few *groszen* and deposited them in a little box placed at the door for *tzedakah*, the expected charitable donation. He washed his hands as ritual dictated and said goodbye to the guard with a nod. We walked along the street leisurely.

We crossed over the bridge toward Wileńska Avenue, and that was when I spotted Eksztejn: handsome, his books under his arm, rushing to catch the "Arbon" bus. My blood pressure and breathing accelerated to a thousand revolutions per minute. I made no attempt to greet him; my father would not have approved. He would have been furious if he knew I was attending the *Shomer* meetings. Walking without hesitating, I maintained a steady pace all the way to the house on Rudnicka Street.

My father, who was leaving the next morning for Nemenčinė, said goodbye to me. I wouldn't see him again until the summer.

***

As the frost came upon Vilna, snowflakes covered the sidewalks and softened the edges of the streets. At the *Shomer*, political discussions continued. But the day trips and planned activities brought together the idealists. An excursion was organized to the forests of Ponar, seven kilometers from the city of Vilna. As I was getting on a bus, I spotted Yudko among the boys. Self-conscious, I urged Mindel not to leave my side until I had enough strength to speak to him. He was older than I was, and at the tender age of sixteen, I felt like a timid little girl, unable to start the conversation. Incapable of moving from my seat, I remained next to my friend until we got to Ponar.

As usual, the wobbling movement of the bus made me feel ill. When we arrived at our destination, Asher, trying once again to get close to me, showed me how to tie the wooden boards to my shoes. They would act like skis and help us glide along the snow. The slope seemed menacing to me.

I began to walk when suddenly my feet got tangled up between the boards, and I fell flat, hurting my arm. I laid on the floor and heard somebody call Yudko Eksztejn, who quickly came to my rescue. I smiled, flustered, as he checked my arm. The thrill of being near Yudko was unrivaled.

I struggled to find my balance as I tried to get up. I felt weightless … I levitated as if I were on a carousel and the metal horses had suddenly transformed into living animals that ran free. I was speechless. Yudko, noting my agitation, abruptly said goodbye. As he walked away, he said, "I hope to see you again. I'm going to the Lux Theater on Mickiewicz Street with some friends from the *Shomer* this Thursday. I hope you can join. We will be meeting at the box office at five in the afternoon."

I didn't think twice. That Thursday, I showed up at the theater box office. There was Willy Hafner, a dark-skinned boy whose father owned a mushroom export company, and Zrulko, whom I had seen a couple of times at the *Shomer* meetings. They greeted me politely. Yudko arrived soon after. He took my hand, and together we entered the theater. My body felt stiff, full of excitement and nerves. I didn't pay much attention to the American film; I could feel my heart palpitating rapidly.

As we left the theatre, Yudko Eksztejn invited me to the Zrovie Café. He told me that he came from a small *shtetl* in Galizia and spoke enthusiastically about his medical studies. He was interested in me and asked about my past. I told him about my grandparents in Anykščiai and my relationship with my father. I felt special and appreciated. Happy!

That was the first of many dates, always in the same café, surrounded by young university students, with just a soda or a cup of tea between us. It was in that café that Yudko taught me how to drink black coffee ... and I left my adolescence behind.

***

The first wildflowers were already displaying their brightness in

March 1931. The city was festooned with color. The streets were replete with ribbons and billboards—inviting people to the annual Saint Casimir's Fair. It was a happy sight.

Yudko and I were drinking coffee on the terrace of the little restaurant we frequented when the religious processions began to pass by in front of us. The crowd was growing, and to avoid the tumult in Lukiškės Square, we decided to walk to the opposite side. The merchants had already set up their stalls on the road: saints and virgins sculpted in wood, beautifully carved crosses, masterfully embroidered linen tablecloths, candies, and trinkets were everywhere. Winter was over, and a festive mood was in the air.

I saw Mrs. Koplevich in the distance, so I tried to avoid her as best I could. I was afraid that she would tell my father that I was alone, unchaperoned, with Yudko. My father would be furious and would likely order me to return immediately to Nemenčinė.

I ran abruptly to the opposite side of the street, leaving Yudko standing by himself in front of the linen cloth stand.

I owed Yudko an explanation, and I thought I would give it to him the next day. However, it would be weeks before I saw him again. I thought about waiting for him at the university gate every day, but I did not dare to do it. My indecision was blurring my thoughts, and my reality was suspended in the air.

***

Time passed, one day melting into the next. The hours ticked between *Chumash*, geometry, and history classes. No one was waiting for me at home: no mother, no father, no siblings. I did not have a family in Vilna. It was just me, a temporary renter, and the landlady.

Yudko still did not appear anywhere, and I did not look for him. Finally, I worked up the courage to go to the next *Shomer* meeting. I was glad when I saw Yudko Eksztejn arrive. I tried to catch his eye to explain what had happened at the Saint Casimir's Fair. Before I could utter a word, he spoke to me in a loud voice, as if he wanted everyone to know:

"Do not worry, Szifra, I understand what happened a few weeks ago. I don't think your father would have liked to know that you were walking alone with a boy three years older than you. Now that the weather has warmed up, let's spend the day together at one of the Valakampiai beaches."

I accepted immediately by nodding and looking intensely into his eyes.

We took the bus from Vilna. I don't know if it was the movement of the wheels, being with Yudko alone, an addiction to adventure, or rebelling against my father, but I felt so alive that day at the river. I knew it was a lost cause; my father wouldn't consent to our relationship. However, the flesh was stronger than the mind, the heart stronger than reason, and my pleasure stronger than my father's mandates. I continued seeing Yudko Eksztejn every day until the beginning of summer when I left for Nemenčinė to be with my family.

***

June was upon us. The constant rain left mud puddles on the streets of Nemenčinė. I opened the door to the pharmacy; the familiar smell of formaldehyde rekindled my desire to become a pharmacist. The *apteka*, with its jars of *Ethacridine lactate*, *Phenobarbitalum*, and tincture of *Geranium maculatum*, lay before me, just as I had left it on my last visit.

My friends from wealthy households went to summer camps in Dieveniškės; others, like Asher, came to our small village to spend the warm summer season with their families, enjoying the refreshing waters of Lake Gela. I couldn't stop thinking about Yudko Eksztejn. On those long, soporific days, I would collapse face-up on my bed, dreaming about him.

I devoted many hours of the day to writing to my family in Anykščiai. I learned that Sonja, my aunt, had joined the Communist Party. Shayna would tell me about her work at the local bank and keep me up-to-date on any news from the family. Abrasha Evenson, my childhood friend, wrote to me from Kovno where he was attending the *gymnasium*. I wrote to them about my progress with the Polish language and about my newly acquired knowledge of medicine and healing. I did not confess my feelings for Yudko, with whom I had plans to change the world.

That summer, I learned a lot about pharmacology by listening to my father and helping him make medicines. I would write down the names of the patients, their ailments, how much they owed, and how much they paid. Every coin earned was put into used porcelain jars. One afternoon, I came upon him burying one of those jars in the garden behind the house.

"Why do you keep the money there?"

"One never knows what the future will bring, and by the way, I don't trust banks. After the banking crisis in America, anything can happen. Everything that I earn in the pharmacy I exchange for gold and then hide it in these jars."

Little did he know that the same gold he treasured so carefully would, years later, save my life.

***

I returned to my usual routine once I was back in Vilna. On the first day of classes, the history teacher explained how Lithuania had been previously and temporarily conquered by Russians, Poles, and Germans. I couldn't concentrate. All I could think about was seeing Yudko at the end of the school day.

The teacher's discussion about Lithuania's deeply rooted traditions was all background noise to me. I could barely hear his lecture about the land where demons and angels lived in caves, about the legends and folklore that culminated in the apotheosis of Christian festivals, and about how the borders were so volatile and variable, changing according to whoever dominated the land.

I lost the thread of what he was saying and started

daydreaming about my Lithuania: the one that had nothing to do with Saint Casimir or the Virgin of Ostra Brama. My Lithuania included my friends from the *Shomer Hatzair*, the Orthodox Jews from the *shulhoif* and the Grand Synagogue; my father's pharmacy and his medicinal potions; and Yudko Eksztejn, the love of my life.

As soon as the bell rang, I rushed to meet Yudko in the small park between Portowa, Jagiellońska, and Zawalna. We hugged—delighted to be back together. Holding hands, we walked cheerfully up Mickiewicz Avenue in front of the elegant Bristol Hotel.

That day, Yudko declared his love to me. The castles of Gediminas suddenly decorated the landscape, the poppies covered the asphalt with their corollas, and the black eyes of Yudko seemed brighter to me than burning coal.

It didn't take me long to confirm that the Lithuania my history teacher idealized didn't exist anymore. Vilna, for better or for worse, was now part of Poland. The atmosphere continued to get harsher. On November 10, 1931, a group of students attacked their Jewish classmates. During the onslaught, Stanislaw Waclawski, a young Catholic, died, and the people, avid for revenge, turned him into a hero. In his name and sheltered by the anonymity of the crowd, Christians rushed to attack any Jew who crossed their path. They destroyed the windows of shops owned by Jews and did not hesitate to break the bones of old Orthodox Jews, easily recognizable by their long beards, black frock coats, and hats.

Community leaders, frightened and surprised, engaged in talks with the authorities without much success. Fear also spread within the *Shomer*. We all talked about it, discussing the measures that we could take, strengthening our ideals of Zionism.

While Vilna burned, I did a balancing act trying to find ways to see Yudko. We would see each other every day after school, losing ourselves in the Bernardine convent gardens. One day, seated underneath the shadow of a poplar tree, Yudko laid out his plan:

"Szifra, I want to spend the rest of my life with you. Next year you'll graduate from the *gymnasium* and obtain your *matura*, your diploma. I don't know whether your father will accept me as a son-in-law, but I would like to speak to him as soon as possible. I would like us to get married and go to Palestine to live. There we can be free, we can work the land and construct our home in an agricultural commune, in a *kibbutz*, like the rest of the young immigrants."

I froze at the proposal. I didn't know how to answer him. I did not have the strength to upset my father and rebel against him. He would never accept it. Moreover, the life that Yudko proposed to me was too risky; survival in the deserts of *Eretz* Israel was difficult, and it would be several more years before Yudko finished medical school and could specialize in surgery. I realized that life at his side could be treacherous.

I loved him, but I didn't know what to do. If I went with him, I would be a disappointment to my father. I wanted to be with Yudko, to be his, to have his arms around me forever, to guess his thoughts, twirl his curls around my fingers, and melt in the seductive abyss of his eyes. But I didn't have the courage. At heart,

I was a coward and didn't have the will to follow him.

Yudko sensed my doubts: "Szifra ... we love each other. That's the only thing that matters."

"But, Yudko," I implored, "my father will do everything possible to prevent me from leaving. Moreover, the journey to Palestine is dangerous. It's impossible to get visas, we would have to travel illegally and take risks—"

He put his fingers on my lips. "Szifra, at least promise me you'll think about it."

To defy my father was one thing, but to risk my life was a concept I was not ready to face. I felt that Yudko Eksztejn was a sentence to a dangerous realm. I decided it was best to break up with him.

A few weeks later, the handsome and fit Roman Fainberg Avramovich, the student chair for all the school sports, was waiting to walk me home after class. As we strolled, a group of girls looked at us intensely, and I noticed their envious gazes. I held my head high, showing off my new admirer.

This soon became a ritual: we promenaded around the city, bought some refreshments, and talked politely. We would then continue our walk until we reached the gate of the building where I lived and said goodbye.

Wishing to bump into Yudko on one of those afternoons, I waited for Roman on a park bench next to the Bernardine convent, which I knew was part of Yudko's daily route. Suddenly, Roman rushed over and took a seat beside me.

As I predicted, Yudko Eksztejn appeared moments later. He gave us a sidelong glance as I tried to hide my true feelings from Roman. I hoped my ex-boyfriend would give me some minimal sign. Even a quick nod would have been sufficient to give me strength, but there was nothing. I was hurt as I saw him continue on his path. Trying to hide my uneasiness, I turned away from Roman and observed Yudko as he walked away.

The next morning, Yudko appeared outside my apartment without warning. Gently, with no sign of ire, he spoke to me and

Shura & Yudko sitting on a bench

kissed me. As if a spell had been broken, we renewed our relationship. I made him promise that he would not speak again about running away from Vilna or about working in the arid fields of *Eretz* Israel. I made it clear that I loved him but couldn't follow him. I wanted him to understand me and accept it. Yudko agreed, but despite my supplication, he insisted upon speaking to my father alone. The plan was set: Yudko would meet my father the next time he came to Vilna to buy raw materials for the pharmacy.

Yudko bravely confronted my father; he spoke of his love for me, of his dreams of being a doctor in Israel, of taking me with him to finish his studies, and about spending our lives together. My father listened in silence, and Yudko waited in vain for an answer, receiving only a brief but courteous farewell without a clear response.

A few hours later, my father appeared at my school during recess and with a tone of sanction said, "I do not know why you got involved with that boy, an idealist, and on top of that, his family is from Galitzia, he is a simple *Galitzianer*... and ... he wants to take you away. I am not willing to accept that you marry anyone beneath your social status, let alone follow him to have a life of misery and hard work in Palestine. Here, you'll find a good husband, a Litvak, a Lithuanian Jew who has a good economic position. A man who doesn't play at being a hero."

My father knew that I loved Yudko Eksztejn, and that if he had given me his blessing, I would have gone away with him after I finished the *gymnasium*. But he didn't leave that door open. The subject was closed. The bell was clanging for us to return to class. I withheld my objection, but when my father turned away, my sobs mixed with the hubbub of the students rushing down the corridors.

I told Yudko what had happened. The school year was ending, and we understood that our parting was near. There was a growing atmosphere of antisemitism, and the university had decreed a more restricted quota on Jews in the careers of medicine and law. For Yudko, the future had plunged after the avalanche; he could not continue his studies in Vilna any longer; he had to look for admission in another country.

We lived our last chapter together for a few more months until he was accepted to the School of Medicine at the University of Bologna. We said goodbye at our favorite park bench. We exchanged looks, caresses, and silence.

He gave me a watch as a gift and added tenderly, "Don't get lost in the mists of time. As you know, I will go first to Italy, and as soon as I can, I will travel to Palestine. I'll wait for you there."

We both cried, wrapped in our sadness, floating in the impossibility of being together. Yudko kissed me and said goodbye. I remained alone, seated on the park bench, watching the sun dampen with my tears.

***

Winter arrived. 1932 dawned amidst fog and frost. I received my first letter from Italy. I read Yudko's words and closed my eyes so I could hear his melodious voice:

Dear Szifra:
The trip to Italy was difficult, but I finally arrived and am now enrolled at the university. The people are very nice. I can manage and be understood thanks to the Latin I learned in Vilna. I would have wanted to live these experiences with you at my side. I miss you.

I will always be waiting for you,
Yudko

I became morose and capricious. I tried to fill the void Yudko had left by buying fancies that my father paid for: a new lace fabric, ribbons to enhance my attire, and colored bows that piled up in my drawers. I had no desire to dress up or to go out with my friends, but I insisted that my father pay for my clothes to be hand-washed every Wednesday.

My father tried to appease his guilt by satisfying my material desires. Spending his money was a form of retaliation. I was angry at him, at the world, and at myself for not being independent and strong. I knew that was a useless mechanism to disguise my frustrated solitude. On the other hand, I enjoyed warm food, white cotton sheets, and a room that I did not have to share with anyone. But when I found myself missing Yudko, I also thought about my family in Anykščiai; I longed for a maternal hug or an affectionately whispered "good night" before reciting the prayer *Shema Yisrael*. No bow, corsage, or stole could satisfy me. I rebelled in my own way; I just couldn't accept my father's judgments.

Nothing helped to open my heart. I was ensconced within my feelings, neither the wide and decorative avenues nor the beautiful chestnut trees surrounding them could help me. The city landscape was choking me. I was boiling with rage. I found myself disinterested in life, not caring about my future.

Everything annoyed me; even the Jewish neighborhood, with its narrow, twisting little streets, no longer delighted me. The ancient ghetto now appeared pale and anemic. It smelled of fish, cooked chicken, stench, and urine. Rather than appreciating the Talmudic wisdom of the Strashun library or the *beth Midrash*, I could now only see beggars and people in rags. Everything looked gray and useless; nothing seemed to make sense anymore.

I wandered listlessly through the streets of Vilna until I suddenly came across the doors of the YIVO, the new Institute for Jewish Research. I entered and found myself in the middle of a cluster of documents, newspapers, and papers lined up in stacks without any rhyme or reason. As I investigated, an article on superstitious Jewish remedies caught my attention. I did not immediately grasp its meaning; the article referred to ritual healings that were used in the *shtetlaj*, the small towns where civilization was most rudimentary.

It read: "The *segulot*, these superstitious remedies, have been practiced by members of the Jewish community for millennia. One common practice is called *bleigießen*, which involves pouring melted lead into a vessel with water to find the cause of the medical problem. The healer, usually a woman, recites Psalms while she performs the ritual. She then 'reads' the shapes of lead created in contact with the water to understand and relieve the patient of his ailment."

The words of that article rekindled my enthusiasm for pharmacy studies, and I immediately wrote an essay for the school newspaper. I was proud to be the daughter of Shmuel Bernstein, the Nemenčinė pharmacist, my father, my teacher, who had shown me the ways of herbs and drugs. He had introduced me to the mortar, the apothecary jars, the beakers, and how to put them to good use.

On my way home, I noticed that at the intersection of the street, the peasants had put a wooden cross to chase the demons away. I was sure then that I wanted to show people that superstitions were not the right path to healing. It was confirmed … I knew then that I wanted to become a pharmacist.

My classmates and teachers congratulated me on the research and for the information presented in the newspaper, but what surprised them most, I was told, was my use of the Polish language. I had managed to produce a substantive essay in a language I had learned not too long ago. Soon after, a letter from my proud father arrived to congratulate me.

I began to count the days until my high school studies would be over. I wanted to apply to enroll at the Pharmaceutical School at the University of Vilna Stefan Batory.

***

I graduated from school in 1932, finished the *matura* with honors, and received a special prize for my essay "Remedies and Superstitions of the Jewish Community in Lithuania." I applied to the university along with my classmates, but only a handful of us were eligible to go on to college.

I was rejected due to the new government-imposed *numerus clausus,* which limited the number of Jews who could enroll in the University of Vilna for careers like medicine and pharmacology.

Like Yudko, some of my friends went to Italy to study medicine while others made their way to the Technion Institute in Haifa or the Hebrew University of Jerusalem. I felt left out—frustrated—at the impossibility of continuing my studies.

My father turned to his friend Zanitzky, a scientist who worked with the famous Professor Moshinsky at the university. He promised a large donation to the institution in exchange for my matriculation. It didn't work. The university closed its courses in pharmacology due to the lack of resources. My future plans turned bleak.

The doors were closing on me. It was as if I was walking through a swamp; the earth threatened to swallow me whole with every step I took. Fate made fun of me, changing the direction in which the arrows pointed. There was no way out! I could hear a loud voice urging me to follow a route, and then immediately it was blocked. My nightmares were constant. I would look for the exit only to be confronted with a boulder that prevented me from continuing along the path. A sudden voice would advise, "Pay attention, there is another road down the archway," but it was always a mirage of my desolate psyche.

To remain in Vilna was no longer an option; I had no work or occupation. It occurred to me that I could go to Warsaw, though my father didn't allow it.

Back in Nemenčinė, my stepmother's house felt suffocating. Every day I would slowly walk to the bank of the Niemen River to think. I would come back without solving anything. I couldn't stand life in the small town. Mornings were abominable and afternoons execrable.

It seemed that my dream of becoming a pharmacist was impossible. The neighbors saw me as a woman of marriageable age, but I was still a spoiled little eighteen-year-old girl. The *balabustas*, the housewives, spoke to me disdainfully. The other girls didn't interest me as friends, and I felt strange at home. Esfir didn't like my presence, and my only refuge was the solitude of my room.

I roamed around the streets and sometimes appeared in the pharmacy to observe and help my father in his work. Apathetically I thought, *Why learn about botanical medicine and medicinal plants, why bother to memorize the names of ointments and infusions, if I can never practice as a pharmacist?*

What was the point of my father teaching someone who had no expectations or future? My professional career had been cut short and truncated. Inertia governed my daily life; idleness imposed itself on everything.

My father suggested that I give Hebrew classes at the village school, so I spent my days teaching runny-nosed kids. The children opened their eyes wide with every new word they learned; they listened in astonishment to the language of the Torah, the language that Ben Yehuda had modernized to be used in *Eretz* Israel.

I had no gift for teaching—the children got on my nerves, and the *shtetl* seemed too small for me. I was exploding on the inside but silent on the surface.

When my father felt my unhappiness, he tried to cheer me

up: "He who works eats bread with butter, but he who works well gets a cake."

I had no university degree; I was a simple Hebrew teacher in a small school in a tiny town. I didn't have the opportunity to be either a good or a bad professional. My options were limited: either I escaped to Italy to be with Yudko or I condemned myself to a meaningless life. I dreamt about him; I kissed the letters that he signed with a *ciao* in the Italian style. I cried over my weakness to make a drastic and definitive decision.

***

Esfir handed me a letter. It was Yudko's, but the postmark was different. Where was he? I locked myself in my room eager to know about his life and anxious to enjoy his declarations of love in private.

Dear Szifra:

You know how I adore you and how much I want to be with you, but I'm now writing to you from this unfamiliar country. I have been offered a job in a hospital in the city of Split, in Yugoslavia. I hope you understand that I cannot let this opportunity pass. I will earn enough money to come for you in Nemenčinė so we can get settled in Eretz Israel. Be patient, and I beg you to wait for me, you are the most important person in my life.

I miss you,
Yudko

Yudko didn't speak to me about dreams or ideals. He asked me to be patient, to wait for him. His words troubled me, and I realized that I had no escape; my destiny was to remain in Nemenčinė and continue teaching Hebrew forever.

The sooner that girl gets married, the better we'll be at home. Tanya is growing fast, and soon she will also have to study in another town, and she will need a good *shidduch*, a good marriage match. Shmuel is no longer young, and it was his intention that Szifra would help him in the pharmacy, but nothing is acceptable to that spoiled girl. She spends her time dreaming about that *Galitzianer*, and if she's not dreaming, she's depressed. I will talk to Shmuel so we can decide Szifra's future and find a suitable boy who will propose matrimony to her.

Soon the parade of potential candidates began—some not so young, some not so handsome, some not so intelligent. Dr. Tenembaum was the first to come to the house. He was an elderly man, probably my father's age, with a protruding belly and thinning hair.

"What do you think of Dr. Tenembaum?" asked my father with an interested tone.

At least my father gave me the option to choose. I was fortunate, not like the other girls who were forced by their parents to marry the best bidder. However, he didn't refrain from promoting me among his acquaintances: a wealthy merchant, an awkward-looking young man, a timid student, a fat butcher ....

I didn't like any of them, and I didn't want to see any of them again. Meetings in cafés, dinners at home, visits to the lake—my father and his wife didn't give up; they began looking for marriageable men from different villages. Tall, short, wealthy, cultured, obese, or squalid, none of them could compete with Yudko Eksztejn.

I became friends with some of the young professors at the school where I taught. Many came from Galitzia. My father wasn't pleased that I associated with them; he insisted they were not of my social or cultural status. He wanted my husband to come from a respectable family, and he wished that they would be Litvak, Lithuanian.

My father was too intrusive. He would search my bedroom looking for letters from Eksztejn and unsuccessfully try to convince me to forget him.

My asthma attacks were more acute and lasted several days. My father prescribed me valerian for my nerves. He was trying to calm my distressed body, but it was all in vain. I felt more and more asphyxiated. Was I such a nuisance in my father's house? Was everyone conspiring against me? I wanted to run away, to flee, but to where? I felt defeated, so I decided to go to the village healer in secret.

"Sometimes I find it hard to breathe," I explained to the healer. "My throat is tight, I'm paralyzed with fear, I feel lonely and helpless. The situation is getting worse every day. Help me, please!"

Without looking at me, the old woman took a pot from the fire and poured the boiling wax into a bowl of cold water. The yellow liquid solidified immediately, creating blobs of wax on the surface.

"Look, my dear, here I see the shape of a heart. What torments you is related to your feelings. It's not a physical illness, but I warn you that if you continue like this, it will become a true disease."

I walked over to see what the old woman was looking at. It was just a ball of wax floating on the water. *Where had she seen the heart?* I wondered. But instead of asking, I just nodded and listened to her advice.

I had written about such unfounded beliefs, Jewish remedies, and superstitions, and yet had still fallen into the same ancient trickeries. My father's science was no longer enough for me. So instead, I memorized the healer's advice.

"Do not stress, your situation will be resolved. You will meet someone who will understand you, and your heart will cease to suffer as much. Stir these herbs in castor oil and then boil them in water. You'll want to gargle the resulting potion, but don't swallow it. Simply rinse your mouth with the solution and spit it out."

I gently cupped the leaves in my hands, paid for the visit, and returned home more serene but with no intention of ingesting the magical brew she had recommended.

When I opened the door, my father was waiting for me in the living room.

"Hello, Szifra. Where did you go?" he asked me without reproach yet distantly.

With immature naivety, I confessed that I had gone to visit

the village healer.

"The one they call the witch?" inquired my stepmother.

"Yes," I replied timidly.

"How can you believe in those *bubbe meises*? They are no more than superstitions. This is a house of *maskilim*, we are logical thinkers. We base our lives on scientific advances," my father scolded me, snatching the herbs and throwing them on the floor.

"Papa, let me explain, the valerian is not helping me, I do not sleep at night," I told him between sobs. "Sometimes I find it hard to breathe. I'm dying in this small town ... I know they are superstitions, and I do not believe in those remedies, but please understand, Papa, I feel so alone."

I withdrew to my room feeling misunderstood. I curled my body, hugging my legs and sobbing while a swelling feeling crushed my bones.

The procession of suitors continued. This time, Mrs. Matilda Poznik, who rented a pension every summer in Nemenčinė, made the arrangements. In the pharmacy, I managed to hear the woman speak excitedly to my father:

"I have a good match for Szifra. You must send her to Vilna to meet this good boy from Lida, Belarus. His last name is Pupko, he is very well educated and comes from a good family."

"Say no more," exclaimed my father. "If you are the one recommending him, there is nothing else to say. I trust your good judgment."

My father knew I would object, so without saying a word, he

took my passport—the only thing that had a photo of me—and went to Vilna to meet Judel Pupko, the new prospect. Once Judel saw how I looked, he agreed to set up a date to meet me.

My father would have to force me to travel to Vilna on the designated day. So, to avoid setbacks, he would go with me himself. I thought about saying that I was sick and, if necessary, pretending I was feverish; maybe I could cough up blood. I felt like vomiting. I would rather stay in bed all day than go to that meeting.

Nevertheless, the specified day arrived, and I could neither force a fever nor produce phlegm magically in my throat. I had no choice but to take the train with my father and go to my aunt and uncle Zinitzky's home in Vilna.

We arrived at the capital and took a *drosky* to the corner of Ulica Miłosierna. From there, we walked toward the old ladies' hair salon, or the *altishkes,* as they were known. My father knew that I could sabotage my date, so he had arranged an appointment with a stylist who would give me an attractive and fashionable hairdo. My father wanted a hairstyle to attract a boyfriend, a hairstyle that would disguise my sad and hopeless countenance, so she fixed my hair with a light perm.

"You're very pretty, Szifra," my father said enthusiastically, "but you have to care about your appearance. I don't like you hanging around idealists who are looking to dig their own graves in Palestine. Those boys from the *Shomer* are libertines, and I will not allow you to follow a life of indecency. Who do you think you are? Graf Potocki?" he asked sarcastically. Then he continued: "You're a good girl, you must make a good *shidduch* and create your own family. Szifra, that boy Eksztejn is not for you. He's a *Galitzianer*, he has some very peculiar ideas. Forget about him once and for all. I'll never accept him in my family."

I felt my throat constrict with emotion. I wanted to run against the wind, to fight for my autonomy outside the social conventions of my family, but, at the same time, I was afraid to fight for my liberty.

Walking back, I felt a sinking feeling, my unhappiness apparent to everybody on the street. Even the blacksmith, the water carrier, and the cart driver avoided my gaze—they could read the heartbreak in my eyes. A little boy playing the tambourine in a corner gave me the strength to reach Aunt Zinitzky's house. There I changed my clothes and waited for the arrival of Judel, the bachelor on duty.

My father had explained to me that Judel Pupko's family lived in Lida, Belarus. He assured me that this young man could offer me a comfortable life. He came from a respected and prosperous family who sold construction materials. I made an effort to play the part.

My father opened the door and invited him into my aunt's apartment. Judel Pupko didn't have an unpleasant appearance; he wasn't my Yudko Eksztejn, but he wasn't bad. He had brought me a fine little box of imported oranges, which were very expensive. I left them on the table as we sat in front of the samovar. Timidly, we started to talk while savoring some rugelach and tea.

We went out for a walk toward the Palais de Dance, where he had made a reservation. A group of musicians played an American song; the sweet melody of "Stormy Weather" echoed on the small dance floor. The conversation felt tedious, and I fell into a bored stupor. Judel invited me to dance, and I thought it was a good idea, but my head was spinning from the glass of champagne I had just drunk.

The dullness was unbearable. I thought the evening was over, but Judel suggested dinner at the luxurious Hotel Bristol on Mickiewicz Street. Memories came swirling back: Yudko Eksztejn had first confessed his love for me outside the front door of that exact restaurant. The place was sumptuous, and Judel spent more than seventy *zlotys* on dinner, but there was no way that I would accept a second date with that insufferable fellow. I refused to accept his offer to accompany me back to my aunt's home, excused myself, and took the bus alone.

When I walked into the house, my father read my face and understood that the date had been a failure. I muttered good night and withdrew to bed.

Before returning to Nemenčinė, we went to the market on Ulica Zawalna. Near the smelly fish stands were hundreds of colorful vegetables on display: onions, beets, carrots, potatoes .... We looked for dairy products and bought a big piece of cheese to enjoy on our way home. My father took me to the book stalls, and, without paying attention to the bitter stench of the place, I stopped to look at the selection of novels. I picked up *Komediantka* by Władysław

Reymont to read on our journey back to Nemenčinė. I wanted to avoid my father's sermon.

I couldn't have imagined the sad news that awaited me back at home. My grandmother had died in Anykščiai on *Tisha'b'Av,* the saddest day in Jewish history. Her death struck me like a diamond cutting through glass. She had been my mother ... and now, she was gone. I thought about my grandfather Shabtai, with his white beard and downcast eyes, as he looked upon my dead grandmother.

I asked my father to go with me to the synagogue to say *Kaddish,* the prayer for the dead. I sat in the women's section, reading *Tehilim,* the book of Psalms. I felt more alone than ever. I would have never thought, not in my most macabre dreams, that in the near future I would be reciting those same prayers on my way to a concentration camp.

While I mourned the death of my grandmother, Hitler was assuming power as Chancellor of the Third Reich.

Chapter Five: 1933-1935

O n one of those cold autumn days of 1933, my father
returned from Vilna with unguents and herbs for the
pharmacy. He was very chatty. He didn't resemble the
serious, white-coat pharmacist I knew.

"I bumped into Dr. Bervenzas, your classmate Lolca's father.
He told me that he met a young man of marriageable age in Lida,
where he now teaches. This young man, last name Pupko, was in
Belgium studying brewing engineering, the family business, but
had to return home due to his father's recent death."

"Pupko? I already went out with a Pupko. Don't you
remember, Dad?"

"No, Szifra, this man is from another family, perhaps a
cousin, his first name is Sioma. We set up a date for you to meet him
in Vilna, where he travels to frequently."

Fearing that I would flee to Italy, Yugoslavia, or *Eretz* Israel
with Yudko, my father had taken my official documents and kept

them in a locked drawer in his bedroom. My father had shown this other Pupko the awful black-and-white photo in my passport; nevertheless, the young man had asked to meet me. He was the next prospect on an interminable list.

I didn't know what my father and the new Pupko had talked about. I also didn't know whether Sioma had asked his cousin Judel Pupko for permission to ask me out. Sioma called me at my cousin Zinitzky's home, where we were staying. I agreed to meet him at the Café Sztral. I could hear his voice on the other side of the line: "The one with the red awning, on Mickiewicz Street, at the corner of Tartar Street, not the one with the green or the white awning. Is that clear?" joked Sioma Pupko with a playful accent and cynical tone.

"Perfectly. I'm going to wear my green coat so you can recognize me," I said confidently.

"I'm colorblind and can't distinguish many colors, so I won't be able to recognize you by what you are wearing. Why don't you carry a newspaper under your arm, so I don't confuse you with another girl."

I looked at myself in the mirror, sprinkled some rouge on my cheeks, and headed in the direction of the café. I walked a few blocks and stopped nervously at the corner of Ratuszowy Square where they sold many different newspapers at the kiosk. I chose one in Yiddish, the *Unzer Shtime*, which, far from interesting me in the proposals of the Bund, would serve as the agreed-upon signal. I put some rice powder on my face, looked at myself again, this time in my compact mirror, wiped off the excess lipstick that had stuck to my teeth, and continued to the indicated site.

A handsome boy walked toward me. I held a challenging look, but he was not intimidated. Abruptly, he pulled me aside:

"Let's sit in the corner, behind the column. Some of my relatives are here, and I don't want them gossiping." And then he formally introduced himself: "My name is Sioma Pupko Kunica."

The relatives were his brother and sister-in-law who had accompanied him from Lida and were watching us from the next table. I asked for a slice of cake. Sioma scrutinized each one of my movements. I carefully cut the puff pastry, trying, unsuccessfully, to avoid the cream from overflowing. Nevertheless, Sioma liked my candor and simplicity, and I was drawn to his self-assurance and *savoir vivre.*

We lapsed into silence several times during the date, and the previously assured and haughty gaze, with which I had greeted him initially, became inhibited and self-conscious. Sioma, with curious charisma, probed me with uncomfortable questions about my past. He wanted to undress my soul, to know everything about my feelings, my grief, my loneliness. In only one afternoon, he made me reveal my most buried secrets.

He spoke of his travels to France, of his life as a student in Brussels, and about his family. Seated in that café, I imagined a new world far from Poland and Lithuania and, for a while, forgot about Yudko Eksztejn. The world that Sioma presented seduced me instantly. I allowed myself to open my heart. It wouldn't take long for me to fall in love with him and dream up our life together. The hours passed by. The Café Sztral emptied. Sioma and I remained alone, without noticing the perceptive and satisfied look from Mitzia and Roza, his older brother and his wife, who remained seated a few tables away from us.

My father was happy hearing a successful report, glad to know I wanted to see Sioma Pupko again. I would stay with my cousins Zinitzky for two more weeks, and my father would return to Nemenčinė to take care of the pharmacy.

The second date took place quickly thereafter, and the third .... We met every day to talk, trapped in seduction and love. Sioma picked me up at my aunt's house in his car, one of the few in Vilna. As we drove around the streets, everyone turned to look at us. He was gallant. He showered me with luxuries and attention. We had dinner in elegant places, ordered the most expensive dishes on the menu, and paired all our meals with French wines. He showed me his finesse as we walked along the streets, pointing out the neoclassical façades of Lithuania and their relation to the architectural styles of Paris. He was a true gentleman. We were eager to share our past and wanted to spend every minute together.

The day arrived when Sioma had to return to his work in Lida, and I went home to Nemenčinė. We said goodbye lovingly and promised each other a future ... I didn't know how long it would be until I saw him again. Twenty-four hours after arriving at Nemenčinė, I received a message from him. He had called the only telephone in the village, the one in the offices of the City Hall. He said that he would arrive the following weekend, and although I didn't feel the same paralyzing shiver that I had experienced when I'd fallen in love with Yudko, I understood that our lives would be intertwined forever.

Sioma came to Nemenčinė. As he crossed the bridge in his car, he entered through the main street in the direction of Švenčionys, sparking the attention of the whole village. Everyone wanted to know who this distinguished person with a car was and what he was doing parked in front of the pharmacy.

Dressed in a black raincoat and a beret, Sioma greeted Esfir and my father and sat down in the

Unknown person poising next to Sioma's car

dining room to speak with them. He told them about his studies of beer brewing in Brussels, the family's industry in Lida, and his desire to conclude his studies in the Flanders' capital. He seemed so intelligent, so worldly.

He referred to me in metaphors, complimenting me by saying that I was like the purest malt, without spikes or stones or impurities. He added that I was not yet a finished product and that he would teach me many things, mold me to become a beer of the highest quality. His eyes shone mischievously as he spoke so audaciously. My father didn't seem to be offended by Sioma's daring personality; on the contrary, he seemed pleased to accept Sioma's outlandish comments as flattery, knowing that they were signs of the great affection he felt for me. I could see a smile forming on my father's lips.

With Sioma now gone, my father turned to ask me if the relationship was serious. I said yes. My feelings were put to the test only a few days later—Yudko Eksztejn had sent me a letter from Yugoslavia. After considerable reflection, I replied to him, telling him about the latest developments in my life, including my probable marriage to Sioma, and I advised him not to write to me anymore. This would be my last letter, I stated, but Yudko continued writing to me for a while. Although I never answered him, I'd keep his missives for the rest of my life, stored like diamonds in a treasured little box. On occasion, I would open them carefully and read his loving words.

***

Sioma traveled continuously between Lida and Nemenčinė. We took walks together around the river and the lakes on the outskirts of the city. Sometimes we would go to Vilna for the day. We enjoyed a good dinner or a simple walk on the riverbank, and when the winter cold was too harsh, we sheltered ourselves in the movie house at the Yiddish theater or by attending Polish performances.

Deep down, I still didn't see Sioma as the love of my life. Unconsciously, I measured my feelings. It took me time to fall in love with the brewer. He was extremely proud and practical and did not understand the inherent loneliness I had always felt. However, I liked his adventurous spirit and his capacity to enjoy life without philosophical questions. At his side, I learned to let go of so many unanswered questions and allowed my fears to diminish, as I opened myself to explore extravagant luxuries imbued in an aristocratic flare. Delighted, I allowed myself to be taken on romantic walks in the park and to concerts by moonlight and to dance the tango as we drank until dawn.

***

Sioma arrived in Nemenčinė on April 1, 1934, on *Prima Aprilis*, April Fools' Day, also known as the Day of the Innocents. The first rays of spring were barely warming the air. As we walked hand-in-hand enjoying the moment, we admired the sprouting poppies that adorned the path on the shore of Lake Gea.

"I would like to marry you," he said to me directly.

I didn't know what to say. *Today is Prima Aprilis, and everyone plays tricks,* I thought.

"You're not kidding, are you?" I replied hesitantly.

"Hah!" Sioma burst out laughing. "Of course not. I already spoke with my mother, and she would like to come and meet your father as soon as possible."

Without waiting for an answer, he planted a kiss on my mouth and sealed our relationship.

That same night, I told the news to my father and *die mutter*.

They embraced me happily, and we toasted to our good fortune.

Sioma's mom, Mrs. Rachil Pupko, and Sioma arrived in Nemenčinė unexpectedly a few days later. Her appearance was elegant. She wore a dark dress embellished with a huge amber pendant necklace. She walked proudly, erectly, as if her long neck could reach the sky. She was different from all the other women I had ever known.

My father wasn't home; he had left early to buy some medicinal herbs. Esfir greeted them, offering some tea and rugelach. Mrs. Pupko examined everything with a keen eye. Once my father arrived, my future mother-in-law's determined and decisive interrogation began.

"Rev Shmuel Bernstein," Rachil began, addressing my father, "could you tell me what Szifra's childhood was like?"

Every response from my father raised a new question from Rachil Pupko: "What happened to her maternal grandparents? How did her mother die? How would you describe the young lady's character?" She asked more and more questions as if it was the Spanish Inquisition. She was preparing the groundwork to launch a poignant and irritating thrust:

"We know that Szifra had a suitor named Yudko Eksztejn. Can you assure me, Rev Bernstein, that this relationship is over?"

My father, undaunted by such indecorous questioning, answered forthrightly:

"I have never seen Szifra as happy as she is now. I assure you that there is no one else but Sioma in her life."

Having clarified all the points and without fully understanding the mysteries of love, my engagement with Sioma Pupko became official. My dowry would be six thousand dollars; two thousand would go first and the rest in a *veksl*, a bill of exchange from the Jewish bank owned by the Burmowicz family. The only detail left was the wedding date, which would soon be selected.

***

On a sunny day during the summer, Sioma and I set out to spend the day in Trakai, a picturesque village where Jews and *Karaim* comprised most of the population. Sioma's car rambled along the cobblestones of Ulica Kowenski, a street lined with wooden houses and pickle stands. We passed the *kenessa*, the humble prayer house of the *Karaim*, which contrasted with the adjacent synagogue with an enormous Star of David on the iron entrance door. The lake in the background garnished the castle ruins. Despite the autumnal cold looming in the air, people were refreshing themselves near the inlet in the middle of the lake.

We parked the car under the shade of a leafy tree. We walked happily side by side. I was entranced by the heaps of freshly picked vegetables piled on an array of colorful carts, ready to be driven to the Vilna market. Sioma bought some pickles, which we bit into immediately. I wrinkled my brow at its sourness and looked up at Simona, who mirrored my reaction. We burst into laughter simultaneously. Everything was perfect.

We rented a little boat and rowed around the lake amidst the medieval ruins. Then we sat down at a small romantic café that had a splendid view of the ancient castle. We ordered some refreshments, and while we waited, Sioma took out a small box from his pocket.

"Here, Szifra, this is for you." With a choked voice he added, "We will spend the rest of our lives together."

A few days prior, he had taken me to a jeweler to get my finger measured, so this wasn't a complete surprise. But I was overwhelmed by the luminosity of the translucent two-karat engagement ring that would unite me with him forever. As he placed the ring on my finger, a light breeze blew my hair over my watery eyes. I will never forget that moment.

***

Winter came and went. Our parents agreed upon November 19, 1935, to celebrate our marriage. Meanwhile, we spent as much time as we could together, going often to the Helios or the Pan Cinema in Vilna. We watched Greta Garbo as *Anna Karenina* at least three times. Each time I would sigh as Count Vronsky fell in love. Sometimes I would sob uncontrollably as the handsome young official hopelessly followed an impossible love. Sioma repeatedly hugged me affectionately without understanding the reason for my tears.

We went to the Yiddish theater to see Blumenthal, Turkov,

and Moretzki, and the various shows written by Sholem Aleichem. We also saw a puppet show by the Maydim group at the Reduta Theater, and in the Lutnia Theater, I felt passionately enthralled with contemporary Polish dramas. I was so sensitive during that period—I could cry and laugh with the protagonists and allow my imagination to get carried away.

On May 12, we witnessed history in the making on the streets of Vilna. The majestic funeral procession for Marshal Jósef Piłsudski, the organizer of the Polish independence, made its way through the city; it was an impressive sight. The heads of the church accompanied the casket, while the soldiers, dressed in black double-breasted trench coats adorned with gold buttons, marched alongside. They would escort their heroic leader to his final resting place.

We sat down at the Café Sztral, the place where we first met, ordered seltzer water sweetened with lemon syrup and a piece of tart, and waited for the crowd to disperse. Asher, my old friend from the *Shomer Hatzair*, saw us and came up to us. His face was distorted, and he asked in an anguished voice:

"Did you hear what happened at the university?" Seeing our confusion, he continued without stopping, chronicling the events in detail like an incessant machine gun. "People from the right-wing extremist group *Endecja* interrupted Professor Ruszcki's class. They came in shouting and then violently separated Jews from Christians. They forced us to sit on the left side of the classroom as if we were lepers or had a contagious disease. They wanted to impose an official mandate to marginalize us. Shlomo objected, and they kicked him in the stomach until he fell on his face. Professor Ruszcki indignantly interceded: 'If Christ were here today, he would sit down on the Jewish side.' Those of the *Endecja* fell silent for a second, but they were not intimidated. They took over the campus and resumed their offenses. Riots broke out all over the university, and several people were wounded. The aggressors took over the administration building and banned anyone from entering; classes have been suspended. We should do something! We must organize a protest. Zrulko has proposed a hunger strike to publicly condemn the vandalism, but I think we should just leave this country and go to *Eretz* Israel, where we have a land that belongs to us and where we can live and work with dignity."

Sioma and I looked at each other in bewilderment. Hints of the *Endecja's* objectives were published by *Gazeta Warzawska*, the newspaper from Warsaw, shortly after: "We will force the Jews to organize their own massive emigration ...." And in smaller font, it read: "We can achieve this; we will not cease until every single Jew has left Poland."

I was twenty-one years old, eager to get married, with a full life ahead of me. I trembled in fear when confronted with extremist groups that, without provocation, committed acts of violence and vandalism against the Jews. Sioma hugged me. We walked to the car and drove back to my house in Nemenčinė.

From that day on, we would hear news of bombs thrown at the gates of synagogues, Jews beaten with sticks, rocks, and metal tubes, and people looting Jewish businesses. Pure hate surrounded us. We tried not to think about the attacks by the *Endecja* or the isolated acts of antisemitism. It was easier to let happiness invade us: to go boating in Trakai, to stroll in the parks of Vilna, to kiss each other until dawn, and to dream of our wedding. November was only a few months away.

Esfir tried to teach me the proper way to run a house. She became nicer to me, as I was no longer a burden to her. She gave me practical advice about life as a couple and even shared some of her recipes with me. I was not accustomed to listening to her; her voice was a dull murmur to me. I tried to avoid her. My thoughts were in Lida where Sioma lived; my mind could only hear the sweet words of my love.

***

My father took me regularly to Vilna. He would go there for work but also to eagerly shower me with all kinds of presents: from perfumes and jewels to satin shoes, feathered hats, and fine fur coats of the highest quality. Everything was exquisite, and everything was for me!

We visited many stores and ended up at Zalkind's storeroom, with its imposing staircase, where my father bought me a hat and a new coat. He then spent forty *zlotys,* an exorbitant amount of money, on a pair of shoes at the Kolponicki shop on Ulica Pohulanka.

Everything was kept in a big armoire inside the house in Nemenčinė. My trousseau was all ready as my wedding date approached.

On one of such trips to Vilna, while I was waiting for my father to finish negotiating with his medical supplier, I crossed over the river in the direction of Šnipiškės and headed toward the cemetery. I wanted to visit my mother. I missed her; I needed her. I would have wanted her at my side to give me advice, to show me how to manage a house and to cook, and, especially, to teach me how to treat my husband. I didn't know what to expect from marriage. I stopped in front of my mother's tombstone. I took a small stone and, as was customary, placed it on top of her grave.

"Dear Mama," I begged in front of her gravestone, "now that I am embarking on a new phase of life, please lead me along the right path." I sighed. Finally, I felt at peace.

I'm going to introduce Szifra to my family today. Almost everyone will be there except for my sister Luba and her husband Aaron, who are unable to come from Brussels. I am afraid that they will find her to be provincial and unsophisticated. My mother accepts Szifra and sees her as the beautiful and insightful girl that she is, but she's still very watchful of her every move. Mitzia, my older brother, with his arrogant and presumptuous attitude, never misses the opportunity to show off his credentials as a graduate of a German university. He will be accompanied by his stunning wife Roza Panvezig. My two sisters, Franya and Aniuta, will also be present. Franya, who is judicious and a little bit difficult, will attend with her second and younger husband Misha Geller. We'll also be joined by

Aniuta's husband Yosif Zaretzky. I am sure that if they don't accept her entirely today, they will eventually come to appreciate her intelligence and charm.

A portrait of the Pupko family, taken prior to 1935.

From left to right: Aniuta Pupko with her husband, Yosef Zaretzky, and their daughter, Fruma; Rachil, the matriarch, seated in a chair, with Sioma on the armchair. Standing in the middle is Mitzia Pupko, the eldest of the Pupko children, with his wife, Roza. Luba Pupko, the youngest, sits on an armchair next to her father, Meilach. And finally, Franya Pupko with her second husband, Misha Geller.

Sioma took me to Lida to meet his brother and sisters. I dressed carefully, leaving nothing to chance, and bought a box of Tilca chocolates to give them as a gift. The entire family was gathered at the door of the brewery on #88 Suwalska Street. The rusty sign that bore the former name of the street, Krume, was still hanging on the doorframe. It was absurd that the straightest street in Lida should be called "Crooked Street."

Franya, to whom I handed the chocolates, greeted me with a sardonic smile. She saw the wrapping and assumed the chocolates were not high quality, certainly not good enough for the standards of her family. She didn't even bother to open the box and instead made an ironic remark.

Sioma had warned me about the impulsiveness of his older sister, but I hadn't imagined the caliber of her toxic poison. He justified her difficult personality with two excuses, both of which were blows to her feminine pride. Her first husband, Misha Bloshtein, a lawyer, had abandoned her, and she had a uterine malformation, which prevented her from having children.

Sioma broke the tense atmosphere by taking me to see the brewery. We first crossed the large courtyard to visit the house.

Then we went through every corner of the factory, including the grain silo, the production area, and the warehouse. The tower was marked with the date of the factory's foundation, 1876, displayed with large numbers at the top, testifying to the great history of the facility.

"Here is where we keep the barley and wheat. The beer that we manufacture is of the lager type," Sioma explained as if I knew the differences. Extending his arms, he continued: "The malt is kept in that tank, and over there, in that room, the beer is fermented ... and that worker is mixing the hops that will be added to the fermented liquid."

He had me try the beer before and after the aromatic flower was added. Enthusiastic, he proceeded with his lecture:

"Only my family knows the exact amounts in the mixture; it's a formula handed down from generation to generation. We have been able to maintain the same taste ever since my grandfather was awarded the Medal of Quality at the Reims Fair. People know the difference between our beer and our competitors, like Papiermejster. They're not as strong as we are or as financially successful. We expect that the next generation of Pupkos will learn and continue making the same recipe in the future and for centuries to come."

Their land extended several blocks. The area included a soft drink factory, a grain mill, and a *tartak*, a sawmill. The lot bordered the river where wooden logs came floating with the downward current until they reached the *tartak*. As they entered, a large circular saw cut the wood. The noise of the machine muffled my fiancé's explanations, so we headed to the soft drink factory. I had never seen so many marvelous things: the bubbling, colored liquids traveled through metal tubes and into individual containers. Between jokes and laughter, Sioma made me try all the different flavors mixed with carbonated water, including the grapefruit flavor they were testing out before sending to the market.

The family was waiting for us in order to begin dinner. My mother-in-law's house was in the center of the factory's patio. She lived with her daughter Franya and her son-in-law Misha. The residence was large and extremely elegant. The walls were upholstered with embroidered fabrics, the floor was parquet, and what struck me the most was a sturdy fireplace with green stucco decorations.

I couldn't hold it in and cried with emotion, "This floor is so sublime!"

"It looks so shiny," my mother-in-law, Rachil, answered, "because we polish it continuously. As you probably already know, we own a *tartak* and a parquet factory."

The Schenkel stove's red-hot coal and the brass samovar's boiling water heated the main room. But the atmosphere was frigid. I shivered with loneliness even as I was surrounded by strangers who would soon become my family.

"Welcome to our home," Rachil said, lifting a beer mug and uttering an endless string of formalities to which I didn't know how to respond.

I felt imprisoned between pompous ceremonies and useless rules of behavior. Without understanding how they did it, they forced me to talk about my participation in the *Shomer Hatzair*. They sought to delve into the details of my past, questioning my friendships and exposing my inner thoughts. I answered resentfully and in monosyllables to this detective-like interrogation.

Franya, with a wicked and envious streak, led the charge.

When the conversation became harsh, she tried to soften it, sprinkling it with anecdotes about how she and Misha had met in 1932. She joyously spoke about the moment when Ze'ev Jabotinsky visited Lida to promote *Beitar*, a right-wing youth group. She kept on applauding the ideals of the Revisionist Zionist organization, talking ceaselessly about Joseph Trumpeldor and extolling the story of how he died defending the Tel Hai settlement in the Galilee against the Bedouins.

"The theater was packed," related Franya. "The people were crowded together in the auditorium to hear what Jabotinsky would say. His speech was fiery. The Zionist leader spoke about a better tomorrow, about immigrating to Jerusalem to work the land. He said, 'Young people must study Hebrew to populate Palestine. That is the future of the Jews.' Near the end of the lecture, totally enthralled, we all yelled over and over again the already famous slogan: 'Hebraization of the Diaspora,' and, in unison, we applauded enthusiastically, cheering our leader."

Franya continued enthusiastically: "On my way home, I walked surrounded by friends who, laughing and exalted by Jabotinsky's words, chose to speak in Hebrew. 'We must do something,' we were saying to each other. Some of the girls exclaimed, 'In Lida, our families only expect us to get married and have children,' and one of the guys said, 'What future can we have here?' In the end, we all concluded, 'Let's join the ranks of the *Beitar*, let us be Revisionist Zionists, like Jabotinsky!'"

Franya kept on going and told us how a young man, whom

they barely knew, was walking a few steps behind them. All of a sudden, he interrupted and said, "Do you think your parents will actually accept? Do you think that they would permit you to go to Palestine? Ha!" And turning his gaze up to Franya, he exclaimed, "Especially you. You are a divorced woman supported by your father. You would never be able to separate yourself from your family or your older brother, who watches over every move you make!"

I could sense her wounded pride as she retold the story. "Do you remember his rage when I told him that I would go to Palestine?" she asked her mother and her siblings. "He was so upset about my utopian ideals. He made it very clear that the future of the Pupkos is here, in Lida, where we enjoy many privileges, where we can afford luxuries, and where we live a life at ease. For him, there was nothing else to add. He was convinced that Zionism was for poor and unemployed Jews. My father lectured me, adding that we support the Zionist movement, but that our family would never go to Palestine to work in the fields. And then he just stormed out of the room."

I relaxed for a moment as I listened to Franya's anecdotes on how she met Misha, her current husband.

However, that respite did not last long; she came back to me and continued: "Szifra, did you ever dream about going to Palestine and working the land with your comrades from the *Shomer*?"

Without letting me answer, she said, threading a web around me, "They indoctrinate you as communists in the *Shomer*, don't they? You know we do not accept the proletariat's government policy in this house."

Sioma interceded for me: "It's been a long time since Szifra attended the *Shomer Hatzair*. When she did, it was a social rather than a political activity. Better focus on your own life and leave her alone. You said you wanted to leave for Cuba with Misha. Go ahead, if you want to, and we will support you by sending boatloads of beer to your Caribbean Island. Maybe that way you'll be able to supplement Misha's salary as a barber."

Franya understood that Sioma, with scathing irony, could win the game. I closed my eyes. The next morning, I would return to Nemenčinė to continue with the wedding preparations. I would be able to rest momentarily from the pressures my new family exerted upon me.

***

The day before my wedding, November 18, 1935, Sioma went to *shul* in Vilna to read the Torah. He was nervous; the last time he'd had the honor of reading the Torah was when he had been thirteen years old, at his bar mitzvah. The tradition specified that the bride should go to the *mikvah*, the ritual bath, so I headed alone to purify my soul without a mother to accompany me. An elderly woman showed me where to leave my clothing. She inspected my fingernails and minutely went over every inch of my body, making me feel violated, manhandled, and even dirty.

She gave me her blessing and told me to enter the tub filled with rainwater. Once I repeated the prayer in Hebrew, she instructed me to immerse myself in the water three times. As the water touched my skin, I heard her say, "You are now a daughter of Israel. You're now kosher, you're a *kaleh*, a pure bride."

My mind wandered; I thought about Sioma, about his family and mine.

"You can't just linger in the water. Get out of there!" the old woman yelled. "These are holy waters; they're not for your own pleasure."

I rushed to get out, dressed hurriedly, and timidly said goodbye.

The ancient custom indicated that from that moment onward, I shouldn't be left by myself. A woman had to stay with me at all times until the moment I walked to the *chuppah*, the nuptial canopy, where my destiny would be sealed. Without any sisters and with my aunt Shayna behind the Black Border and my mother and my grandmother deceased, I had no one close to me. I felt alone; I was touchy and irritable.

In less than twenty-four hours, I would cease to be Szifra Bernstein and become the wife of Sioma Pupko, heir to a brewery, a sawmill, and a soda factory. I loved him, and that should have been enough, but I also understood that from that moment forward I must submissively resign myself to married life. Despite my anxiety, I imagined Sioma waiting for me at the end of the aisle by the *chuppah* with a reassuring smile.

I slept restlessly, thinking: *Will the love between us last forever? Will I be a good wife and mother? Will I know how to manage a house?* But most of all, I thought about how much I missed my grandmother Leah.

***

"The doorbell, Szifra!" my aunt Zinitzky shouted. "Can you go and open it?"

I got up lazily, consoling myself a little: *Sioma loves me, and today I will marry him!* I opened the door and found myself face-to-face with my father. We embraced each other, crying with emotion.

"Szifra, it's time for you to get ready," he said to me. "Rabbi Rubinstein is waiting for us."

I took the hairbrush with the tortoise-shell handle, a gift from my father, and smoothed my hair. I then put in some hair rollers and my white cloqué dress, made especially for this important day. I applied rouge on my cheeks to reduce my pallor, applied red lipstick, and tried to smile. My father kissed my forehead when he saw me dressed up. We went to the rabbi's house where the wedding would take place.

Sioma signed the *Ketubah*, the marriage contract written in Aramaic, in a small room filled with about twenty guests.

My father walked me to the *chuppah* where Sioma was waiting for me. I followed the tradition—which seemed old-fashioned to me—of circling my husband seven times to the beat of the prayers. Sioma lifted my veil, took my hand, and placed the ring on my finger, saying, "*Ani le dodi ve dodi li.* I am for my beloved, and my beloved is for me." As part of the ceremony, we drank from the same glass of wine as we heard the different blessings from the rabbi. Sioma concluded the ceremony, like all bridegrooms, by stomping on a glass in memory of the destruction of the Temple of Jerusalem. The people cried, *"Mazel tov!"* Mitzia, Roza, Aniuta, Yosif, and all the family congratulated us. We walked to the Hotel Savoy on Ulica Sodowa where my father invited all the guests to a banquet and a party.

Holding onto the loving arm of Sioma, we walked together down Rudnicka Street, turning down Zawalna until we reached the corner with Sodowa and entered the hotel's salon. I greeted the attendees with a smile, but I was sad that my maternal family had not been able to attend the wedding—it was still impossible to cross the Polish border.

We had dinner, danced polkas and mazurkas until dawn, and then took a *drosky* to the train station. From there, we would travel to Warsaw by train. In a small suitcase, I carried part of the trousseau that my father had bought me for my honeymoon: two French sweaters, four dresses, and another one for the reception that my mother-in-law would give upon our return from our honeymoon.

After only a few hours, we were in the central station of the Polish capital. From there, we took a car that drove us through Marzalkovska Street, a main street illuminated by a beautiful spectacle of lights. Then we finally got to the Hotel D'Angleterre, where we would be staying.

No one had ever explained to me what would happen on my wedding night, and I was afraid. The little that I knew came from my friends' gossip. Stiff and nervous, I lay down on the bed. Between touches and sweet kisses, Sioma wrapped me in hot pleasure and guided me as a child. Our love for each other was sealed between the sheets.

We strolled around the streets and squares, visited monuments and museums, and bought furniture, rugs, and draperies for our future home. In Kraków, we walked along Rynek Glowny, the main square, and through the Sukiennice fabric market. I enjoyed seeing the people, the vendors' hustle and bustle, and the proud, majestic, and marvelous city hall. I admired the walls of the old metropolis, Wavel's castle hill, and the cultured environment of the Jagiellonian University.

We crossed the Wisla River to reach Kazimierz. The Orthodox Jews, dressed in black trench coats, wearing long beards, and absorbed in their thoughts with their eyes cast downward toward the pavement, reminded me of the Jews from the Vilna *shulhoif.* I could feel the Jewish spirituality in the air. Although the synagogue of Rabbi Remuh was the most visited, there were numerous prayer and study houses, one after the other, crowded into Kazimierz's limited space. Between the metaphysical and the earthly, Sioma and I felt ourselves to be the main characters in a poem by Mickiewicz; we were Tadeusz and Zosia, the eternal lovers who enjoy a walk around the city.

We traveled to Zakopane, an elegant ski resort. From the window of our small hotel, we could see the Tatra mountains with their snowy peaks. Sioma was a very good skier, and I was a novice. Nevertheless, he encouraged me to try, so I let myself go from the top of the hill, sliding down with fear, to end up happily in Sioma's arms.

Shura on her honeymoon in Zakopane

We explored the local area in the afternoon, eventually coming upon a beautiful waterfall that lightened up the mountainous horizon. The landscape was crystalline. We walked to the edge of the falls, listening to the water and the wind sing, and enjoying the fragrance of the wet leaves.

Upon returning to the hotel, we found a message from Mitzia, Sioma's older brother. He urged us to return to Lida immediately; an accident had taken place in the brewery: a worker had fallen from a ladder. He was receiving care, but he would be incapacitated for several months, and Sioma's presence was immediately required to take charge of the situation.

My husband's face turned somber; we would have to take the first train back to Lida. Reality struck me; I did not know what the future had in store for me in my new home. It was the beginning of a new stage in my life. Our honeymoon was over.

***

"Welcome to the family. You're a Pupko now!" Rachil greeted us affectionately as she handed me a small box that contained a diamond strung on a gold chain. I was shocked by the unexpected gift. The stone was so bright! I felt appreciated. As Rachil clasped the necklace around my neck, she started to explain the condition of the worker and what needed to be done.

She led me to her house in the backyard of the warehouse. She kindly showed me to our "temporary rooms," as she said, until we had our own house. That left me with an uncomfortable feeling of displacement and a sense of not belonging anywhere.

The following morning, as soon as Sioma opened his eyes, he sensed my uneasiness and suggested, "Let's go to Belgium. My sister Luba lives there, and we can sell my share of the brewery to Mitzia. We will begin our independent life."

I had no objection. We would move away from all the family pressures, and I could learn to speak French. I immediately agreed. Of course, Mitzia objected. Sioma was indispensable to the family business. I would have to adapt to my new situation, and I would have to learn how to live with my new family.

***

My mother-in-law was planning to have a reception in our honor.

About seventy snoops will turn out, I thought, *all wanting to meet me and hypocritically celebrate our wedding that happened weeks before in Vilna. They will come to drink and eat the free food offered and to inquire with whom the young Pupko heir has fallen in love.* Although my opinion didn't matter, I cooperated with Rachil in making the arrangements.

The tables were arranged with white linen tablecloths and wildflowers in the shape of a horseshoe. One by one, guests with blurred faces were introduced to me. I shook hands with the Wieners, and I greeted the Kaplinskys and Mr. Leibl Stolowitsky, the *buchalter,* the brewery accountant, who was accompanied by his wife.

My mother-in-law wanted to introduce me to all of Lida's society. From chair to chair, I walked politely like a pendulum, smiling with a maniacal rhythm, listening to a continuous sugary praise of the Pupkos. *How ironic!* I thought. *Rachil always wears that amber necklace, with an insect stuck inside—an ancestral prisoner. Will I also become a fossil trapped within petrified resin?*

Moreover, if I were honest, I couldn't forget Yudko Eksztejn. I imagined him still an idealist, in Yugoslavia, not that far away, planning his odyssey to Palestine. I saw him, with his curly hair flying to the rhythm of the wind, with his focused mind always aspiring to reach the horizon ... I couldn't accept things as they were, so I embroidered my days with illusory fantasies, completely removing myself from my reality.

In the following months, I set out to explore Lida. The city was surrounded by two rivers: the Dziekanski and the Lida. The southern part of the city was bordered by the castle ruins. King Gediminas had built residences everywhere, and Lida was no exception. Legend had it that there was a treasure beneath its foundation, but the remains were cursed, and if somebody dared to dig, they would inevitably die. Nevertheless, every day, when the church bells marked noon and school ended, a flock of boys would venture to play inside the ancient fortress.

The economic boom was everywhere; you could see it in both elegant shops and the marketplace. But there were also plenty of soldiers living in military barracks around the city. Their stench of alcohol and sweat would inspire fear in the population. They sometimes turned violent and abusive, and I would try to avoid them at all costs.

As I went walking and learning my way around Lida, little by little, I fell in love with my adopted city.

I would spend hours in my mother-in-law's living room during the winter. I learned to observe every minute detail in that cozy room: the old fireplace with its interesting ornaments, the big table, and even the samovar in the corner. I admired mostly the oil painting over the chimney mantle signed by the painter Joger. He depicted the brewery in 1916. I would look at it closely; it had a beautiful glow, and there was some magic in the conveyed linear perspective where you could see the bridge that connected the *tartak*.

One of those cold and dark afternoons in January 1936, as I

was helping pluck goose feathers, Franya turned suddenly to her sister Aniuta and exclaimed, "Aniuta, don't you think that the name Szifra is coarse and provincial?" They were talking as if I weren't there. They mixed words in Russian and Polish along with an occasional word in Yiddish.

"It would be best to call our young sister-in-law Szura, a more aristocratic name. It is short for Alexandra, associated with the Czarina Alexandra Feodorovna Romanova, wife of Czar Nicholas II," Franya continued.

I could see that the servants were paying attention to the conversation and waiting for my reaction.

"I love the name," I said jokingly before Aniuta could reply to her sister, "but don't you think that before changing it you should ask Sioma if he agrees?"

"Szura, dear," answered Aniuta, pitying my naïveté, "it was Sioma himself who suggested it and asked us to bring it up to you. So ... welcome to our family, Szura!"

I raised my eyes. Now it was my mother-in-law's turn. "You are very pretty ... Szura," she paused to get used to the new name. "Szifra doesn't suit your new status, your dignity as a Pupko. Szura is sophisticated, less Jewish, a name that will inspire you to be more self-assured as you assume your place as a genuine lady of our family."

I acted nonchalantly because I was disconcerted. I left the goose half-plucked. I excused myself and went to seek refuge next to the malt tanks. I felt like an old dress that needed to be mended and repaired to be fashionable. Not only had I changed cities and adapted to a new lifestyle and role, but now I was being forced to use a new name. I pondered everything, then I paused and accepted: Szifra was left behind, and from that day forward I would be known as Szura.

I went down the back street of the brewery. The road seemed narrower; the cobblestone lane was the opposite of the broad, wide avenues of Vilna. I missed cosmopolitan life, the theaters and cinemas and the parks with their leafy trees and chirping birds. Most of all, I missed the diversity of more than one hundred synagogues tucked in one area. I turned onto Suwalska Street and stopped in front of the building where Sioma had rented the apartment to which we would shortly move. I smiled at the prospect of leaving my mother-in-law's house and having my own home. Calmer, I returned to the brewery.

"Szura ..." Sioma said to me. My new name, sweet upon his lips, resonated without appearing strange: Szura Pupko, that was me. With this simple gesture, I completely broke free from my past. I would no longer be Szifra Bernstein, the one who had known Yudko. Now, I was Szura, the wife of Sioma Pupko.

Chapter Six: 1935-1939

We moved to the rented apartment and became neighbors of a Dr. Zaltzin. The sofas and cupboards arrived from Warsaw as did a big dining table that barely fit. In a gesture of extravagant luxury, Sioma ordered the installation of a bathroom with a bathtub and sinks. Since then, taking a bath has become one of my favorite delights.

We hung copper pots and bronze trays—gifts from my mother-in-law—on the kitchen wall. We placed a new wooden mortar and pestle next to the stove and filled a small canister with ladles. Very soon, I learned to make salads with cucumbers, potatoes, and beets, marmalades and fruit jams, and assorted stews.

We had a panoramic view of the city of Lida with its more than forty thousand inhabitants. From our small apartment, I could see the puffs of gray smoke emanating from the fireplaces of the Ardal rubber shoe factory. The city was growing, and we were an important part of it.

Sioma had introduced me to the Bedzowski family, owners of a shop on Suwalska Street, a few blocks from the brewery. They sold everything from military uniforms to household goods, fine fabrics, mink fur, Persian lamb leather, and even Karakul. Mr. Bedzowski was a born businessman; he turned every item into a necessity for his clients, and I became one of his best. I would choose fabrics of different prints and textures, which Podosky, the tailor, would turn into beautiful stoles and coats designed especially for me.

Life went on. Once a week, my husband invited a group of friends to the house to play poker, *chervone* crul, or *bekladanka*—a kind of gin rummy. He socialized with all kinds of influential people with whom he loved maintaining close ties: wealthy businessmen, government officials, military officers, and prominent locals like Karchmer, who became a good friend of ours.

At first, I went to great lengths to host them, serving luxurious meals to flatter them. I would prepare a beautiful table full of red caviar, cold meats, sardines, blinis, chocolates from the Goldstein grocery store, and Pluto's candies from Winogradov's delicatessen. But over time, I stopped liking those extravagant get-togethers. I stopped liking having those men in my house, invading my space, boasting around, and filling the atmosphere with tobacco.

Sioma and his friends bet large sums of money on their card games. It was customary to play cards once a year during Chanukah, the festival of lights, to honor the Maccabees; but Sioma played at least once a week. His behavior irritated me, but without being able to change it, I gave in. I convinced myself that it was good that Sioma was at home with me.

Regardless of my hesitation, I continued to serve them gastronomic delicacies beautifully displayed on fine crystal and offer them Stock Cognac and vodka without focusing on how quickly the bottles were emptied. Sometimes those men brought their lovers or their wives, alternating between them. After dinner, I would usually excuse myself and go to bed. There was no point in waiting for Sioma, who would come to bed at dawn.

***

It was around Purim 1936. I had a strong suspicion that I was pregnant. It was a happy day. I prepared food for the poor, made charitable donations, and went to a friend's house to exchange *shalach manos*—baskets filled with treats. I wanted to surprise Sioma with the news, so I also prepared a romantic dinner with candles and flowers.

Sioma had gone out with his brother-in-law, Yosif Zaretzky. Hours went by, and he didn't return. As I was waiting for him, I dozed off on the couch. At five in the morning, the door opened. The smell of barley, yeast, and malt announced Sioma's presence. Sioma entered stealthily on tip-toe, thinking that I was asleep. He was returning from playing cards with Karchmer. When he saw me open my eyes, he apologized for the late hour. There was no way to fix the situation. He noticed the specially arranged table with flowers, the *hamantaschen,* and the cold dinner. Sioma couldn't stop asking for forgiveness.

It was in those moments of rage that I thought about Yudko Eksztejn. I wondered about the kind of life he had in Palestine, and I compared it with my life in Lida, a small town where everybody knew everything about each other. I lived with a family that meddled too much in my affairs and couldn't stop thinking about how life with Yudko would have been different. Trying to accept things as they were, I assured myself that I was better off in Lida. If I were in Palestine, I would spend my days harvesting vegetables and suffering the poverty of idealists. I was happy to assume the role of "Mrs. Pupko," wife of Sioma, the coveted and respected young brewer. I confessed to him that I thought I was pregnant. He hugged me tightly, declared his love again, and promised to take care of me and our child. He was very affectionate, and I swallowed my pride.

Sioma took me to see the doctor the following day. Desiring to celebrate, he went out to buy red caviar and vodka. We announced the news to the family during dinner that night. I would soon become a mother.

"Mazel tov!" they shouted almost in unison, wishing us good health and fortune. I could sense Franya's hypocrisy. It was so palpable; without being able to hide her jealousy, she gave me a kiss wishing me good luck. I could see that she was sad and angry because she had not been able to conceive.

Without waiting for my consent, my mother-in-law firmly announced that she would send Yenka, the maid, to our apartment to help me.

"She'll know what to cook to feed you properly," she said. Then she ordered, "Every day you should have a glass of beer. The malt is very healthy for the baby." She went on, "And beware of looking at unpleasant things to avoid your child being born with defects." In a flurry of myths and commands, Rachil continued to dictate her beliefs, imposing behaviors based on the purest primitivism. She felt as if she was the owner of the sole truth and had the right to impose it on everybody, especially me now that I was pregnant. "Do not go outside; be careful not to have any frights because it causes deformities to the baby; close all the windows and small doors to avoid any ill wind that can bring you harm; watch out for any direct sunlight; don't look at the moon because there are evil spirits that can be harmful to the baby; don't you dare go to the cemetery during the pregnancy because some stray soul can find its way onto the unborn baby." And on and on it went.

Seeing my confusion, Sioma interrupted the litany: "Mama, leave her alone, you're frightening her. The doctor has said that she and the baby are healthy and that we should not worry."

Luckily, Rachil fell silent after that.

***

I had morning sickness, and Sioma would stay in bed with me until late. His older brother, Mitzia, condoned this; he would come to the house to throw pebbles at the window, forcing Sioma to get up and go to work.

I did not have a very busy routine. I would slowly get ready to have lunch with my mother-in-law and her daughters. During one of those meals, Franya said in dismay, "Are you not afraid to bring a new life into this violent world?"

"What do you mean, Franya? We live well, we need nothing, I do not understand your question."

"Haven't you heard the latest news from Vilna? On March 17, there was an organized protest against antisemitism. Many Jews gathered in the Zydowska and Niemiecka streets to rally. They were naive to think this would be a peaceful event. Defenseless, they were attacked by uniformed men on horseback. The demonstration was a total useless failure ... it surprised those who still believed that they lived in a country of laws, democracy, and freedom. And you, pregnant as you are, don't realize the danger?"

I was annoyed at her remark. "Nothing is going to happen to us, this was an isolated event," I answered.

***

We soon moved to a house specially built for us on a plot of land next to the brewery. As my belly grew, I planted and harvested vegetables in the small garden behind the kitchen. Yenka and I prepared delicious salads using our homegrown lettuce and radishes.

I started buying superfluous household decorations, following the example of all Pupko women. We had imported cutlery and pieces of porcelain along with new pots and pans. I also started to dress more elegantly, wearing new shoes, fur coats, and fancy hats. Sioma loved to spoil me; he would bring me a necklace or a ring or even a simple banana that would have cost him a fortune.

Very often, we ate dinner at my mother-in-law's house. She loved to serve us farfalle with a little bit of butter. Whatever the meal was, it was always accompanied with some beer. I enjoyed strolling along the banks of the river Lida, reminiscing about my days in Nemenčinė. I would walk from my house to the Europejski hotel, where Jabotinsky had been staying for years, only to drink seltzer water and get away from the brewery and the scrutiny of the family.

Sioma's sister Luba, who lived in Brussels, wrote to us regularly. She told us about her deteriorating relationship with her husband, Aaron. Rachil was saddened by it. Aaron had been a promising, intelligent, well-educated, and tenacious young man. He was a textile engineer but was struggling to find a job. He was resourceful and had studied dentistry to save his family's financial situation. But an abyss was slowly separating Luba and Aaron. The only thing keeping them together was their son Anatole. Luba complained bitterly in her letters. My mother-in-law wrote to her on several occasions urging her to get a divorce and return to Lida as soon as possible. Luba's situation became a topic of discussion between the family. Everybody had an opinion about it. Her love life, as with everyone else's private life, was constantly scrutinized during those dinners at my mother-in-law's.

***

June's suffocating weather was unbearable, but Sioma brought shaved ice every day to refresh my drinks. To have ice was a luxury, and I was grateful for that gesture. The brewery had an underground room built to conserve blocks of ice harvested during the winter. They barely lasted through the summer, but it was a great asset to be able to sell cold beer on hot days.

I felt lethargic. The inactivity and the exaggerated care of my mother-in-law overwhelmed me. Occasionally, I had the energy to go to the movies with Sioma. Sometimes Aniuta and I would walk to the Paris Hotel where we drank *tsikorye*, that brownish liquid that substituted coffee.

One day, as I was returning from Mr. Bergman's Stara pharmacy on Ulica Sadove, I ran into a group of young men blocking the small entrance to Mr. Levinson's shoe store. They shouted, "Don't buy from Jews, they are dirty people, they take advantage of you, and they always overcharge you!"

I was scared to challenge them. I was in front of the store, and they kept yelling aggressively, "*Jid*, Jew." I chose to shelter myself inside the shop, so I passed through them and entered. Once inside, I was frozen, petrified. I stayed there waiting for the mob to leave. As it turned out, hours passed, and the crowd didn't dissolve. I was afraid to go back home by myself, so one of the store's employees went to fetch my husband to pick me up.

SHURA

Sioma arrived with Mr. Stolowitsky, the brewery bookkeeper. I hugged Sioma and cried. I feared for our future and for the baby that I was carrying. When we left, a young man yelled at us: "Jewish pigs!" I did not feel safe anymore.

I have many responsibilities in the factory. I oversee all financial issues and do the accounting. I receive the salary of an ordinary employee, but sometimes the Pupkos have extravagant requests unrelated to my work. Once, before Sioma got married, Mrs. Rachil came to my house in the middle of the night. An argument between the two brothers had escalated; they were violently fighting, and she asked me to intervene. Without hesitation, I went immediately. I have a personal relationship with them, but I often question my role as a - *170 -uchalter* acting as a mediator in family squabbles. Just today, I was called for another task outside the office: I had to escort Sioma to the Levinson's shop to help his wife Szura get out of there.

***

We traveled to Vilna in October so I could give birth there. In Dr. Sevliza's clinic, located on Pohulanca #4, a baby girl was born. It was October 21, 1937.

My mother-in-law, fearing that some evil influence might overtake us, took the umbilical cord along with the placenta and hurriedly buried it in a hole in the brewery's garden. Then she attached small pieces of paper on which she'd written Psalms to the curtains of my house to protect us. She relied on amulets and superstitions, and even though I did not believe in them, I let her have her way.

"When a baby is born, it can be taken by Lilith," said Rachil, "that is why you have to give her a name as soon as possible. So that Lilith cannot claim her as her own."

It seemed like she was eager to fill my mind with fear, and her behavior caused me to want to spend more time in my father's house in Nemenčinė. My anxiety was subdued by avoiding any thoughts about the macabre, non-existent beings about which my mother-in-law spoke. Nevertheless, I was unable to sleep. Sioma, aware of my suffering, wanted to hire a woman to help me care for our beloved child, whom we had started calling, affectionately, Maszinka.

The superstitions and orders coming from Rachil did not end.

"No outsider should look at the baby during her first week of life. It's bad luck," my mother-in-law scolded her son. "Only her parents and grandparents can see her. Tie a red ribbon on her little arm to protect her from the evil eye. And you, Szura, try not to have a fright! If your milk dries up, you won't be able to nurse her."

Rachil's mood changed as often as a windswept cloud. She could be jolly and smiling and then, without warning, sour and demanding.

"She's such a pretty little girl," she commented as my daughter closed her eyes, "but the Pupko surname doesn't have any descendant yet to bear the name. My husband, Meilach, *zirchono lebracha*, blessed be his memory, still has no one named in his memory. Mitzia has Noya, and now Sioma has his baby girl ... but what I want is a male offspring, a boy who will preserve our family name."

Looking into my eyes, she pleaded with me: "Let's hope the next one is a male. I would have wanted to celebrate a *bris*, the ritual circumcision, so the Prophet Eliyahu could come to visit us. But don't get me wrong, I love this beautiful baby."

Relatives and friends showered me with kind attention, yet I was tormented, wondering whether I would be capable of raising my little girl.

When the baby was a week old, Sioma and the other members of the family went to the synagogue to give her a name, as

Shura & Sioma with Masza as a little girl

was tradition. My husband had the honor of being called to read the Torah. We named her Masza after my mother Masza Nechama. I could feel my mother's presence next to me, now living through my daughter. She would protect her against all evil and especially against the Angel of Death.

On Friday night, we celebrated the arrival of *Shabbat*. We brought little Masza in a baby carriage to my mother-in-law's house.

We passed by Rabbi Reines's famed yeshiva filled with rushed scholars ready to participate in the holiness of *Shabbat.* The *-173 -habbos* goy, the young gentile man who helps on Saturdays, had turned on the lights of Rachil's home. As we entered, one of the senior employees in the factory greeted us. As soon as he saw the carriage, he smiled, giving Sioma a friendly pat on the back:

"When your grandfather was a baby, he was taken out in a wooden cart, but this girl travels in such an elegant carriage!"

At dinner, everyone spoke about the growing antisemitism and the hard economic situation that was approaching. Rachil, jovial and determined, exclaimed, "Don't worry. Beer will continue to be sold; the harder the times, the more people will drink. When the Great War ended and there was a prohibition on the sale of alcohol, Meilach and I managed to make light beer at home, and we sold it on the black market. Don't put on such long faces. We will survive."

Franya might have been right; it wasn't the best time to have brought a child into this world. Despite everything, Sioma and I would protect her. I couldn't have imagined what awaited us on the other side.

Aniuta said that in Vilna she came across graffiti painted on the windows and walls of Jewish establishments. When one store owner tried to remove it, he was beaten up.

"What I can't understand," Aniuta wondered, "is how the police didn't even intervene. I'm worried, very worried."

I fear for my grandchildren, especially the newborn daughter of my youngest son Sioma. Times have changed. If Meilach were alive he would know what to do, but now I am the head of the family, and I don't know how to act or how to find the strength to overcome the crisis and the hatred. I hope that this explosion of antisemitism is transitory as it has been in the past.

I wrote to my grandfather announcing that he had had a great-granddaughter. I then began writing to Anykščiai weekly, sharing every little detail of my daughter's doings: a smile, a babble. There was no response for a while. Finally, I received several late letters at once. With his typical handwriting, my grandfather complained that the sales in his grocery store were diminishing constantly and the people who owed him were not paying; every day he tried to make sense of the red numbers and his increasing debt. In one letter, he talked about Sonja and her romantic relationship with Justas Paleckis, the leader of the Communist Party who would become the president of Lithuania, and that Shayna was still working at the bank. He wrote that my uncles Yosef and Leibn Rapoport—children of a previous marriage—who had made a life for themselves in New York, were coming to visit him in the spring. My grandfather hadn't seen them in years. Yosef was a pharmacist, and Leibn had his own women's clothing store. I could feel his excitement just by reading his words; I was happy for him.

***

1938 began with a cruel winter. Masza made my day worthwhile. She was growing up in a sheltered household. The ever-present Rachil was very fond of her, and she would impose her outdated ideas by giving her a sip of beer foam every day. According to her, it would make Masza's bones healthier. To my mother-in-law, beer was good for everything.

The frost was very strong. My lungs were weak, and I had to be hospitalized to prevent more asthma attacks. I stayed in a clinic in Szczawnica, one of the oldest thermal towns in the Carpathian Mountains. The picturesque valley of Grajcarek had a longstanding tradition of curative baths. I could see the view from my room. Every day I was subjected to various treatments that helped open my bronchi. The therapy also included plunging into the sulfurous spring to take advantage of the rich minerals that the water carried. I needed that respite, and I even enjoyed the healing process.

When I returned home with Sioma, my mother-in-law gave me an envelope that had arrived that same morning from Anykščiai:

Dear Szifra:

Yosef and Leibn came to visit us from America. Your grandfather Shabtai was very happy to see them, but after their departure, he became deeply saddened. His grief was so great that he fell ill and died. I am sending some photos that my father left, along with the letters you wrote to him. He loved you so much and thought of you as his daughter. I hope we can see you soon and meet Masza.

I love you,
Shayna

Shanya's news hit me hard. I hadn't seen my beloved grandfather since I'd left Anykščiai as a young girl. I could no longer embrace him or tell him how much I loved him. I couldn't get out of bed; I couldn't breathe. My dear Shabtai was no longer with us, but he would forever be in my heart.

To distract me, Sioma proposed to go to the opera in Vilna and leave Masza at home with Rachil. The theater, built in 1902 and located on Ulica Wielka Pohulanka, was packed. They were playing *Eugene Onegin*, inspired by the novel in verse by Alexander Pushkin with music by Piotr Ílich Tchaikovsky. I imagined being Tatyana, the character in the opera, resigning myself, like her, to always be faithful to my husband. I felt lucky to have Sioma at my side, a man who loved me so much.

After the performance, we strolled through the city. We passed the Sztral Café on Mickiewicz Avenue, lovingly remembering our first meeting. Back then, the café had been visited by many of our Jewish friends, but that was no longer the case. One afternoon, the waiters refused to serve a Jewish man. They posted a sign in Polish on the main entrance: "To each his own." This was a chauvinistic and racist slogan displaying the paranoid and mythomaniac patriotism that Poles began to believe in. The Jewish community of Vilna decided to appeal to justice. They were not heard or answered by the court, so they joined together to boycott the restaurant.

We returned to Lida at dawn. We were awakened by the *click-click* of pebbles against our window. It was Mitzia calling his younger brother. I managed to hear my brother-in-law's voice of alarm. He said that a group of people were demonstrating in front of the main gate of the brewery. People were yelling insults against the Jews, demanding that we be banned from selling any type of grain, flour, or beer. They were accusing us of stealing their bread, infecting the air they were breathing, and polluting the space where we had been for centuries.

I saw how Sioma, little by little, submerged into a worried state. The police were aware of what was happening that morning, but they didn't arrive until night. We were living under a false sense of equilibrium. Our fragile balance was about to be disrupted.

***

In the spring of 1938, at my father's insistence, Masza, Yenka, and I went for a few weeks to visit him in Nemenčinė. My father enjoyed giving his granddaughter fresh eggs, laid by the hens that same morning. Esfir would keep quiet most of the time, uttering one or two polite words here and there. Enjoying the good weather, we would walk along the rocky path leading to the lake. Pushing my daughter's pram as she babbled some words, I would take in the scenery and tranquility amidst the singing birds. I was happy.

Some days I would take advantage of the proximity of Vilna to go shopping and leave Masza in the care of Yenka. I was fascinated by the ermine collars imported from France, the colors of the feathered hats from Florence, and, of course, the shoes from

Warsaw. Everything was within my reach, in abundance, and without limits. I would lose myself at the movies. The cinema allowed me to enter fantastic worlds. I enjoyed watching the splendid Greta Garbo in *Camille* in the small Edison movie theater, I cried with Bette Davis performing in *Jezebel* in the crowded Nirvana Theatre, and in the Malenke Theatre, I traveled to Brazil with the handsome Clark Gable in *Too Hot to Handle*.

My beloved Szifra has changed so much; her name is now Szura, and she wears ermine and silk. There is hardly any glimpse of the simple and humble girl that attended the *gymnasium*, the little girl I knew. Today she is a lady, a wife, and a mother. Sioma spoils her; money comes easy to them. I don't think they know the meaning of it. I can't bear to see how much my daughter spends on hats and shoes. Even in these moments of instability, they squander money without thinking twice. It is not for me to judge, and yet I do. I cannot conceal how much I repudiate their superfluous purchases.

***

My mother-in-law offered to take care of Masza for a couple of weeks while Sioma and I vacationed in San Remo. We traveled by train to Italy via Warsaw. We shared the cabin with a German businessman from Frankfurt. He was proud to tell us about his country. Without knowing that we were Jewish, he praised National Socialism, the German movement Hitler had led since 1933, and how fast he was propelling his homeland toward progress.

"Hitler is a charismatic and passionate leader," he pointed out. "His energy is contagious. He's captivating the entire population."

We were alarmed to learn that educated and prominent people could blindly admire Hitler. In our view, he was a madman who exalted the superiority of the Aryan race. He ignited the idea of national pride, instilling Jewish hatred and absolute racism. We chose to ignore it, opting to believe that the situation surely wasn't as alarming as people said. We were on vacation; I preferred to forget about Germany and that lunatic.

Flanked by mountains dotted with red gabled roofs, the town of San Remo beautifully contrasted against the blue of the Mediterranean. It was a fabulous place. We felt free. We missed Maszinka but were confident that she was in good hands. We enjoyed the food, the sea breeze, and the exotic vegetation.

"What a beautiful plant, with spikes to protect it!" I said to Sioma.

"It's a cactus. Turn around and smile!" He clicked the camera button, immortalizing the moment.

We stayed in Warsaw on our way back home. While we enjoyed the parks and boulevards, we heard rumors of what was happening in Germany. It was said that

Jewish children were being expelled from public schools and Jews could not go to public parks or restaurants. We didn't want to believe it. We thought it was unfounded and exaggerated gossip.

When we reached Vilna, the Jerusalem of Lithuania as we affectionately called it, we found out that we had been mistaken. Many German Jews had taken refuge in the city fleeing Nazi persecution. Jews in Germany were treated as second-class citizens. They could not sit on park benches; they had been expelled from the universities and fired from their jobs. We heard terrible stories that multiplied every day. The people who had arrived didn't have any legal documentation allowing them to stay. Being in Poland put them in a precarious situation.

We tried to convince ourselves that adverse circumstances were confined to Germany. We believed that we lived among friends in Lida. Christians and Jews coexisted in peace with each other. We couldn't fathom that we would need to seek refuge in another country.

Bella Stolowitsky, the daughter of the brewery accountant, told us that in her *gymnasium*, a school run by the government in Lida, a young man had made a cruel comment about the Jews. The teacher was frustrated and admonished him to be quiet. The incident calmed us down and made us believe that everything was fine ... and we went on with our daily routines.

***

Masza learned to walk using the brewery as her playground. Yenka watched over her with zeal as she chased the chickens, plucked their feathers, and was entertained just by following her own shadow.

One day, a letter from my father arrived. As I read, I could sense his anger.

Dear Szifra:

Yudko dared to come to Nemenčinė. He came directly from Yugoslavia and asked permission to take you back with him. He has a good position as a physician, but he is very naïve. He had the nerve to tell me that if you agree to go with him, he will adopt Masza. He had the temerity to bring flowers! I nearly slapped him for his insolence, I never thought that he would dare to return after all these years. I forbade him from visiting you, I just wanted you to know. I advise you to be careful. Don't get involved in a complicated situation from which you will not be able to escape.

Take care,

Your father

I should have destroyed the letter, but I didn't. I don't know why. I hid it among my things, afraid Sioma would find it. Yudko was really in love with me. We had not seen each other or had any contact in years, yet the image of his elongated face and his smooth hands were imprinted in my memory. He had come to get me; he still wanted me ....

I ran out of the house; I needed to breathe. I crossed the wooden bridge over the creek and headed toward the military base at the end of the street. I felt the spring breeze on my face and tried to understand what was happening to me.

In my frantic escape, I didn't realize how far I had run. I came to my senses with the aroma of Boruj Kolkasky's bakery. I realized there was nothing to decide.

The reflection of a rainbow in a puddle became distorted when I stepped on it. I watched the small waves vibrate until the movement subsided … I went back along the market street, past the synagogue with its silver dome, and returned home. This was my place, alongside my husband and my daughter. It was absurd to continue entertaining silly fantasies of lost loves. It was useless to keep on stirring murky waters. I had my duties as a housewife. Rosh Hashanah was approaching, and we were having people from Slonim coming over to stay at our home. They didn't have enough people to complete a *minyan*, the minimum number of males required for the prayers in their village. So, they came to us.

***

We were accustomed to the daily exercises from the military base in Lida, but more and more soldiers were seen on the streets. Trucks full of uniformed men arrived continuously in our city. We were worried.

It was rumored that the Jews in Germany were being attacked in large numbers, the windows of their shops had been smashed and smeared with offensive signs, and the synagogues had been vandalized and burned. The Jewish refugees that had arrived in Vilna had no money and no work. The Polish government wanted to expel them. And the police searched everywhere looking for them. The situation was difficult. They had nowhere to go. Some of us wanted to be oblivious to what was happening and acted in a very naïve way. But war was imminent; it was 1939, and people were not afraid to show their hatred toward us.

Nevertheless, we sought a respite ... we planned a vacation to Krynica. We longed for poppyseed cake and brandy, wishing to enjoy life away from the daily routine of Lida. We hoped to govern our fears and conceal our worries. We just wanted to float through a languid and sleepy river; I was eager to plunge into thermal waters with healing properties. I thought that all troubles could disappear or at least stay clouded for a while.

Krynica was famous for its natural springs. A variety of treatments were offered for distinct ailments. It was very popular to plunge into different pools and have a crenotherapy treatment or corporal massage. It was also recommended to drink the source water, rich in sulfur and minerals; people claimed it could cure any disease. They even had the pungent water bottled with the Zuber label.

"*Tatu's*! Daddy," Masza hugged her father goodbye as we left our little girl in the care of her grandmother.

Approaching our paradisiacal destination from afar, I fixed my eyes on the luxurious hotel we would be staying in. After dropping our suitcases in the room, we took the funicular up to the snowy peak. We were on top of the world. At the summit, we felt alienated from the current events. We thought that we were in control of our destiny, we even thought we could fly.

We strolled through the town. The cobblestones echoed our steps. Among the flower vendors, a young man shouted the latest news: "Hitler annexes Austria. All of Europe in chaos!"

Sioma took a *grosz* out of his pocket and bought the newspaper. He read the headline subtitle out loud: "Germany has taken the first step, and we are on the verge of war." The article anticipated the risk of Poland being attacked by the German power. It also issued safety measures for the population in case of an invasion and announced the simulation of an aerial attack on the 14th of March.

Trying to enjoy our stay, we were pampered with good food and great service, but the perturbing news kept on coming. The current events were slowly affecting our psyche. Little by little, like a drop of water making a dent in the ground. We shortened our trip and returned to Lida. As we arrived, we saw that everyone was preparing for the military maneuver that was to happen the following day. They covered all the doors and windows with black cardboard, cloths, and tablecloths, using whatever they could find. The sense of danger was contagious. The first thing I did when we arrived home was hug our little girl. I hid my anguish with tears.

Chapter Seven: 1939-1941

B y early 1939, we knew that armed confrontation between the great powers was imminent. There was much to do in advance of the military simulation. We managed to find blackboards to camouflage and protect the house windows in the event of an air raid. We bought gas masks from the streets, one for each member of the household—seventy *zlotys* for the adult size and fifteen for children. Then we waited fearfully for the sounds of sirens.

The alarms resonated continuously and thunderously. We put on our masks, and I placed the small one on Masza's face. The airplanes were flying low, making tiny spins and sprinkling the city with tear gas. The air was dense. People ran to find shelter in their houses or elsewhere. Masza whimpered; she was frightened, and the mask bothered her. She didn't understand what was happening and why there was such a commotion. I also couldn't stand the mask for long; I was having an asthma attack and had trouble breathing freely. Frustrated, I took off my mask before the drill had finished. Sioma forced me to put it back on, worried and wishing that the alarm would stop shrieking and everything would go back to normal.

After the military operation, as if nothing had happened, the Edison and the Nirvana cinemas maintained their regular schedule, Bedzowski's store opened its doors, and Sioma returned to the brewery to resume his workday.

Antisemitism had escalated to an unmanageable degree. A group of Poles gathered outside the kosher butcher shop, protesting against the ritual slaughter of animals for Jewish consumption. A few days later, the senate voted to abolish the right to perform the *Shechitah* rite.

Ze'ev Jabotinsky, the founder of *Beitar*, was coming to Vilna. He had become an absolute celebrity in the Jewish world. The event was taking place at the Mars movie theater, and Franya and her husband went to hear him speak.

When they returned home, they were so excited that they kept on interrupting each other as they recounted the event. They said that more than two thousand people had gathered there. The passion and energy in the room had been palpable. Jabotinsky's words were powerful and captivating, leaving a lasting impression on their minds.

"Jabotinsky looks a little older, I think he must be about sixty years old," noted Franya.

"But he is more vigorous than any young man," her husband

corrected her.

Jabotinsky spoke for two hours solely in Yiddish. He expressed great concern about the growing antisemitism. He urged everyone to immigrate immediately to Palestine. He mentioned the White Paper and the prohibitions imposed by the British government, which prevented Jews from immigrating to *Eretz* Israel. "If we want the Land of Israel, we have to fight for it." The famous leader spoke of the impending war and insisted on leaving Europe as soon as possible.

"While I was listening to him," Franya said, "I could only think to myself: here in Lida, we have our lives, our livelihood. How can we leave all this? The brewery, the sawmill, the soft drink factory. It would be absurd! Moreover, it would be very risky to leave the country illegally."

***

Toward the end of August 1939, months after the drill, we tried to convince ourselves that the political situation wasn't so bad—that the newspapers exaggerated. We rationalized that the Germans had always been civilized and orderly, and that it wasn't in their nature to behave in such a bloodthirsty, primitive, or violent manner.

German Jewish refugees arrived constantly. Many were stranded in Zbouszyn, the border between Germany and Poland. Others managed to get to Lida. In an effort to avoid any problems with the authorities, the Jewish community crowdfunded around eighty thousand dollars to get the refugees out of the city. The task became impossible. Nobody wanted to give them asylum; they were "displaced Jews."

Yet we still refused to believe that a fatal destiny would reach us. We took for granted with unshakable certainty that the recently signed non-aggression agreement between Russia and Germany, two great powers with opposing ideologies, would last. The pact between Ribbentrop and Molotov provided certain credibility that we could continue living in peace in Lida.

We continued vacationing with luxury. We went to one of the most elegant and refined Polish spas of the day. On the way, we stopped to shop in Warsaw: a couple of sweaters, a jacket, a pair of shoes, hats, furs, and a raincoat. Sioma and I strolled the streets until sunset, enjoying the gardens at the Palace Lazienki, better known as the Palace on the Water, where we paused to admire Friedrich Chopin's statue. On our way back to the hotel, we passed by the Great Synagogue of Warsaw on Tlomacka Street; little did we know it would soon be destroyed by the incoming war.

The hotel, with its renowned thermal springs, was decorated with stained-glass windows, a beautiful hand-painted vault with Renaissance-style angels, and numerous stucco ornaments with gold leaf inlays. White-gloved waiters offering cold meats, breads, and petit fours whizzed throughout the dining room. The guests were dressed in the latest styles and enjoyed all the frills offered at the hotel: the famous tea ceremony, nightly balls in the main salon with a live orchestra, and an all-day service of delicious appetizers and exotic drinks to satisfy every palate. It was hard not to feel excessively optimistic. At that very moment, we were living in a world of endless fantasy.

An unexpected letter came from Rachil. Attached was a letter from Luba, Sioma's sister who was living in Brussels.

Dear Mama,

The situation in Belgium has been deteriorating very quickly. There is increasing talk about an upcoming war. People blame the Jews for everything, even the declining economy. They accuse us of being capitalists, of taking advantage of others, and accumulating wealth that does not belong to us. No matter what good we do, we are blamed. At the same time, they say that we are stubborn communists who seize their property.

Aaron managed to obtain documents from the British army that allowed him to leave for London. Despite our deteriorating marital situation, he has promised to try to get papers for me and our son Anatole so we can go with him. In the meantime, we will send the boy to live at the home of Marie Antoine, the woman who works in our house. Her family lives in a small village in Flanders, and our son will be out of danger in the countryside. I don't want to waste any more time, so I've gone ahead and initiated legal procedures to obtain travel permission to return to Lida. I hope to see you soon.

Miss you,
Luba

We were having dinner at the hotel when a young man dressed in a black suit entered hurriedly into the dining room. All eyes were on him, following his every move. He approached one of the diners and whispered something in his ear. Pale and distraught, the man got up without finishing his meal. The buzz spread until it reached us: Germany had invaded Poland!

"Let's go home, Sioma," I implored. "We don't know what is happening in Lida. I want to be with Masza as soon as possible."

We intended to take the first train out, but others were just as desperate as us, and the tickets had sold out. This was a turning point in everybody's lives. People from different backgrounds—nationalities, cultures, religions—were all congregated in that train station at that exact moment. Our differences didn't matter. We were all united in our uncertainty and despair.

We couldn't get tickets that day or the next. We kept going to the station day after day in the hopes of finding a way back home. So, we waited, anguished until we could return.

When we finally arrived, Lida was boiling; it was a powder keg. The smells of charred coal, sweat, and fear generated a stench of death. On our way to the brewery, we saw the destruction the German aerial attack had left in its wake. People were running aimlessly with suitcases and packages. Some of them had come from the small villages that bordered the city and were seeking shelter in the homes of relatives or friends. We saw small fires, houses in ruins, destroyed buildings, holes in the streets, and shattered windows everywhere. But most of all we perceived fear: selfish fear, violent fear, visceral, animal fear.

The family waited for us in the dining room while Masza slept in the adjacent room. They were discussing which country they'd prefer, Russia or Germany. One of Sioma's sisters was disdainful of the idea of German antisemitism and racial hatred; she claimed that the Germans were civilized people. "They will surely treat us better than the Russians. The Germans are capitalists, they are very disciplined and organized, they would never think of expropriating the brewery." In general, the family judged the Russians as unscrupulous Bolsheviks, communists eager to annihilate the bourgeoisie and all good taste, destroyers of capitalism.

Everyone had an opinion. Mitzia recounted how Mr. Leibl Stolowitsky, the brewery's accountant, lost his home. He saw his house burning down during the bombing. He ran toward the river with his children and wife. Such was his concern about saving his family that he didn't realize the hot piece of iron encrusted in his chest. Nothing stopped him, not even the pain or the smell of his own burnt flesh. The Stolowitskys lost all their belongings and went to live temporarily with relatives. They were left with nothing but the sour taste of death.

Rachil took charge of the situation. The next morning, she ordered the family and the workers to help her sort out household items, clothing, and furniture.

"We are living in critical times, and we have to prepare. We'll need cash to get by," my mother-in-law said. "Promissory notes and money in the bank will be useless. We need the mobility of bills and coins. We must sell everything we can. Whether the Germans or the Soviets arrive in Lida first, I am sure all they'll want is money. We must be prepared to distribute it strategically."

By mid-afternoon, Jews, Poles, and Belarusians were coming to buy our trinkets, knickknacks, and nonessentials at bargain prices. Rachil demanded that either Mitzia or Sioma take a train to Brussels as soon as possible to bring their sister Luba back to Lida.

"Mama, that is impossible! They're not issuing any travel visas, and all government offices have closed. Europe is burning, and I don't think we realize the magnitude of the situation," exclaimed Mitzia.

"Moreover, we cannot just leave our families unprotected," interrupted Sioma. "Luba will find a way to get here. If Aaron went to London, it would be easier for her to mobilize on her own. Surely, she's already on her way, so stop worrying."

Lida's sky was sporadically covered with warplanes. The noise from the turbines was deafening. The ground was constantly rumbling. It rained sawdust. Everything smelled of gunpowder. When bombs dropped, people ran in terror with no direction, order, or reason. People sought shelter where there was none.

The sky would turn black and the pavement red with blood, flesh, and bones. Beggars playing the violin at the corner of Szkolna Street ceased to exist. All we breathed was panic and chaos.

The Soviets knocked on our door on September 17; they were occupying Lida. Russian tanks paraded down Suwalska Street.

People welcomed them with cheers and applause. We watched from afar, doubting the goodwill of the usurpers. The spectacle of tanks, horses, and soldiers on foot took over the entire avenue. A light rain interrupted the pompous demonstration of Soviet dominance. The Bolshevik flags, fluttering in the wind, now turned into soaked rags. It all felt like a metaphor.

A military truck full of soldiers announced "Freedom, Equality, and Fraternity." They believed they were our saviors, but the tragedy had just begun. Lida, which bordered Lithuania, became an escape door. Many Jews fled to Vilna, where the sickle and hammer flags were raised on all public spaces and buildings. The Bolsheviks, drunk with power and envy, were fast to impose their ways; nothing could stop them from seizing what they found in their path. They were rude and merciless, especially to the Jews and the wealthy.

A few days later, Russian officers arrived at the brewery to requisition the production. We were informed that it was our duty to provide drinks for "the people." Every week a Soviet detachment arrived to take the whole lot, continually demanding that we produce more and more. Soon the factory was forced to work overtime. They recorded everything with precision—the inventory, accounts, and, of course, profits. We were at their service.

They celebrated the anniversary of the Russian Revolution on November 7 and chose our house—barely used and just large enough—for their festivities. They ordered us to prepare a banquet with geese, red caviar, and other delicacies. It was also my birthday.

Wearing an all-black maid's uniform, I celebrated by entertaining a group of scoundrels, a forced and submissive smile stamped on my face. There, in my own home, beer and vodka flowed like water without consideration. The sight was nauseating: their noses were red from the alcohol, and their bodies, with protruding, oversized bellies, reclined on our sofas. The new "masters and lords" lacerated my dignity with every minute that passed.

"We are not in mourning, on the contrary," Sioma said after the senior officer asked him to sit at the table and have some vodka with them. My husband spoke Russian and with his charisma had gained the confidence of the high officials.

"Today is my wife's birthday and the anniversary of the revolution," Sioma told them, raising his glass, "two noble causes to toast to."

They all raised their glasses and toasted to my health: "To the wife of comrade Pupko."

Mishka, one of the Russian officers of the NKVD, the People's *Kommissariat* for Internal Affairs, and a Jew, whispered in Sioma's ear: "Stalin's communism will soon be the law."

"I think I know what you mean," replied Sioma, naively. "We will continue paying our taxes and contribute to the Russian government."

Mishka didn't even try to suppress his laughter. "You're an idiot. They'll take everything away from you: the factory, the furniture, the house, the car ... everything! This is how the regime works, everything is for 'the people.' You better start getting used to the idea."

Sioma's visage changed.

Once the dinner ended and the soldiers had left, Sioma said to me in despair, "Sell everything you can tomorrow. Put out everything, absolutely everything. Let's take advantage of how much we have. We do not need fine china, crystal, or ornaments. Get rid of it all!"

My sisters and mother-in-law joined the sale. We even sold Sioma's car at an absurd price. With limited gasoline, he would ride a bicycle instead. We put sheets, silverware, tablecloths, and lamps up for sale at bargain prices. Everything was to be sold except for a curtain I hoped to use to make a dress for myself.

***

Two Russian engineers appeared at the brewery, along with the *poletruk*, the director of the Bolshevik youth. They sought to collect taxes—imposing a very high percentage and demanding immediate payment. While they weren't legitimate, we didn't have an option but to accept their claim and pay. At least we still owned the brewery.

Days later, a manifesto was issued announcing the nationalization of the banks and industry. Interestingly enough, they didn't confiscate the factory. We were still living on the property and working as usual. But our freedom was waning, breaking us down irreversibly. The regime prevailed and grew stronger. The intimidated mass yielded without questioning the abuse of the invaders. To celebrate the first official event, they forced all Polish children to recite the Bolshevik oath.

"*Klatva* ..." the chant began vigorously. From the youngest children, like my little Masza who wasn't even three years old yet, to the teenagers and adults, we sang the hymn and applauded communist heroism. I didn't know how to read Russian, so I mechanically chanted along: "*Klatva ya rodvzini* .... I promise to defend my homeland ...."

"We have come for the bourgeois," cried the Russian officials storming into the brewery office. "They are guilty of all human misfortune. We are looking for Elimelech Pupko, better known as Meilach. He is an exploiter of the masses."

They had with them an arrest warrant for my father-in-law. The papers they showed implied that he would be taken to Minsk or Moscow for a minor interrogation, but it was known that in reality, the objective was to transfer all prisoners to the work camps in Arkhangelsk, in northern Russia.

The communists, who were bureaucrats after all, did not know that Meilach had been dead for years. If they learned of their mistake, they would take Sioma and Mitzia. Given the danger, the Pupko brothers fled that very night. They hid in the home of a Polish farmer who used to sell them barley for their beer production. Roza, Mitzia's wife, and I stayed behind in the brewery along with our children Masza, Noya, and Meilashe. But we feared they would want to apprehend us, too. Sioma and Mitzia were fugitives from the communist regime and were on the wanted list. According to the Russian code, if they tried to escape, they were worthy of forced labor; if they couldn't find them, the penalty could fall on us. We didn't lose any time: the next morning, we went on our way to Vilna, which was still an independent city. Rachil and her daughters stayed in Lida, as they were not at risk.

We started the journey on foot. The snow was up to our knees. Noya was walking ahead, almost blurred by the whiteness of the landscape; I carried Masza in my arms, and Roza carried Meilashe. Friends who lived near the train station sheltered us for the night. Sioma and Mitzia were waiting for us there. Together again, the four of us discussed our options. Sioma wanted to get as far away as possible and quickly, but Mitzia, fearing to end his days in a forced labor camp, preferred to surrender and work for the Russians.

"I will be an exceptional proletarian, I will become a *stajanovietz*," Mitzia insisted.

"I'm not going to work for the Bolsheviks, I would rather escape than accept their oppression. There must be another solution … in the meantime, let's go to Vilna to gain some time," Sioma said with aplomb.

We had one thousand dollars in the bag. Sioma would travel alone to Nemenčinė to pave the way and inform my father that we had escaped from the communists and were headed to Vilna. I was afraid to separate from Sioma. I kissed him hard to keep him close. We had to take advantage of the darkness of the night to escape.

"Sioma, Sioma! Wait for me!" yelled Mitzia as he rushed after him. "I'll go with you, you're right!"

Two days later, they sent a *drosky* to pick us up. Roza, Noya, Meilashe, Masza, and I left at night. We were afraid of being intercepted by the army, as we didn't have legal papers, and they could stop us from crossing the border into Vilna. Luckily, there were no mishaps. The *drosky* dropped us off at the train station in Vilna where my father, Sioma, and Mitzia were waiting for us. We were hungry. My father brought some cheese—a lavish treat—to share with us.

We rented a small apartment on Ulica Pohulanca, where the Tarbut school used to be. I knew the street well, but a lot had changed since my time there. The building had been originally designed with large apartments, but it had since been converted into a tenement. Each room housed a family, and the bathrooms were communal. Cleaning was scarce, and there were always plumbing problems that were never resolved. A nauseating smell would reach the far corners of the room. My father sent us a sofa and a bed for Masza; our friends, the Frydmans, lent us a cupboard to store the few pieces of clothing we had brought. I didn't complain; this was far better than being in Lida under Russian rule.

We received news from Lida that was not encouraging. They had nationalized many businesses including our competitor Papiermejster, the Korona chemical plant (where they made inks and dyes), the olive oil and poppy seeds industry, and the nail and screw factory. The Pupko brewery had somehow been spared, likely because it was a smaller enterprise in comparison with the others. We knew the situation was temporary and could change rather quickly.

Everything in Vilna was scarce, and the shortages made people desperate. Long lines formed in front of the grocery stores. One day, in Tchatski's shop, I managed to buy a slice of chocolate cake to share with Sioma and Masza. When I arrived home, our little girl was asleep. We tried to wake her up to eat the cake together, but she was too tired. Sioma and I were so hungry that, without thinking twice, we ate it all. There wasn't even a crumb left for our daughter. I felt so guilty and selfish that when Masza woke up, with tears streaming down my face, I begged for her forgiveness. Half asleep, not understanding what I was talking about, she looked at me with queasy eyes while I stuttered through my apology.

Vilna was growing without respite. The population had reached two hundred fifty thousand inhabitants, mostly refugees. There was no food or merchandise in the stores. The need for basic items and food increased violence and theft on the streets. From time to time, we would receive precious packages from my father with butter, honey, and even some chocolate for Masza.

Antisemitism was a contagious evil. The practice of painting offensive graffiti on the doors and windows of Jewish businesses eventually spread to Vilna. Signs displaying "*Juden*" accompanied by stars of David discouraged potential buyers. Posters and banners were posted all over the university demanding the expulsion of the Jewish academics. Stones were thrown at Orthodox Jews while the authorities feigned dementia and turned a blind eye. The growing hatred encouraged people to veer away from us Jews. It was said that we smelled due to an illness that corroded society.

I did not want to believe the abhorrence and hoped to return to the luxuries we had enjoyed in Lida. I lived in a false harmony. I would picture the family playing cards with friends, smoking cigarettes, and drinking vodka. We complained about the shortage of food, the insecurity on the streets, and, of course, the war, but we continued to seek mundane pleasures. Despite everything, we laughed and sang.

A letter arrived from Rachil explaining that the dangers in Lida had subsided. The Russians were not interested in the brewery as it was too small for them to care about it. Rachil asked us to return as soon as possible. The Soviet officers liked Pupko beer and wanted more of it. We needed to go back to work at full speed.

Ignoring Rachil's urgency, we postponed our return until February 1940. But by then the atmosphere in Lida was tense. The conditions worsened quickly. Peace was an absolute lie, a fabrication of the mind. We were the object of hatred everywhere: we were Jews.

Vilna along with all Lithuania was annexed to the Soviet Union. Its independence vanished; the Bolsheviks had reached us once again. We looked for escape routes everywhere. Someone told us that two-hundred-dollar exit visas to Japan were available in the city of Kovno. From there, you would be able to travel all the way to Arkhangelsk in Russia and then to Kobe where a Jewish committee would welcome you. We heard that the Kushelevich family had already managed to get to Japan. There was still hope.

Thanks to the armed conflict, the previous impassable dividing lines between Poland and Lithuania had now disappeared. So, in the meantime, we fled to Anykščiai, the Lithuanian village of my childhood. I had not returned since that night when, as a young girl, I crossed the Black Border with the smuggler. My uncle Meyer was waiting for us at the entrance of the village. He recognized us only by the photos that I had sent from Lida along with my letters.

Anykščiai had changed drastically! The narrow streets were all blurred in my memory. Now they were filled with Lithuanian military men—with their white bands around their arms and auras of superiority. Meyer and his wife Leye welcomed us to their small house behind the bridge. Their daughters Froike and Frida offered their friendly smiles to Masza. A few days later, Mitzia and his family came to Anykščiai. They were equally fearful of the arrest orders enforced against the Lida bourgeoisie.

A smuggler gave us an official visa that belonged to a Tzipit Alexander. We only needed to change the name on the document in order to use it. We got a special liquid that washed the ink away; then we wrote our names. It was dangerous business.

"I do not want to go to Japan," I complained to Sioma. "I'm scared. Besides, what am I going to do in an Asian country where I can't understand their incomprehensible language or even read their signs?"

"It will be temporary until the war is over. We must get out of here. Your father sent us money for the ticket, and he gave me a watch to sell in case of need."

"Yes, I know he has given us his blessing. He also advised that once we get there, we can make do by selling or even finding a way to manufacture Karakul coats. But still, I am afraid. I don't want to leave this continent."

Sioma stroked my face with tenderness. Deep down I knew that going to the East was our only escape.

***

Sioma went often to Kovno, where the occupation government was organized, hoping to find our names on the record of approved visas. He checked the list week after week, but our names did not appear. Our anxiety grew every day.

Fed up with the lack of news, one day, Sioma hid some dollar bills between the leather and the felt of his shoes, intending to bribe some communist functionaries. But he never got the chance. In just a minute, our situation changed drastically. Sioma was arrested and imprisoned in the infamous Yellow Jail. Located on the border of Lithuania and Prussia, the building had originally been constructed before the Russian Revolution to protect Russia from a possible German attack. Sioma presented the issued visa that he carried with him. Unfortunately, the NKVD had initiated an investigation to arrest anyone with forged documentation; Tzipit Alexander's visas were fake. Sioma was detained and handcuffed immediately.

He was charged on counts of fraud and treason and therefore lost his right to a trial. He could be executed at any moment.

We begged my aunt Sonja to intervene with her communist friends. We learned that Abrasha Evenson, my childhood friend with whom I had sled on the streets of Anykščiai, had joined the NKVD. We thought that maybe he could help us, so I went to him.

Commandant Abrasha looked fearsome in his uniform. The numerous insignias were evidence of his high rank. Through his gaze, I still recognized the child with whom I'd played long ago. I begged for his help. He was sorry to learn that Sioma, the very same man he had arrested the night before, was my husband. He promised to try and help.

Seventeen long days and seventeen endless nights, multiplied by hours, minutes, and seconds, passed by before Sioma returned to my uncle's house. I heard him arrive at dawn; I was half-asleep as he kissed my eyelids. I wanted to ask him a thousand questions as I caressed his head.

He recounted his release quickly, almost out of breath: "In the middle of the night, two Russian officers entered the jail. Under the pretext of interrogating us, they removed me and another prisoner out of confinement. I feared for my life. Then they separated the two of us. Abrasha Evenson identified himself as your friend and Judel Perelman as the brother of an acquaintance of yours before giving me back my freedom."

I hugged Sioma tighter than I ever had before, and I didn't let go for the rest of the morning. My uncle Meyer woke us up with the news that the Soviets had assassinated the prisoners who had shared the cell with Sioma. It was a miracle that Sioma was still alive. He felt reborn. God had given us a new opportunity. Although there was a shortage of food in Lithuania and Belarus, we were able to celebrate Sioma's return with bread and milk—a gift from the owner of a mill on the outskirts of Anykščiai.

We returned to Lida a few weeks later. The family was forced to adjust to new realities: Franya's husband enlisted in the Russian army, Aniuta's daughter was accepted to the *gymnasium,* and Sioma and Mitzia worked in the brewery under orders from the Soviets. We decided to enroll Masza in the Russian school where she could learn the language and receive a communist education. Her indoctrination process would begin at an early age.

We were soon invited to a school performance that celebrated an official Soviet commemoration. As we sat in the audience, we could see our little Masza standing in strict formation, firmly reciting a hymn along with other children: "*Yesli zaftra vaina* .... If the war begins tomorrow ...." As soon as the festivities ended, I went to my daughter and congratulated her for her accomplishment without revealing my true feelings. The education she was receiving made me nauseous.

All the adults were forced to register their vocation at the command headquarters. Those who held professions were called "bourgeois exploiters." The officials savored their triumphs against the well-to-do and sent many of Lida's businessmen to labor camps without explanation. Sioma's and Mitzia's names were on their blacklist as "social oppressors and enemies of the people."

We knew that it was just a matter of time until both brothers were arrested. We decided to flee again to Nemenčinė where my father could still take us in.

It was dangerous to travel as a group, so I traveled ahead first. When I arrived, I was greeted with the news that my father's pharmacy had closed. The antisemitic outbreaks were no longer sporadic; they were targeted and calculated. All Jewish-owned businesses were banned as part of a new law. Our non-Jewish neighbors and former friends became wolves in sheep's clothing; their hands were transformed into thorny claws, their grimaces showed us their pointy teeth, and their body language indicated disgust. Nemenčinė ceased to be a peaceful summer destination; hatred had corroded the otherwise harmonious community. I didn't rest until I saw Sioma and Maszinka arrive the next day.

"You must get away from here as soon as possible," my father begged us. "The Germans are approaching, and they mustn't find you in this town. The Russians aren't any better. Germans, Russians, or Lithuanians—all of them, for different reasons—want the Jews gone. They will imprison or shoot anyone without legal documents or any person who does not live here permanently. Flee, hide wherever you can." He paused to take a breath and said emphatically, "Sioma, you must think of a safer alternative for the sake of your family. It is not the time to hesitate. You must act quickly and escape now!"

We headed back to Vilna. We were in desperate need of

shelter and safety. We found the *Yerushalayim* of the North in a miserable state. The heart of the city had stopped beating. Thousands of refugees were living on the streets. Wood or coal for the stoves was scarce; people fought over the few supplies sold at exorbitant prices in the black market. We were fortunate enough to find a roof over our heads. We rented a small place in an apartment building. We still were some of the lucky ones, thanks to my father's occasional package of chicken and veal. But it wasn't enough; we were always hungry.

We moved from one place to the other; we were wanderers.

***

My menstrual period was late. "I can't be pregnant!" I said to myself. "I don't want to bring a new life into this belligerent world." I wept until I collapsed.

That night, lying in bed, I whispered into Sioma's ear, confessing my fear. Tears streamed down my face and into my mouth as I mumbled my distress. It was June 1940; we knew that German troops were getting closer to Vilna. Lida was still under Russian rule, and an infant had no chance in this upside-down, *meshuggener* world. We doubted every decision we made. Every step we took raised questions. We lived defying danger every day. We had our daughter, who was almost four, to think about. She was constantly exposed to the dangers of war and defenseless. I didn't want to add more to the equation.

Sioma and I decided to wait a week before confirming my pregnancy. The time came. My previous decision hadn't changed, and I said without blinking, "I want an abortion."

Sioma nodded. He did not try to convince me otherwise. "We'll go to Dr. Sedliza's office."

I held my breath all week until the agreed-upon date. The doctor was waiting for us in his office on Pohulanka Street on the second floor of a building with a neoclassical façade. In that deteriorated and unadorned office, the traffic of souls prevailed— children who would never see the light of day.

The nurse came out: "Dr. Sedliza will receive you now, please come in."

The specialist explained that the procedure would not be painful and told my husband to wait outside. Everything happened so quickly. As we left the office, I felt a seaquake within me. I had killed my child, murdered my baby. I had left him breathless, inert … dead! The sunny, crystalline day cut through my empty entrails like a sharp knife. To no avail, I tried to convince myself that I had done the right thing. Nothing could comfort me.

We took the tram back to the apartment. The rattling of the tracks crushed and ground my guts. I felt sick to my stomach. When we finally arrived at the little rented room, I ran over to Masza. I squeezed her tightly, kissed her, and hugged her until we both surrendered to sleep.

***

Despised by all social strata and nationalities, many Jews in Europe became homeless nomads. With nowhere to go, we tried our luck in Anykščiai once more. My uncle Meyer welcomed us, along with Mitzia and his family, to his house.

A few days later, we managed to rent a furnished house from Mr. Koplevski. The house was nestled by the river, surrounded by the forest, and situated along the route to Utena. Sioma thought it would be a good idea to buy geese and raise them in the back of the farm. The process of fattening them was very slow, but it was a good business to get us by. We could use almost every part of the animal: the liver would be sold at a good price, the skin fried and served as a snack, the fat used as a spread on bread, and the meat used as a great source of nutritious protein—especially beneficial during the winter frosts.

We gave our names—Sioma, Szura, and Masza—to our three new geese. It was a fun little game we played while watching them squawking in the backyard. Sioma was a stubborn, fat goose; Szura kept on spinning around aimlessly; and Masza only followed his mother. Our fates, like those of our three geese, were doomed.

We slaughtered Sioma first and sold his feathers to pillow makers. Then it was Szura's turn. Whatever part we didn't sell from the plump thing, we ate, enjoying the fat mixed with honey. Masza was the last one to go. What we earned from them enabled us to buy wheat, rye, and flour. Unfortunately, the money made from selling the geese was insufficient, and thus Sioma was forced to look for other sources of income. He sold empty beer bottles and tried to trade flour in bulk. Uncle Meyer also taught him how to dye clothes in indigo so he could sell them, too.

Mitzia worked in the shoe felt factory and received a few coins per day as payment. Sioma, on the other hand, had managed to buy some sacks of wheat flour to sell at retail. To help his brother, he divided the profits between the two of them. I didn't quite understand the fraternal relationship between them. At the expense of everything else and at the cost of his own family, Sioma would continue to support Mitzia and his family. It was a disadvantage, but I refrained from making any comments.

I'm tired of being a simple day laborer. I have a profession: I studied engineering in Germany. The communists pretend that we are all equal, devoid of any distinction or individuality. My brother Sioma has been very generous to me, Roza, and my children Noya and little Meilashe, but I cannot stand the insecurity that we feel here in Anykščiai. I depend on the goodwill of my brother and that of my sister-in-law's aunts and uncles. My mother called us from Lida, exhorting us to return. She assures us that the situation is stable and insists that it is our duty to work at the brewery while this frightening situation is resolved.

Mitzia and his family returned to Lida; we decided to stay in Anykščiai. We learned that my aunt Sonja had followed the Lithuanian communist government to Leningrad. My grandparents had never understood their daughter. She was now Justas Paleckis's secretary and had joined the march along the river Neva with him. That proved to be an almost fatal decision for Sonja, as she was shot and wounded by a German bullet from air raids. She managed to get to Odessa almost on all fours.

***

We heard on the radio that the Germans had attacked the Soviet Union. The hoarse voice of Foreign Minister Molotov echoed through our room. The date was June 22, 1941. We knew that the aerial offensive would soon come to Anykščiai. The sirens sounded while attack planes bombarded the city. The roar of the bombs was deafening, and the gusts of fire from the Luftwaffe, the German Air Force, tinted the sky. Many people tried to reach the Russian-Polish border, but the German planes sprayed a black toxic liquid on the transports, leaving many dead. There was panic and confusion all around. Everyone ran, aimlessly seeking refuge anywhere they could: a cave, perhaps a ditch, the shelter of a leafy tree, or crouched in a useless embrace. There was no escape; the flash of those lights announced the end of the world.

On the side of the road, where we could see stacked piles of inert bodies and houses burning, we could also see the Lithuanians, in their despair, opening their homes to the Germans. The soldiers walked through the doors exhibiting their power with triumphant demeanors.

That day in Anykščiai, the *Szaulists*, members of the most antisemitic Lithuanian group, raged their hate against the Jews of the town. They locked most of them inside the old synagogue and beat them mercilessly. People reported that the slaughter was brutal. Blood flowed in the *shul,* rocking like the tides during a lunar eclipse, and the legs and arms of victims floated in their own bodily fluids. The blind frenzy of antisemitism that had accumulated over centuries clouded over any hint of reason. This group of pro-Nazi volunteers would later form part of the Einsatzgruppen—the infamous special killing unit who assassinated thousands of Jewish men, women, and children in mass shootings after forcing them to dig their own graves.

Along with a few other victims, my uncle Meyer was able to buy his freedom and escape the carnage at the synagogue. We were lucky that Koplevski's house was on the outskirts of the city, far enough from the feast of death. Meyer, along with his wife and daughters, Froike and Frida, and my aunt Shayna managed to safely join to us. Fearing for our lives, we barricaded ourselves in the house. From the window overlooking the road, we saw the German troops marching toward Leningrad.

A group of soldiers settled in front of the house. They set up a tent adorned with the insignia of the skull, the *Totenkopf,* that identified them as the motorized troop. We saw a group of Jews getting beaten as they were mandated to wash the Nazis' vehicles. A peasant speaking with a husky German officer seemed to point to our house as if to say, "There are more Jews in there."

We jumped out the back window and escaped in only a few seconds. As soon as we began to run, we were intercepted by a

Lithuanian commander, a leader of the *Szaulists*. He took us by surprise and pushed us to the wooden area nearby. Wild mushrooms and berries covered the ground. I panicked. Fear took hold as I felt fluid trickling down between my legs. I shook uncontrollably. He pushed us farther into the woods until we reached a spot where other Jews were being kept—Jews who, like us, had escaped the massacre in the synagogue. We'd been hauled to a *żydu stowiła*, an encampment erected to concentrate the "fugitives." About a dozen Lithuanian combatants monitored our every move; their hateful stares threatened to assassinate us under any pretext.

We hugged each other tightly and formed a fragile cluster, threatening to fall apart with the least effort. It was cold, but we shared our fear and the little heat that came through our bodies. After three long days and three eternal nights, my uncle Meyer, with a sheepish expression and a bull's body, asked me to obtain permission from the Lithuanian commandant to go to the house to get his *tallis*.

"Szifra," he still used my childhood name, "I know that you speak Lithuanian very well. Take this ring and ask Commander Pulawiczus (by then we had figured out his full name—Dalys Pulawiczus) to let you go to Koplevski's house. Today is Tisha B'Av and the anniversary of the death of your grandmother Leah. I need my prayer shawl to say *Kaddish* for my mother. If they let you go and you manage to get to the house, bring my shawl, our fur coats, and anything else you think might be useful here in the woods."

My uncle continued: "Do you remember where we buried the

objects before we were caught? Let's hope you can bring them back so we can try to buy our liberty. Be careful, Szifra, and good luck!"

I did as I was told and asked permission from the commander to fetch a coat from Koplevski's house. I was afraid to go alone, and it somehow occurred to me to request that two *Szaulists* under his orders escort me.

I began to explain that we were not from Anykščiai. "My last name is Pupko, we are from Lida, and we are here on a visit," I went on, trembling.

"From Lida?" the commander exclaimed curiously. "My mother-in-law worked for a Pupko from Lida! Are you the Pupko of the brewery?"

I did not know if the reply would benefit or condemn me. I opted for a less compromising strategy: "We will be very grateful if you help us …." With a subtle gesture, I let him know that we would pay him well.

"I will not send you with a *Szaulist* because he will probably try to take advantage of you. I will accompany you myself. Come later tonight, and I will take you."

I was startled; I did not know whether I should trust Pulawiczus or not. He could also harm me. But something in his gaze calmed me down. I returned to where my family was gathered and told them about the conversation with the commandant.

My husband reacted instantly and took me aside: "You have to go back to him and tell him that you have a husband and a daughter. Beg him to help us. I feel this is going to get worse; if we do not get out of here soon, we will not be able to save ourselves. We need the help of Koplevski to hide us. We must hurry and take advantage of this opportunity!"

I approached the Lithuanian officer and said, "I have a coat of Karakul, Persian lamb brought from Astrakhan that will suit your wife very well, and also my husband's Omega watch for you. No one knows where I have hidden our valuables except me. If you help us get out of the Anykščiai forest, you will be handsomely rewarded."

The official accepted without hesitation.

We waited for darkness to come to cover our movements. Pulawiczus led me through a patch of the forest that I immediately recognized. I could see from there the road that led to the village. We stealthily knocked on the door of Koplevski's house. As he opened the door, I explained that I had come to collect my things and those of my uncle. He wasn't surprised when I also asked him to help me hide for a few days; on the contrary, he accepted complacently. In the shadows, making sure nobody was watching, I crept under the foundation of the house, right to where we had buried some of our belongings. I wouldn't be able to take everything with me, so I placed some of my uncle's sacks aside, hoping he would also be able to escape. There it was, the *tallis* he needed so badly to pray for my grandmother's soul, carefully folded along with his coats and suits—prized possessions that he would never get to see again.

Crouched in the makeshift hole, I waited for the commandant to bring Sioma and Masza to me as we had agreed. It was already very late at night. The minutes and the hours seemed eternal on the clock of my anxiety. It all smelled like wet earth.

From my hiding place, I saw Pulawiczus, clad in military uniform and a winter jacket, staggering toward Koplevski's house. He could barely walk; he was drunk. Masza's little face peeked out from beneath the commandant's coat. He had kept his word and handed my daughter over to me. I hugged and kissed her without stopping. I could not let her go; I didn't want to be apart from her.

I dug up Sioma's watch and gave it to Pulawiczus as payment.

"You still have to bring my husband," I said, reminding him of the Karakul coat for his wife in exchange for Sioma.

The hours passed; I was desperate. It was almost dawn when I saw Sioma arriving through the thick fog. I handed over the coat to Pulawiczus and implored him to help my uncle and his family. He was not interested in any other goods that we offered. He was happy with what he had and said it was not worth the risk. I dared to ask for one last favor.

"We need to send a letter to Lida. We must let them know that we're fine. Is there a way that you can get someone to take it personally?"

He somehow procured a motorcyclist. We paid him fifty dollars, an exorbitant sum, to take the written message to the brewery. Finally, feeling the embrace of Sioma, I allowed myself to succumb to exhaustion, and I fell into lethargy ....

That same night, while the whole town slept, Sioma and I

retrieved two more watches and a hundred rubles. The Nikolai coins were almost growing roots in Koplevski's land. We did not know if we would need them in the future, but no one could know about their existence.

Explosives rumbled and echoed in the distance; the continuous gunshots and the constant noise of fear was making me mad.

We remained hidden under the earth for a few more days to escape the *odium judaicae*, the instilled hatred of the Jews. Koplevski came down every day to feed us, bringing soup and bread. When the night was stark and without stars, he allowed us to go into the house. We couldn't light any lamps or fire, so we tried to warm ourselves in the dark. The constant fear of being discovered kept us quiet. We spent most of the time in the underground hole. Dampness and cold pierced through our bones, but we were grateful to be alive.

Good news appeared in the form of the young man who brought us a note from Lida. It was written by Mitzia. The message said that the whole family had gathered in the brewery. We were the only ones missing, and they were anxiously waiting for us.

Pulawiczus was true to his word and ensured that no German came near Koplevski's house. He even got us documents to travel. He procured fake papers for my husband and daughter. But we were afraid to use them, and we preferred to use the international student card that Sioma had from his time in Brussels, which did not indicate his Jewish identity. Pulawiczus's wife gave me her Lithuanian identification card that attested she was Catholic. Not only did she lend me her identity, she also gifted me a chance for survival. As we planned to pass through Vilna on our way to Lida, we sewed the dugout coins to my corset to hide them.

We decided to travel separately once more. Fearing that someone could identify me as the granddaughter of Mr. Rapoport, I would travel alone with the papers of Mrs. Pulawiczus. To avoid any setback and increase our chance of escape, Sioma and Masza would be escorted by Pulawiczus to the train station. They would go to the Švenčionys station, north of Vilna where we would meet up later. We said our goodbyes without hugs or tears, quickly, without stopping to think about the danger. But the uncertainty of whether or not we would ever see each other again lingered in the backs of our minds.

The airstrikes continued incessantly; there was no truce, no respite. We had left my uncle and his family in the camp. I prayed constantly for their escape. Once again, without success, I tried to persuade Balys Pulawiczus to help them and bring them to us. All my attempts were useless; he had no interest in saving my uncle Meyer, his wife Leye, his two daughters Froike and Frida, or my aunt Shayna ... they were destined to die.

The *Szaulists* were murderers, animals who insulted, mistreated, and spat on the Jews. We would later learn that they used axes and sticks to murder them. The ones who survived the beatings were killed at close range. Almost like a game, the

Szaulists fired until they ran out of bullets. The Jews of Anykščiai, among them Shayna, my uncle, and his family, succumbed to their avarice. Their lights extinguished.

Through the window of the moving train, I see Jews being harassed by Nazi soldiers. They seem to be repairing the sleepers joining the rails, but I can't see clearly. The scenes pass quickly through my eyes, like gusts. I pray that Szura is safe and doesn't have any mishaps. I hope she is at the Švenčionys station and has found transport for all of us so we can get to Vilna together. I am afraid that my student identification isn't enough for the officers, and we still must go through the border and checkpoints. I have carefully instructed Masza to answer only to her Polish name Marisha. She must keep quiet and not utter a word in Yiddish. Despite her young age, I know she understands we're in danger. If our hunters sense our real identities, our deaths are a sure thing.

Lady Pulawiczus placed a necklace with a cross on my neck. In exchange for her generosity, she received a gold bracelet, one of the few mementos from my mother. It hurt to let go of the one thing that tied me to my mother, but life was worth more than any heirloom.

I slept in a haystack next to a horse and a cow. Screaming on the inside, I took a deep breath, inhaling the putrid odor. I needed all the strength I could get to face the following day. At dawn, Pulawiczus's wife came to pick me up. Her massive body led me to the train station. There was no emotion in our farewell other than profound gratitude.

Although Pulawiczus charged for his services, I would be forever thankful for what he did for us. He granted us the opportunity to be on the side of the living.

I passed through Zarzecze en route to Vilna, all while pretending to be Catholic. The night concealed my anxiety. I had to find a wagon to pick up my husband and Masza at the train station, but I did not know how or where. In the darkness, I distinguished the roofs of the churches of San Casimir and San Augustus. As I began to walk, I encountered a Polish officer holding two ferocious guard dogs; he was guarding the neighborhood. He greeted me courteously, and I decided to approach him. I placed my engagement ring in his hand and begged him to help me get a *drosky* to the Švenčionys station.

The policeman disappeared with my jewel in his pocket. I waited nervously, beginning to think that he had slipped away and would never come back. A while later, he appeared around the corner. He was walking alone ... without a *drosky*. He returned the ring to me apologetically; he couldn't get a cart, he said. I did not insist, and I put the ring back on my finger. Disillusioned and frustrated, I went to the house of Sioma's cousin Fridl Kowiwienska and spent the night there.

Fridl told me that the *chapuni*—a violent Lithuanian group who exchanged Jews for money—had come to the house a few days earlier and taken her husband and brother. She was terrified; she had no information of their whereabouts and feared for their lives. I was just as nervous, feeling like I was being consumed from the inside out. I didn't sleep at all as I waited for news.

***

Between tears, I opened my eyes and found Sioma and Masza standing in front of me. This time, I cried with joy.

"Szura, my dear, we've had so much luck, you have no idea. Balys Pulawiczus accompanied us to the train station. He was guarding us from a distance when two *Szaulist* officers began to approach us with the intention of hurting us. Pulawiczus came first and demanded my documents. As if his role was to scrutinize me, he reviewed my papers and pushed aside the *Szaulists* who demanded to see them as well. To mislead any officers, I had given Masza a basket with eggs and bacon in it. But the subterfuge didn't work; the two officers were determined to stop us."

"I thought Pulawiczus knew the Lithuanian chief of the station?" I interceded.

"I do not think so, but Pulawiczus reasoned with the officers and offered to escort me to the city of Utyan, you know, Utena, to hand me over to the authorities there."

"Was Masza with you at all times?"

"Yes, she was very well behaved. She didn't speak a word, as I had asked her to. However, while they were questioning me and deciding what to do with me, one of the uniformed men approached Maszinka, or Marisha as I baptized her temporarily. My heart dropped when he asked her in Yiddish: '*Meidele, farshteist Yiddish?*

Little girl, do you speak Yiddish?' Falling directly into the trap of the *Szaulist*, Masza, having understood the question, answered in perfect German, 'Nein.' Miraculously, the train was already in motion. I pulled her hand and jumped onto the train. From the platform, the *Szaulist* shouted that the girl was Jewish. Commandant Pulawiczus saw what was happening and was quick to board the train as well. People looked at us suspiciously, but no one betrayed us. Pulawiczus disembarked the train a few stops later and left us to face our destiny. You can imagine that I was very scared."

"What luck, I'm glad you arrived well!" I exclaimed, prematurely deducing that this was the only mishap.

"Not so fast, Szura. On our way, I spoke to a Polish man who agreed to rent a carriage in Vilna to travel from the Švenčionys station to here. Traveling with someone who wasn't Jewish would help us go unnoticed, so I convinced him that, since I had a small daughter, it was safer for him to travel with us. It was very early when we left. We arrived at the Pospieszkach-Antokol bridge at around eight o'clock in the evening, ready to cross the river. And that's when the authorities stopped us again. One of the officers took my documents. He sensed that something was amiss. He threatened to send me to the Ukiszki jail. As you know, no one comes out alive from that place. He pushed me aside and tied my hands while I begged him to let me free, telling him that my daughter Marisha was in the carriage."

Sioma was still very agitated while he recounted the rest of the story of how Masza saved his life. Masza got out of the cart and approached the officer. In perfect Polish, she said, 'Dear sir, it is very late, and I am very tired and hungry, I want to eat and go to sleep. Please release my *tatu's!*' I think she touched his heart. The officer, feeling some kind of compassion, threw the papers to the floor and muttered under his breath, 'Go to hell, I never want to see you again!'"

I was so relieved that in the end, Sioma and Masza had arrived safely. We hugged each other tightly, though no caress was enough to show the relief I felt in being reunited with my family.

We stayed in Vilna for the time being. The Germans occupied the city shortly after, on June 24, 1941. They placed signs throughout the city announcing the new Nazi laws. The authorities imposed irrational prohibitions and mandates on the Jews, enforcing nightly curfews, forbidding sites, and even deeming sidewalks off-limits for Jews—they were now reserved only for "first-class citizens." On top of all that, they also ordered Jews to pay the Germans a tax of five million marks in gold and jewelry.

We believed that by cooperating with jewels and money, we still had a chance to survive. We were deluded. It would not have mattered if we had collected a mountain of diamonds and rubies; the Germans of the Third Reich were insatiable. The oppressive Nazi flag, decorated with the swastika, now fluttered on the façade of the Vilna cathedral; the *zloty* was replaced by the Deutsche mark, and our fate—life or death—hung at their whim.

***

The news ran from mouth to mouth. A Jew that came from Nemenčinė told us about the misfortunes that took place in my father's village. He said that the Lithuanians in Nemenčinė, proud to wear the white bands on their arms, aligned themselves fully with the Nazis and acted as faithful collaborators. The Jews were forced to dance in front of the synagogue while the *Szaulists* plundered the compound. The ones who did not dance were harshly whipped. The Lithuanians made a pile with the sacred scrolls of the Torah and prayer books and burned everything in a pyre.

"To witness the shame the men felt in front of their women and children—it was unreal, almost sadistic. All dancing, naked, trying to cover themselves while crying from embarrassment and fear," the man remembered anxiously. "The tragic incident took an infernal tone, as the agitators, in a fiery frenzy, uncontrollably beat the Jews with their batons until they stopped dancing their last dance. There are no words that can express the horrific scene ...."

"How did you manage to see everything? Where were you at the time?" I interrupted, on the edge of a nervous breakdown.

"I was hiding, watching from the sidelines. I saw them being forced to take their clothes off. The *Szaulists* kept feeding the fire with the removed garments. All naked, moving, never stopping, the Nemenčinė Jews, including my whole family ..." at that point, his voice broke in an agonizing cry, "... became actors in a horror show. The Christians who were not involved in the massacre just watched.

They became accomplices. No one raised their voice in objection. Entranced by the hatred of that macabre theater scene, they witnessed the denigration of the Jews of Nemenčinė, forced to participate in a despicable new rite."

"They killed them all?" my husband inquired.

"Everybody was moving around the pyre with their heads down. Showing their flesh, feeling terror and humiliation, while trying, in vain, to dodge the attacks. Those who had not been beaten to death were forced toward the woods. In a disorganized row, every Jew from the town—men, women, and children—walked deeper into the forest. The mothers squeezed their infants, fusing into each other, the fathers struggled not to let go of the hands of their kids, and the older people shook as they struggled to walk. A young man tried to escape, but he was shot instantly. I tried to think of a way to help them, but I didn't know how." Interrupting his own speech, the Nemenčinė native fell silent for a moment. Sobbing, he then continued slowly, "The *Szaulists* forced them to hurry until they reached the woodlands. I followed the death parade with my gaze until I could no longer see them. Then I sneaked out from behind the church wall where I was hiding. As I ran away, I heard shots in the distance; their screams still ring in my ear. They're all dead ... I'm alone in this world."

Sioma hugged him, trying to comfort him. It was a tragedy—so much vile, so much irrational and evil wickedness—it was unbelievable.

"Do you know if Shmuel Bernstein, the village pharmacist,

was among them?" I asked in a whisper.

The man looked down, confirming with a movement of his head. "Dr. Shmuel was there; I recognized him by his height. I vaguely remember his hard countenance, his troubled face turning constantly; he seemed to be looking for something or someone."

"Were his daughter and his wife with him?"

"I do not know. There were a lot of people, I cannot say for sure, forgive me ...." He politely said his goodbyes and left.

I can't believe what is going on. I recognize the faces of many of those who are beating us, but I do not understand. They were our neighbors, I treated them in the pharmacy, we would talk to each other amicably on the street. What the hell happened to them? Where does their hatred come from? They stare at me. I know him, I gave this man medicine for his stomach ailments, and for this other one, I prescribed a remedy for his skin. That lady who is watching in silence, I recommended valerian for her nerves. I remember that she didn't have money to pay me, so I accepted a hen she offered. Someone is shouting my name telling me that I can be saved, he waves at me, but it is too late. I am surrounded by my people, Jews like me. The forest shelters us, the *Szaulists'* blows break our bones, the bullets clatter around me. Where is Tanya and Esfir? Where is Szura and my grandchild Masza? Ah, what a fortune! From the corner of my eye, I see Esfir running to the other side. I hope she is with Tanya, but I don't see her. Run, save yourselves! Save yourselves! They beat me up, I can feel the blows, I see their anger and don't understand. Nothing hurts anymore.

SHURA

We didn't have a body to mourn ... I couldn't even say a proper *Kaddish* for my father.

***

We received a letter from my mother-in-law urging us to return. The officers who had taken the brewery were requiring that the Pupko brothers come back to take charge of the production. We debated for a few minutes whether to return or not, but by the afternoon we were in a horse-drawn carriage heading toward Lida.

Leaving the city of Vilna was no easy task. There were many checkpoints along the metropolis where we would have to provide our non-existent travel permit. *Chapuni*, Nazis, *Szaulists*, White Poles, Russian Bolsheviks—they were all against us just for being Jewish.

We managed to get to the outskirts of the city by sneaking through the less traveled streets—alternate roads that we knew were barely watched by the German army. It was a longer winding route, but it was safer. We encountered military convoys of beardless young soldiers marching on the roads. I wished to get home with no mishaps. We were drifting, looking for freedom, trying to break the padlock of history. Destiny, now run by the poorest and most malevolent instinct of the human being, seemed inescapable.

By nightfall we arrived at Ponyevezh, a town just outside of Lida, where we had once rented a house during a summer. We were only a few kilometers from the city, but we decided to stay in the small town overnight, as it was much safer to travel back to the brewery during daylight.

Chapter Eight: 1941-1943

We arrived at the brewery on August 23, two months after the German army had marched victoriously through the streets of Lida, expelling the Soviets. The Wehrmacht, the German armed force, had taken possession of the area. They had placed the main offices of the regional commander at the *gymnasium* and converted the Great Synagogue into an arsenal. By then the Nazi flag waved on all the buildings across the city.

A German guard opened the door to the brewery's patio. Rachil rushed to meet us and lifted Masza lovingly. The Nazis had declared "Temporary Laws," seizing all the properties that had belonged to the Jews. By decree, our house and the brewery had become theirs overnight. The Nazis had moved the family into a small cellar behind the water tank, which would now also become our living quarters.

"From now on," the soldier said, "you will follow the orders of

SS Engineer Lochbhiler."

Rachil filled us in, explaining that the Nazis had appointed a committee with members of the Jewish community "to watch over the best interests of the Jews of Lida." The Judenrat, as it was coined, consisted of fourteen people: the appointed leader was the teacher Kalman Lichtman. His first task had been to recruit men to work on the city's outskirts. In the following days, the work was also extended to women. More and more people, or rather more Jews, were required to serve the Nazis. We quickly became their slaves and lost all our rights.

"We have been lucky to remain in the brewery," said my mother-in-law. "We have not been required for other jobs, but nothing is certain—the situation changes constantly. The Judenrat designates more people every day. They follow what the Nazis demand of them: Jews to wash the sidewalks, brush the stones on the street, work on the train tracks, or any other denigrating task they can think of. I'm hoping we can all remain working within the brewery."

Mitzia had arrived a few days earlier. When he came to greet us, he told us what he had heard people say on the way to Lida. His fear resonated through his rushed words: "I met some peasants on the road who told me they saw a ... a ... wounded woman on the path from Ponary to Vilna. They stopped to help her, and she informed them of what had happened in the city. The Germans gathered the Jews under the pretext they would be taken to work in a secret place. They were forced to cover their eyes with rags while they walked in a line on the road to Grodno. But they didn't take them to work; the Nazis brought them to the forest in Ponary and shot them all. The woman who recounted this harrowing account had somehow fallen into the death pit without being shot. She survived the massacre hidden by the dead bodies that covered her. She managed to escape at night, taking advantage that the *Szaulists* were drunk on their hatred and alcohol. Wounded, she finally arrived at the Jewish hospital where she reported the crimes. But nobody could do anything."

Mitzia continued: "But it doesn't stop there. Do you remember the construction in the middle of the forest that the Russians started to build in 1940 to store fuel? They never finished it and left huge holes in the ground. Since the Germans entered the city, that abandoned foundation has become a massive tomb. Week after week, the *Szaulists* drive trucks overloaded with Jews to the site. The Jews are pushed out of the vehicles and forced to walk to the edge of the ditches. In fear, hunched over by the constant blows, they are shot one by one and fall into the hollow area. In a cascade of inertia, gravity attracts the bodies to the void, rapidly filling the space."

Mitzia inhaled heavily before he continued. We listened attentively, becoming more frightened by the minute. Sioma and I looked at each other impatiently, not fully comprehending what we were hearing. We wondered if by not acknowledging what was happening around us, we could control it somehow or at least keep those atrocities from happening to us.

"From what I was able to understand," said Mitzia, "after each massacre, the people who live around Ponary come to take the clothes off the dead and steal anything they can find from the bodies to sell in the market. Those scavengers make a profit from everything. They are vultures taking advantage of the Jewish misfortune. A pair of boots are sold at one hundred and twenty rubles, and stockings in good condition can reach a good price. People have lost any sense of humanity."

Sioma interceded: "We know that the Nazis are the brains behind these horrors. They have cunningly managed to find useful fools who work for them. Those *Szaulists* are Lithuanian braggarts who don't mind doing the Germans' dirty work."

"It's true, the Lithuanians are wearing the furs they steal, they don't care if they are a dead woman's clothes. They are the first in line to rob, they take rings and any gold objects stained with blood … the blood that they have spilled with their hatred and violence. Then they drink to celebrate or to forget the crimes they've committed. I have informed the Jewish community in Vilna of what is happening in Ponary. They already know through other witnesses. They don't know how many people are dead. They don't have the power to do anything. The problem is that the German government is colluded, and they enjoy our hardship."

We were stunned, standing before an abyss …. I had no time or energy to cry; I couldn't even try to find my relatives. I still had hopes that my sister Tanya would appear in our doorway at any moment. It was the end of August 1941. I could feel the lack of oxygen in my lungs; the asphyxiating atmosphere emanated from every crevasse of the walls, even from the stinking sewers of the city.

We seldom received any news at the brewery. The rumors we managed to hear were disturbing. In our own city, the situation worsened. A few days after the German occupation of Lida, the Jewish intellectuals and leaders were forced to gather in the main square where the market was usually set. Doctors, lawyers, teachers, rabbis, and even the *shochetim*, the butchers, were there. About two hundred prominent people in the community were pushed together into the open space. They were dictated to walk through Suwlaska Street, in front of the brewery, then into the edge of the forest, where they were shot. For more than an hour, the people in the nearby town of Stoniewicze heard the shots and the cries of the victims but did nothing about it.

***

Our house was occupied by German officers. It made me sick imagining them sleeping on my sheets, eating at our table, licking my silverware. They allowed us to get some things and take them to our assigned dwelling.

We settled in a corner of the storage area, and soon enough, we were called through a loudspeaker to meet in the brewery yard. Engineer Joachim Lochbhiler introduced himself. The tall and husky Nazi officer would be overseeing the running of the brewery and supervising the production. Lochbhiler made sure we met his assistant Herman Fischer, a medium-statured man with a small mustache barely drawn above his upper lip. While Lochbhiler spoke, Officer Fischer was busy looking down at his black notebook. He wrote down each of our names and assigned tasks for each of us to work in the brewery.

The engineer was educated, but he was still a usurper, a stranger who had taken over our house and our livelihood—ruthlessly ruling over us. I was tasked with cleaning the rooms, scrubbing the lavatories, and disinfecting the toilets. Roza, my sister-in-law, would have to cook for the Nazi officials who came to visit and, of course, clean the kitchen. Sioma became the storage keeper and also supervised the extraction of malt from the barley. The other members of the family were ordered to work in the various stages of the brewing process, such as fermentation, storage of grains, and processing hops.

Additional people were brought in to work at the brewery and forced to share the space with us. That very first night, curled into a fetal position, I dreamt of my father. I felt myself dying in slow motion. A vicious fire embraced me—a similar inferno to the one that had been ignited during the Spanish Inquisition, the same bonfire that had consumed the Torah scrolls at the synagogue of Nemenčinė, devouring our past and our traditions. My nightmare recreated the image of the Jews forced to dance in the town square, harassed by the *Szaulists'* clubs and by the high-caliber guns of the Nazis. They danced around the flames as our sacred books burned.

Dragged by tenebrous winds, they moved in circles. Sullied and abused, they were pushed toward the forest to meet their end. We lived a nightmare—like a Chaïm Soutine painting where the trees are crooked and the characters' faces are deformed. The Jews were puppets in this Dance of Death; their oblique eyes and their disproportionate ears haunted me ... I woke up sweating. Overwhelmed and feeling lost, I focused on the steady rhythm of the breaths of the strangers sleeping nearby. I tried to convince myself that our situation was not as bad as my dream.

***

New rules were enforced each day. One day's mandate was that every Jew must stitch a yellow patch on their shirts. The instructions were very specific: a ten-by-twenty-centimeter rectangle with a circle and a "J" drawn in the center to distinguish us as Jews. Rachil sewed the badges onto our clothes. But the order changed rapidly and constantly. Soon after, we were forced to sew instead a star of David, the *Judenstern*—yellow as the sun, standing out, imperturbable on our sleeves. Rachil went right back to work, unstitching the old fabric applications one by one before threading in the new patches. After a few days, the engineer allowed us to not use the yellow star, deeming it unnecessary since we would no longer be leaving the brewery premises. We were protagonists of the most absurd spectacle: first being the respectful owners of a thriving industry, then becoming slaves. I had to suffer the harassment of our jailer, who threatened us with punishments like licking the corners of the toilets to make them shine.

Soon the daily work became routine, never pleasant but consistent. They fed us a miniscule food portion: a cooked potato a day and a hundred and twenty-five grams of bread. It was an exact ratio, not one gram more. Their unkindness was a constant reminder. Remembering the past was futile, and thinking about what we'd had before was torment. We had to focus on our survival. We were still alive.

It was the end of November 1941 when an announcement came through the loudspeaker: all of us Jews had to pack our things. We would be relocated and were only allowed to carry one bag per person. Could one fit an entire life in a suitcase? I was debating what to bring. What was essential? I packed toiletries, photographs, some clothes, a warm coat, and the *Likutei Mizmorim*—the prayer book that my grandfather had given me.

"Only fifty pounds," repeated the loud voice, "take only the most needed items."

What is indispensable? Indispensable for what? I wondered. We went down to the brewery yard, as we were told, with the *luvianka* in hand. We were ready to leave when Engineer Joachim Lochbhiler ran to meet us, intercepting our path.

"Wait, you must not go with the rest, I need you to work at the brewery."

Sioma turned to look at me with a hopeful expression. We had been awarded another day to live at the brewery! The rest of the Jews were crammed into a segregated and guarded area of the city. They used wire and timber to close it off. Later, it would be called the ghetto.

Thousands of Jews would end up living in the designated neighborhood, sharing latrines and breadcrumbs. The Nirvana cinema on Lidska Street was converted into a communal kitchen. The Germans divided the space with mathematical precision by fitting the maximum number of inhabitants inside the smallest possible rooms.

The Jews couldn't roam freely; they were forced to stay inside the designated zone. Anything that was left in their homes, including furniture, paintings, souvenirs, ornaments, clothes, or even the smallest kitchen utensils, was confiscated.

We could see what was happening from the window of the brewery tower. From there, I caught a glimpse of the barbed wire fences that surrounded the ghetto on Postowska Street. The guards with their dogs lurked, watching the prisoners' every step, effectively preventing any attempts to flee. If anyone tried to separate from the herd, they were beaten with the rifle butt; if they tried to escape, their days swiftly ended with an instant shot.

The evacuation from the city, or *aussiedlung,* as the Nazis called it, was a "massive success." In just one day, all the Jews of Lida, including those living on the outskirts of town, were relocated to the ghetto and made to live inside packed, monitored living spaces. According to the German government, the casualties were minimal.

Sioma and Mitzia presented themselves at Lochbhiler's office. My husband persuaded him to bring in more people—more workers, more hands—more Jews who could be saved from the atrocities of the ghetto. They would supervise the hydraulic pipes of the factory. The whole system had to be properly maintained during the winter to prevent ducts from freezing. Lochbhiler would have to ask the *kommissar* for permission, but it was worth the effort.

It was agreed that the brewery would take in an additional forty-two people to work and live with us. The brewery was a sealed vessel, where we were starved, mistreated, and had no freedom, but anything was better than being in the ghetto. We helped choose who would come to the plant to work. In the lot, there were former employees, our acquaintances, and many women who had lost their husbands to the army during the Soviet Occupation. Their gloomy faces showed their uncertainty, not knowing if their husbands had died or were still fighting at the front.

We made room for the newcomers in the cellar, our shared living space. The group included our friend Mr. Kutchinsky and his family; and the former *buchalter*, the accountant of the brewery, Leibl Stolowitsky, and his family.

***

At the very top of the brewery tower was a large and impressive number: 1876. This was the year the brewery was founded. Every time I'd gaze at it, I was reminded of the mark the Pupko family had made in this city and encouraged to go on living. I would dream about those glory days when the czar had granted Nosel, Sioma's grandfather, permission to produce beer. Life was a wheel of fortune; I had to believe that better times would come. For now, we were slaves in our own cages.

They forced us to perform useless, insulting jobs only to make fun of us, to tire us out, and to keep us constantly moving. We were made to carry stones from one place of the yard to the other without any purpose, take empty boxes to the factory gate, and haul sacks of sand to the sawmill. We were just like Sisyphus, pushing a boulder uphill knowing that the stone would always roll back down to the bottom, where we would start again. We were building nothingness under the most perverse hatred.

I had to scrub the floors and the walls of the cellar, but no matter how hard I cleaned, everything was still dirty. The grooves absorbed the grime, and I struggled to go over every crevice between the tiles. Masza would sit nearby and watch me mop the floors. She sometimes coughed without relief. From time to time, I would stop my chores to hug her and try to ease her pain, but the phlegm lingered in her lungs. One night, while everyone was trying to sleep, one of our bed neighbors screamed in alarm: "The girl has *koklush*, that whooping cough will infect us all! Take her out to the patio to sleep."

What I first considered an insult later seemed reasonable. The nights were not yet cold, the air outside was pure, and she might benefit from it. Sioma installed a small bed in the courtyard for Maszinka, where I could watch her from my window. Every night, I would gently pat her back, intending to alleviate her agitated breathing. Her chest convulsed as she coughed through the sleepless nights.

Upon seeing the cradle in the yard, Engineer Lochbhiler offered me a jug with a thick whitish liquid, apparently milk.

"Frau Szura," he said politely, "it's mare's milk, and it is known to cure whooping cough. Give her a little bit every night, you will see that she sleeps better."

I thanked him for his kindness, but I distrusted him. *I'm a Jew, why should he help me?* I could not understand why he would be different. Through the next three weeks, Engineer Lochbhiler brought mare's milk daily until Maszinka's cough subsided.

***

Beer production was necessary: beer for the German soldiers to drink themselves senseless and forget about their crimes, beer to mitigate hunger, beer in exchange for eggs or vegetables, beer for a glass of milk or a piece of cheese. But food was scarce. The dulled skin of my chest reveled every single section of my vertebrae. The bones drew their exact shape behind my thin thighs. I weighed less than forty-nine kilos. Sioma and I shared our servings with Maszinka, and she, with her few years, already understood the situation. She barely bit into her ration, giving us what was left on her plate. We would refuse, of course, and she would slowly eat the little that was left.

The women whose husbands had been forced to join the Bolshevik army longed for someone to trust. Some of them, like Sula, with a plump face and bright eyes, trapped and alone, accepted the compliments of the officers when they visited the brewery. Very soon, trying to survive, she surrendered to the pleasures of the flesh and gave her body to them. Seeking to attract the best bidder to her bed, she only wanted a better dinner, probably an extra blanket or a larger piece of bread.

Riva, on the other hand, still believed that her husband was alive on the Russian front but was seduced by Engineer Lochbhiler. She thought that under his protection she could live more comfortably in our imprisonment. Lochbhiler not only shared his attention in bed but also his food and the sweets that he occasionally received from home. Little did she know that her fate would still be to die under the Zyklon B. Her body would be discarded in the crematory furnaces of Majdanek. But at least at that time, her life was a little bit less miserable than the rest of ours.

No one judged those acts of infidelity; we were more concerned about our daily tasks and the food we got each day. We weighed the immediate results of any act. The equation was easy to understand: in exchange for libidinous games, you could receive a double portion of bread or the leftovers of a cake eaten the previous night by Nazi officials. Basic necessities were more important than loyalty to a husband who had probably died in a ditch.

***

The windows dawned with frost, announcing the cruel winter of Belarus. The sunset, at such early hours, began to depress me even more than before. I closed my eyes for long periods, trying to avoid noticing what was happening around me. An occasional shot in the near distance would disturb my senses, a scream in the night accelerated my bloodstream, and a silenced groan disrupted my nerves. But dawn came every day, the sun breaking the silence. The work continued in the brewery under the unconditional auspices of the Nazis' cruelty.

The engineer assigned me more tasks. I would now also be cleaning the brewery laboratory and other rooms around the factory. The skin on my hands, before smooth and silky, became as rough and hard as untreated leather. My heart also hardened; every day the freedom we longed for seemed more and more distant.

A factory technician put together a clandestine shortwave radio. Every afternoon after work, a small group of us met secretly to listen to the news from London and Moscow. It was a glimpse of extramural life—a window that allowed us to peek into the reality behind the myth of the German victory. Thus, we learned that Soviet guerrilla divisions were fighting in the distant mountains of Altai. Fooled, we dreamed about a German defeat. We wished that, like Napoleon, the Nazis would succumb to the harsh Russian winter. The radio was kept a secret. Every night, Michash Stolowitsky, the son of the former brewery accountant and electrician's assistant, disarmed it and hid it.

When the work became unbearable, we tried to focus on positive thoughts. Continuous nightmares clouded our minds, so much so that closing our eyes was sometimes a torment on its own. On the nights when we couldn't sleep, we wished for liberation. It was better to take an illusory optimism as our anchor.

The nights were appeased by the kerosene lamp that I had been allowed to take from our house. Engineer Lochbhiler had also let me pick up some books to read. Regardless of my roommates and without concern that there was a shortage of fuel, I spent the long hours of the night reading, imagining other worlds, placing myself in remote times, or thinking about imaginary characters described by Mickiewicz and Bialik. I recited from memory the Hebrew songs from my childhood and hummed their melodies. When I was able to sleep, my slumber would give me little peace, and my grandfather appeared. I would sit on his lap and stroke his long white beard.

***

Bella Stolowitsky, the *buchalter's* daughter, went out every morning from the brewery to the ghetto on the opposite side of the river. She would head over to the Judenrat so she could be assigned some work. Likewise, in the opposite direction, some of our friends left the ghetto to come to work at the brewery. Bella complained to her mother, explaining how scared she was every time she left the brewery by herself and came upon a Nazi soldier. Some days she worked on the train tracks, carrying coal back and forth all day long. Other days she'd wash the sidewalks of the market square or carry heavy sacks of sand. She would witness the constant assassinations; people were murdered at random for a minute offense or for no reason at all. If they didn't work fast enough, gasped or grumbled, or dropped the packages they were carrying, the Nazis' rifles reacted immediately. Every minute was a feat of survival.

Bella's mother begged Engineer Lochbhiler to get her a job inside the brewery. The days passed, but nothing changed. Bella became desperate. She had been assigned to cut bushes in a mountain house taken by the *Gebietskommischer* Hermann Hanenberg, the commissioner of the area. She heard laughter and cries of pleasure on the other side of the fence and discovered Hanenberg with some women naked in the pool. His sadistic fame preceded him. Bella could be punished without cause, but even more so for peeking behind the shrubs. She became afraid to leave the brewery again and asked Lochbhiler to help her out. The engineer took pity on her and got her a job in the brewery lab to evaluate the taste of beer and the quantity of alcohol in it.

Soon after she took the job, she discovered a couple covertly making liquor at the lab. In exchange for vodka, eggs, and sugar to produce the sweet drink, Bella was sworn to secrecy— receiving an occasional lump of sugar as payment for becoming their accomplice by association.

***

The days passed slowly. Masza followed me while I scrubbed the tiles and cleaned the rooms. She sat in the corner, watching me in silence. Roza cooked every day, preparing morsels and delicacies for the Nazi commanders, while Franya washed the clothes of the SS officers in the gendarmerie. Hours went by bleaching the mold stains on the walls, mopping off the greenish liquids that dripped under the pipes, and vigorously cleaning any trace of Nazi boots off the floor .... One more day.

We heard that some of the Jews who had fled to the woods had returned to the ghetto. They couldn't tolerate the harsh conditions in the forest. We had learned this from a seventeen-year-old boy whom we sheltered one evening. He had secretly entered the brewery through a grille on the street near the river and stayed the night in the storeroom.

"I am part of a group of about fifty young men and women who have provisionally camped in the *puszcza*, the densest area of the forest. We couldn't stay locked up in the ghetto and do nothing! The Nazis are capable of anything! That is why we decided to flee. We prefer to live in the wild where we can be free and fight for our lives rather than live in the confinement and cruelty that the Nazis impose on us. We will fight with all our might."

"And why did you come back?" Mitzia asked.

"We need supplies: drugs, blankets, shoes, and food. I will try to enter the ghetto to grab all this, and then I will return to the forest with my comrades. The Bielski brothers, from the village of

Stankiewiczi, organized our small group. Tevie is the oldest and the most capable; we live under his authority. We aim not only to survive but to execute strategies to fight and defend ourselves."

We gave him something to eat, and then he slept for a few hours. Before dawn, he was gone. His shadow was scarcely drawn on the wall of the brewery courtyard. He scurried along the riverbank, entered the ghetto, and then returned that same night to the brewery.

"I do not understand the logic," he said before leaving for the forest, "my relatives refuse to leave the ghetto. They say that the Nazis can't do without them, thinking that their work is indispensable for the Third Reich. Some of them manufacture shoes for the army while others work at the military hospital. They showed me their official papers and their work permits where their itinerary is recorded: day, hour, minute, and second when they leave the ghetto and return. They are under the illusion that as long as they are productive, they will be protected. Why can't they see beyond their noses?"

"You see," said Rachil, "it is dangerous for everyone to leave. If some escape, we will all be punished. Here in the brewery, and your family in the ghetto, we have a ration of food, however meager, we have a bed, even if it is full of lice and fleas. In the forest on the other hand, what can one live on? You are young and ready to fight. We neither have weapons nor do we know how to combat. We are old; we are not suited to take that kind of risk. But don't worry, your family will be fine."

"I don't think so!" he snapped in disagreement. "Many rumors are circulating about how the Nazis intend to murder all Jews, and since they have no scruples, I think they can do it without thinking twice. I have begged my parents to escape with me, but they can't be convinced. I'm afraid I will never see them again."

He said goodbye politely and disappeared into the land of wolves. Every night we saw new shadows go out of the ghetto through the brewery patio and vanish into the woods seeking the camp of the Bielski brothers. There they lived covered by mud and bushes, collecting wild berries and mushrooms to feed themselves. They were like goblins—using the brewery as a bridge between the forest and the ghetto. They hid between Suwalska and Postowska Street and then ran away, without being seen, toward the pine and birch forest.

We didn't believe that fleeing into the rough vegetation—the unknown—was our best option. We saw it as jumping into the void. We were not rebel fighters; we were not communists or idealists. We differed from the revolutionary ideas in vogue and never considered joining the brigades of Russian partisans. We were aware of groups attacking German trains and were informed about their every movement, but joining them wasn't for us.

***

I focused all my concentration and energy on cleaning the rooms I was assigned to in the brewery. The tiled floor in the machine room was the most difficult; the vapors dampened the slabs, making it difficult to remove the layer of fungus that accumulated and caused the pavement to be slippery and unsafe for the workers. I made sure to scrape every inch.

As I was kneeling, I discovered a dark circle on the floor. I passed the cloth over and over again to try to scrub it out. The stain remained stuck to the tiles. I washed and scrubbed, but the soil persisted. I used my fingernail to scratch it and tried to use a spoon, rubbing it desperately in vain. My frenzied anguish was eating me up. I was alienated. I did not realize that someone was watching me. Suddenly, I felt Engineer Lochbhiler's hand on mine. I was startled at the intimate gesture. As he helped me stand, I sensed his lustful look. Without losing my common sense and my dignity, I withdrew immediately, exiting the room—fearing any harmful consequence.

From then on, I tried to avoid Engineer Lochbhiler whenever I could. One of those summer nights, when the heat wouldn't let me sleep, I went for a walk. I passed the courtyard and reached the edge of the river, near the *tartak* where the wood was cut and prepared for the railway sleepers. It smelled like freshly cut logs. The wood shavings on the floor looked so inviting, I just wanted to lie on them. As I was thinking of our situation—prisoners inside what used to be ours—a hoarse voice frightened me:

"What are you doing here?" It was Lochbhiler.

"I came to get some fresh air."

"It's dangerous for a woman alone …" he said suggestively.

Maybe he had seen me leave the warehouse and had followed

me here. He had been kind to me and my family in the past, but I had sensed that he had other interests.

"You're right," I said in alarm.

Trying to escape the compromising and awkward situation, I tried to get out of the *tartak,* but the engineer got in my way. Aware of my nervousness, he stepped aside and let me out. Sweating, I reached our room where Sioma snored, huddling our little Masza. Luckily, our roommates slept, too, and no one had noticed my absence. I was safe from Lochbhiler's advances for now. He appeared to be a good man, I supposed since he didn't want to force me. But that night, my heart beat incessantly; I couldn't fall back to sleep.

***

The death toll in the ghetto continued to rise as 1942 began. People suffered and died for various reasons—typhoid, lack of hygiene, malnutrition, and infections—but at the end, the suffering and deaths were all due to one thing: an unjust and inhumane confinement exacerbated by the endless abuse of their oppressors. The *Chevre Kadisha* did not rest; they removed the bodies from the streets while the living tried to maintain their routines. There were some signs of joy like songs and music and the occasional smile. Efforts were made to be optimistic, to continue with everyday life, to be creative, and to go on. We prayed and hoped that the war would be over soon.

Sioma was given permission from the engineer to visit the ghetto. He would wear his star on the lapel of his coat to be easily identified as a Jew. Carrying the access papers that Lochbhiler provided, he was able to smuggle in tobacco, medicines, and beer. Inside the ghetto, he found his friends playing cards. He listened to their complaints: there was not enough food, they slept in small, crowded rooms, they quarreled among the families, and illness was rampant. They told him of all the deaths and murders; they cried about the relentless mistreatment and forced labor. They tried to console themselves with the delusion that they were necessary and indispensable to the Germans. They reasoned, if not them, who would work for the Nazis?

Absurd jobs were given to the Jews, like chasing rabbits during a Nazi hunting outing. Enjoying an easy target, the prisoners were to facilitate accurate shots for their jailers. The Nazis scoffed at the Jews as they ran restlessly behind the hares. Terrified, the Jews obeyed the Germans' orders, fearing wounding lashes, hurtful blows with sticks, or shots of grace.

Sioma returned crestfallen. He wanted to help his friends, and so he came up with an idea to recruit more workers: "Engineer Lochbhiler, there is a lot of work here at the brewery. We need manpower. It would be beneficial to employ ten more people from the ghetto. And it won't cost a penny to the Reich."

"Do you think it is necessary?"

"Definitely." Sioma procured a list of names for the engineer and continued: "If we employ these people, we will have better performance in the brewery."

Lochbhiler knew no one was needed at the brewery, but he consented to help. A few days later, the engineer called Sioma to his office, the same room that had once belonged to Sioma's father and older brother.

"I have the official documents with the names of the people on your list. Leopold Windisch, the regional *kommissar*, has already signed them. Bring the new brewery workers as soon as possible, before somebody gives a counter-order."

Those ten chosen left the ghetto to come work at the brewery. Among them were our friends Chaim Weksler and Shlomo Brody. Sioma hugged them and welcomed them to our humble abode.

***

On Sunday, March 1, 1942, a group of Belarussians from Lida abruptly entered the brewery. Beating us with clubs, they corralled us into the courtyard. The violence was beyond any reason. With no mercy, they hit my mother-in-law from behind, and she fell to the ground.

Lochbhiler demanded an explanation from them. They had orders to take us with them; we had to serve as witnesses for "something." They hauled us out of the brewery to the empty place where the market used to be. The Jews of the ghetto were also dragged there. The Nazi flag waved over the old *gymnasium*. Leopold Windisch, the local *kommissar*, was strutting as a proud leader. One by one, we saw people we knew killed in front of our eyes. We were forced to watch the murder of Kalman Lichtman, the professor who had been appointed head of the Judenrat. He was shot in cold blood for helping people get work papers. Others, who were accused of having falsified documents, were killed to teach the rest of us a lesson. Some of our people were commissioned to retrieve the corpses and clean the newly spilled blood from the floor. We returned to the brewery with devastated spirits, still smelling the horror of what gunpowder and hatred could do.

***

Windisch, the *kommissar*, came to the brewery regularly to supervise the production. We would tremble at his presence. He would insult us and order us to serve him promptly, denigrating us with grunts and shouts. We were his prisoners, his servile slaves.

We contented ourselves thinking that our situation was better than others—at least we could eat the meager leftovers left by the *kommissar*. Nevertheless, we were at the point of starvation. My body was exhausted. I was very thin, and I felt my health declining. Every movement was a struggle, but I had to preserve my energy for work—to clean and scrub without rest or payment, as dictated by the Nazis. I couldn't slack. I had to work to survive.

I stopped menstruating.

***

I would wake up in the middle of the night with severe asthma attacks, my lungs assaulting me. Without oxygen and soaked in sweat, my gaze would search for Sioma. He would stroke my hair while I tried to breathe. His caresses helped me alienate the anguish I felt. I consoled myself that we had Masza with us, that the three of us were alive. What else could we ask for?

Could we survive? Could we continue swallowing their dirt forever? We had become accustomed to everything: the smaller portions of food, the deaths, the ill-treatment, and the absurd jobs. When there was the smallest difference in our routine, we didn't know how to handle it. A puff could demolish our fragile souls. Routine would take over, and order prevailed at the end. We often had news from the ghetto: people lived in crowded, filthy spaces, suffered hunger, and fell ill due to typhoid and fevers. Death was an epidemic.

We lived in constant danger. The engineer often tried to find me alone. As much as I tried to avoid being on my own, I often found myself cleaning empty rooms. Whenever possible, I would ask Sioma to accompany me.

One day, just as I was about to wash the windows in the laboratory, I felt a presence behind me. It was Lochbhiler. He approached me from behind, took a newspaper, and delicately showed me how paper was more absorbent and worked better to dry glass than the cloth I was using. I became tense, and he realized that. My nervousness made him take two steps back. When he left,

I took a deep breath. I was never sure if I could trust the engineer, but deep down, I knew he was a good man and would never force me into doing anything I did not want to.

***

None of the dogmas we had kept sacred had any sustenance. Prayer was not effective, as we had presumed—marriage ceased to be the strength of a couple, *kashrut* did not save us from malnutrition, and sacralizing *Shabbat* did not guarantee our lives under the Nazis— but my mother-in-law still kept certain rules of *kashrut*, refusing to eat the chicken we'd get clandestinely in exchange for yeast or beer. It was the only safeguard against evil left for her, a residue of freedom and autonomy in front of the rifles that threatened to rip us from life. She preferred to die of hunger by her own choice. No one dared to argue with her, not even her children.

Each person did what they could to survive. Decisions were made individually, and any approach was accepted as valid and respected without conditions or judgments. If Riva wanted to share her bed with Lochbhiler in order to get some candy, so be it. If Sula wanted to lick the boots of the sadist Windisch, none of us would intervene. When my brother-in-law Misha was selected to be the barber of the *kommissar* and obtained woolen blankets for the winter, we understood that he had to take advantage of it.

Sioma, Masza, and I lived bottled up in the now, in the minute, and even in the second, concerned about facing the uncertainty of tomorrow. Nosel, the grandfather of Sioma and founder of the brewery—whom I had never met—was often in my dreams. With his long beard and black cassock, he would smile at me, reassuring me, telling me that tomorrow was going to be better. But the reality was different: we were living in a constant agonizing nightmare.

We knew that Lochbhiler protected us, but our lives hung by a thread. We were in a precarious and fragile situation; we were at the mercy of the whims of a German serviceman, and we followed his every instruction to prevent any possible disagreements or misunderstandings between us, the engineer, and the other officers. There was no freedom, no compassion, no respect for our lives.

Kaletco, a German officer under the command of Windisch, visited the brewery to inspect the production and ensure the Jews were following Engineer Lochbhiler's orders. He was looking for something, but we did not know what. Lochbhiler was nowhere in sight.

The soldiers who had come with Kaletco started to shout aggressively at us to congregate in the courtyard and stand in formation. They began questioning us incessantly: "Where do you live? With whom do you share a room? Who lives in the big house?"

Sioma dared to ask the reason for this new action. The answer he received was a blow to the head with the butt of a rifle followed by several punches to his belly and another few to the face. A tooth flew out of his mouth as if it was a seed. Chaim Weksler attempted to stop the hailstorm of strikes, but a soldier shot Chaim immediately and injured his leg. No one moved. Blood streamed from Chaim's leg, marking a dark red groove on the ground.

Kaletco simply ordered everyone back to their jobs and then exited the brewery as adamantly as he had entered, enjoying his arbitrary manifestation of absolute power. Sioma, broken, morally and physically, massaged his cheek and stomach. Others helped Chaim. We were trembling, as we made our way back to our workplaces without a sound, trying not to cause any more disturbances. One more day ….

***

The lingering scent of fermented grains impregnated Sioma's clothing and body. The pungent odors in the cellar stood in the way of any advances of marital desire, though we still occasionally longed for carnal love, and I would let Sioma embrace me just to be close to him, to feel human. These moments were rare but pointed to the fact that even amongst the most adverse circumstances, we still yearned for each other. We desperately tried to maintain a minimal sense of peace and love to keep us united.

Reason loses its threads in times of war; life is incongruous. Perhaps even Freud wouldn't have understood having moments of passion in hell. In those instances, when my hair brushed against his chest, we felt as one, amalgamated, regardless of the dreadful circumstances we were in. When we made love, I wanted to scream into a frenzy, to run outside naked, to take off the yoke that was drowning me. They were minutes, seconds of feeling free, feeling him inside me; I wanted to roar and cry, to laugh and babble the name of my beloved husband, to appease my inner thoughts ... but I remained silent, repressing the savage lust in me, remembering that we were sharing a room with other people; this brought me back to reality, to the stench of acid, hops, and yeast.

The German guards and the Belarussian police assigned to look after the brewery were suddenly called to the front. We understood that there was a new danger. Lochbhiler devised a plan of self-defense among the workers of the plant. My husband was given a new role as a sentinel, and at least that gave us a momentary freedom of movement inside the factory.

Passover was approaching. We managed to bake *matzeh* in secret to commemorate the holiday with the unleavened bread. On the day of the celebration, we covered the windows of the laboratory with cardboard and organized a *seder*. We recalled the ancient story of the liberation of the Jews from the hands of the Egyptian pharaoh. As we read the *Haggadah*, we followed the prayers and drank *meduz*, a clandestine mead that replaced the traditional wine. The story of Passover transported us back to ancient Egypt: the adventures of Moses and how the Israelites had longed for freedom. There was no need to eat bitter herbs to remind us of our people's slavery in Egypt, as was prescribed by the *seder* book; we had our own pharaoh seated in the pyramids of the Third Reich.

***

On Tuesday, May 5, 1942, the German government ratified a new law demanding that all Jews in Lida hand over anything of value by that Friday. The death penalty was imposed on those who did not comply. We didn't see the advantage or benefit of delivering our valuable belongings. Instead, I placed my ring, three hundred dollars, a pair of gold coins, a diamond necklace, and a few teaspoons of vermeil inside a matchbox. Then I hid the little box near the distillation column.

The situation worsened by Thursday, May 7. Sioma was on duty stationed on the factory roof with a Belarusian electrical engineer. Misha returned from work and gathered us to relay the news. My brother-in-law had encountered an intoxicated and talkative guard who had just returned from a dinner with some German potentates. The guard had heard that something serious was about to happen to all the Jews in the ghetto. "The Nazis have set up two days to seize everything from the Jews. They won't act before stripping us bare," Misha said.

"You're wrong, they could act now. They are capable of anything," Sioma contradicted.

That night, we decided to wake up every Jew who slept in the brewery to weave together a plan. Sioma and I went up to the brewery tower and gazed out into the ghetto. We noticed unusual military movements. A group of Nazis sealed the perimeter, putting in place a wooden fence with barbed wire. Another detachment was busy building a cement wall with broken glass on the top, restricting any access into and out of the area.

By dawn, the ghetto was fully surrounded by the police and SS soldiers. Shootings began as soon as the sun peeked through the horizon. Through the window of our room and the gloom of daybreak, we saw dozens of shadows entering the ghetto. We could hear the shouts of the Jews as they were shoved through the main gate of the ghetto. Stumbling down the street, pushed by the soldiers, they were led to the train station.

We ran to hide in a *maline*, a small refuge that was set up as a secure place. We stayed there until Engineer Lochbhiler came to tell us that the danger had passed.

Everyone was evicted from the ghetto. We named this day the great *Schita*, the great butchery. After that day, there were very few Jews left in the city, including us who remained inside the brewery.

A week later, the Nazis closed the smaller ghettos located on the outskirts of the city and filled the Lida Ghetto once again. Four thousand Jews were transported from Woronowa, Iwje, Radun, Zholudek, and other smaller villages nearby. For some reason, they imprisoned the Jews from Szczuczin in the old prison on Third of May Avenue, separate from the other Jews.

We tried, once again, to resume our routine inside the brewery. Again, we were under the pretense that having work documents would ensure our salvation. Everything was very uncertain; there were illusions in the air. We were eager to look forward, not back.

Always alert, watching from the tower, we observed what was happening behind the fence of the factory. This time, there was some kind of movement taking place in the Jewish cemetery. They were removing the tombstones and desecrating the graves. The slabs, inscribed in Hebrew with the names of the dead, would now serve to modernize the streets. They became building materials; who cared if the ancient tombs remained anonymous? There would be no more Jews. The Messiah would no longer come to resurrect the forgotten bodies.

In addition to what we had witnessed, other atrocities took place across the country. Lochbhiler would later recount what had happened in the ghetto of Vilna: the Nazis had taken captives, mostly children, women, elders, and a few men, to Stoniewicze, where they had prepared large ditches in advance. As they arrived at the site, they ordered the victims to undress and herded them to the edge of the pit, facing their predetermined tombs. In an instant, the burst of machine guns illuminated the scene. It was a monstrous mass murder. Somehow, some survived among the corpses. Realizing their luck, they waited until darkness fell. They rose in silence. Not knowing any better, they went back to Vilna. Like ghosts, they penetrated the ghetto just to avert the others and to sleep amongst Jews locked in a prison. The following day, the Nazis sprinkled chlorine on those who lay dead in that execrable common grave and then covered them with dirt.

***

Gentile peasants, who would sometimes come to exchange their products for beer or any other goods they could obtain, served as news carriers, informing us of the whereabouts and achievements of the partisans, the resistance that was fighting intensely. We knew that groups of guerrillas and paramilitary forces were nesting in the nearby forests. They were fierce fighters who attacked the Germans by surprise, acting at night.

The farmers feared them. They would stampede into their humble houses, demanding food and threatening to kill them if they didn't comply. We were also informed that the Russian resistance troops had organized a successful surprise attack, derailing a train on the outskirts of Lida. With their ingenuity and homemade bombs, they altered the flow of transports carrying armaments and provisions to the German soldiers fighting in the front. For as little havoc caused to the Reich as it seemed, the news gave us hope.

One night, as we winded down from an exhausting day of work, the few lights left on in the brewery all eclipsed at the same time. Total blackness enveloped us. The silence of the factory was disrupted by our cries of astonishment and fear.

Engineer Lochbhiler was calm; he explained that something had happened in the energy terminal and tried to quiet us down, saying there was no reason to be frightened. A few hours later, a military courier advised Lochbhiler that there were suspicions that the blackout had been an act of sabotage. Apparently, the Russian engineer, who operated the electrical station, had cooperated clandestinely with the partisans. He cut the wires before fleeing to the forest with his Soviet comrades. We rejoiced at the magnitude of this feat. After all, we thought we still had a chance to survive in comparison with the people fleeing the ghetto.

Most families were not eager to venture into the dark forest. Russians and Poles hunted down one another, making the whole area very dangerous. For the few Jews who dared to hide between the bushes, mud, and dung, only those who could procure a weapon would be admitted to the paramilitary brigades.

We learned about some young people who had bought contraband weapons for large sums of money in the hopes of joining the partisans operating out of the dense forest of Lupuczanska. My husband and Mitzia decided to buy two rifles and two handguns just in case and hid them behind a distillation column.

There were days when we thought of escaping and others when we decided it was better to stay. We rationalized that joining the fighting militia was impossible, as they only accepted fighters, not families with children. Besides, if the rest of the Jews who worked with us heard of our plans, they'd denounce us, fearful of reprisal. After a while, we stopped discussing the issue and realized it was better to stay in the factory. Through our clandestine radio, we heard the Russian and English predicting German failure, giving us a burst of confidence that the war could end soon. We didn't want to make any rash decisions and risk what we still had. After all, we were all alive, and the whole family was together.

For a while, the mass murders slowed down. Silence was no

consolation. It suggested a premeditated tranquility before the last lunge.

***

Sioma spent long hours talking with Lochbhiler. They drank beer, sometimes vodka. One day, our protector told Sioma that he was being transferred to the front, and they had assigned another officer in his place. We feared the worst; the Nazis' goal was to annihilate us from the face of the earth.

It was July. Engineer Lochbhiler assembled us on the patio. The heat was nauseating, even more so with the cauldrons constantly boiling around the factory.

"Today is my last day at the brewery. I'm being sent to the front to fight. They will send Eherenreich in my place. He belongs to the Nazi party and is a faithful follower of Hitlerian ideas. Please, take care. I wish you good luck!"

Lochbhiler shook hands with Sioma and Mitzia, and to everyone else, he said his goodbyes with a nod. It was an odd feeling, but we were going to miss him.

It dawned earlier than usual when Eherenreich arrived the following day. His brutality preceded him. His gestures and sarcastic tone frightened everyone, especially Masza, who ran away to hide during formation. Conditions inside the brewery grew harsher and crueler by the minute.

Eherenreich, who always wore his swastika band, proudly

displaying his adherence to the Nazi party, knew absolutely nothing about brewing engineering. This turned out to be a blessing in disguise: he needed us.

Every day, he would approach Mitzia and Sioma to ask questions about various processes. He didn't understand anything about the compression of ammonia or the importance of hops or malting. He had only tried the beer once it was bottled and ready for consumption. The more they tried to explain the chemical reactions, the more frustrated he became by his inability to absorb so much information. Instead, he strutted around the brewery showing off his little friend *fräulain* Merrkel, a cheap whore who couldn't count to ten, and demanded reverence from all of us, becoming more vicious as the days passed.

By winter, my hands, once manicured and smooth, were weathered and bleeding. The cold was so extreme that it was unbearable, freezing everything, even my fingers. One afternoon, a soldier arrived with several posters. He hung them on the walls with glue that smelled of rotting resin. A reward of fifty thousand Deutsche marks was offered to anyone who turned over Tevie Bielski, the leader of the partisans' group operating in the vicinity between Novogrudok and Lida. Dead or alive, they wanted him captured.

We had heard that Bielski was a man of contradictions: rude but compassionate. He was a warrior who attacked without warning. I envisioned him as a kind of Robin Hood, one who helped the unprotected but was seen by the authorities as a wanted criminal. Tevie wasn't only fighting to implement justice in the world; his war was to survive. He was fighting along with other Jews to seize back the simple right to exist.

By year's end, we realized we had let Chanukah slip by without celebration; unlike the Maccabees, we lacked the oil for a miracle. Christmas brought drunken soldiers and rape. Seduction danced with Death. Another year of confinement had passed, and for us, one more day of life.

1943 began with hope: the new exploits of the Bielski and their *atriad*, their military detachment of partisan resistance, filled us with joy. Tevie and his group had managed to steal a horse from the *kommissar* of a nearby village. The high-ranking civil officer was beside himself; he was enraged and wanted to trap the partisan at all costs. His agents sought information from everywhere. A group of soldiers came to the brewery. Shouting threats, they violently interrogated each one of us. Nobody knew anything about the issue, so they left and went to the ghetto. We heard shots ... some innocent people paid with their lives for the robbery of the equine treasure.

We gathered in secret to receive updates from our clandestine radio. All attentive, we could hear Stalin's determined voice: "We have fought hard to repel the enemy; our brave soldiers have saved the city of Leningrad. I urge our partisans to fight relentlessly in the woods. The Soviet Union will be victorious!"

We relished the minute of joy. But this victorious moment quickly turned sour. A few days later, we learned that there had been an uprising in the Warsaw Ghetto and that the Nazis, in retaliation, organized a massacre. The ghetto was reduced to rubble. The Jewish rebellion had been a manifestation of dignity. More than three hundred thousand Jews had been deported from the Warsaw Ghetto; three hundred thousand innocent victims were killed between July 22 and September 12, 1942. As a reaction to the deportations and assassinations, between January and April of 1943, a covert group led by Mordechai Anielewicz fought courageously against the Nazis, facing them with bullets, sticks, and stones. The fighters succumbed one by one to the modern Germanic machinery, which was much more sophisticated than the few firearms and rudimentary weapons the resistance was armed with. They died with pride, inspiring other uprisings in other similar confinements: the Jews would not go like sheep to the slaughter.

The sound of Eherenreich screaming orders and the occasional shower of gunshots snatched our powerless, pathetic peace. The Nazis were relentless in their goal of murdering Jews. We lived in a state of panic, but not enough to convince ourselves to flee into the woods.

One day, Engineer Lochbhiler unexpectedly arrived at the brewery—it was a great surprise! Our old protector had returned from the front and wanted beer for his troops. Sioma ran to provide him with several boxes, which his soldiers took gratefully.

Before saying goodbye, Joachim Lochbhiler approached Sioma and whispered a warning: "Get out of here as soon as possible! The end is near. There are plans to destroy the ghetto and annihilate all remaining Jews in the area, including those working in the brewery. I can't help you other than to tell you that you must flee to the forest! The resistance forces are hiding there. They attack the German army fiercely and constantly. You'll be safer among them. We have not been able to repel them. As I see it, it is your only way out. Save yourselves!" He wished us good luck and walked out of the brewery through the patio.

Death, with its life-scavenging scythe, seemed to be leaning on the doorway, lurking like a hungry jackal ready to attack at the slightest misstep. Our time was running out.

Chapter Nine: 1943

In April, we heard reports that five thousand Jews were murdered in Ponary, a forest on the outskirts of Vilna. In July, the rules in Lida became stricter than before. The Jews were barred from working outside the ghetto. Rumors trickled like crumbs. More isolated than ever, we barely received any information from the outside world.

It was around three o'clock in the afternoon on August 16, 1943, when I heard a truck stop in the courtyard. A group of Latvian soldiers descended and began beating Chaim Weksler, who by chance happened to be there. I understood we had to flee and ran to fetch Masza. We hid in the small cellar that served as a *maline*. Two others joined us.

My mother holds my arm tightly. We run and hide in a corner. She places her finger on her lips, signaling me to keep quiet. Where is my dad?

There are soldiers everywhere. They shout sullenly in German: "*Shmutzige judenbunde, raus!* Dirty Jewish dogs, come out!"

Although I don't understand what they mean, I know they hate us. Oh, no! They have found us! They use the butt of the rifle to push us out! I'm scared! Where is *tatu's*? Where are they taking us? Don't let go of me, Mommy, don't let go!

A few minutes later, a German guard appeared before us and ordered us out. They dragged us toward the courtyard. Masza wept silently, and I hugged her tightly. Amid blows and cries, we were gathered with the rest of the people in the open area of the brewery and were ordered into a formation.

"We came from Slonim," said one of the officers in a husky and authoritative voice. "We bring papers that accuse you of poisoning the beer. You are all under arrest."

We looked at one another incredulously; it could not be true. "We didn't do it, please, please, let us be," I pleaded.

A sardonic smile was his answer. His despicable grimace made me fall back instantly. "The Christians on this side and the Jews here." They separated us, pointing at us with their rifles.

Minutes later, Sioma appeared behind us, wet and shivering, covered with a blanket that I assumed someone had given him. I later found out that he had sensed the danger while walking by the brewery gate and had run to the river to escape. Nevertheless, we were glad to see him and be together again.

They are coming for us! Run, save yourself! I have to get to the river to try

to escape; I have to warn Szura that we are in danger. I'll sneak out that window! Ah, there is a drainage pipe that flows into the river, it can be a good hiding place. The Latvian soldier has seen Riva's daughter and shot her, poor thing. Now he has seen me, and he is coming after me. He is aiming his rifle at me. I will die here! I close my eyes, and the young man shoots ... I'm still alive! It is a miracle; the mechanism of the soldier's rifle is stuck. I am in luck! I spoke too soon ... he's got another gun, and he's going to shoot me!

I shout in German and demand, using an authoritative tone, "Take me immediately to the brewery director. Right now!"

I'm soaking wet; I'm so cold. Eherenreich shows me the documents accusing us of poisoning the beer. They state that this was done as part of a conspiracy by the resistance fighters. Leibl Stolowitsky, the former accountant of the brewery, has also been brought into the office; they use him as a guinea pig, forcing him to taste the beer that is supposedly poisoned. Nothing happens to him, and yet they are pushing us both toward the yard.

"Women in a row and men in another," the soldier ordered.

From here I can see how they separate the Jewish workers from the others; they all look scared. The Nazi shouts. I plan to flee; no one has seen me. They've caught my father, but how? My father is just the former accountant of the brewery, he has nothing to do with the poisoning issue! I can see him among them; why should they need my father? He is only an employee of the factory. Michash, my brother, is there, too! They are taking them! They came looking for the Pupko family, and they got them already, including the children. I do not know why they take my family; the

Stolowitskys don't own anything. Oh! I think the SS officer just saw me; they discovered my hiding place! From the yard, the soldier points my way. I'm going to surrender before something worse happens; I do not have the strength to stay alone and see how they take my family. Maybe I can get away if I go down the stairs swiftly before they find me. I'll try to escape through the river. Somebody is coming ... I better hide behind the boiler. As I hear his footsteps on one side, I move toward the other silently and rapidly. He has not seen me. I go up the stairs to the attic where the grains are stored; there, I can hide until they leave, and then I will run to the forest. They won't find me among the barley grains, and they will probably leave soon. Here, amid cereals, I find the silence of death. My heart beats very hard. I cannot stand it anymore ... I cannot survive alone, a young woman without any protection, without my father, without my entire family.

Bella Stolowitsky was being pushed by one of the soldiers toward us.

"Get in the truck! Hurry up, we can't wait anymore," cried the Latvian soldier. "Turn back, I will kill whoever dares look at the road."

Chaim Weksler could barely walk; he swayed on one foot, and yet he was herded with the rest of the men. They were in formation, following the orders of the SS officer.

Franya stepped forward to speak with the *kommissar*. "My husband Misha is Windisch's barber, and he is not here. I beg you to let me go with him."

Surprisingly, the SS officer ordered a soldier to accompany

Franya. They disappeared behind the gate to the Nazi offices …. We never saw her again.

From the corner of my eye, I caught a glimpse of Sara Stolowitsky, the wife of the brewery *buchalter*, her little daughter Chana, and her niece, running. They had managed to hide without being seen. The rest of us were lined up in a death row.

I was holding Masza as we were shoved into the truck. The rest of the children were walking beside us. Yenka came into my thoughts. She had worked with the family for many years; months ago, she had offered to help despite the risk of being killed if she was discovered. My sister-in-law Aniuta and I took advantage of the confusion:

"Run to Yenka's house," we urged Fruma, the oldest of the children and already a fifteen-year-old girl. "Take your brother and cousin and hide there."

I overheard Noya, the daughter of Mitzia and Roza, telling Masza with a mixture of fear and certainty, "You can't come with us, we're white, and you have dark skin. If the Nazis see you, they'll know you're Jewish, and they'll kill us all! Go back to your mother before someone sees us!"

Fruma and her little brother Dzozik nodded, acknowledging what Noya was saying. Masza, only four years old, understood that she was not wanted by the rest of the children and burst into tears.

A thousand scenes passed through my mind in a matter of seconds; it might be true what the children said. But there was no time to lose, so I hugged her and then pushed Masza to run with her cousins toward Yenka's house. We walked to the truck without turning back. I took a deep breath ... at least my little girl would be safe. But I couldn't stand the separation.

When I saw that my husband was being sent on another transport, I pleaded with the Nazi officer in perfect German: "Commander, please, can you send us all together? We want to be with our men."

"You will meet sooner or later, everyone will go to the same place," he said mockingly.

We got on the truck and were ordered to face each other, with our backs against the windows. As we started to move, we saw people from the Lida Ghetto walking between Nazi officers. They carried small suitcases and wore several layers of coats, one on top of the other. We learned that the ghetto had been liquidated once again; there were no more Jews left in Lida.

The truck crossed the river Lida, driving us toward the building used by the Technical Organization of Germanic Troops. It was formerly known as the "Old Burnt Prison," located on May Third Street. That day, it served as a space where Jewish women and children arriving from different ghettos were held temporarily.

We were thrown into a filthy room full of insects. People before us had defecated in the corners. The stank had attracted a great quantity of buzzing flies. From time to time, we heard the strenuous shouts of our watchmen as they opened the door and gave a hostile welcome to a new tenant. "Nothing they say can penetrate my being, nothing that they do to me can hurt me," I kept repeating to myself.

The light came in as they opened the door once more. A human wreck, still clutching her suitcase, was forcefully pushed in. I was somewhat relieved knowing that my little girl would not be witnessing this horror. *I'm not alone,* I reassured myself. *I have my mother-in-law and my sister-in-law Aniuta with me, and I hope Franya has found her husband.*

The door opened again. This time it was our children who were being hauled into our prison. Distraught to see that she hadn't been able to escape, I hugged Masza tightly.

Fruma, in a choked voice and between spasms, described what had happened: "We ran to the building where Yenka lives. She welcomed us into her small room. We hid under the feather quilt of her bed, but the Nazis soon arrived. We were frightened, but none of us emitted a sound. They broke the furniture, opened and closed drawers, emptied them, and searched every corner looking for Jews. They ran from one place to the other, shouting, looking in every room. Suddenly, one soldier pulled the quilt and laughed when he found us. We were then loaded onto a truck that brought us here."

Fruma could not stop crying; Aniuta hugged her, trying to soothe her.

"Fruma, my little girl, do not worry. We are all together now, we will find out how to get out of here."

"Mama, it was not my fault, I wish they had not found us, but there was nowhere else to hide. Yenka's bedroom is very small, and we did not find another hiding place. I wanted ...."

"Hush, hush my girl, sh ... sh ... calm down now."

Masza sat on Rachil's lap. She embraced her granddaughter tenderly and between tears began to pluck out the lice that had made a home on the child's head. One by one, with her nails, she picked out the eggs deposited there; one by one, the minutes passed between uncertainty and fear. We even tried to bribe the guard with a watch that Aniuta had managed to bring. He took the watch but turned his back to us.

Some people who arrived at the holding depot had brought with them some personal belongings and toiletries; we had not been given the time to do so. We asked permission to return to the brewery for them. Luckily, the guard who had taken the watch put us on a truck and instructed that we could only bring one suitcase, only one. He warned us that we would first stop at the ghetto to pick up the orphaned children remaining there, and then we would go to the brewery. In the meantime, Masza stayed with her grandmother.

The ghetto was desolate.

"Hurry up, pick up the small children quickly!" they ordered us.

Two or three children were wandering by themselves down the ghetto street. I took one by the hand and guided him to our transport. I spoke to him lovingly, as if he were mine, trying not to show the pain I felt inside.

When we reached the brewery, I took my beige coat, thinking about the coming winter. I also took a blanket, some clothes for Masza, and, without thinking if it was necessary or not, my tortoiseshell comb. I had to hurry, as the furious screams of the German soldier were banging in my ears. I ran out, closed the door, and climbed back into the truck.

We spent the night inside the jail. The next day, we were joined by the last group of people taken from the ghetto. A little girl who sat beside her mother was crying; a young boy grumbled and cursed his fate. We, the women of the brewery, kept close as a separate clan.

"They told us they would take us to Lublin," said one woman.

"I don't think so. We'll go to some work camp," corrected another.

After three days crammed inside this pestilent place, the Nazis finally allowed us out to breathe some fresh air. They pushed us to walk down the cobbled street, as we were forbidden to step on the sidewalks. They treated us worse than any animal!

In my best German, I addressed the commander who had arrested us in the brewery: "Sir, you told me that our husbands were to meet with us."

"That's right, and I'll keep my word," he said in the same mocking tone as before. "They have already brought them from the prison of Syrokomli, and they will travel in the same train car as you."

They ordered Rachil, Aniuta, and her children Dzozik and Fruma to join the people who were coming from the ghetto. Roza, her children, Masza, and I were taken aside. We were then brought to the train station and grouped with the rest of the Jews.

SHURA

When we arrived at the station, our husbands were already inside the train car. We would travel in cattle cars, which had previously transported animals; we were seen as lower than any beast. As we were hurried inside, they pushed more and more people into the already crowded space. Through the open car door, we saw wounded German soldiers coming from the Russian front. The sight—evidence that the Russians were fighting, that they were close, and that the war might be nearing its end—made me rejoice. But in the meantime, we were in this stinking, tight place, and we had our morale shattered. It was the pestilence of hatred ....

Tatu's is inside the train! I feel calmer now. At least I'm with both my parents; I have one on each side, and they'll take care of me ....

A soldier was checking my suitcase. He glanced inside and saw my tortoiseshell comb; without any shame, he put it in his pocket. The doors of the car remained open; they were waiting for more "load." There was no room for anybody else, but more and more people came. The heat was unbearable. We were very thirsty. Uncertainty and fear incited a vivid discussion inside the train:

"Where will we go?"

"They say we will go to Lublin, but I doubt it, they do not need us to work there."

"Yes, I'm sure, they'll take us there or at least nearby."

"Don't be so gullible! Their goal is to kill us all. Don't you realize it?"

There was a locksmith in the car who stated that once the bolt was closed from the outside, it would be impossible to escape. Another thought an axe would come in handy to break the door from the inside or to break the floor of the car. It occurred to somebody to ask permission from the Nazi officer to allow us to go fetch some water. To our luck, he agreed. He allowed one person to come down and bring a bucket for all of us. How sardonic; we were more than fifty individuals—one bucket could barely satisfy half of us. There was a well a few steps away, next to some peasants' houses. Bella, the brewery accountant's daughter, was the one chosen to go fetch the water. One of our travel companions lent her his coat; it was a few sizes too large on her, and it would have enough space to hide an axe or any other tool she found. She stepped out of the cart and walked to the well.

A guard is coming! Oh wait, it is the Frenchman who was on the train tracks when they forced me to shovel coal!

"Please help me! I need to get an axe!"

"Do you want to kill me with it?" he asked.

"No, I'm trying to save myself! Help me!"

"Go near the well, wait for me, I'll see how I can help you," he promised.

I fill and empty the bucket with water a hundred times. I fear that someone will discover what I am doing. Where is the Frenchman? Ah, there he comes at last! He explains that he had to cut off the handle of the ax so I could hide it under my coat. With the treasure under my arm, I go back to the train. Everybody is waiting for me.

The car was pandemonium! We waited a long time for Bella. We thought that she wouldn't make it back, that she had been caught. The locksmith was losing his mind, hitting himself against the walls. His visage had changed drastically, and there was no way to calm him down. They tried to soothe him to no avail. Bella finally returned at the last moment with an axe hidden under her arm.

Dusk came, and the Nazis closed the doors of the car. We heard the lock and the engines of the locomotive but felt no movement. I realized that it was not our train moving but the one next to us. We waited in stillness ....

Our train started moving later that night. I was holding Masza by the hand. The sound of people praying and moaning in agony multiplied around me, making me dizzy.

The straw on the floor smelled of urine, and the sultriness overwhelmed me, but worst of all was the feeling of uncertainty—a weight that tormented everyone. We were around fifty souls made up of families, older people, and little children like Masza. Were they really taking us to work? Where was God? Was He claiming us back to His bosom?

"We have to escape," Sioma said to me. "The axe will not help us in any way, we have to find another way out of here."

Shemah Israel, hear us, Lord! I shouted the ancient prayer internally, pleading to God for mercy. *Aren't you listening to us, Lord?*

I did not find God in that moment. My husband repeated that he was not going to die without a fight. He would not give up. It was more than evident that if we stayed, we would die sooner or later, but I was tired of suffering. I was exhausted from the ambiguity of the situation and fed up with feeling fear. I had given up. If my destiny was to end up in the hands of the Nazis, then so be it. We had been suffocated by the Nazi yoke for years. Living between fear and utmost mistreatment, we had tolerated too much. To know yourself dead while still alive was torture; I couldn't do it anymore. I succumbed to tiredness and fell asleep.

Sioma was arguing with some men about the possibility of escaping. Someone thought of making a hole in the floor of the car. It was too dangerous; with the train moving quickly, we would fall on the tracks and die crushed between the steel wheels.

As they assessed different options, in a moment of clarity, my husband said to his brother Mitzia, "I believe that the barbed wire that obstructs the small window of the car can be removed. Michash, the accountant's son, is thin enough to slip through that window and remove the bolts from the outside."

"Why do you think my sixteen-year-old boy should risk his life?" shouted Leibl Stolowitsky, the boy's father. "My son does not have to be a hero, look for someone else to do it!"

"Look, Leibl," Sioma said hurriedly, "we're moving away from the area that we know; this is our only chance! The night is not so patient, and the sun will rise again. We have no choice, no one else has Michash's size nor his ability to execute the job."

"I will do it," Michash interrupted.

The boy climbed on the shoulders of two men in order to

reach the small window. With difficulty, he managed to fit himself through it. Luckily, his feet reached the step outside the door. His back was against the wall of the moving train, but he'd have to turn around to open the lock. Suddenly, a noise came from outside ... it was Michash, trying to open the bolt. One screw was out. We waited in silence. Another screw was out—*crack*. From inside, the men helped to slide the door. And, suddenly, it opened!

The wind blew in, and I felt almost revived. Everybody was hesitant to jump out. I did not utter a word ... I wasn't thinking. I was suspended in nothingness ... I didn't want to jump, I couldn't. Masza, sensing my indecision, let go of my hand and with a survival instinct grasped the hand of her father, a father who promised her a future and not a death sentence. She turned to see me with scrutinizing eyes, and her decision became firm. As little as she was, she understood that staying with me meant suicide. With Sioma, she would have a chance. She chose life.

My husband would jump, but he waited his turn .... There was no looking back; the train was on its course. The danger increased exponentially as the seconds passed. "Dear God, my religion forbids me to say your name in vain. In my mind, I can see the unpronounceable letters, those that are read in the subconscious, but I've never said them out loud. *Hashem*, The Name. I invoke your blessed name, help us."

One, two, three, four, five seconds—they passed quickly. Everything was black, uncertain. The night, the girl, the forest, the fear. I fell on the wet ground, and the rustle of what sounded like a gun buzzed near my ear. The heat of a bullet grazed my arm. I heard the Nazi soldiers' shouts echoing from the roof of the train. The noise moved away in the distance, at last, lost in the dusky night.

Did I jump off the train? I wondered. *I got off the train! I don't know how. Is it possible that somebody pushed me?* I hesitated for a few seconds. My beige coat must have stood out in the darkness. I had felt the gunfire close to me, three bullets in total; I had counted them. *Did the others jump, too?*

I got up without a scratch. The train drove away quickly as I ran into the woods. A few minutes earlier, I had not realized that the darkness provided a miracle, and the obscurity of the forest offered its arms to save me. The moonless night frightened me. I felt disconcerted. I was all alone in the absolute silence and the total blackness of the forest. The creaking leaves under my feet were my only companions as I walked through the woods. But the trees were a dubious shelter.

I eventually curled up against a fallen log, but then I heard dry branches crushing nearby. It could be a wolf, a Nazi, a Russian partisan, or a White Pole—all just as cruel and rapacious. I couldn't sleep; I was overly alert. The minutes passed; the noise dissipated. I was afraid, but I struggled to stay awake until sleep finally overcame me.

Where is Szura?

"Szura! Szura!"

Someone tells me that she jumped out! Mitzia jumped with Meilashe, who is just a baby, and Roza followed them. We approach a

military checkpoint.

"Close the doors!"

They have noticed that the bolt is open! A soldier opens the door abruptly.

"Has anyone jumped?" he asks with cynical humor.

We lower our gazes and shake our heads. No one dares to look at him directly. We do not make a sound, afraid that our trembling voices will give us away. The soldier leaves and locks the door. We're bolted inside the car once more; it cannot be! We can't give up! I must persuade Michash to go through the window again. The young man is terrified, but his father is worse. He does not want to know anything about it and argues that it is too risky to open the door again.

"Michash," I say, "if you're not able to open the door again, at least save yourself."

This phrase convinces him, and one more time he climbs out the window. Noya, Mitzia's daughter, believes that her father, mother, and brother have been killed by the bullets fired earlier. There is no way to calm her down. She hugs Mrs. Weksler, who caresses her. I approach her and try to convince her to jump, but she stomps her feet firmly.

My leg hurts, and the butcher who was going to jump with Masza wants to stay on the train.

"Noya, listen, jump with us, I beg you."

There is no convincing her; she is paralyzed. She shouts that she no longer wants to live without her family and that she will not jump.

Michash has managed to open the door again, and the seconds start to tick. The wind of freedom opens our lungs once more.

"Noya, please jump out, come with me and Masza."

I try to push her; but she responds violently, hitting left and right.

She clings more firmly to Mrs. Weksler. Michash, his sister Bella, and their father have already jumped. There is confusion and chaos in the car. Chaim Weksler has stepped aside; he has an injured foot preventing him from jumping. He knows that he can't be saved, that he is doomed. He's completely silent as he walks away from the door. A couple I do not recognize has just jumped. Meanwhile, Noya kicks and grips Mrs. Weksler's arm even harder.

"We will take care of her," Mr. Weksler assures me.

I have a moment of doubt, but I must decide quickly. I take Masza by the hand and cover her head with my palm to protect her from the fall. I place myself on the small step that protrudes from the door of the car, and I throw myself with Masza in my arms: a leap into the void. We roll on the ground, turning and spinning until we finally come to a stop. We are covered with shrubbery.

"Are you okay? Are you hurt?"

Fortunately, Masza replies, "Nothing hurts, *tatu's*. I'm fine."

I woke up and decided to walk deeper into the forest. I heard someone approaching and quickly hid behind a wide trunk. But then I heard the familiar voices of my brother-in-law Mitzia and his wife Roza, who were walking carrying their son Meilashe. I was so glad to see them. Surely, they had jumped at the same time I had. We walked through the forest together and very soon came upon some Russian partisans. They were drunk but invited us to their food. They gave us three loaves to share—but not without first taking Mitzia's boots as payment for their help.

We ate the wild mushrooms and strawberries that we

foraged by the road and which had just begun to sprout. We walked without a course, staying away from the nearby villages for fear of being discovered or killed by the peasants.

I hoped that Sioma and Masza had jumped off the train. The worry was eating me alive. My dry tears contrasted with those of Roza, who couldn't stop crying for Noya. She also didn't know if her daughter had managed to jump off the train, but she maintained hope. *At least you have Meilashe and your husband with you,* I said to myself, addressing my sister-in-law in my thoughts. *I have nobody.*

We wanted to reach a partisan camp in the forest. We knew the Bielski encampment couldn't be far. Dusk was creeping in. As we walked along the edge of the woods, we glimpsed a little light blazing. The house belonged to a Polish family, sufficiently far from the city. We quietly approached the house and knocked on the door. A man, whose face seemed weathered from long days of work under the sun, opened the door.

"Sorry to bother you at this hour," I said, "we've been walking all day and have only eaten a small portion of fruits from the forest floor."

He signaled with his hand to stop talking. He looked first at Mitzia, and then he turned his head nervously to each side of the house, making sure there was no one else around. He welcomed us into his abode and gave us soup. He explained that we were near the Mosti train station, and that this area of the forest was regulated by Russian partisans. He explained that the Germans seldom raided the woods and advised us to find a hideout under the stars. He provided us with blankets and agreed to let us spend the night in his barn but demanded that we set out before dawn. We were doubtful of our new landlord's intentions. Would he betray us, or did he genuinely want to help? We decided to take turns standing guard throughout the night.

My father forces me to walk. He carries me for a few minutes, gets tired, and then makes me walk again. I'm exhausted. Michash occasionally offers to carry me. I'm hungry, but I do not complain. I walk, and I walk some more. It seems like we have walked in circles all night. The man from Warsaw who jumped with his wife says he knows how to read the sky; he assures us that he recognizes the Polar Star signaling where north is. Everything looks the same to me. There is a dim light in the thicket of the forest, and we follow it. Bella is chosen to approach and ask for guidance. She speaks fluent Polish, and they will not be able to know if she is Jewish or not. Bella is very brave! She goes quickly and returns with milk, especially for me, and bread that the peasants gave her. She tells us that they directed her to walk to the opposite side of where we are headed. They have said that we are close to a Nazi camp. If I sharpen my eyesight, I can see the lights flashing in the distance. I'm very tired, and I'm scared ....

The peasant turned out to be a good man, and we were able to continue on our path.

More than three days passed, and we still knew nothing of the others. We came across a group of partisans. They asked if we had rifles, guns, or any other weapon. When we answered that we didn't, the leader of the group, using his battle jargon, clarified to Mitzia, "Women and useless people unable to defend themselves have no place in the *partisanka*."

Mitzia explained in perfect Russian that we had jumped off the train and begged his permission to join their group, even if it was just for a few days while we waited for the rest of the family who had probably jumped, too. The partisans allowed us to stay temporarily. They shared a few morsels of their food in exchange for work. We helped with everything we could: we brought wood from our surroundings, cooked, and washed. We tried to spend our time doing whatever they asked us to do instead of thinking and worrying. I was still waiting for Sioma and Masza. Roza's tears of grief—mingling with the mud of the dense land, crammed with pines and birches, around us—foreshadowed an ill omen.

We asked a peasant for directions. We haven't stopped walking all night. At dawn, we lay down to sleep by the river Niemen, the same river that flows from Lithuania to Belarus. I think of Szura ... have they shot her? Is she safe? I want to think that she is. Soon we will find her! At night, we follow the stars; I recognize The Great Bear constellation that directs us north toward where the Bielski's camp should be. A young man is approaching, and I ask him where we are. He indicates that we are in the Bialoposka area, which is controlled by the White Poles, warning that they are violent men. We are in danger! He advises us to cross to the other side of the river, where we can find the Russian guerrillas, including the *paritisanim*. The river here is mighty, and its torrent is strong. The

Germans have either taken or destroyed all the boats. The young man is willing to help us; he will bring his small boat to take us across. He warns that the boat is old, deteriorated, and has a hole; he doesn't know if it will hold the crossing. The boy walks away, and we are left waiting.

Daylight blinds me. Nevertheless, I see a brawny man approaching from a distance. He wants to know what we are doing there. He realizes that we are Jews and offers to bring us food. Who can we trust? Is he an informer? Who's the enemy? Does he truly want to help us?

More than an hour has passed, and the young man who had promised the boat does not return. Will the Nazis come for us? The Germans pay peasants and any civilian for every Jewish head they deliver. Alas, the boy returns! He brings a basket of food with him. He explains that he tried to find a better boat or raft but found nothing. The damaged one will have to do. I share with him that a man approached us inquiring about who we were, and the boy makes a grunt in response and looks dismayed.

"We can't trust him, he probably went to inform the Germans, we must hurry," he says worriedly.

With a bucket, we draw the pooling water out of the boat while the boy strongly rows away from the riverbank. Masza is on one side, and Bella sits next to her to balance the weight. We finally reach the other side of the Niemen. We thank the young man and pay him with what we have of value: a razor with its blades and a flashlight. We never asked for his name, but we will forever be indebted to him. He saved our lives.

The days passed, and all I did was wait …. I asked myself with overwhelming guilt, *Why did I jump? Why did I leave them?*

SHURA

Where could they be?

The smell of pines and conifers oppressed my chest; I could not stop the pain, it was intolerable; I couldn't breathe.

We jumped off the train with Sioma Pupko and his daughter. We crossed the river with the help of a young man, but now ... what awaits us? What can we do in the forest where hunters stalk us everywhere? Who are our allies? The Germans are not; the Poles aren't, either. Help from the Russians is completely unreliable. My father has been a humble accountant for the Pupko brewery. How will he survive in the dense forest? Michash, my brother, is strong and young; he will have no problem joining the partisan fight. My chances are slim as a woman; I don't have many alternatives while living in the forest. On the other hand, we should help Mr. Pupko with his little daughter Masza. We help him by taking turns carrying her around, and I pamper her, probably too much, while her father rests. But her sluggish walk slows us down and puts us at risk.

We get a glimpse of the little house the young man told us about. He explained that the owner has an arrangement and collaborates with the partisans of the *Atriad* Legalszczyk. He warned us that his son is a recalcitrant antisemite friendly with the White Poles who hunt down Jews. We must be certain that the son is not in the house before approaching. We search for a bicycle. That would be the sign that he is home. Not without hesitation, we decide to knock on the door. With my looks, I can pass as a Catholic girl, and besides, I speak fluent Polish and Russian. I check for the bicycle inside as well—I don't see it—and I decide to speak to them in Russian. The peasant invites me inside, and I share with him our story. He offers me food. Suddenly, I hear three shots nearby.

"Do not worry," the farmer assures me, "it's the partisans honoring a dead comrade."

A man with the red insignia of the Russian army is welcomed in by the farmer. I learn that he identifies himself as a Pole. He is a friend of the peasant, his name is Wojciechoski, and he is active as a partisan. I also tell him about how we jumped from the moving train. He suggests heading eastward, into the deeper, denser area of the forest where he says a *partisanim* camp is located. Wojciechoski and the peasant offer to walk us part of the way.

My family, along with Mr. Sioma and little Masza, are hidden behind the bushes, waiting. I shout, "*Tovarich!* Comrades!" signaling them to come out of their miserable hiding place. We follow the generous partisan who, on horseback, leads us through the woods and the swamp. The afternoon begins to cool. Maszinka does not complain, but the rags that cover her little feet are soaked. The girl moves me deeply; she suffers, but she does not say a word. She takes her father's hand, and with that, she seems content. Night is descending. The leaves that cushion the earth lighten the horse's steps. I think of my mother and my little sister Chana who stayed at the brewery. The thought that the Nazis have taken them away makes me feel anguished. I'm afraid of the great possibility they've been murdered. I miss my mother! But we must continue; there is no other alternative.

We found that most Jews had been admitted to the *partisanka* based on their communist ideas or due to a quota they provided, which meant that they owned a weapon. It was nighttime on September 22. We were seated around the campfire trying to warm up. Silently, I welcomed my misfortune ... I felt alone in the world, without my husband and without my daughter. It had been seven days since we had left the train. *Why did I jump?* The question continuously circled through my brain, tormenting me and piling up with thousands of other questions.

Someone offered me a small pot of hot soup. I took it automatically, but I froze before swallowing it. Holding the humble bowl to my lips, I thought about how life goes around, and how much I had been forced to change …. Today, this pewter cup represented something more precious than the fine crystal glasses I had once cherished.

I'm soaked, I'm cold, and I do not have shoes. We walked a lot, a lot …. Where are we? My dad says this is the Naliboki *puszcza*, near the village of Kletishche. He tries to reassure me that we are not far, but I am cold and hungry, and I want to sleep. The river was freezing, and I can't get myself warm again. Where is my mother? I want to get to wherever we are heading, but where is that place? I'm tired; all I want is to rest.

The fighters eating beside us, always on alert, suddenly moved swiftly; they heard someone approaching. They stood abruptly, with their rifles in hand, as I snapped out of my reverie. A horse appeared, walking toward us.

After greeting the leader, the partisan directed his attention to me: "We brought her husband and daughter." It was then that I saw my beautiful Masza climbing down from the horse.

What joy! I felt indescribable happiness enveloping me! I ran to hug them. The bitter salt that had previously stained my cheeks turned into sweet honey moistening my lips. The clock was handless; time stood still. Eleven survivors had jumped off a moving train; it was sealed in time and space. I kissed my husband and my daughter desperately. Masza was soaked; I asked if someone had some extra clothes for Masza to change into. It was getting dark, and the night air had a bad countenance. Mitzia hugged his brother, asking incisively for Noya, his daughter. He had hoped that she had jumped off the train with Sioma.

"Mitzia ... I tried to pull her with me," my husband attempted to explain, "I wanted her to jump with us, but she was reluctant to do it. There was no convincing her otherwise. She clung to Mrs. Weksler and fought me off. When you, Roza, and Meilashe jumped, we heard shots and thought that all of you had been killed. She was terrified. There was no way to make her jump out into the unknown. She kicked and hit. She was out of control, completely beside herself. No matter what I said or did, I couldn't persuade her ... time ran out ... and she stayed on the train ...."

"You should have pushed her, you should have made her jump," Mitzia reproached furiously, flustered and distraught.

"It was impossible, I swear, Mitzia."

"You say this because she's not your daughter ...."

Roza whimpered inconsolably. Sioma was speechless; he did not know what to say. Our daughter was with us, but our niece was not. Noya remained amongst the stinking straw of the train car at the mercy of the Nazis. Was she alive? Would she be harmed? They'd had only a few seconds to decide to jump or stay on the train. The decisions made in those split seconds had fateful consequences.

SHURA

Noya's parents had trusted that Noya would jump after them, but she hadn't. Destiny mocked us; no one could have predicted the result. Sioma stood downcast. I hugged him in silence.

Mitzia and Roza, with Meilashe in their arms, turned away from us. A mother's moans of sorrow and pain ripped through the darkness of the night. Roza wailed inconsolably, crying out for her daughter. At dawn, Mitzia, Roza, and Meilashe left for a camp of Jewish families who lived in the surrounding forests.

We asked for detailed information about the Bielski camp, where we knew they also accepted families. The leader of the *atriad* told us how to find the Bielski brothers' *partisanka*. Leibl Stolowitsky, his son Michash, and the couple from Warsaw joined us. Since Bella had attained a gun, she would stay at this camp to fight.

The partisans only accept those who have weapons and are capable of fighting. I speak several languages to perfection, and I have neat handwriting. Throughout childhood, my teachers were wowed by my academic skills, but what good is that now here in the forest?

My father looks tired and old. Here he is—not in front of his accounting books or working with numbers in his head—but in the wild. To survive in times of war, you need unscrupulous men. My friend Yaakov has promised to help me, and he gave me a rifle so I can be accepted into this group. As I see it, to join the partisans against the Nazis is my best option.

Am I seeing visions? It seems like my little sister Chana and my cousin are here! And my mother, too! How did they get here? They tell me that they hid in one of the *maline* in the brewery and waited to make sure that no one was around before running into the forest. And now, here they are! I am elated! My family is finally united; however, I must bid them farewell again shortly, for Yaakov will be introducing me to the commander of the *atriad*.

Two partisans escorted us outside the paramilitary camp and instructed, "Go south without passing the road, go into the forest, and hopefully, you'll find the group run by Tevie Bielski."

We were afraid to go back into the woods. There were many dangerous areas dominated by the White Poles who were fighting against the Germans while also happily taking part in the killing of Jews. We had no choice but to follow the directions provided by the leader of the *atriad*. We wandered around the Naliboki forest until we found the Bielski camp in the densest *puszcza*. It was Yom Kippur. We did not fast, we didn't cleanse our souls in celebration of the holy day, but we prayed with all our might, asking for God's help.

Chapter Ten: 1943-1944

The Bielski camp was located behind the railway lines, tucked into a clearing among a marshy swamp. One had to cross the tracks watched over by soldiers from Vichy France to reach the camp. We were hidden but ready to cross at a moment's notice. We heard shots near us, so we waited. We had to be cautious and ensure no one was around before proceeding. When we finally managed to cross, we ran deeper into the woods until we arrived at a partisan surveillance post, where we were detained.

"Tell us the *parol*, the password," the paramilitary ordered.

"We do not have the *parol*, we escaped the *akcja*," my husband told them.

Somehow, they believed us and let us pass.

The *partisanka* was in the middle of the *puszcza,* the thickest area of forest. The camp resembled a hamlet amid wild, overgrown bushes. Everyone in the camp had a role and was busy doing something, minding their own business: a woman watched over a suspended cauldron, some *partisanim* ate, others were sawing through a log, while another carried wood.

Upon our arrival, they gave us soup and handed us some blankets. Soon, a group of people gathered around us; most of them were from Lida. They wanted to hear our story. They asked if we knew anything about their relatives and friends. We told them what we knew about the liquidation of the ghetto and the train cars. They were hungry for details, but we didn't have any more information to provide.

While we ate, a tall, stout man with broad shoulders and a friendly gaze came forward to greet us. Tevie Bielski introduced himself as the *komandir* of the *atriad*.

Shmuel Amarant, a thin man who wore glasses and a professor of history, approached and informed us that the improvised underground huts were called *ziemlankas* and assigned us hut number eleven.

The modest abode was almost flush with the ground, and from the outside, we could only see a small hole covered with spruce branches. To enter, we had to bend our heads and walk down two steps. Once my vision acclimatized to the half-darkness, I noticed the gabled roof, held by logs placed in the middle of the room. It smelled of plants and humidity. There was a small iron stove that also served as the heater; it had a long tube attached to it that allowed the smoke to escape through the roof. The only pieces of furniture were the beds, which were made of long wooden planks covered with straw, and sacks of flour filled with dry leaves. It was a gloomy space lit with only a few rays of light that entered from a tiny window.

About a thousand people were living in the camp, each assigned to some kind of trade. The historian introduced us to Shlomo Volkowysky, a lawyer from Novogrudok who offered to be our guide. He took us to see the construction of a new *ziemlanka*, a space that was better conditioned for the impending crude winter; then we visited the *varshaten,* a workshop where shoes were made to later be exchanged for a variety of other goods made by other partisan camps; next was the rudimentary kitchen, where they prepared food for the entire community; and finally we entered the office of Tevie Bielski, the *komandir.*

The *partisanka* was a tightly organized space. Men took turns leaving the camp every week on missions called *zadache.* They raided abandoned villages and hamlets to bring back food, tools, kitchen utensils, and windows, and once, they even brought a stove.

There was a special faction of the partisan group that sabotaged railroad tracks or power stations, weakening the German front. These tasks were organized by Azoel Bielski, head of the armed forces and one of Tevie's brothers. Zus, the second brother, was Chief of Reconnaissance and in charge of group security. They explained that Sioma, like the rest of the *malbushim* (a term used condescendingly for the people who had no weapons), would not be compelled to participate in such dangerous missions. This statement reassured me greatly, as I preferred Sioma not to risk his life. We had suffered enough.

There were rules for everything in the forest: when to eat or use the kitchen, how to receive our daily food portions, and, of course, where to work. *Komandir* Tevie Bielski expected everyone to follow all his orders to the letter. Yes, we lived in a burrow infested with mosquitoes among marshes and wild beasts, but we were free. We were no longer victims fearing the claws of the executioner.

***

The campfire was extinguished. Before it went completely dark, I could hear the whisperings of a couple of men in the group. "They probably have jewelry or money, they own the Pivo Pupko brewery in Lida and have amassed a great fortune. Somebody must tell them that to become one of us, they are obliged to give up all their possessions for the welfare of the commune."

I walked away, trying to ignore the rancid comments. We had brought nothing with us. Even if we had been kings and dukes before the war, today the Pupkos were pure fiction—an evocation of a glorious past. Our riches had disappeared at the hands of the petty and wicked Nazis. How could they demand payment from us? We did not own anything. Our only possession was our naked bodies.

I picked up Masza and walked by *Komandir* Bielski's cabin. Again, my ears didn't fail me, as I picked up a conversation between Azoel and his older brother: "Tevie, why did you accept these bourgeois? They are arrogant and think of themselves as noble, but in reality, they are *malbushim*, people who lack fighting skills; they are as useful as a pair of old, worn-out pants. In addition, they bring a small girl with them. The woman is pretentious, and she will not get her hands dirty by cooking or doing any of the everyday chores. These people pose a problem for us. We have discussed it a thousand times! We need men to fight, not more families to take care of!"

"Shut up," Tevie said slowly. "You do not know if what you say is true. We must save every Jewish soul no matter how we do it. We must welcome them; that is our only chance of survival. Even if we are brave and fight, our weapons will clash with the coldness of the world. We must preserve our humanity and moral values and try to help our Jewish brethren."

I ran to tell my husband what I had heard. "People are hypocritical, they do not want us here," I complained. "They still believe we are rich and fail to understand that our prosperous and wealthy past is now family lore."

Tevie had a good heart; he understood that the key to survival was being united. We were all Jews; the Nazis wanted all of us annihilated. Nazism had forced us to join forces, regardless of our worldviews, our economic, social, or cultural conditions, and much less our professions. We were all just humans. Orthodox or liberal, members of the *Beitar* or the *Shomer*, communists or capitalists, Revisionists, Zionists, Bundists, even assimilated ... we as Jews were all doomed to suffer the same fate.

My parents and my two brothers are together, and I have decided to stay here, with Yaakov. He is very brave; he loves me. He has provided me with

a rifle with which I can fight along with the *partisanim*. Tonight, he has left on a mission against the Nazis. Surrounded by the darkness of the night, I'll wait for him in front of the fire. I do not know when I will have to fight, but soon the comrades will treat me as their equal—although today, they still don't accept me fully because I am a woman and a Jew. I am sure that Yaakov will help and protect me; he has an important position within the *atriad*. My family left with Sioma Pupko and his family. I am certain that they are already at the Bielski camp. I wish them luck, and I'm hopeful we can reunite soon!

Yaakov has not yet returned from the *zadache* ... too many hours have passed. Finally! There comes one of his companions who's returning from the mission. He says that Yaakov and the others were caught in a barn where there was a Jewish family hiding; the Poles arrived and killed everyone, including the peasant woman who owned the place. Yaakov took his own life before the Poles could shoot.

"He died a hero," said the comrade.

Yaakov, Yaakov .... Where are you? Will it now be my turn to fight?

***

We settled in hut number eleven, the space that had been assigned to us on the first night. We shared the room with about forty other people. Our neighbors, arm in arm, looked at us with disdain; our presence meant a more overcrowded *ziemlanka*, less oxygen, and less food.

I dreamed that I was on a boat on top of a mountain; the waves were huge, and I was alone. I felt faint, but something told me that tomorrow would be better. A question hovered in my subconscious: *How can the riverbed reach the top of the mountain if the slope leads the water to the opposite side, toward the sea?* I found the answer in my dream ... it had to go around the world to start again.

Sioma woke at dawn and took a glass of *tsikorye*, a chicory beverage prepared in a large pot. We asked how we could help. People looked at us with envy, and I perceived their resentment. They assumed we were rich, arrogant, and not willing to work hard in an *atriad* of communists. They forgot that we were also Jews like them, fleeing from the same enemy.

No one spoke to us. Professor Shmuel Amarant was the only one who advised us: "Start by collecting logs from the forest to light the *ziemlanka* stove. If you are productive carrying *suchostoi*, the dried branches for the fire, you will soon be accepted by those of barrack number eleven. Do not worry about others. We have all kinds of people here, including survivors who are far from being well-educated. Try to ignore their offensive comments."

It was difficult to block out everything. We had barely escaped German hatred just to find ourselves among the antipathy of our co-religionists.

Sioma had to participate in a mission and bring food to the camp.

"Pupko, you're not a combatant, you are just a potato thief!" I overheard the hurtful comments of his companions.

The essence of human beings did not change in the marshes

or the prairies. The struggle for power, authoritarianism, the inability to give in, and lack of empathy was the norm in the *partisanka*.

I joined the other women collecting logs in the surroundings. They spoke of the recent conflict between two sides who quarreled over the command of the *partisanka*. One group was made up of the Bielski brothers and their close colleagues, and the other was comprised of the followers of Kesler. The internal battle had not ended well. Kesler had been killed during the brawl. From that moment on, no one had objected to the leadership of Tevie Bielski. The ones who supported Kesler had gone off to another *atriad*. When we'd arrived at the camp, the murder had not been forgotten: the gossip, the problems, and the disputes were still circulating.

The *partisanka* was shaped by an avenue-like field that joined the *ziemlankas* together with the kitchen area and the workshops. It was a central space where the *partisanim* gathered during the day. I settled the logs where they had indicated and moved toward the bakery, a small cabin with a rudimentary mill. There I received two pieces of bread, one for me and one for Masza. From the trunk of a tree, they had improvised the breakfast table— it was there where I waited for Sioma to return.

A few hours later, he arrived with the other comrades. They brought back a hen and several sacks of flour, which they had found in an abandoned farm. Luckily, they were able to avoid any form of confrontation. That night, I slept hugging Masza, sheltered by the heat of Sioma's body.

When I awoke, I kissed my daughter and carried her near the Berezyna River, a tributary of the Niemen River, to relieve our accumulated liquids. When we returned, we heard a young woman calling the kids: "Children! Come near, it's time to learn!"

Masza wanted to join the children who followed the young woman.

"We have organized a small school," said the lawyer, Shlomo Volkowysky. Csesia was a teacher originally from Novogrudok, and in the camp she exercised her craft: she taught, organized games, sang with the children, and coordinated plays that they performed for us. Masza would be in great care.

Masza began making connections with the other children in the camp, and her face shone with joy. She ran through the central field of the *partisanka,* chasing after the other children. The boots I had been given for her were enormous and did not allow her to walk steadily, but they were better than the wet rags that had covered her feet when we'd first arrived at the camp. She stumbled with every step, but her glow and joyful laughter softened my heart. Nothing stopped her.

***

News came from Vilna. An armed revolt had broken out in the Vilna Ghetto on the first day of September. This was a blow to German pride! Jews who refused to surrender fought head-on. But just as it had happened in Warsaw, the ghetto was liquidated by the Germans soon after. Some of the clandestine members were able to flee and joined forces with Russian partisans. We were heartbroken by the image of the Jews who had been murdered or deported, but we applauded the bravery of the Vilna fighters. Despite our ambivalence, we danced with joy. We sensed that the end of the Nazi regime was near.

Life in the *puszcza* soon became routine; insects and dirt attached to our skin. The sky was constantly covered with warplanes performing reconnaissance trips. We never knew if they were routinely inspecting the area or planning to attack us. To avoid being spotted, we would run to hide in our huts, camouflaged between leaves and branches—becoming part of the landscape.

***

I found Leibl Stolowitsky, the former accountant of the brewery, working with the blacksmiths. He looked old, tired, and very overwhelmed. His wife, Sara, took care of their daughter Chana and their orphaned niece. Michash, his son, had grown in just a few weeks—he was now a man. There was nothing left of the boy who had slipped through the small window of the train car. He was now one of the young *partisanim* in charge of dangerous missions. Mr. Leibl Stolowitsky greeted me courteously and asked about Masza.

"She's fine, very thin, but she's doing well. And how is Chana?" I reciprocated.

"She is at the clinic, she's got dysentery. We're very worried about her health," he said.

Typhoid, scurvy, boils, and dysentery—illnesses proliferated by the lack of hygiene and the scarcity of food—were our everyday reality in the *partisanka*. Some, like Chana, recovered, but many others died. It was the law of life. I thanked God a thousand times for Masza's health and our good luck.

Medicine in the forest was limited to home cures: a powder smeared as a disinfectant, boiled milk injected to accelerate the immune system, and ash and urine baths to ward off lice.

"You know, Szura," Sioma said, "we could make a *stolpski*, a soap to improve the hygiene of the camp. It is a simple process that I learned while studying brewing engineering in Brussels. I can use animal fat, tree ash, and a little resin to produce soap."

Before I could respond, my husband led me to Tevie Bielski's *ziemlanka*. The *komandir* was having breakfast with his wife Lilka. Attentive to the explanations Sioma gave, Bielski gladly accepted the plan and instantly gave orders to a couple of subordinates to be ready for the task.

In the farthest section of the camp, in a small hut next to the clinic and kitchen, a brown greasy mass would be made and cooked on a bonfire. It would then be cooled on slabs of wood where it would solidify into a rustic soap.

The power in the *atriad* was hierarchical. At the top of the pyramid were the Bielski brothers and their friends. Then we had the young men from Novogrudok (the native town of the Bielskis). The rest of us, who mostly came from Lida, were at the end of the chain. There was even a song explaining it: "I don't advise you to go to the eleventh *ziemlanka*," said the chorus, "the *intelligentsia* lives there; Polish is their *muttersprache*, their mother tongue .... The *geschichte* teacher is treated the best; he teaches history and is given the thickest soup with lots of pieces of dough."

But thanks to Sioma's inventiveness, our status improved radically. We went from being *malbushim*, low-class citizens, to "the engineer, the engineer's wife, and his adorable daughter." The dentist from Minsk, who shared our *ziemlanka,* suddenly started speaking to us; a couple from Mir sang songs to Masza. Tevie invited my husband assiduously to take vodka and sausage in his hut, sharing sugar and *shinka*, a tasty bacon, with him.

I started working with my husband on producing soap. We took resin from the trees, burned wood, and melted the fat in a copper kettle. The success of the soap factory was resounding! It was not a commercial soap like the one with the name of the famous opera singer Kipras Petrauskas, but it did the job of disinfecting and cleaning the skin, helping to prevent infections and diseases.

Winter came, and the first snow fell. My dried-up hands, aged at twenty-nine, kept turning the mixture of ash and grease. The melted soap bubbled up, and a rising feeling of envy around us began boiling in the air.

***

The area of the *puszcza* where the camp was situated was very dense. It consisted of a forest of conifers, birches, and pines. I soon learned to distinguish the best woods to make the fire burn faster. The splattered oaks gave variety to the landscape, and deer often approached the camp. Squirrels joined their little hands on the fringes of ferns, and birds rested on the branches of the pines.

Despite the sanitary measures, respiratory diseases, from a common cough and cold to severe lung infections, plagued the camp. The women who worked in the improvised infirmary applied wet cloths to the sick to lessen their fevers. The one doctor in charge applied compresses on pustules and inflammations at the same rate that he practiced abortions. They were busy filling pillows with straw and trying to feed the people under their care as best as possible.

I learned a song today. Csesia taught it to us. I will sing it to my parents at night; I'm sure they'll like it! *"Klimu Woroshilov pismo ya nopisal* ... **To Klimu Woroshilov I have written a letter ... my dear brother will go to the Russian army ... if he perishes, I will take his place and his rifle ...."**

I longed for privacy with my husband. In the underground mud and log house, where we lived, we were always surrounded by people. We talked about trivial matters while we tried to cover ourselves from the cold, snuggling to find body heat. There were twenty beds, one next to the other.

I did not get used to the crowded conditions; I had trouble sharing the little oxygen we had under the surface of the earth. It was often that Sioma would turn to me smiling and stroking my forehead. In our secret code, I would understand his gesture: the three of us were together, that was all that mattered. Nevertheless, I felt claustrophobic and nauseated, and I cursed the lichens that shrouded my dreams.

A pinch of hope was added with every new day. But there were times when my stomachaches were unbearable. One morning, the cramps attacked me by surprise; I was starving, and I could not help the tears rolling down my cheeks. Masza stroked my hair. We went out to collect mushrooms—the same ones that grew inside the *ziemlanka*. They made me sick. I promised myself that if I got out alive after the war, I would never eat champignons, truffles, or chanterelles ever again, even if those delicacies were prepared by great chefs.

Szura cries of hunger. She doesn't say that to me, but I know she suffers. I do not know how to help her to prevent her empty stomach from causing her so much pain .... My poor wife. I hope the Allies will arrive soon; I fervently wish that peace reigns again. We long for peace.

***

The morning fog had dissipated. Seeing myself in the mirror of my imagination, I groomed as best I could. I ran my hand through my hair, wet my face with the water from the bucket outside the *ziemlanka,* and drank *tsikorye* with bread soaked in water.

Sioma had risen earlier to go and prepare soap, and Masza was playing with the other children.

"Are you Mrs. Pupko?" two Russian partisans pulling a cow approached me and asked. "This cow is for your family. Comrade Karchmer, of *Komandir* Dubow's *atriad*, has learned that you are here and has sent this animal as a gift."

I thanked the two young men and sent greetings to our dear friend from Lida, who had instantly become our protector. I was excited to receive such a gift and ran to look for Sioma to tell him. But I was soon surprised to learn that our new wealth would have to be donated to the community. The only benefit we would enjoy would be receiving the first cup of milk for my Maszinka.

I pulled the cow behind the corral where Tevie's horse was kept. A comrade milked the cow and handed me a small jar. I quickly and carefully carried the white liquid to my *ziemlanka.* I boiled it and gave it to Masza to take a few sips. I drank a little bit of the precious milk and then shared it with my husband. He smiled at me, enjoying the taste of it. Every day for weeks on end, the cow gave us her abundant milk ... until the day they had to sacrifice her for the meat.

We were given small pieces of fat and beef that we chewed with pleasure. I tasted the thick broth with the aroma of conifers, stewed with the morning leftovers and seasoned with mud and spices of the forest, a culinary delicacy in these circumstances. They used every part of the cow and didn't waste a single piece; even the skin was tanned in the *partisanka* workshop and used for making shoes.

Whenever possible, Karchmer sent us gifts of food that we

gladly accepted.

***

The carpenters were hammering wood, the blacksmiths were melting metal, the hairdresser was shaving somebody's beard, and my husband and I were mixing ashes with fat. It was a typical afternoon—until we heard gunshots nearby. I ran out of the makeshift workshop immediately, looking for Masza. Luckily, I found her just a few steps away.

"Run, run!" people were shouting vehemently.

"Leave everything as it is."

"Save yourselves!" others warned.

"Let's go into the woods, into the marshes. Fast!" Tevie ordered.

Sioma and I took Masza's hand. We followed our leader, who, despite his characteristic leather jacket, was barely distinguishable from the dense undergrowth and the mud of the swamp surrounding us. We all tried to hurry, but the older ones who had difficulty running stayed behind.

As we ran, the *puszcza* became denser and the mud deeper; in the swamp, our flight became increasingly difficult. The shots resounded behind us. We could not afford to stop. Tevie guided us; he knew each trunk and branch of the trees we passed. The thicker the forest became, the greater the chance of survival. But the advance was slow, as the blackish viscosity covered us to the waist.

Sioma carried Masza on his shoulders as we tried to advance. Finally, the bullets dissipated in the distance. We did not stop moving despite the thick, sticky water that prevented us from running. Every step I took weighed on me, as I tried to keep my mind clear to escape successfully.

Tevie led us to higher ground in the swamp, a kind of island where we spent the night safely. It was not until dawn when the sentries returned from the camp, asserting that the enemy had vanished. Only then did we set out on our way back to the camp.

When we arrived, we quantified the damage caused by the White Poles. Right away, Tevie organized groups to temporarily relocate us to another site in the forest.

***

Two strangers arrived asking for Sioma. They identified themselves as Russian comrades.

"Where's the chemist?"

"I am his wife, what can I help you with?" I replied politely.

"We come on behalf of Victor Pachenko, head of the *Atriad October*. We want soap."

I recognized the name Pachenko; he was reputed to be a fair man. I went to look for a few bars of soap and handed them over. In return, they gave me a liter of vodka, bread, and *shinka*, a mouthwatering pig's leg. Unsurprisingly, several people in the *partisanka* demanded that we share the *shinka* with everyone.

"I'll give you the vodka, but I'll keep the *shinka*. I will save it for my family," I said firmly, handing over the bottle of alcohol.

My actions had consequences. A few days later, my husband was accused of stealing fat destined to produce soap. How dare they even suspect us? We were suffering just like everyone else.

"We've never taken an ounce of that fat," I said.

The denunciation was a pretext to take away the responsibility of the soap workshop from my husband's hands. Tevie himself ordered Sioma to withdraw from the post, arguing that his presence was no longer necessary to secure production. One of Tevie's friends replaced my husband. Without further ado, we were stripped of the little privilege we enjoyed.

Food was scarce. When we could find some meat, it had to be preserved under the snow. We consumed it little by little in small slices every day. Unfortunately, brawls and camp gossip only increased. In the harsh conditions in which we lived, people lost the little civility they had left. Education faded in the face of hunger. Tevie continually intervened in clashes, especially when the disputes swelled into violent blows. Our leader suppressed the feisty with threats and severe punishments, throwing them into a makeshift "jail," a much-needed place in the camp where thieves and bullies were locked up for hours, sometimes days, and even weeks. There was only one authority, and it was Tevie.

***

One night, the Bielski brothers were drinking heavily. Zus Bielski shouted at Sioma, "Hey, Pupko! We need you!"

Tevie gave him a friendly smack in the back, welcoming him to his cabin to play cards with them. I didn't know where Sioma was until much later that night when he came back to our *ziemlanka*. The incident of the *shinka* had been forgotten; they had re-accepted him into the exclusive circle of comrades.

To enter Tevie Bielski's *ziemlanka,* one had to go through a beautiful door stolen from a neighboring town. The elegant windows had belonged to a manor house in Novogrudok, and the mud walls, covered with wooden logs, were decorated with maps. In the center was a desk with a typewriter, which was transformed at night into a card table.

From that night on, Sioma snuck out of our room to join the card games in the *komandir's* bunker. In that hole, dug underneath the earth, he enjoyed the exclusive camaraderie as he played poker with the Bielski brothers and his associates.

My husband enjoyed those hours of recreation with the head of the *atriad*. They played poker, smoked cigarettes, and drank samogon—the moonshine that accompanied their jokes. They also cursed and talked about the theories of life. Tevie, with his usual slow manner of talking, pausing with commas and dots between words, weighed on every idea, every project, every vision of the future while Zus laughed wholeheartedly at every chance. Sioma, on the other hand, entertained them with anecdotes of his life as a bourgeois, with the *savoir vivre* that he learned on his various trips before the war. Regardless of the different worlds from which they came, destiny had united them here, in the forest among wolves—a place in which they shared bets and alcohol.

When our teacher Csesia shows us a new Russian song to recite, I try to forget the hunger I feel. When I play in the yard with my friends, I try to disregard the pain in my stomach. Today we have built a beautiful castle in the snow! My hands almost froze, so I had to run into the *ziemlanka* to warm them a little. When I came out again, I saw that someone had stepped on our castle. It doesn't matter, tomorrow we will build another. I am so hungry! I ate a piece of sausage; it was disgusting to see that it had worms, but I ate it anyway. I am very cold; sometimes I can't feel my feet. My whole body is freezing. I only have a small blanket to cover my hands, but it is not enough. My boots are so big that I often stumble; I have so many blisters on my feet that I don't count them anymore. I don't tell my mom as she will only worry—she already does what she can for me.

Masza never took off her coat, ragged and three sizes too large. Her pale face, starved and sad, blended with the white landscape around her. Tears would often roll down her cheeks. Her swollen lips showed the beginning signs of scurvy. We lived in terrible conditions, and I was constantly suffering from asthma attacks, but how could we complain? We were free in the *puszcza*. We were alive! The three of us were together!

I grabbed my daughter's hand as we approached the bonfire, joining the others. Some talked, and others drank *tsikorye*.

Together we sang a song that became our hymn and gave us strength: "*Zoj nit kein mol az du geist dem letstn veg* ... Never say that this is the final path." The song spoke of hope, of longing, and of the future. "Here we are ... a better tomorrow will come soon!" The leitmotif of the anthem pushed us forward.

For the first time, I felt one with the group of Jews around me, refugees like me, miserable and sad as I was, all yearning to survive to build a better future.

***

A new year had begun: 1944. The frosts would not let us rest; it was the crudest winter we had faced in the forest. Afternoons were dark, and we spent many hours inside the damp *ziemlankas*. We avoided turning on the stoves to try to save some coal, but it was also difficult to keep the wood dry. The never-ending cold nights made our bodies shiver constantly.

"Mama, Mama."

I heard Masza as if in a dream. I opened my eyes. She wanted attention and demanded protection.

"Mama, do you hear those noises?"

I heard the howls of a hungry wolf prowling around the camp.

"Mama ... they are the gnomes of the forest. They tickle and play with the animal, making it howl so loudly that the trees shake. Mama, I can see the gnomes every time a lightning bolt illuminates the sky. Their eyes sparkle. I can make them out through the window. Do you see them?" exclaimed Masza, pointing to the only window of our subterranean house. "Do you hear them, Mama? They laugh and jump, they wave at us."

"Yes, *mein kind*," I comforted her tenderly without judging her fantasies. "Place your head on my lap and go to sleep."

The pack of wolves was close. I held her hand, and a disturbed sleep overcame me again.

My mother has fallen asleep again; she cried a lot today. I am frightened by the noises, but I reassure myself by thinking that the gnomes take care of us. They are friends of the wolves, and they make them happy by giving them sweets. Mama promised me that tomorrow we will go together to look for dry branches and wild strawberries! I'm terrified of those wolves and their constant howling.

In the morning, Sioma fetched firewood, and I left the *ziemlanka* to wash Masza's and my hands with ice. She ran with the other children while I went to the kitchen to help prepare a stock of leftovers to warm our malnourished bodies. Moments later, I was at the shoemaker's hut. The previous night, I had asked him for boots for my husband and some *volikes* for my daughter.

"Ma'am, it is impossible," he explained, "these yellow ones you see here are to supply the orders of other *atriads*; we have to fulfill our commitments. The Russian comrades demand a certain number of shoes, and they are our priority. You will have to wait for yours."

While we argued about my urgent request for the new boots, we heard a big fuss coming from the central "avenue of the camp." Several men appeared through the pine trees; they were coming from a *zadache* and carrying an injured man. The young *partisanim* were agitated, interrupting each other as they recounted the failed mission: they had reached the hamlet. Looking for supplies, they had snuck up to a peasant's farm to steal some chickens. To their surprise, the door had no padlock. They had opened it and entered, trying not to make noise. In the darkness, they had seen some shadows moving. They had not had time to react as the rifles in front of them had fired. It was an ambush! The peasant had informed the Nazis that the Bielski *partisanim* were scavenging food from that area. The soldiers had been waiting for them all along. In the midst of all the confusion, the *partisanim* had returned fire without strategy or purpose, without even knowing who they were counterattacking.

"Let's get out fast, I'm hurt!" one of them had shouted.

They'd run off across the field and fled into the woods. Two comrades had carried the wounded man to the *partisanka*. Blood gushed out from his chest. Desperate, everyone came running to give him words of encouragement. Dr. Hirsch checked him and almost immediately walked away disconsolately. The partisan died before our eyes. The men said *Kaddish* for him.

How could I demand new boots in such circumstances? Nothing mattered anymore other than the fortune of being alive. Masza continued wearing boots three sizes too big, and Sioma wore the old shoes he had brought from the brewery.

Tevie was furious at the failure of the raid and sad about losing one of our own.

"This will not happen again," he grumbled, "we'll teach that peasant who the Bielski are."

That same night, a group of *partisanim* went to the man's house and set fire to his property. It was the law of the jungle, the only way to earn respect. The Jerusalem of the Forest, as we began to call our camp, was no paradise at all. It was more like ancient Babylon, ruled by severe codes of behavior that imposed discipline on those who misbehaved. The rule was revenge: an eye for an eye, a tooth for a tooth.

***

Sioma's turn to go out on a mission came again. I was terrified of the dangers of those *zadaches*! I preferred not to think about it. The partisans risked their skin each time they sneaked into small settlements. Sometimes they were lucky—finding abandoned villages where they could collect food and useful objects or encountering peasants who gave them bread or utensils without resistance or reproach. If they were fortunate, they would get away only by threatening the villagers with their rifles and pistols. But sometimes, in order to enforce authority, they had to use more violent tactics. Most of the time, the *partisanim* returned to the camp with potatoes, beets, barley, sacks of wheat flour, honey, and even livestock.

Sioma left with his companions at night. Three days later, they returned, pulling an old horse as a reward. The animal would serve not to plow or to be mounted on but as much-needed meat.

Csesia, the young teacher, taught the children a verse to be thankful for the succulent fibrous delicacy. I imagined that our banquet was composed of duck breast and not the putrid, rubbery pieces of horse meat. We all chewed joyfully. That day, with our bellies full, we slept satisfied.

***

I continuously felt helpless, unable to offer more food to my little girl, who was increasingly malnourished. Questions and memories tormented me: *When will this hell end?* I was tired; nothing made sense. *What happened to my uncle Meyer and his family? Is it possible that my father was saved? Where is my aunt Shayna? And Noya? What about my sisters-in-law? Could they have escaped?* I was afraid of the answers. I replayed the different scenes again and again: the separation from my mother-in-law at the train station, Noya in the cattle car clinging to Mrs. Weksler, me jumping off the train into the abyss, the nights I spent alone in the forest .... It was better not to think. I occupied myself in the kitchen, stirring up brothy concoctions.

"What's the use of your education? You won't get anywhere in this place knowing Hebrew," said the lady in charge of supplying the slimy broth we ate daily, interrupting my thoughts. For her, perhaps rightly, the *intelligentsia* was useless in the *puszcza*, where the only skill required was a useful trade and the ability to fight. I refrained from answering; the smell of decomposed skin from the tannery struck me. I tried to focus on the little poem we had dedicated to Azoel Bielski: "Azoel is the strongest, Azoel is a *gibor*, a hero, a *bracha*, a prayer of God; Blessed is the place where he sets his foot." That was my way of trying to erase the uncertainties that polluted my mind: delete the past and stay in the present.

A loud noise was heard nearby: two bullets shot into the wind. A group of *partisanim* had brought back three German soldiers as prisoners and shoved them into the center of the *partisanka*. The comrades had left yesterday, right before dawn, for a mission. After walking for hours in the muddy snow, they had taken refuge in a barn and waited for evening to fall. They had taken two sacks of wheat flour and one of barley. Upon leaving, they'd heard footsteps. The owner of the farmhouse had realized he was being robbed and begun to shoot. In less than a minute, they were surrounded by Germans. They'd abandoned the booty and managed to sneak out through a back door. As they'd fled, they'd encountered three drunken Nazi soldiers who, paradoxically, surrendered immediately.

As we moved closer to see what was going on, one of the captives, a fair-haired young man with blue eyes and a straight nose, resisted, spitting at his captor.

"You will never dare to disrespect me again," said the

comrade as he slapped him.

Tevie Bielski ordered that their pockets be emptied; one of them carried a photograph of an Orthodox Jew with a long beard and *payes*.

"Why do you have this photograph in your possession?" asked one of our men.

"I keep it as a souvenir, a reminder for when the war ends and there is no Jew left on the face of the earth. I'm hoping I can make some money from it, as it will represent how Jews looked before they were an extinct species."

Our men rushed to hit him; their kicks and punches rained over the prisoner.

"Stop!" cried Bielski. "We are not like them. These men must die with respect, as they deserve. They must be shot for their war crimes. Now, everyone, go to your *ziemlanka*," he ordered.

They took the Nazis where we could no longer see them. Moments later, we heard the shots being discharged from a distance.

***

We had not eaten meat for weeks. It was February. Finally, one of those missions returned with a huge loot: a dead cow wounded in a firefight. The *komandir* was shocked to see the dead animal on the ground, staining the snow. The *partisanim* had not realized that they had left a path of blood on the white snow.

"The party is over," Tevie declared. "The red clues, spilled like a path, will lead the Germans right to us. Get ready! We have no time to lose; they will find us in a few minutes. Take all the arms, we must flee into the depths of the forest!"

The whole camp disappeared in a blast ....

Where are my parents? I have to run, but my legs are too small!

"Please, sir, can you help me, take me by the hand?"

He does not help me, and he walks away. Each step I take is a struggle; my feet sink into the snow, and sometimes the snow reaches up to my waist. It is impossible for me to run.

"Please, ma'am, take my hand and help me go faster!"

I hear bullets! Where are my parents? I'm scared!

I found Masza running with the help of a lady. Eventually, Sioma caught up with us and carried Masza. We accelerated our frightened steps into areas where there was almost impenetrable vegetation. We heard screams, a sudden turmoil of words, then the deafening noise of bullets. We hid as best we could behind some trees. Sioma shouted something that, amid the commotion and fear, I couldn't understand.

We stayed put in our spot until we could barely hear the bullets in the distance. Little by little, the harsh sounds dissolved into the darkness of the night. We returned to the camp at dawn. It was desolate; the local police, under the command of the Nazis, had stolen everything, even our livestock. Security was reinforced immediately. We were left without dairy and meat. Scurvy and dysentery spread quickly without medicines or proper nourishment.

***

As the weather grew warmer and more pleasant, the campfire we relied on to keep us warm was no longer necessary, but it continued to burn, serving as the center of the camp where everybody met up at night. As the sparks dwindled, adults like us retired to our huts. The young people lingered and took advantage of the dark.

As I endured the stinging of hundreds of fierce mosquitoes and scratched at the sores left by the bloodthirsty lice, I remembered the tales from my childhood and the stories of the *shaides*. They were spirits that lived in the *puszcza* and appeared suddenly just to frighten people. Now we were part of that fantasy world, inhabitants of the forest; we had become *shaides*, fearsome souls who strolled through the villages, stealing livestock and provoking acts of sabotage against the Nazis. We wanted to survive; we wanted the war to end soon.

***

March 1944. What seemed like an illusion of butterflies falling from the sky became an allusion to hope. In broad daylight, small parachutes rained from above; the floating blankets lightly fell all around us. The spectacle filled us with great excitement.

"The Russians sent us food!" cried a woman.

We ran to the clearing where most of the gifts had landed. It was disappointing to see that there was no food; instead, we found weapons. Azoel and Zus approached first to inspect the objects and announced that the weapons would be distributed to different groups: first among our resistance warriors and then to other *atriads*. We worked all morning organizing the explosives and rifles, and afterward, we waited for further instruction.

That night, in our crowded *ziemlanka,* Sioma lay down next to me. The other souls who shared our space made it difficult for us to have any kind of intimacy. Masza fell asleep, and Sioma whispered in my ear: "Let's go outside! There is no danger, there is only silence."

We had slipped out of our temporary dwelling on a few other occasions, but I was especially tired that night, and my nose itched from the smell of the mothballs that had arrived with the package of explosives. I'd come to understand long ago, during our captivity in the brewery, that sexual desire is an instinct that does not die easily. Fear of being extinct from the face of the earth is not enough to erase the longing for lovemaking. On the contrary, it was precisely on these occasions that the stimulus became more vigorous and the desire more powerful and exciting.

Sioma stroked my breasts as if they were his property, smiled lustfully, and without further questions, led me out of the cabin. Bright fireflies lit the way. Sioma placed a blanket over the mud. I wept feeling his tender caresses; I wept for fear, for joy, for anguish, and for the uncertainty of our present and our future. I cried for my father and for Noya, for my mother-in-law Rachil, and for my sisters-in-law. I sobbed for my uncle Meyer and for his family, and for all the Jewish people who were suffering. I had cried countless times before, but that night I felt guilty for surviving. I asked myself, *Why me? Why us?*

We returned to the *ziemlanka*, smelling of sex, blood, and smoke. I carried inside me the epidemic of war, where moral boundaries didn't exist, where people didn't fear the forbidden and lost any respect for the sacred. How could we enjoy anything, even sex, if we were all pawns in an inexplicable game of chess? How did I allow myself to shout out in pleasure while being a puppet in the hands of hatred? In front of us, I could only see a cruel and pathetic fate.

***

The holiday of *Pesach* was approaching. *Matzot*, unleavened bread, was prepared in the furnace as the atmosphere in the camp grew more festive. I had difficulty joining in the merriment. I doubted God; I doubted my identity. Where was Moses to part the waters of the Red Sea? We were sinking in a sea of dead. *Where are you, God?*

With the warm weather, typhoid fever spread through the *partisanka*. The clinic, under the instruction of Dr. Hirsch, couldn't handle the epidemic. They were forced to isolate the sick, but there were no medicines to cure them, and the deaths were adding up.

Notwithstanding our bleak environment, the reports

received through the partisan radio were encouraging. The Russians were winning at the front. We believed the end of the war was near!

We held a *seder* together around the campfire. I fixed my hair and my daughter's with wildflowers we had collected. We counted the ten *makot* (the plagues God wrought upon the Egyptians), sang songs from the Haggadah, and ate *matzeh* instead of bread. *Pesach* redeemed us.

The evening celebration ended, and we retired to our *ziemlanka*. As I rested my head, I grazed my earlobe only to realize that I didn't feel the metallic piece of my mother's earring. My grandmother had given it to me so that my mother's presence would always be with me. I had never taken it off, especially after losing its pair long ago.

"I lost my earring! I lost my mother!" I panicked and shouted without caring if I woke everyone in the room. Fate was playing a trick on me! "Sioma, I lost my earring!" I exclaimed, desperately searching the muddy floor. Despite the pleas for silence from the people who wanted to sleep, I continued with my frantic cry: "Remember, Sioma? This is the earring I've never taken off! It was a gift from my grandparents! It was the one that belonged to my mother. The only thing I had of hers. Do you think that it could have fallen in the woods or near the fire?"

Masza woke up and soon understood the problem. She knelt beside me and helped me search for the earring. My head was spinning. I had lost my entire family; this was all I had left ... a memory, a token, a breath or a sigh of what a mother meant.

"Mama, is this what you were looking for?" Maszinka gazed up at me with her jet-black eyes, holding the little earring in her hand. "I found it at the entrance of the *ziemlanka*."

I hugged my daughter, exhaled with relief, and laughed at how nothing made sense: we were fleeing from the Nazis, we were constantly on alert for the antisemitic Russians, we were hiding from the White Poles, and we lived with many hardships in the forest. But I had been blind with concern and anguished over a simple earring. That night, I dreamed that I was in Anykščiai, in the house of my grandparents. I saw Leah and Shabtai; I hugged them and kissed them lovingly. They offered me Tilca chocolate, and its taste lulled me until dawn.

***

May 1, 1944, Labor Day: a holiday for all *partisanim*! We ate *shinka* to celebrate! Eating ham was not a sacrilege against the Judaic law, it was survival—it was one of the few options in our meager diet. Someone brought a guitar and a mandolin. We distributed *samogon* and danced kozachok on the "main avenue" of the forest. It was just a simple path, but we decorated it with red banners to enhance the ambience. The atmosphere was full of jubilation and leisure. Shmuel Amarant, the historian, asked for silence so we could listen to the words of the song.

"Never say that this path is the end," a young girl sang in

Yiddish, immediately grabbing our attention.

The bonfire captured the strength of hope. The harmony of our voices slowly lifted our spirits until the notes resounded with force: "Because the gray sky covered the sunlight! The moment we longed for will surely come; they will hear the sound of our march. We are here; *Anachnu po!*"

We kept on singing—unafraid of being heard. We were proud of who we were. We were proud to be Jews.

***

There was time for everything in the forest: time to be afraid and time to immerse oneself in philosophical, eternal questions. Would the Messiah ever come to end Jewish suffering? My grandparents had taught me that with his arrival, all the hardships of the world would end. If the prophecy was correct, should we wait for his coming? He'd take us back to our homeland of Israel and end all sorrow and pain. But my initial thoughts would strike back: *if the Messiah has not arrived yet, when we Jews are suffering more than ever, then he will never arrive.*

In the *puszcza,* we understood that our only solution was to fight, for neither the Messiah nor God, nor anyone, would come to save us. No religious belief was solid enough to withstand the cruelty of war and the extermination of our loved ones. If we survived, we would need to establish ourselves in *Eretz* Israel and rebuild our homeland all on our own.

The few Orthodox Jews in the camp prepared an area in the improvised tannery for worship. I never went. Religion was not my forte; it was a reminder of my past in Anykščiai—something that belonged to Szifra and not to Szura. What did I care about the Messiah or Eliyahu, the prophet, who never came to the Passover seder? We lived underground, like moles in holes. We surfaced sporadically to take in some air only to return to the mud moments later. I left all rituals, superstitions, and fanaticism to others. What did prayers and following the laws of *kashrut* matter now? We had more pressing concerns. I spent my days thinking of the land of Israel, my happy days at the *Shomer Hatzair*, and Yudko Eksztejn, my boyfriend from long ago.

***

I never thought that the sounds of war could seem encouraging and inspiring. But that summer, as the front crept closer to us and the explosions trembled onto the Earth's surface, I was filled with longing and hope.

The summer was in full swing! We knew the Allied forces were fighting nearby—the explosions became louder and louder.

"Alert! Alert!" shouted one of the sentries guarding the camp. "Our comrades have encountered a group of German soldiers fleeing the front! We have caught four of them, and nine have died in the skirmish. Make way for the prisoners!"

I left the kettle on the fire and saw from a distance what was happening. People began circling the prisoners who knelt in the center of the *partisanka* with their hands tied behind their necks. One of the *partisanim*, in a moment of impulsive hatred, spat on the face of a prisoner. Revulsion flowed through his pores. One by one, others followed, seeking revenge, shouting, kicking, and slapping the prisoners. The unrestricted blows were vindictive strikes against the entire German nation, against its cruelty, against the complicit humanity that silently allowed our families to be massacred. It was an act of catharsis, perhaps even redemption. They continued hitting the German soldiers, breaking their noses, smashing their heads, breaking their teeth, and crushing their testicles. It became an unbridled horde ....

A young *partisaner* shoved his rifle into the mouth of one of the soldiers, saying, "This is for my brothers and my parents!"

He silenced the man with his gunshot.

The bullet exited through the back of the soldier's head. He instantly fell. The other three soldiers, moored in their places, wept in fear. One of them stained his pants, urinating himself. Rage burned through the camp; an uncontrollable temper of revenge was palpable in the air; it was a feverish dance, an angry and irrational vengeance. The bullets penetrated through the mouths of each one of the soldiers, symbolizing vengeance for all the Jews murdered by the Reich.

As the days passed, camp life returned to how it had been before. We tried to forget the horrific event. We complained once again about the usual things: the scarcity of milk, the mosquitoes and lice feasting on our blood, how no one slept well at night. In the days that followed, we received more news of the Russian onslaught: more groups of German soldiers were fleeing the front. We celebrated every rebellious feat of the partisans. If we learned that a train had been derailed or that they had besieged a group of German soldiers, we rejoiced.

One morning, a group of about a hundred German soldiers ran into our camp as they fled from the blasts caused by another group of partisans. On their way into the camp, they killed five people who were still sleeping in their hut. Our comrades quickly pursued them and shooed them off, pushing them to the outskirts of our camp, where the fight continued. Terrified, and on high alert, we waited around an hour until we were told the area was clear.

***

August 10, 1944. We heard horses and tanks approaching. The Red Army arrived, their sickle and hammer flags fluttering in the wind. Their entrance caused a commotion of glee in the camp.

"The war is over!" the soldiers cried as they came out of their armored vehicles. Their contagious exhilaration brought hugs, laughter, and uncontainable tears of happiness. Pure joy.

Chapter Eleven: 1944

O rders came from the highest command of the *atriad* groups: Bielski was asked to start the march the following morning after dismantling the camp. This would be our last night in the *partisanka.*

It was one more night filled with anguish: What would we find in Lida? Who had survived? A multitude of ambivalent thoughts congested my brain. We did not sleep much. We knew the German army was retreating; the roads were a no-man's land, and they were still dangerous.

Tevie didn't want us to be seen as thieves of wheat and hens, usurpers of towns and villages; he wanted to exalt our image as warriors, righteous servicemen who fought against the Nazis. We were commanded to leave most of our things behind and only bring what was indispensable.

As we set out on the march toward Novogrudok, one man took a wagon and packed things to carry with him. Why did he do it? Why was he not following the *komandir's* orders? Bielski's guards noticed the *drosky* full of objects and immediately alerted Tevie. With an authoritative gesture, the *komandir* demanded that he leave the cart. But the man challenged our leader and continued to pull it. Without thinking twice, right in front of everyone, with the backdrop of Lake Kremin, Tevie blew the man's brains out. His wife let out an uncontrollable wail as her husband fell in front of her and her son's feet. Her cries did not cease as she walked all the way to town.

No one said a thing, but we all thought that Tevie had gone too far. He had abused his power when it was no longer necessary; the enemy had already been defeated.

Our group was walking slowly and in disorder; we marched with children and older folk who had overcome the hardships of war. German prisoners were traveling with us because Tevie had promised the high command to take them to Novogrudok. From there, we would leave for Lida.

We saw corpses of soldiers and civilians scattered along the roadway. The landscape was desolate, roads and bridges had collapsed, and everything was in ruins. The smell of decay was nauseating, and I tried to shield Masza's eyes as much as possible. We hastened our steps, trying our best to keep up with the group. We walked stealthily, afraid of being attacked by surprise. Other *atriads* approached us, intermittently absorbing our group within their ranks as they passed us by. All of a sudden, we saw Bella Stolowitsky marching with her partisan group. She shouted with joy as soon as she saw us and ran to hug her family.

We were walking on inhospitable land, uncertain of our future, but along the way, confusing us with Russian troops, people came out to greet us. We were one thousand two hundred people who had survived in the *puszcza*. One thousand two hundred souls, under the command of the Bielski brothers, who had been saved from the clutches of Nazism. One thousand two hundred homeless Jews.

We walked asphyxiated by the smoke of forest fires, carrying ashes in our eyes and mud in our ears. The parade was less than triumphal. Hearing sporadic shootings, we were mistrustful and apprehensive. We feared what we would find in our home.

We traveled for several days until we reached the river Niemen. As we approached the urban ruins left by war, we saw that all the houses in Novogrudok had been destroyed. We wandered through the area that used to be the ghetto, and we cried with our companions who once lived there. Some survivors faced the stark reality of returning home to find their dwellings either knocked down or occupied by strangers. German prisoners were secured behind a fence; they looked at us fearfully, just as we had looked at them not long ago: from captive to imprisoner.

At dusk, we gathered atop the hill of the ruins of the old castle, and a flag of the Red Army fluttered victoriously. There were triumphant speeches, and a certificate of gratitude was given to us for our participation in the fight against the Germans. There was still a lingering feeling of emptiness; mutism overcame many of us as we looked at a landscape of forgetfulness, blood, pain, and death. Those of us from Lida said goodbye to our comrades from the *puszcza* and focused on our journey ahead.

A few days later, we reached the outskirts of what had been our city. There was nothing left: the houses were all burned, and most buildings had collapsed when the city had been bombarded. It was hard to remember what the streets had looked like before the war. We could not distinguish where the main synagogue, the Winogradov store, or the Nirvana cinema used to be.

The tombstones in the Jewish cemetery were desecrated; only scattered pieces of the stones were left. Some Hebrew-inscribed marble and granite slabs had been made into the foundations of new houses. Cows now grazed on the fertile ground that covered the bones of past generations. There was no way to distinguish the tomb of Meilach, my father-in-law, but Sioma said *Kaddish* nevertheless.

We were fortunate to find that the brewery had been abandoned. The Germans had fled, and no one had dared occupy it. The house that had once been my mother-in-law's was in good condition. We fixed the main room and rested there until the following morning. We ate beetroots and drank the beer we found leftover in the factory drums. It had been a year since we had seen the rest of the family. We waited impatiently for them to arrive. We didn't know their whereabouts. A few days later, Mitzia and Roza arrived with their young son Meilashe.

Meilashe is more distracted than before; he has changed a lot. Where is Noya, his sister? Where is my grandmother Rachil? And my cousins Dzozik and Fruma? Where are they? Where are my aunts Aniuta and Franya and my uncles? Only my uncle Mitzia and my aunt Roza returned with Meilashe. My parents say this is our family. They say that

being together is important, but most of them are still missing .... My aunt Roza cries a lot. She has found one of Noya's dresses and gave it to me. My mother dyed it blue so that when I wear it, it will not remind Roza of her missing daughter. The dress is very beautiful; the fabric is soft and shiny, and I like the feeling of it on my skin. I wait for Meilashe to come and play with me, but he does not come. He is sitting in a corner and biting his nails. Maybe he misses his sister .... Where is she?

Several weeks passed, and yet no other family members returned to the brewery. I wanted to know who had survived in Anykščiai, so I traveled there in a carriage along with a few other people.

When I finally arrived, I went to where my grandfather's grocery store had been. An old man stopped me and prevented me from knocking on the door.

"I am Perchik." I remembered him, he was "the beggar" of the village.

"I am Szifra Bernstein, the granddaughter of Shabtai Rapoport."

"I'm glad to see you! I remember when, at the beginning of

the war, you brought your husband and your little girl. Listen, don't knock on the door, you won't find anything .... Another family is living in your house now, and they will not be happy to see you. Come with me, I have things for you, objects that belong to your family."

He took me behind an alley to a humble house and handed me some photographs. After all I had cried over the past few years, I imagined I would have no more tears to shed, but I started sobbing instantly when I saw those pictures again.

"Everybody is dead," Perchik confirmed. "They were killed at the hands of the *Szaulists*."

Perchik handed me pillows, duvets, and furs that belonged to my uncle Meyer. I thanked him and left with my memories.

I found a wagon to take me and my new "riches" back to Lida. How heavy my heart was! I was distressed and dizzy with an accumulated sadness. My aunt Sonja and I were the only surviving members of the Rapoport family .... What a paradox! She had fled to Russia in search of communist ideals, provoking my grandfather's wrath. Her rebellious action became her ticket to life.

I arrived in Lida by dawn. Bewildered and feeling painfully hollow, I walked back to the brewery with my head down.

Sioma admonished me as soon as he saw me: "Where have you been? I went mad, I thought the Lithuanians had killed you, you do not know the stories I have heard .... Jews who are returning to their own homes to reclaim their property are being murdered. Szura, dear, I was struck with fear thinking that you could have been killed in Anykščiai." His rage decreased slowly until, finally, he let out a big sigh: "I am so relieved to see you back." Then he hugged me with all his might.

It was not easy finding food in Lida. Lacking flour and butter, the bakery could only offer stale bread. There was no money or raw materials available. Many stores were empty or abandoned, and the town square, formerly surrounded by beautiful houses and thriving Jewish shops, was now a gallery of demolished brick walls and shuttered windows. The scene was suffocating.

Almost all the buildings in the area had disappeared: the synagogue, the library building, the town hall, the city garden, the so-called "new synagogue" opposite the Chassidic Kizbishe, the Stolarske (the great building of Talmudic studies), the house for the elderly, and even the bridge over the river had been destroyed ... everything was just dust. Only the wide-walled church had survived the bombing, but it stood in a deplorable state. There was nothing left to suggest the long-gone greatness of the city of Lida. Even the sewers reeked of poverty, and the chaotic atmosphere on the streets invited violence. The stench of fear, evil, hatred, and death still hovered around .... *God, why did you allow this horror to happen?*

An order came from the Soviet army: all partisans must enlist in the military. The war was not over, and the Germans were fighting back on the other side of the river Vistula. They wanted— and needed—to recruit young people to go to the front. Sioma rejected this order, having his own motives for defying it. He was distrustful of the Soviets and believed that there were still lists circulating that pointed out the "bourgeois and capitalist" citizens. No doubt, he would be marked as an enemy of the Union of Soviet Socialist Republics. He stayed home, helping me clean, and worked on the brewery machinery to see if it could produce beer again.

We began to work, but a few days later, the Russian authorities seized all private property. They promised they would provide secure jobs for us working in the brewery, but Sioma did not trust Stalin's promises. There was envy and absurd demands for equality based on the communist ideal. We were in constant fear, afraid of being sent to Siberia.

There is a psychic working in the Lida market who reads cards and predicts the future. She has told me that she can visualize a prison, but she also glimpses a long journey by sea. She has advised me to leave Lida as soon as possible. But I have not decided what to do yet. This is the place where I was born, my home. Here, I have my future assured. I was awarded a medal of honor for my performance as a woman combatant with the partisans, and I have been invited to be part of the Komsomol, the youth communist organization. The new government confiscated the Pupko brewery, and my father has not been able to find work as an accountant. Instead, he has been designated to work as a laborer in a rod factory. When asked for another position, his boss told him, "Leibl Stolowitsky, the country requires you to do this job; your duty is to work to the best of your abilities." My father is weak, and his health is failing. I keep hoping they will relocate him to an office job soon. My brother Michash, on the other hand, is working in a workshop as a carpenter, receiving food stamps to help my father. I am happy I have been granted a good position: I am the assistant to the workers' wages manager of the Komsomol. My boss trusts me and gave me the key to the cash box in case he needs me on payday. I cannot complain; I have my family and a stable job.

We decided to travel to Nemenčinė as soon as possible. Before leaving Lida, we searched for valuables in all corners of the brewery. We had hidden some jewelry and other small treasures before being transported on the train. I found my engagement ring in the matchbox where I had left it, and Mitzia found his mother's mink shawl under a trunk. Behind the distillation column were some pearls that had belonged to Franya and some three hundred dollars in cash! We scrutinized every inch of the house and factory, trying to find the teaspoons of vermeil and the diamonds we had hidden, but we never found them.

We split everything equally between us. The money was the easiest; the pearls were given to Roza, and the mink was granted to me. When I tried it on and saw my reflection in the mirror, tears came rolling down my face, burning my dry cheeks. Would I ever be able to wear the fur that had belonged to my mother-in-law without crying? We did not want to accept that she was dead. There was no body, no grave, no *shiveh*, no death certificate. Rachil, the matriarch of the family, appeared in my dreams every night. We prayed *Kaddish* for her and began to plan our escape.

***

Mitzia, Roza, and Meilashe came with us to Nemenčinė. I knew my father was dead, but I wanted to make sure. The city was riddled with grief-stricken souls wandering aimlessly, hundreds of people moving from one place to another, carts crowded with people not knowing where to go, and thousands of shadows looking for relatives cremated in the Nazi furnaces. Death hovered over us, its face atrocious. It was hard to believe the limits of human evil, and no one wanted to accept what had happened to us.

We didn't understand the magnitude of what had happened during the war ... a war still ongoing. As we advanced, the desolation increased; overgrown grass covered the abandoned ruins of the destroyed houses. We crossed the bridge that was on the brink of collapse. I could see the pharmacy from that point with the *Apteka* sign still hanging on the door.

I felt the inquisitive eyes of the townspeople, a resentment that pierced the skin. I had returned to the place of my birth to die a little more. Agnieszka, who had previously worked at my father's house, was inside my old home. She opened the door, faking a smile in greeting. All I wanted to do was run away, but I needed to know the truth. I needed to know my father's fate, to check the facts, to hear the testimony of someone who had seen him die.

Agnieszka was annoyed to see us; my father's house was now hers. Sioma reassured her that we did not come to live there; we were only searching for our family. Esfir arrived a few days later. There were no hugs or tears, just a nod, a small gesture of understanding. We were bound by loss and desolation.

She told me my little sister Tanya had been murdered in the woods along with my father. Esfir had managed to hide in a peasant's house while the *Szaulists* had killed the village Jews.

"Szifra," she said in a whisper, "do you remember that your father used to keep coins hidden in medicine bottles at the pharmacy? He buried them in the neighbor's property. If you and your husband help me dig, we may find enough money to start a new life."

We began planning a strategy for how and when to dig up the treasure. We decided it was best to do it at night, and we needed to involve Agnieszka in carrying out our plan. Mitzia would help excavate; we needed strong arms to do it in a single shot and take advantage of the dark. However, I didn't want him to receive a portion of it ... I didn't want to share my father's inheritance. That money was mine and my stepmother's, no one else's. We could have paid any man to help us, but it was risky. If somebody found out about our wealth, we could be assaulted the instant we stepped out of the village. In the end, I had no choice but to agree to give Mitzia a small amount as payment.

Agnieszka met us at dusk, right before the first star appeared. We walked through the back of the pharmacy to the neighbor's lot, where we thought my father had buried the jars. The moonless night was perfect for our cautious mission. We found two shovels and used any tool that could help us dig. We would have done it with our bare hands if necessary.

We started in a corner of the yard. After digging for more

than half an hour, we found nothing. I remembered my father always mentioning the importance of *Yerushalayim* and its location on the map, so we stood as if we were looking straight ahead at the synagogue ark. We scoured the west edge of the land, in front of the small fence that divided the property, but we also found nothing.

My stepmother suddenly remembered that the jars had been buried near the water drum that served as a bath. Silently, ensuring that nobody saw us, we walked down the small alley that ran through the back of the pharmacy. At the first blow of the shovel, Sioma broke a ceramic jar hidden in the ground. We stared at each other in complete silence. We quickly came to our senses and removed the soil with our hands. We discovered several jars of porcelain filled with gold coins. We paid Agnieszka and gave my brother-in-law what we had promised him. The rest of the coins were distributed between Esfir and me.

People would start waking up at any moment. If anyone heard of our feat, we could be killed. We said goodbye to the maid, hid all the coins inside our underwear, and ran far away from the village. We scurried away like thieves, fleeing without anyone intercepting us. We took what belonged to us: an inheritance that my father had saved during all those years. That money would help us begin a new life far away from there.

Years later, a rumor became a legend in Nemenčinė. It was said that Agnieszka had left the village shortly after the end of the war, just after a visit from the pharmacist's daughter. They had seen her wearing gold teeth, a denture specially made in Vilna. It was rumored that the Bernstein family and Agnieszka had found gold hidden in the grounds of the old pharmacy, and with the treasure, the former servant had turned rich overnight. Agnieszka never returned to town, but the legend subsisted over time.

Esfir came with us to Vilna. The city, now in Russian hands, was restored as the capital of Lithuania. When we reached the market on Kalvariska Street, across the river, we saw a vibrant metropolis. Without a glimpse of remorse, the people had taken many objects from the Jews, knowing that some were returning, and they offered them to the highest bidder. No one seemed bothered about selling stolen items from our murdered families.

The Soviet government instituted a voucher system for giving out food and clothing. Basic resources were scarce. There was no work for refugees like us, and the vouchers were impossible to obtain. International aid organizations were not yet settled in Vilna; to buy food, our only option was to use my father's gold. We hid the coins inside soap bars and used them only for emergencies. When we needed some money, Sioma would cut a bar, and the glowing gold would appear within the greasy mass.

As the days went by, our fear of being sent to Siberia grew. With one stroke, we could be imprisoned as capitalists. If we left our work site, we could be accused as deserters. Even though the war was still on, the Russian government was rapidly organizing its bureaucracy. Every day, the rules and standards of living became more and more strict.

On the streets of Vilna, where I had spent the happiest days of my life as a teenager, ghosts from my past appeared constantly. The Jewish Quarter no longer existed; it had been left abandoned in a ruinous state. The Strashun library, once so renowned in the Jewish world, had been dismantled. The more than one hundred synagogues of *Yerushalayim shel Lita* had been converted into cellars. The old *shul-hoif* was empty; it held only the memory of its past students, who had all been assassinated during the war.

No one trusted even their own shadow; suspicion lingered everywhere. The concept of surviving as a family seemed strange to many people, as most had lost at least one member. The other survivors looked at us with resentment, whispering between them. Instead of seeing it as a miracle, they doubted our victimhood when they saw that all three of us were together. I was disturbed by the looks and comments of friends and acquaintances filled with envy, suspicion, and hatred.

***

Time was against us. The communist system spread its arms everywhere, searching for informers and snitches; they circulated calumnies and incriminated traitors. We knew we needed to leave Vilna as soon as possible; blabbermouths and envious folk were soon to deliver Sioma to the authorities, condemning him to a life of forced labor in Siberia.

We returned to Lida. Mitzia argued that he could be a *stakhanoviste*, an exemplary worker. He tried to persuade Sioma to register at the offices of the Russian government. My husband refused and instead obtained a permit from the commander-in-chief of the Russian government to travel to Białystok via Grodno. Before leaving, he persuaded Mitzia to go with him.

Esfir, Roza, Meilashe, Masza, and I stayed locked in the brewery and waited patiently to receive news from them. We knew the plan: once they reached Białystok, Sioma and Mitzia would send for us, and we would flee together … never to return to Lida or any country governed by the Stalinist regime. It was not long before a Russian commander arrived to accompany us to Białystok, where we met our husbands.

My boss enters the office with three officers … he says there's money missing from the box. The officers overturn benches and desks looking for the money. I am being accused of committing robbery! "Stolowitsky! You and I are the only ones who have the key to the box." He argues that since he's not the thief, then it must have been me. But I am innocent! But because I am Jewish, in the eyes of the *Komsomol,* I'm immediately guilty. It is my word against his. They will prosecute me, and I do not know what will happen to me. I must flee as soon as possible. If I wait any longer, they will come to arrest me. The most prudent thing is to leave today and escape to Białystok where I have a friend who may be able to help me.

Chapter Twelve: 1944-1945

We said goodbye to Esfir in Białystok. Eventually, she would go to South Africa, where she had relatives. I would never see her again. The industrial city of Białystok was regaining strength after its destruction; there was ceaseless activity, and the survivors of the massacre were coming back from different areas eager to help each other locate family members.

Sioma and I, together with Mitzia and Roza, went to an office set up by the Jewish Refugee Center to inquire whether any of our relatives had survived. The line started inside a small room furnished with a simple desk and typewriter. It extended out more than two blocks down the street and continued growing. Every single Jewish survivor was looking for someone.

A man stood at the door guarding the entrance. He welcomed us and asked for our names.

"Sioma Bernstein and Mitzia Shapiro," replied the two

Pupko brothers, using their wives' last names. They feared that the name Pupko would alert the Soviet authorities and they'd be arrested as capitalists. No one could be trusted.

The hungry survivors of the concentration camps resembled ethereal shadows, always trembling and unable to stand still. There were endless lists of surnames and volatile addresses that changed every day. There was no news of Noya, Franya, Aniuta, or Aniuta's husband Yosef Zaretzky ... no member of our family appeared on any list. Nor did we know anything about Luba or of her son Anatole, who had stayed in Belgium during the war.

Day by day, Roza's disillusionment grew deeper and deeper. She wanted to find Noya and prayed for her miraculous resurgence. We searched in every newly formed aid institution, leaving no stone unturned. She was lost forever. There was no way to cheer Roza; none of our efforts were fruitful. Everything fell into a void.

We began a pilgrimage to different orphanages in search of Noya. When we reached these houses, children would often approach us, eager for affection and some kind of security. Hundreds, perhaps thousands or hundreds of thousands, of children had been orphaned by the war. Some would ask for any news of their parents; others were too small to remember them, but there was a deep sadness nestled on their faces.

In one of these institutions, a little girl hugged my husband and wouldn't let go. She had beautiful, expressive black eyes. She begged us to take her with us. Sioma insinuated that he wanted to adopt the child, but I convinced him that we were not in a position to feed another mouth. I was not prepared to have another daughter. After my earlier abortion, I knew I couldn't fathom raising another child. In the end, I won the argument with a strong "no." We left the orphanage downcast with a dose of guilt.

We headed to Bielitza, Poland, where we continued to look for our relatives. Warsaw had not yet been liberated; the war continued on different fronts. Traveling was dangerous, but nevertheless, we moved through snow-covered roads in search of our family. Weighing the risks, the desire to find survivors—to find our loved ones—was stronger than our fear. The journey lasted more than two months. We passed through dozens of cities, always with Mitzia, Roza, and Meilashe by our side.

We arrived in Lublin in the dead of winter. It was February 1945. The city smelled of ashes and death. Emaciated and battered humans, their souls torn to pieces, roamed the streets of the city. The living shadows of men, women, and children carried the burden of incomprehensible horrors suffered in the Nazi extermination camps.

Lublin reeked of putrefaction, and the smell of scorched human flesh and bones blew from the neighboring Majdanek camp, located near the border of Ukraine, only four kilometers from Lublin. It was in Lublin where we learned that the crammed train we had escaped from in the summer of 1943 had been headed to the Majdanek extermination camp. All of our family, including Noya and all our acquaintances, had been killed on arrival.

The stories we heard of Majdanek, a neighboring field in

sight of Lubin's inhabitants, were unmentionable. Before the Red

Army arrived on July 24, 1944, the Nazis had stormed out, taking with them more than a thousand detainees in an unprecedented death march. Because of the speed with which they'd fled, they had left the camp completely intact. The evidence of the crimes committed was ever-present. The Russians quickly discovered, with horror, the gas

Noya Pupko

chambers, the barracks, and the crematory ovens. They also verified the use of Zyklon B to make the annihilation of Jews faster and more effective.

The Russians found mountains of shoes, clothes, eyeglasses, and accessories—all of which served as accounting tools. Hundreds of thousands of Jews had been murdered in that camp, and their belongings were all that was left of them. The Russians stared in stupor and horror in the face of evil. They also found some prisoners who had stayed hidden in the camp. As they set them free, the lost souls roamed the streets of Lublin wearing their camp rags. All of this was just the tip of the iceberg; the Nazis had done so much more to the Jewish people ....

My brother Mitzia cannot bear to hear what the people of Lublin tell us about the massacres in Majdanek. He closes his eyes, but suddenly his pain intensifies. The smell of burned bones that still lingers in the air pierces through his nostrils. Roza can't look me in the eyes; she feels

guilty for the loss of her daughter Noya. Outwardly, she blames the Nazis—who are nothing more than cold-blooded murderers! Silently, she blames her husband and me. She doesn't speak ... doesn't say a word. Her eyes are always glassy; her gaze says it all. Mitzia says goodbye to us; he, Roza, and their son will travel to Bucharest. The farewell is heartbreaking. I do not know when I'll see my older brother again, I do not know when ... I do not know anything anymore.

Among the rubble of such wickedness, the three of us, Sioma, Masza, and I, settled into a rented room in Lublin. We sold the pillows and duvets that I had brought from Anykščiai. I kept the money we earned from the sale under my bra for safety. We were constantly afraid; there was violence everywhere. People starving to death, with nothing to lose, took what they needed or wanted. Everything was scarce. Even the most honorable person was willing to do anything to obtain a loaf of bread and feed his family. For those who were already thieves, it was an easy opportunity to take advantage of the naive. I slept with my hand on my chest, guarding our treasure.

The Pupko family has escaped from Lida; they are wanted for being capitalists and bourgeois. All of their properties have been officially confiscated. Bella, my daughter, has been forced to flee as well. Her boss has blamed her for stealing, but it is an absolute lie. She has gone to Italy and plans to take a boat to Jaffa. Michash, my son, insists on leaving as soon as possible. There is no work here for me either. As the former accountant of the Pupko brewery, all doors are closed. I die a little every day; the Soviets make me work as a rod loader, carrying rods from one side of the street to the other. I am saving enough money to escape to *Eretz* Israel, where I will start a new life!

***

My menstruation had not been regular for a long time. I did not pay much attention to my lack of bleeding until I felt my womb growing ... I was pregnant again. The war had left me wounded emotionally. My mind was plagued with monsters and nightmares from the underworld. I wasn't prepared to bring an innocent life into this world, so I decided to have another abortion.

We hired a doctor to perform the procedure. This time, the process was much simpler; I knew what I was getting into. Afterward, alone in my room, I sobbed again for our loss and asked God to make me sterile. He didn't listen.

I used the little energy I had left to keep going. The *Bricha* group was formed to help Jewish survivors, offering a clandestine passage to Palestine. Abba Kovner was the leader of this organization. Fondly remembering my Zionist days in Vilna, I tried to locate him unsuccessfully. No one knew of his whereabouts.

Leaving Europe for Palestine seemed to be the best option, so we signed up to join the *Bricha* group alongside many others who wanted to establish the Jewish State. We knew that the journey would be challenging. There were officials at every border who had to be bribed, and it was necessary to know which places had to be avoided ... the war was still fierce. We traveled in trucks and trains to Prague, carrying fake documents, a bottle of rum, and the gold coins inherited from my father, still hidden inside the soap bars. From there, escorted by a young member of the clandestine group, we set off by bus to Prešov.

We arrived on April 12, 1945, the date of President Roosevelt's death. We stayed only a few hours before traveling to Bucharest. The aerial bombardments had left the city destroyed. We stayed in a small hotel and waited for an illegal boat to take us to Palestine. We survived with the canned food and checks distributed by the JOINT. We met acquaintances who, like us, had survived the war. With them, Sioma organized a support group of survivors, and together we met once a week. Some told stories, some remained silent, and others made jokes about our misfortunes, asserting that a sense of humor is the last thing a Jew should lose. Mostly, we comforted each other, and together we recited the prayer *Shejeyanu*, thanking God for allowing us to reach that moment.

I saw myself in the mirror. My gaze was no longer that of a young bride; my body was hollow and empty. My only dress was tattered, just like my soul. Bucharest offered a change, a respite. I bought a gray and blue shantung dress in Rovel's shop. For the first time in years, I felt like a dignified woman.

Life flowed more pleasantly. I learned how to trade goods in the black market and exchanged the cans distributed by the JOINT and the UNRRA for other basic products. I traded the Spam for a kilo of flour, a canned soup for fresh vegetables, and a box of cigarettes for a liter of milk. The Russian authorities turned a blind eye to the illegal trade, even letting us swap goods in the "open bazaar."

We met some young people who had been imprisoned in the Auschwitz camp during the war. They wore numbers on their forearms branded by the Nazis, as if they were cattle. With them was Baruch, a child marked by the same burning iron. Masza and Baruch soon became friends.

In the privacy of our hotel room, we took one gold coin from the soap bar. The extra money provided us with small luxuries like slices of cake, chocolate, and even movie tickets. One day, we went to watch *Tarzan* and invited Baruch to join us. Seeing Johnny Weissmuller fly from vine to vine to rescue his beloved was inspiring. We began to regain our faith in love.

From that day on, Masza and Baruch spent their afternoons playing together. They chased one another in the hotel's corridors, pretending to be Tarzan and Jane in the African jungle. Baruch was completely alone in the world. As I watched him play with Masza, I hoped he would regain the smile that had been brutally snatched from him during the war.

We met Yosef Klarman, who organized *Aliyah Bet*—a code name for the illegal immigration to Palestine. Klarman explained that the British controlled the area, and very few Jews were allowed entry to establish themselves in the land of our ancestors. We wanted to be part of the selected group and told him we were willing to take the risks, but there was no way we could convince him. "We want young men," explained Yosef, "*Chayalim*, soldiers ready to fight. The war in Palestine is going to break out at any moment, and you are a family, you are not fighters."

We chose to stay in Bucharest and wait for the conditions to change. Our longing to go to Palestine seemed like an impossible dream. Zionism had become an ideal from my past, along with the now Doctor Yudko Eksztejn. The Szifra of the *Shomer Hatzair*—who had recited poems of Bialik—and even the Szura of the *partisanim* was gone. There was now only Mrs. Pupko, Masza's mother and Sioma's wife, a survivor who wanted to forget about war and suffering, a woman who longed for a better life ....

The next few months would be filled with constant traveling from one week to the next as we tried to figure out where we could settle. Looking for work or some livelihood, we traveled again to Prague. We were able to buy five hundred stockings to sell on the black market. We did so well that it was worth repeating the dangerous operation.

We traveled once more to Czechoslovakia, this time making sure to dress elegantly to avoid suspicion. We bought more stockings and added a tablecloth. We changed trains in Strasbourg and purchased a seat in the first-class compartment. A distinguished-looking man, who was already seated, began to talk to Sioma. His foreign accent betrayed him, and the conversation continued in French, which my husband spoke fluently.

"I would love to return to Brussels to finish my degree as a brewer engineer," Sioma told him. "When my father died in 1935, I suspended my studies and came back home. Then I got married and the war started, and my education was left unfinished."

"But you can have a better future if you have a diploma in engineering. Perhaps I can help you," the man responded politely. "I am the consul of Belgium, and there is probably some way of getting your papers in order. If you come to Brussels, look for me." He handed us his business card, which we kept as a valuable treasure.

Eventually, as we settled in Brussels, we contacted the consul. Sioma would have a chance to finish his career and get his degree. The diplomat explained that the process would not be fast or simple because we had no documents. Nevertheless, he was eager to help; he declared us *Belges in disant,* "temporary Belgians." We waited patiently.

During this time, we traveled to the Bavarian Alps. We were accepted into a Displaced Persons camp in Bad Reichenhall, in the Berchtesgaden area. Through some hurdles, I was admitted to the nearby improvised sanatorium for asthmatics and people with tuberculosis. The clinic had a nearby spring used for curative purposes and was run by Englishmen. I went willingly with hopes that the healing water would improve my breathing.

The makeshift hospital was arranged in a cellar with beds aligned side by side. We were to lie in them to receive oxygen early in the morning and at night. We were required to do walks along the village pathways and bathe in the hot springs. Sioma continued his travels to find money-making opportunities: he bought and sold wood from Bratislava, Czechoslovakia, which turned out to be a very productive business. While I was being treated, Masza was looked after by a woman in the village whom Sioma paid with food and cigarettes bought from the black market.

This lady cooks fruit throughout the day and smokes the cigarettes my parents bring her. She takes care of me while my mother is treated in the sanatorium. She's good to me, but all she does is cook jams and jellies to sell in the village. I get bored in this house. Sometimes I play with a girl who lives in the adjoining house, who has a newborn baby brother. The baby is very funny; he moves his little hands when you rub them. I wonder, how are children born? I'm going to ask my mom when I visit her at the clinic later this afternoon.

Masza came to visit me every day after lunch, and together we enjoyed the clean air. Clever and inquisitive, she asked me, somewhat inopportunely, how babies were born as she accompanied me on one of my usual walks.

"The children," I answered, "are brought by a stork."

Masza was dissatisfied with my answer. She folded her arms in protest. "It is not true. Storks build their nests in the trees. They are mothers of birds, not of children, I have seen them!" She gave me the cold shoulder and stayed silent for the rest of the day.

As I left Masza at her boarding house, I managed to tell her that she was still too young to understand certain things. My daughter was no longer listening to me; she said good night and closed the door behind her.

***

There was a prisoner-of-war camp guarded by Americans in a village near Bad Reichenhall. I learned that Engineer Joachim Lochbhiler, the SS officer who had protected us at the brewery, was included on the list of prisoners.

As soon as I could, I ventured to the camp. There was a fence with barbed wire that surrounded the site. From the outside, you could see many Nazi prisoners resting in the courtyard. I approached the gate, but a guard stopped me, saying that the entrance was forbidden to civilians. I explained that an ex-SS officer who had tried to help us during the war was on the list of prisoners, and he was not meant to be there. I do not know how he understood what I was saying, but he allowed me to speak to the officer in charge of the camp.

"Ma'am, you're looking for Officer Lochbhiler ... let me look for his record and find out if he's here." After a brief pause while he was searching for the paperwork, he said, "Ah, yes, here it is. He was captured fighting on the Belarusian front. He has a high military rank, and we can't let him go just because you have requested his release. We need evidence of his humanitarian acts. Is there anyone else who could testify on his behalf?"

"My husband, the Stolowitsky family, and my brother-in-law, but besides my husband, I do not know where the rest are."

"Would you be willing to sign a paper that would make you responsible for the liberation of this gentleman ... Lochbhiler?"

"Of course," I said firmly, ready to sign the paper the officer handed me.

I was happy to help clear the name of Lochbhiler. When Sioma returned, we consulted with the Jewish agencies to see how we could speed up the liberation process. We learned that the Stolowitsky family had already provided their testimony. We weren't given details regarding Engineer Lochbhiler's liberation, but we never forgot his name or what he had done for us.

***

By the middle of July 1945, I ended my stay at Bad Reichenhall. Masza and I waited for Sioma to collect us at the entrance of the clinic. We travelled to another Displaced Persons camp, this time in Klagenfurt, Austria. These lands contained myths of winged dragons. Between the hills, Hitler's shadow, Goebbels's fame, and the macabre evidence of Mengele's experiments were all around. Ravenous antisemitism had seeped deeply into the soil of the land. We would have preferred to be somewhere else, to run away, to be shielded from all the atrocities, yet we had nowhere to turn. We were wanderers, unwanted nomads. At least here we were able to secure temporary lodgings, as Klagenfurt was now controlled by American and English troops.

Poppies painted the roadside red, but their colorful nature was not enough to cover the vast cemeteries exposed to war, pain, and misery. We were housed with at least six other Jews. The temporary rooms were in poor condition and unsanitary. We were free to come and go from our shared chamber as we pleased. The doors were always wide open, but we were confined within an area fenced with barbed wire. A commander named Benjamin, who came from *Eretz* Israel, visited Klagenfurt to encourage Jews to migrate to our ancestral home.

We learned that the Allies had just destroyed the Japanese cities of Hiroshima and Nagasaki. We didn't know what the future consequences of the atomic bomb would be, but we rejoiced at the news. The Germans were finally defeated!

Benjamin informed us that soon a convoy would travel to Palestine via Italy. He invited us to join the group. Once again, we knew the trip would be illegal and clandestine. The British government continued to control that area of the Middle East and closed its doors to those who sought refuge. The *Bricha* group organized an intricate communication network, collecting knowledge of the best and safest routes, which meant friendlier borders and checkpoints with looser security. Under the protection of these young Zionists, we would go to Italy and wait for a ship to take us to *Eretz* Israel.

I long to go to *Eretz* Israel to work the land and to fight for our rights as Jews. I worry for Szura; can she stand the rigors of desert life? Her anxiety attacks have become more frequent, and when they strike, I don't know what to do for her. The world has become completely *meshuggener;* it has turned upside down! The washerwoman has become a prostitute, the housewife a street sweeper, the carpenter a priest, and a bomb has erased an entire city in Japan. Communists are looking for capitalist crumbs inside the walls. The Poles continue to murder Jewish survivors returning to their hometowns, and the Lithuanians hunt for treasures left behind by Jewish families. The world, no doubt, is crazy .... But, at last, the war is over. What next? What future awaits us after surviving the massacre? Poverty, hopelessness, loneliness? I am worried for my daughter Masza. I hope that in Palestine we will have a better life.

Chapter Thirteen: 1945-1946

Once a vibrant, industrial city, Udine had also suffered through the struggles of the war. We could see destruction everywhere: in the pointed arches of the Gothic monuments, where there used to be a cobblestone street, now there was rubble, but above all, we could see the devastation in people's faces. We could feel the process of dehumanization and insensibility that had affected everyone. The ancient splendor of the medieval city, with a castle on the hill, was no longer palpable. Along with the other refugees, we waited patiently for the *chayalim*, the Jewish soldiers dressed in civilian clothes, to take us to Bologna. We would then proceed to Florence to board a clandestine ship headed to the Promised Land. We languished as we waited, and we still checked lists of survivors in the hopes of finding our family and added our names to each list in case anyone came looking for us.

Once we reached Florence, the group we arrived with from

Udine dissolved. The young leaders announced that they could no longer take us to Palestine with a child. It was too risky. We decided right then to take the next bus to Rome. We traveled all day and only had a loaf of bread to eat between us. At one of the stops, Sioma removed a gold coin from one of the soap bars and ran to buy some plums for the trip. He made it back just in time before the bus started again.

Rome's fountains, grand avenues, and glorious past of caesars and conquerors captivated me. After Mussolini's death, the Romans were experiencing a renaissance. Soon enough, they would teach us how to smile again.

We settled into a small apartment overlooking a building with a portrait of Madonna painted on the wall. The Mediterranean sun was a blessing. We had food thanks to the biweekly packages sent by the JOINT, which included condensed milk for Masza. I sold the canned goods on the black market and traded them for fresh produce like I had done in Bucharest. Thanks to the UNRRA and their check from Banco di Roma, we were able to pay our rent.

Sioma fell sick one autumn afternoon and was quickly diagnosed with meningitis. His fever was very high, leaving him dizzy without respite. He was overwhelmed and complained of acute pain in his neck and body that prevented him from raising his head. For days, he slept in total darkness, as he was sensitive to light. Every morning, I gave him freshly squeezed orange juice to drink, as prescribed by the doctor, hoping he would recover soon.

He grew seriously ill, and I was afraid I could lose him. After all the struggles we had overcome, it was unthinkable for him to succumb to meningitis. I prayed to God, the same God I had fought during the war, for his speedy recovery.

Sioma slowly began to feel better. He asked me to get a typewriter so he could write his memoir. During the next three months, he wrote a couple sentences each day, remembering the most insignificant details of our captivity at the hands of the Nazis and our salvation in the forest. Eventually, once he fully recovered, he abandoned the task of writing and decided instead to embrace the joy of living in Italy, a country bursting with song and bliss, with fields of lavender and sunflowers.

The first day Sioma was able to leave the house, we went for a stroll on the beaches of Ostia. We met up with new friends from Lida who had survived the miseries of the war like us. The winter winds of the Adriatic blew in from the horizon. Standing in front of the waves, with my eyes wide and

Shura, Sioma and Masza in Ostia, Italy, enjoying a beach day with some friends

unblinking, I welcomed the future. I opened my arms and gave myself to the new day. Masza ran to the shoreline, and without caring how cold the water was, she took off her dress and jumped into the waves. What a joy it was to watch my daughter play! The white foamy folds of salty water caressed the sand in a rhythmic beat; I saw the future as I watched the horizon; I knew that we had to go on.

In January 1946, we moved to an apartment on Largo Pietro Vasareti Street and enrolled Masza into a government school. Every morning, she walked to school to study Italian. The first book she read in that language was *Pinocchio*, a story written by Carlo Collodi about a wooden puppet that comes alive.

Some afternoons, we would meet up with a few other Lithuanian survivors in a café nearby. We played cards, talked, and tried to erase the traces of our past sufferings. Trying to leave our nightmares behind, we established a rule: we only allowed ourselves to talk about the present and our dreams for the future. There were continuous discussions on whether we should emigrate to Palestine, emigrate to the United States, or remain in Rome. These conversations were mere words; there were no visas, no entry permits, and no authorizations to emigrate. Nevertheless, we were hopeful, and we were alive.

We went out often to entertain ourselves, to be with friends, or just to stroll around. On those days, we would leave Masza alone in the apartment. She did not have many friends to play with, so she would sit near the window and watch the world from above.

My parents have gone out again. From this window, I can see into a neighbor's apartment. I see a pair of dolls on a bed, one of them dressed

as a nun. They are beautiful! I would like to have a doll to hug and care for. A girl just poked her head out the window and spotted me! She is making a signal, maybe she is inviting me to play! What a thrill! But I do not know how to get to her building. I see an opening in the fence with a stone doorframe. Maybe I can play with her. If I'm counting correctly, I think she lives on the third floor.

"My name is Masza," I present myself to the lady who opens the door.

"I am Mrs. Dauria, I believe you are here to see Maria Luisa. We are heading out to church. Where are your parents?"

"They are not home, they will return later," I answer Mrs. Dauria.

"Maybe you want to join us for Mass?"

I know my parents will disapprove, but I don't care, so I walk with them to church. I imitate the ritual; I cross myself, and I hear the prayers in Latin. As we return, Mrs. Dauria insists on accompanying me to my house. My parents are back already, and I introduce them to the mother of my new friend Maria Luisa.

Masza had met a charming girl, Maria Luisa Dauria, who invited her to her house every afternoon. On many occasions, she accompanied her friend to Mass. I did not object; however, I wondered if it was right for a Jewish girl to learn the *Pater Noster* before learning to pray the *Modé Aní*, the Jewish prayer that is said daily upon awakening. I didn't care much; on the contrary, it comforted me to know that Masza was learning some Catholic rituals and prayers to be prepared in case there were new attacks against us Jews. Masza, with her dark braided hair, olive complexion, and big eyes, could pass as a Catholic Italian girl. The Dauria family became good friends of ours as well.

All over Rome, we saw American soldiers, their uniforms contrasting against the ancient buildings of the Eternal City. They'd drink in the cafés and laugh out loud through the streets, openly expressing their victory and relief to be away from the battlefield. One afternoon, while we were out walking, I was startled by the laughter of some drunken American soldiers who, despite the cold January weather, ate lunch on the restaurant's terrace. One of them approached Masza and tossed a chocolate bar up to her, then he raised his head and spoke to Sioma: "I am being sent home tomorrow, and I have a coat that I'm not taking with me … I'd like to offer it to you."

Sioma turned to look at me without understanding why the soldier wanted to give it to him. Nobody gifted anything in those days.

Trying to speak some words in English, I asked the soldier, "That's a joke, right?"

"No, not at all, take it! It will keep you warm for the rest of the winter." Reaching out, he handed Sioma the coat.

"Thank you very much!" my husband exclaimed excitedly, putting on the coat immediately. "It fits me perfectly!"

A photographer, who usually worked on that corner, immortalized the moment with a snapshot. We bought the photo to remember the generous encounter.

***

I had trouble passing by the butcher's shop, as the smell of meat—the stench of dead flesh—made me nauseous. It evoked memories of the war carnage and induced a rush of visions: the image of my father, along with all the Jews from his town, harassed and pushed to the outskirts of Nemenčinė to be murdered; my father lying dead on the grass, all his bones broken from the deadly beating, his face smeared with mud; hundreds of bodies sharing a common ditch. As I walked by, I tried desperately to ignore my aversion, not to faint, and to brush away the nightmares piercing my brain. I arrived home sweating. I threw myself on the bed and closed my eyes to forget ….

Everything affected me; I constantly suffered a mixture of emotions that fluttered at the slightest whisper. An uneasiness crawled inside me, producing uncontainable tears or senseless laughter. The fragile order with which I tried to rebuild my life could easily disintegrate at any moment.

Yet again, my mother has suffered another one of her attacks. She remains in her room, lying on the bed with her eyes lost in space. I've called her, but she doesn't respond. She does not want to be bothered. She asks me to go and play and let her rest. I know she's not tired; I know she suffers. I can see her chest moving up and down—she is not breathing well. I know that it is best to leave her alone. I approach the window. My friend Maria Luisa Dauria is there! I make a sign to beckon her. I am happy to go to her house. I hope she lets me play with the doll dressed as a nun.

Chapter Fourteen: 1946-1947

By the end of 1946, the Belgian consul fulfilled his promise
to provide us with official papers, and our visas finally
arrived. Even though he retired and no longer worked for
the government, he sent a letter from Brussels advising how to
complete the documents so Sioma could be admitted to the
university.

We prepared to travel to our new home, the capital of Art
Nouveau. Since the war had broken out in Lithuania, we had not
heard from Luba, my sister-in-law. We were deluded with
anticipation thinking that she had managed to hide in some corner
of Belgium and save herself from Nazi cruelty. With a palpitating
hope that she was alive, we bought her a scarf of crimson silk. The
warm tone would suit her dark complexion.

Once we arrived in Brussels, we contacted the former consul
to thank him for his help. We settled into our new home and
immediately inquired about Luba's whereabouts. We quickly

located her husband, Aaron Brawerman, who had survived the war while fighting with the English army. He explained that shortly after he had departed for England, Luba had left their son Anatole with some friendly peasants. A few months after that, she had been deported to Auschwitz. The red silk scarf tangled between my fingers ....

Anatole was saved by posing as the son of the farmer, hiding in the Flemish countryside, and using Jean as his name. He was instructed in basic Catholicism so he could pass as a non-Jew. At the end of the war, when Aaron went to collect his son, the boy refused to go with him.

"Anatole didn't even respond to his birth name. He did not want to come with me, he just clung to the cross that hung around his neck and cried that his name was Jean ... that's how he's been baptized!" Aaron told us how he tried to explain to his son the terrible events that had happened in recent years. "Anatole ran into the bedroom of his foster home, shut himself in, screamed, and denied his past. Bellowing, he repeated the Catholic prayer tirelessly, screaming intermittently that he was not a Jew. I tried to convince him without success. I finally gave up and left. I've been back to the farm several times, but every time I go, Anatole refuses to see me. I do not know what to do."

Sioma comforted his brother-in-law and promised that we would visit his son as soon as we could.

***

We enrolled Masza into a boarding school administered by nuns. She would be able to visit us on weekends. She was happily growing up. She forgot her Italian and learned French. Meanwhile, Sioma was advancing in his studies of brewing engineering.

We continued to use the few gold coins still hidden between the soaps to survive. My husband partnered with an acquaintance in a small record factory, but it was unsuccessful. Earning money was not an easy task. I would stroll down Avenue Louise, looking at the display windows and imagining myself in those beautiful dresses. I remembered the mink stole that had belonged to my mother-in-law and decided to incorporate it into a coat to modernize it. I bought a hat adorned with feathers and went to a dressmaker to have some dresses made. I wanted to be an elegant woman again; I wanted to reinvent myself once more.

I do not know who I am. They say I am a Jew, but I pray with the Rosary. I don't want to go and live with my biological father; I hardly know him. I feel comfortable living here in the countryside, in this land, near these cows, in this place where time passes between sowing and the harvest, amid the trees that I have grown to love. My name is Jean, I am Catholic, and I love Anne. In my mind, I have a vague image of my mother Luba, I remember her hands and her caresses, but I have no memory of her features. Aaron claims to be my father. He couldn't control his anger when I answered that I was happy in the countryside and that I wanted to stay here. He says that I was not born a peasant, that I am the son of an educated and learned family. He insists that he wants to help me, and he has tried to persuade me to go with him. I do not want to hear his screams anymore. I don't want to suffer anymore. My mother died in Auschwitz … and the only one who understands me is Anne. Today, my mother's brother Sioma came to visit with his wife Szura and his daughter Masza. They asked me things I did not want to answer, or rather, I don't know how to express my answers. Masza repeats that she is my cousin and that I am a Jew. The only thing I want is to be left alone. When I grow up, I will marry Anne, and we will have a beautiful family.

Anatole saw us approaching and didn't know where to hide. He was an introverted young man with an elusive look. Sioma explained to him that we wanted the best for him, that we wanted to help him, and that we had accepted his choice of faith.

"It's all right that you love Anne and want to follow the Catholic faith. We respect you," my husband said. "You will always be Anatole to us, our nephew, the son of my sister Luba. But no matter what religion you profess, I want you to know that you were born a Jew, from a Jewish mother; your blood is our blood."

"Can I call you uncle then?" asked Anatole without lifting his head. With a filial instinct, Sioma embraced him immediately.

We visited Anatole several times during that year in Belgium. One time, he even agreed to come to Brussels to spend a weekend with us and Masza.

Our relationship with Anatole grew over the years. He stayed in Brussels, married Anne, the love of his life, and became a great man.

SHURA

***

Life in Brussels was good. When we could, we would go out to eat. Our landlords became our friends, and we often spent pleasant evenings in their flat listening to music, talking, and laughing. Once, we even had dinner at the elegant Palace Café.

Sioma was finishing his studies when we received a letter from some relatives who had moved to Mexico before the war. They invited us to live with them, promising good job opportunities where Sioma could be successful in a thousand and one ways. They described the nice weather in Mexico and spoke about the ever-smiling people there. But ... who wanted to go to an unfamiliar land, where they didn't know the language or even the currency? I imagined a completely inhospitable country, but there were not many other options for us.

Our Mexican family procured visas for us. In early October 1947, we began our travels to the land of maguey and *chile,* by way of New York. I would become a poppy among cacti.

Chapter Fifteen: 1947

We flew to New York on October 10, 1947. Once we landed at the airport, in the center of the arrival tumult, a familiar face stood out. He had a photo hanging around his neck—the image of my grandfather. Immediately, I recognized my uncle Leibn Rapoport. In America, he was known as Leo. He took my suitcase and kissed my forehead just as my grandfather used to do. He stroked Masza's hair and gave Sioma a handshake.

He brought us to his apartment in Brooklyn, and his wife served us a succulent dinner. Life was different in America: the war had not happened there. The Holocaust was distant and alien; they didn't suffer the torture of a past. We left Lithuania behind and thought of Italy and Belgium as temporary safe havens. We saw in front of us a welcoming and possibly happy future.

The entire Rapoport family, who lived in New York, gathered that same afternoon in the small apartment. They asked us thousands of questions: about the war, about our survival, and about what had happened in Europe. They were eager to hear any news from Brussels and what we knew about the concentration camps. They interrogated us about every factor of what we had witnessed and the horrors we had experienced.

It was the first time we shared our story with people who were completely removed from it. For them, the battles and the slaughter were as distant as Mars. They had seen pictures of the extermination and concentration camps that American soldiers and journalists had sent back. No one, not even us, really understood the magnitude of what had happened or how our family had been assassinated. We continued to ask ourselves what had occurred to us as human beings and how that kind of massacre was possible.

Our American family felt guilty for not having foreseen the signs of what had been about to happen; they regretted not having done enough in time to get us out of there. Now, they wanted to help us. They didn't want to offend us by just giving us money, so my uncle bought from us the tablecloth we had purchased in Prague as a way to ease his conscience. In our view, they had nothing to atone for, but the five hundred dollars he provided would help us start anew, and we were grateful.

New York was a big city with immense structures shading its streets. The Hudson River passed alongside it, with shipyards adorning its sides, and cargo ships carrying all kinds of materials and products paraded up and down.

My uncle went out of his way to make us comfortable: he bought all kinds of food for us to try, took us sightseeing along Long Island, and showed us around town. For ten days, we enjoyed touring the metropolis, using the tram system to travel everywhere. The bright billboards announced the titles of the new films, women wandered around wearing warm coats and showing off their beautiful hats, and men ran to work. I was amazed. The city pulsed with energy. I was mesmerized!

Masza, like me, fell in love with the most modern city in the world. She kept on saying that she wanted to stay in New York. There was no time for dreaming; a long-distance call from Mexico directed our future. We had to act quickly and travel to the capital of the Aztecs very soon. The visa that our relatives had processed for us would expire the next day. That is, October 21.

Before we left, my uncle gave me several items of clothing from his shop. We said goodbye with regret and boarded our flight to Mexico. We didn't know a word in Spanish, but our souls opened, grasping the moment.

Chapter Sixteen: 1947

Our arrival in Mexico was not what I had expected. I envisioned that a landscape of cacti and maguey would receive me as I came out of the plane. I imagined a city populated with *rancheros* mounted on donkeys or horses. It was a great surprise to find members of the Pupko, Darzon, and Winer families arriving at the airport in large cars to greet us.

That day, October 21, 1947, we cried with joy. We instantly adopted Mexico as our new home. I learned to eat pineapples and papayas, mangoes and bananas, and other exotic fruits like mamey, *chirimoya*, and guava, and, of course, I became accustomed to eating tortillas and *chile*. These new flavors seduced my palate and slowly dissolved the bitter tang of my past. But how could I forget the tastes and smells of my Lithuania, my distant Lithuania? Would I ever be able to return?

I practiced counting in Spanish, and I became used to the melody and rhythm of the language's soft words. Only the essence of what we once were remained. From that essence—that breath—

a roar of strength was born. The weeping willows along the canals of Xochimilco hugged me. In the spring, the violet jacarandas laid their leaves on the floor, placing a carpet where I walked. This terra incognita became my home: a land where the sun is ripe and the cacao flower grows; a place where people smile for no apparent reason at all; a warm oasis bordered by two huge oceans, covered with pyramids and secrets, mysteries and flowers, crafts, and color. In Mexico, spring is not a season; it is a state of being. The winters are fused with autumns, and the summers are showered with rain. I loved Mexico from the very beginning. Mexico welcomed us without question and opened its arms to us, allowing us to be reborn.

Sioma became Simon, and I remained simply Shura. I learned to cook Veracruz-style gefilte fish with *chile güero* and tomato sauce. The comforting smile of my grandfather Shabtai persisted in my dreams, and the warmth of the arms of my grandmother Leah soothed me during the nights. The Castilian-Mexican tongue, which confuses "z" with "s," aided in alleviating my pain. The honeyed language with its tranquilizing rhythm slid easily between my teeth; it became part of me and my new life.

Mitzia, along with Roza and Meilashe (who later became known as Michael), settled in Canada. The Stolowitsky family established themselves in New York, where Bella, Michash, and Chana successfully reinvented their lives in the American style.

I learned that Yudko Eksztejn fought with the resistance in Yugoslavia. When he managed to reach Palestine, he fought for

Israel's independence. After the war, he became a doctor in Israel.

I keep his letters; they have been with me all this time, treasured in a drawer on my bedside table. Sometimes I read them when I need to travel back in time. I recite his words by heart—they allow me to remember, to suffer, to weep, and to be reborn in that forbidden love that happened long ago in the distant peacefulness of my youth.

Today, I yield fruits in Mexico, and over the years, I have grown roots here. The strawberries of the forest of my Lithuanian past have transformed into sweet prickly pears of thorny cacti. From my balcony, I'm infused with the sounds of my adoptive country. The alleys of the City of Palaces, with its courtyards full of bougainvillea and hummingbirds sucking pollen from the flowers, open in front of me. Our new home allows me to forget, at least from time to time, the tortuous path of my past: Anykščiai, the Niemen River, the massacres in Ponar, the partisan struggle in the *puszcza* of Naliboki ... all of it is in my heart.

I breathe; I can finally breathe.

Shura and Sioma, years after the war, vacationing in Venice, Italy

Epilogue

fter living through wars, assassinations, robberies, Nazism, communism, and the Perestroika, the Rapoports' house still stands erect in Anykščiai. The building that served as a pharmacy for Shmuel Bernstein in Nemenčinė is preserved. The Pupko brewery in Lida became a major brewery in Belarus. The old coal stoves were replaced by gas ones, the *droskys* previously pulled by horses were substituted with automatic cars, and the kerosene lamps were abandoned to accommodate electric ones.

The feelings, the suffering, the yearnings of a young woman, and the losses of loved ones remained forever in her memory.

Rapoports' house in Anykščiai. The photo on the top was taken in the early 1900s; the photo on the bottom, taken in 2005, shows the same house still standing, during a visit by Shura's children and grandchildren. Standing in the modern photo is Masza Pupko (now Masha Cohen).